Iskandar

# Iskandar

And the Immortal King of Iona

MIKE BIRD

RESOURCE *Publications* · Eugene, Oregon

ISKANDAR
And the Immortal King of Iona

Resource Publications
An Imprint of Wipf and Stock Publishers
199 W. 8th Ave., Suite 3
Eugene, OR 97401
www.wipfandstock.com

ISBN 13: 978-1-62032-646-6
Manufactured in the U.S.A.

# Contents

# Contents

# Acknowledgments

IT IS NOT OFTEN that a theologian sets out to write a novel. But herein is my first attempt to move from the genre of non-fiction to fiction. This novel started out as a series of bed time stories that I told my eldest daughter Alexis. She enjoyed the tale, its suspense, surprise, and asked me to commit it to paper. Thereafter, between 2009–2011, in north Scotland and eastern Australia, usually on a Sunday evening, I wrote the first drafts for this novel. What I hope can be found in these pages is an entertaining fantasy story of betrayal, revenge, brotherly love, redemption, the triumph of good over evil, all infused with an eclectic mixture of religious themes.

I have to thank several people for the development of this novel. First, my daughter Alexis, for listening to my stories and for encouraging me to write them down. Second, to Ovi Buciu and Elke Speliopoulos for reading over a draft of the novel. Third, to James Ernest, my Baker Academic editor, for taking the time to read over the novel and to recommend some publishing options. Fourth, the good folks at Wipf & Stock, for accepting the novel for publications in their *Resources* series.

Mike Bird
Brisbane, Australia.
September, 2012.

# Map of the Kingdom of Iona

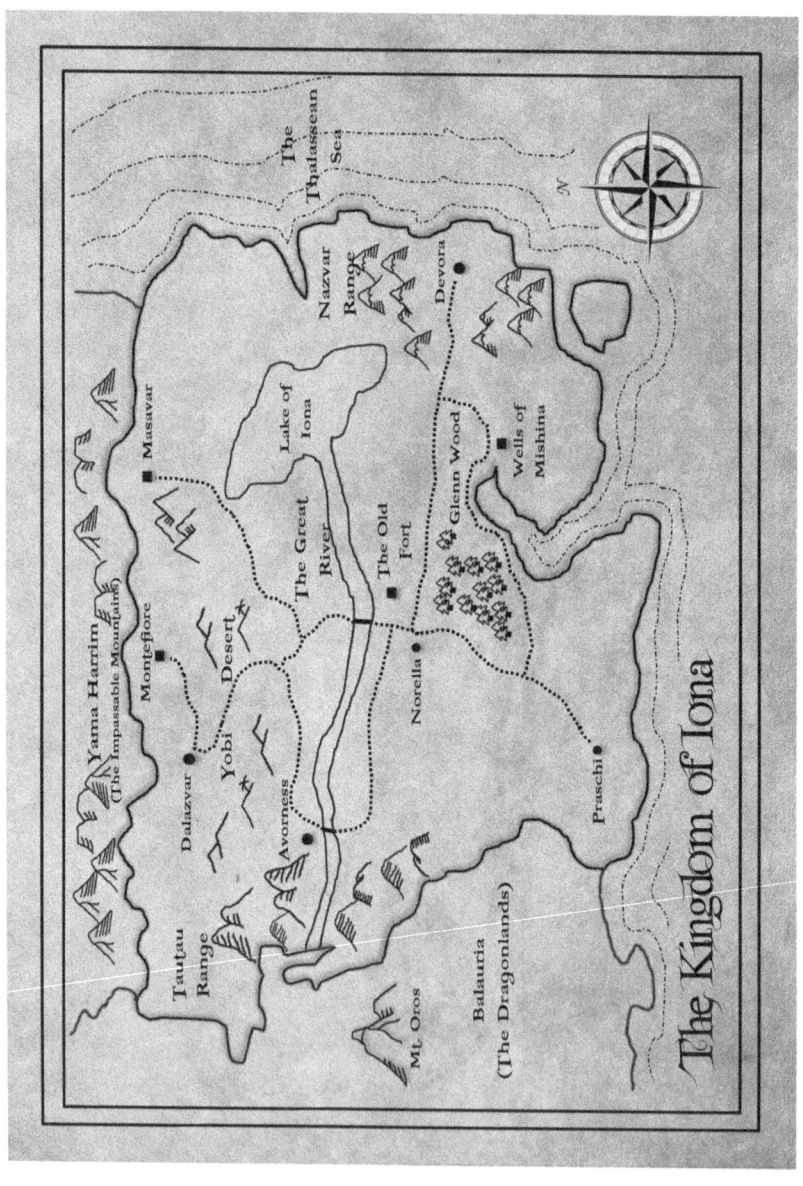

# Chapter 1

## Morpeth, Prisca, and the god Marduk

IN DAYS LONG SINCE forgotten, when gods and goddesses ruled the hearts of men, when races and beasts long since extinct shared the land of earth together, and when mystery and magic were still believed, there existed the kingdom of Iona. Iona was a land wedged between the great mountains of the west and the ice deserts of the east, whose inhabitants lived under the monarchs of Iona. They ruled a land of ten cities, a hundred villages, mysterious woods, and immense lakes. The land was continually filled with strife where warlords and warlocks battled one another for land and power, trampling over anything or anyone that got in their way. Every weapon in the arsenal of man was put to the vocation of death, war-hammers or wizardry. All were used in the civil wars of Iona. Until the kings of Iona brought peace through mediation or the intervention of their own standing army. It was a land where the demi-gods of the seventh heaven tormented men for their own sport and used them as pawns for their own games. The kings interceded with the gods as priests, offering sacrifices and taking oaths, in exchange for blessings and deliverance.

Until there came a king. A ruler who knew neither the limitations of a priest, nor the place of man in the design of the created order. His name was Morpeth son of Malthasar and his wife was Prisca from the river tribe of Avorness. They worshipped the old pagan god Marduk with a zeal that outstripped the most pious of priests. No sacrifice was too great for their god. They offered the flesh of many condemned criminals upon the fiery altar of Marduk's temple. Their piety and devotion did not go unnoticed by Marduk. In a cool winter evening, on the one day of the year when the king and his queen entered the hallowed sanctuary at Montefiore to offer incense and intercessions for the realm, Marduk appeared to them in a shining light. He revealed himself to them in the form of a Minotaur. Morpeth and Prisca froze in terror at the spectacle and cowered on their knees before him alone in the holy place beyond the eyes of others. Marduk commended their love for him and offered them the one thing that no mortal had ever been offered before: immorality and divinity. Marduk offered to make them gods, members of the pantheon, a right that was his alone as the highest god of the pantheon. But their divinity would have a price. To prove worthy of the divine administration Morpeth and Prisca would have to sacrifice their children to him and prove their loyalty in blood. They had six children, three girls and three boys, princes and princess of the kingdom of Iona. Morpeth gasped back at the offer.

"Your divine eminence, you offer so much, but you demand what we cannot possibly give you. I would sooner die than break the slightest hair of my sons or daughters. I beg you, my lord, take back your offer, for such a thing cannot be sought by any father." Prisca's eyes flooded with tears at the prospect and she softly nodded in agreement with Morpeth. But Marduk grinned knowingly at them. He spoke and his voice echoed like an unholy thunder that shook the pillars of the temple.

"No, Morpeth and Prisca, you are my chosen instrument. Immortality itself will change your mind and you will learn that the blood and flesh of your children are a small price to pay for what is set before you." Marduk drew near and breathed upon them with a wind that smelled of a mixture of lilies and dung. Immediately Morpeth and Prisca received the highest power of the heavens. They become more than human, but not fully divine. They were constrained still by their human form, but exceeding it in abilities in every respect. They were now immortal, yet still vulnerable to death should their head ever be severed from their body.

Immediately they felt a power move through their veins and into their lungs, into their heart, and into their brain. Like a delicious poison working into their body, they could feel the sinews and bones drinking from that which moved within them. As the king and queen lay in an ecstatic state before him, Marduk spoke again.

"You are now immortal monarchs of Iona. You have tasted the power of my realm. Part of that power is yours to share now, the rest only when you grant me the sacrifice that is duly mine. I offer you immortality and divinity, a place with the gods for all time. Fill my sacred cup with the blood of your children and I will let you drink from the wells of divinity forever. Now go and make your choice."

And the god vanished into the darkness. Morpeth and Prisca were left their shivering in fear and perplexity, wondering if it was but a vision or a dream. But most of all they felt the insatiable hunger growing within them, a hunger for power that drove them instantly mad. Priests heard the commotion and came into the temple and were unable to console them or restrain them. The king and queen remained in a demented state for three days, screaming, laughing, tearing their clothes, crying, rolling about like mindless beings, striking themselves with the sacred vessels of the temple. They could occasionally be heard screaming for pity, begging for death, and embracing one another with tears. For three days the priest kept watch for them outside, waiting for them to return to their senses, to summon assistance, to call for a healer, or simply to die from the madness of seeing things not fit for man.

Then, on the morning of the third day, there was only silence for two hours. One of the priests dared to enter to see what had become of them. No sooner had he begun to ascend the staircase than Morpeth and Prisca walked out of the temple, having the appearance of soberness and control of their senses once more. The priests bowed and asked the king if he needed anything. Morpeth held his wife's hand tightly and smiled. "Bring me my children," he replied.

The priests of Marduk sang their ancient chants in a language no longer known to any tribe or clan. They stood in a circle around the sacrificial table made of stone and ivory and inscribed with the laws of their religion. The priests were wearing robes of white linen with golden seams on the edges. The gold trimmings glistened from the reflection of the torches in the dark room. Their chanting grew louder and faster and they would stomp their feet every few moments. Then the chief priest, Amoz came to Morpeth and inquired:

"My Lord, it is now time to offer the sacrifices," he said with his head bowed.

Morpeth looked at him, "Good, the hour is upon us." He turned to his right and nodded his head to a large dark man, a Scythian slave. The slave left the room and returned a moment later with two other slaves carrying six children between them. The children were unconscious and were dressed in red garments. The slaves laid the lifeless children down on the table and all but one of the slaves then promptly left the room.

Amoz's eyes widened with shock and surprise. Looking confused at Morpeth, he said: "My Lord, what is this? These are your children. Why do you place them on the table of sacrifice?"

Prisca came to Morpeth's side and replied, "They are to be our offering for this day. Fear not priest, we shall kill them but for a moment, and once divine, we shall raise them back to life."

Amoz fell back aghast and spoke in desperation, "Surely not, my lords. You can do no such thing. To sacrifice innocent blood would be to desecrate the altar before us all. I beg you to reconsider this."

"This is what our master Marduk commands of us. We shall obey," said Morpeth.

"We must obey," Prisca added.

"No," shouted Amoz defiantly, "You can do no such thing. It is madness. The gods require mercy, justice, and love not the sacrifice of innocent children."

"We know the gods, priest. We know Marduk. And this is how we shall please him and he will make us gods if we do this pious act." Prisca spoke sternly with a hint of annoyance in her voice and she gave Amoz an angry look.

Amoz fell before Morpheth and Prisca's feet.

"But this is sacrilege and I beg you to stop now. You are not in your proper minds, power has corrupted you. Let us stop this. Go and reason with your brother, my lord. He will show you the error of your ways. I beg you, master."

Morpeth leaned down and placed his hand on Amoz's shoulder and picked him up. "Leave the matter to us. It is for us to decide the rites and rituals of our beloved god Marduk. I hold the power of life and death over all subjects in my kingdom, even over my children." He placed a dagger with an ivory handle in Amoz's hand. "Take this and do what you must do. I will reward you with riches beyond your imagination."

Amoz looked at the children. They looked lifeless and pale, obviously drugged. His mind cast back to the time when they were each born and dedicated to Marduk and the service of Iona. Their faces were full of innocence and completely unaware of the horrors about to befall them. Amoz turned around quickly.

"No," he said in a voice that the king rarely heard. "No, my lord. You will not sacrifice these innocent ones in the temple while I am high priest. No god, king, or man will make me defile my own soul. I shall not be party to this nor shall I let you do something that is unheard of in priestly lore.

I will not let you and your queen do something that, when in right mind, you both will regret." And with that he presented the dagger back to Morpeth. "Forgive me lord, but I will not do this. Nor shall you!" Morpeth's face remained stale, unmoved, and unstirred.

"Well, then, priest. I see your mind is made up. You leave me no other choice."

And Morpeth took the dagger and thrust back into Amoz's stomach. "Now you will die, my priest."

When Amoz collapsed, the cohort of priests around the table stopped their chanting and gasped in horror as they scurried towards the back wall quivering in fear. They muttered something between themselves. Morpeth and Prisca knew not what they said. Despite his wound, Amoz began crawling away towards the entrance unnoticed by Morpeth and Prisca who were now fixated on the shivering priests.

"Perhaps we should teach them a lesson, Morpeth," said Prisca.

"Perhaps we should, my beloved," he answered.

Prisca smiled to herself and stepped towards them. Waving her arms in a circle she uttered some magic words and with that a violent wind, stronger than any storm, rushed through the room. What seemed like a mini tornado grabbed one of the frightened priests and spun him around and threw him against one of the pillars of the temple. And then Morpeth put his fist into his palm and lunging forward a ball of fire launched from his hands and landed on one of the priests, consuming him in an instant blaze. The priest screamed in agony as he was incinerated. The rest of the priests scattered over the temple and cowered behind or under anything they could find as the bodies of their two colleagues lay on the floor before them.

"Now let that be a lesson to you all. I am not a king like an ordinary man. I am the immortal king of Iona and you shall do my bidding. Now return to your posts if you wish to live. Refuse and you will die like those you see before you."

The priests froze for a moment in their place, but then, one by one, with great hesitation and ever watchful of Morpeth and Prisca, they returned to their places and began singing again. Behind them, Amoz was crawling towards the entrance and he yelled in a raspy voice.

"I curse you Morpeth, you demon. I curse you Prisca, you heartless witch. By the name of the benevolent god Vetrius, I curse you. I swear to you this day that by the hand of your own child, you shall die. May he be given a double portion of your power and may he use it to avenge us all from the evil and madness that now grips you. I curse you both. May enmity reign between you and may your own offspring rise up to destroy you."

"Get that dying dog out of here, would you?" said Prisca to the Scythian slave, who nodded. He went over to Amoz and kicked him in the stomach. Amoz rolled down the staircase and remained at the bottom, motionless.

"Now let us begin again," said Morpeth. He and Prisca joined in the chanting, preparing themselves for divinity, putting the faces of their children out of their minds. But little did they know that Vetrius had already granted Amoz his wish.

The Scythian slave took up the duty of the priest. The dark figure stood over the children in the dim lit room. Morpeth and Prisca were a few feet away from the table upon which the children were laid. Finally, Morpeth yelled, "Do it" with a sense of hesitation and hunger in his voice. His eyes closed, his face turned away from the children, and he gripped Prisca's hands.

The slave looked down at the motionless children and taking a knife from his side he plunged it into the chest of the first of the six children. The first to die was Brutoi, a six year old boy, who bled to death in this drug induced sleep. The slave's face barely moved except to blink from the blood that spurted back at him. When the dagger struck the child, Morpeth and Prisca instantly felt an immediate sense of ecstasy and terror as if some enchanted substance had entered their bodies. The Scythian turned to the next child. A girl, whose name was Karla, only eight years old. He did the same to her and immediately the colour faded from her face. Again Morpeth and Prisca grimaced in a mix of pleasure and pain as a power slowly ebbed into their bodies. The slave moved to the next two children, Izza the five year old girl and Crestin a nine year old boy. They died while their parents wept tears of pain and joy.

Only two children were left now. The twelve year old Jakov and the two year old Iskandar. They lied together side by side. Jakov's arm and leg draped over his younger brother as if he were already trying to shield him in his sleep. The slave once more raised up his dagger to strike, but he did not hear the arrow that pierced his heart. He dropped the blade to the ground and himself fell lifeless upon the tiled floor. The sound of steel and stone woke Morpeth and Prisca from their ecstatic state. They turned around to hear the sound and in the doorway they saw a figure in full armour and six men behind him all holding cross bows.

"What is the meaning of this, Morpeth?" yelled the armoured man. "Have you gone mad?"

It was Fallkirk, Morpeth's brother, general of the army. Fallkirk walked up to the altar and saw the bodies of the dead children that made him twist his face in grave sorrow.

"What have you done, man?" he cried in anguish.

He scanned his eyes quickly over Jakov and then to Iskandar. He noticed that they were both still alive and that gave him a flutter of hope. He took Iskandar's face in his hands and stroked him softly feeling great sorrow for the boy, the youngest boy. Then turning around he looked at the king and queen filled with a mixture of grief, agony, and rage. He walked forward towards Prisca and Morpeth who themselves had not yet moved and the two simply stared back him with no emotion at all on their faces.

"When the priests told me what you were doing I did not believe them. How can you bring your children to this grief? Your children, Morpeth! My nieces and nephews! Your own heir!" His voice accelerated in speed and rose in pitch to the point of fury. "Your own children, Morpeth! What evil has beguiled you, man?"

But Morpeth was silent. He just stared blankly at this brother. Staring into the eyes of his brother, fixated on the pupils hidden inside the darkness of the visor of the royal helmet. Finally, he moved towards Fallkirk and spoke.

"My dear brother. You know neither the power of Marduk, nor the power that already flows through our veins. And from now on you shall no longer call me your brother, nor even your king. You shall call me your Most High God."

Fallkirk drew his sword and stepped towards Morpeth. "I don't know what oppressive poison afflicts your mind. But you are no god. If it bleeds, if it dies and stays dead, it is not a god. And I will make you bleed if I have to brother." Then glancing back at his six companions he nodded and spoke, "Seize them both. The king is out of his mind and the queen is no better."

The six men moved towards Morpeth and Prisca armed with a mix of crossbows and swords. Morpeth's face showed the first sign of any emotion: anger.

"So it is treason and idolatry then. You dare cross your king and your god".

"You are no god, Morpeth," cried Fallkirk.

"No?" retorted Prisca. "Then here and now feel our divine wrath." With that she waved her hands and once more a fierce wind blew over the six assailants and knocked them off their feet. Fallkirk himself was pushed back towards a wall. Through the wind one of the soldiers fired a crossbow dart which was deliberately blown off course. Prisca saw the dart swirling through the air and waving her hands again she directed the wind to carry it back to the soldier with greater force than which it was fired. The other soldiers also fired their darts only to have them blown far from their intended target. The soldiers drew swords and tried to rush them during a lull in the wind. Morpeth stepped forward and sent forth a ball of fire that narrowly missed one of the soldiers but ignited the curtains at the rear of the temple, beginning a smoky blaze. Prisca cast further wind in front of them in tandem with another fireball from Morpeth, creating a huge blanket of flame that fell upon the remaining four soldiers sending them crashing to the ground in a consuming fire.

Fallkirk could only look on in disbelief as the room began to fill with smoke. Morpeth and Prisca then turned towards him and the two began circling him to his left and right .

"See, I warned you, Fallkirk. You are dealing with divinity not royalty now".

"Kill him Morpeth. He shall be the next sacrifice to our genius and glory," spoke Prisca.

Fallkirk could only stand behind a pillar of the temple, coughing more as the smoke filled the empty space with its intoxicating fumes. Just then two fireballs crashed into the pillar that Fallkirk was hiding behind. He ran to the next one along the deep hall of the temple. The wind gusted around him like a gale. The wind and fire set further vessels of the temple ablaze so that the heat and smoke was almost unbearable. Visibility became more difficult for all. Fallkirk looked around the room and noticed that the wooden beams at the far end of the temple were on fire. Picking up a brick he threw it at Prisca only to see it come flying back at him and slam into the wall behind him. More fireballs flew through the air as he jumped from pillar to pillar. Other items, bricks, golden pots, bronze saucers were also scattered around the temple as the winds bellowed.

"You cannot escape Fallkirk. There is nowhere to run, my brother," taunted Morpeth. Fallkirk kept moving. The heat inside his helmet was now unbearable and he was short of breath. Finally, he ran for the exit only to be gripped by the wild wind and was slammed into the wall. He slowly rose up, coughing, feeling the steel of his helmet almost burning his face with its heat. He could vaguely make out Prisca and Morpeth standing in front of him. Fallkirk drew his sword and confronted them.

"I will not die here Morpeth. Not now, not like this."

"You don't have a chance, silly mortal," said Prisca scornfully.

"Come now, my dear. He is family, royal family at that. He deserves a noble death."

Fallkirk looked up at the burning beams above him then stared back at Morpeth.

"No brother. You will not kill anyone else today. Your end is as certain as mine."

"I find that very hard to believe, Fallkirk, considering where you're standing".

"Really," said Fallkirk. "Then feel this."

Fallkirk launched into the air and using his sabre he cut through the burning beam above him, sending parts of the ceiling crashing down. Morpeth and Prisca fell back as shards of burning lumber, stone, and debris fell around them and even on them. Morpeth dropped his sword and staggered away in shortness of breath. Looking to his right he saw the two children Jakov and Iskandar on the altar. Hesitating for a moment, he turned towards them, dodging further beams that began falling all around him. Fallkirk picked up the two children, placing one over each shoulder and ran to the exit down the stars. He felt the cool air hit his lungs and he tried to breathe deeply even as he coughed up black phlegm. Wasting no time, he ran down the stairs. At the bottom of the stairs, Amoz grabbed at his ankle, clutching at his leg as Fallkirk tried to run.

"Help me too," said the old priest with desperate grasps for breath.

Fallkirk looked down at him in pity. He was already burdened with the two children, but he reached down and helped Amoz up. Further rumbles and explosions could be heard inside the temple behind them. Fallkirk carried the children and dragged Amoz out of the temple complex as smoke started bellowing out of the various windows and entrances. Coming to his horse, Fallkirk collapsed to the ground and opened his front visor so that he could breathe better. Amoz crawled over towards Fallkirk.

"Thank you master Fallkirk," he said with a weak and whispery voice. "You have saved us all from the monsters."

"The king and queen are dead. The royal line is decimated. I hardly call that salvation."

"Dead?" Amoz's face weak with mortal injury looked confused. "They are not dead master. Morpeth and Prisca will survive. You cannot kill them with fire or burning wood. But they are trapped for the moment and it will take them days to get out. But you rescued the children master Fallkirk. They are the two pillars of our deliverance."

"What do you mean? I just saw half the temple collapse on my brother and his wife. That was after he used some power, some strange power not of this world, both to burn me half alive and to blow me into the next kingdom."

Fallkirk leaned forward and gripped the priest by the garment.

"What happened in there priest? What is going on? How do you know Morpeth isn't dead?"

"The god Marduk has made them demi-gods. Your brother and your sister-in-law are no more. They are no longer human, but are immortals. More than human, but not yet gods."

"How did this happen?"

"Marduk promised them that if they sacrificed their children to him, that he would grant them divinity. With every child that died, they grew more godlike, more divine, and less human. You cannot stop them with wood, stone, or steel. Only severing their head from their body can kill them. Otherwise they shall live forever."

Fallkirk let go of Amoz. He leaned back and paused for a moment.

"And what of the children? How can they save us?"

Amoz coughed, sputtering blood, nearly choking in pain. He looked back at Fallkirk.

"My time is short. But this much I know. Marduk is not the only god of the pantheon. His self-indulgent interference in the affairs of men is matched by the mercy and compassion of Vetrius. I begged Vetrius for revenge for this evil, I pledge my life in exchange for it, and Vetrius has answered my prayer."

"How do you know this?"

Amoz coughed some more, his chest tightening and his body convulsing slightly. He grabbed hold of the children's arms and rolled up their sleeves. On the forearm of Jakov and Iskandar was a tattoo of two intertwined snakes.

"Do you see this mark General Fallkirk?"

Fallkirk leaned forward to look at the arms of the children.

Amoz explained to him: "The children had no tattoos before this day. This is proof."

"What is it? What does it mean?"

"It means, master Fallkirk, that both children are marked by Vetrius. He watches over them and he is for them. They are marked as his servants to bring justice to this land. Not all the power of divinity and immortality has passed into the bodies of Prisca and Morpeth. And what remains, that is given to these two. The same power of your brother now flows in the body of these two boys, especially the younger, he has a double portion of this magic. They and they alone have the power to destroy Morpeth and Prisca."

"How can this be?"

"The how is not important. What matters is hope." Amoz convulsed again and felt his life slowly ebbing away. "You must take them, hide them, and prepare them to destroy Morpeth and Prisca. They are our only hope, master. There is no other hope for us. If you fail and Morpeth kills them, he will be a god, and he will unleash terror on us all. Divinity will make him mad even further, murderously mad. Take them Fallkirk . . . you must . . ."

Fallkirk grabbed the priest by the garments and shook him.

"What else priest? What else can you tell me?" But Amoz remained silent. He was dead.

Fallkirk leaned back on his elbows, feeling confused and stressed. He was startled to hear sounds of rumbling inside the temple and he could feel the rumble beginning to move closer. Prisca and Morpeth were not dead and they were not content with staying in there either. In a moment of release, Fallkirk hugged the two unconscious boys and wept. He wept for them and for himself. He especially embraced little Iskandar, the youngest of the family, for whom he had a special affection. He kissed him on the forehead as he feared what the future held for the boy now. It was a day of evil, a day of confusion, and now a day of destiny as well.

Feeling drained and somewhat disoriented, Fallkirk put the two boys on the front of his horse and then mounted it himself. He looked into the open plain and the mountains beyond the great river. He closed his eyes and kicked the horses with his heels. If the priest Amoz was right, and he was the only one who had made any sense of the madness of what had happened in the temple, then there was only one thing Fallkirk and the boys could do: get as far away as they could from there. Go somewhere where they would never be found and pray to Vetrius that Morpeth and Prisca would never find them. At full gallop he rode on, not knowing what fate stood before them.

Before the day ended, Morpeth and Prisca emerged from the burning rubble looking strained, but more angered than injured by their misfortune. They continued to feel the ravenous hunger of divine power and resolved to seek out their last two children and finish the sacrifice that they had promised Marduk. On return to their castle at Dalazvar, they organized their army into scouting parties to find Fallkirk, Iskandar, and Jakov. But it was too late. The three had disappeared and were not seen again. Months and years passed and Morpeth and Prisca's rage at the escaped trio became insatiable. They systematically sacked every village, town, and city in the search for them. Many warlords rebelled in their local districts and civil war followed led by a group called the Freedom Legionnaires who lived in the forests and deserts. Morpeth and Prisca fought side by side with their troops. Using their immortal powers they seemed almost invincible and they put down all respective threats.

Yet no victory over insubordinate cities or crushing attacks of the Freedom Legionnaires could bring them what they wanted. Eventually, in their frustration Morpeth and Prisca turned on each other. After a few years of failure in not finding the two boys in their relentless hunt, Prisca tried to have Morpeth beheaded in his sleep by an assassin. When the plot was uncovered, Morpeth had Prisca bound and imprisoned in the Masavar fortress. With her hands perpetually bound, she was unable to use her powers and was as helpless as any other prisoner. They did not see each other or speak to each other for eight years.

Nobody knew what happened to Fallkirk and the children. Some of Morpeth's advisors thought that Fallkirk crossed the western mountains and he lived in the wilderness as a hermit. Some said that they simply died in the Yobi desert plains. Morpeth learned that destroying up to half his kingdom had not rooted out the fugitives, and neither did he have the troops to fight continual civil wars. So he stopped sacking towns in his quest, but chose a more subtle course of action. Instead, he sent soldiers to scout the wilderness and ordered his spies to look for children who were of the same age as Iskandar and Jakov and to see if any might be them. Eight years passed and the soldiers found nothing in the wilderness but strange ferocious animals and uncivilized tribes of the Tautau. The spies likewise could find no children who matched the description of Jakov or Iskandar, until one day . . .

# Chapter 2

## The Tavern of the Motley Bulldog

PRASCHI WAS A SMALL village in the southern hinterlands of Iona. Cattle grazed in the countryside, farmers planted and harvested their crops, and village life centred on the market place. Praschi was far enough away from most of Iona to be free from its civil wars and strife, but close enough to walk to the highways leading to the north, west, and east. On this one sunny day, little Bobbascow was carrying his bucket to the well. He was enjoying the walk along the dusty road. He felt the warm beams of sunshine fall on his freckly face, and he listened to the sounds of the world around him. It made him sing. Suddenly, he heard the frantic noise of hooves coming. Around the bend came a blur of brown and silver at a ferocious speed. Bobbascow just about got knocked over by several speeding horses. Just before they were on top of him he dived to the side of the road and narrowly avoided being trampled. Rolling over, Bobbascow looked around at the horsemen heading away from him. They hadn't even bothered to slow down to avoid him. It was like they didn't even see him.

"Typical," he murmured to himself. There were three horses, and they were imperial guards. He recognised their insignia. A green dragon's head surrounded by flames. He'd heard of them, never seen them before, and wondered what they were doing in Praschi. Nothing ever happened there. To make matters worse, Bobbascow realized that he was sitting in a pool of mud that soaked into his pants and made him feel very uncomfortable.

"Oh, fig nuts" he said to himself. He looked around for his bucket and he noticed that it was in the middle of the road and had been trampled on. It was now broken into pieces. He sighed. He'd have to return back to the Inn not only without water, but now without a bucket as well. Wringstone the Innekeeper would not be happy. He might even give Bobbascow a kick on his bottom for failing his task. Bobbascow sighed again and slowly turned back towards the village centre. It was a lonely walk back to the Inn especially when he knew what was waiting for him now. He wondered how he might explain it to Wringstone. He knew all too well that saying imperial guards broke it might not be believable.

Bobbascow walked through the town and waved to everyone he knew. The baker, the blacksmith, the other boys of the town playing in the street. They all knew Bobbascow. Many felt sorry for him. He came to Praschi on a slave train as a child and was sold into servitude. That was why he now worked for Wringstone at the Tavern. It was called, "The Motley Bulldog". Wringstone named it after his pet bulldog called, incidentally, "Motley." Wringstone loved "Motley" more than anything else in the world even though he was a vicious and stupid animal. Wringstone valued the dog far more than Bobbascow. In fact, Bobbascow often wondered if one day Wringstone might kill him and feed him to Motley in a drunken rage. The only thing that prevented that from happening was the other servant, Talkai, a tall, gingery, and lanky man who had also been sold to Wringstone. He was a nice man though. Like an uncle to Bobbascow. Bobbascow could not remember not having Talkai around. Talkai was very fun. He was kind of clumsy, always falling down, breaking things, and getting into trouble. But best of all he was always kind to Bobbascow and they looked out for each other. They had to. Working for mean old man Wringstone was terrible. The best thing about Talkai was that he always getting into mischief and Wringstone spent all his time hollering at him and not at Bobbascow.

Bobbascow opened the door of the Inn and walked into the foyer area. It stank of stale beer and the smell of onions from the kitchen.

"What took you so long?" came a voice from the dark corner of the room. It was Wringstone. He sat on a stool eating his breakfast. As he spoke Bobbascow could see that egg and corn were all over the black beard that covered his rounded face. Bobbascow and Talkai would often joke about how many chins they thought Wringstone had under that beard.

"And where's that water I sent you to get?".

"The bucket broke, master Wringstone. I got knocked down by imperial guards."

"What? Imperial guards knocked you down? In Praschi? Let me guess, they were on their way to the wedding between a lady Dragon and a fat frumpy pig and they just happened to knock you over? You silly child. Do you expect me to believe that non-sense. You were wasting time playing and you probably left the bucket in some meadow. Or sold it to someone for little penny. Didn't ya, you little git!"

"No, master Wringstone. It's true."

Wringstone pushed his plate to the side and stood up. His short, stocky frame caused the floorboards under his feet to creak.

"One of these days, Bobbascow, I'm gonna give you your due. Servants might have rights, but only when there's witnesses around. Mark my words, Bobba, I'll clobber you to death one of these days," he said shaking his fist an inch from the face of Bobbascow who tried not show his fear.

Just then Talkai walked in carring a pig on his shoulder.

"Master, you'll never guess what I saw in town?"

"What?" grumbled Wringstone.

"Imperial guards, here in Praschi. Would you ever have thought?"

He took the pig to the back of the room and then threw it into the backyard like it was a sack of potatoes. "

"Don't throw the pigs!" yelled Wringstone.

"Master, don't worry, they bounce, just like cringo balls." Bobbascow laughed. Wringstone just shook his head as he did at most things which Talkai did and said.

"Where did you see them?" Wringstone said to Talkai.

Talkai was now behind the bar and started to clean cups with a rag.

"Just up the way of the main street. They were outside the turnip stall of old man Kingston. They looked very serious."

Wringstone's face showed an air of concern.

"Something ain't right. Imperial guards don't come to Praschi without a good reason."

Wringstone walked out of the front door and looked up the main street. Sure enough, just as Talkai had said, he could see three imperial guards. They were dismounted from their horses and standing in front of the turnip stall. Wringstone had seen them many times before. He was a veteran from the Munic wars over ten years ago. He'd seen more than enough of the king's imperial guards for a hundred lifetimes. He knew who they were and what they could do. They were the king's personal messengers, close bodyguards, and specialized in executions of political dissidents. The imperial guards were all too efficient in their work. They were people to be avoided. Wringstone could see the three of them, armed with swords at their side, and they were talking to a man wearing a brown cape and a red hat. Then suddenly, the man with the red hat pointed straight at Wringstone who was but 100 yards away. The three riders turned and looked straight at him. Wringstone froze and his heart began pounding. It got faster and faster as the three men in green tunics began walking towards him.

"Oh no," he said to himself. Somehow he knew it was going to be a very bad day. He went back inside at once.

Wringstone went behind the bar and looked inside a cabinet. In it was a sword and crossbow. He pulled out the crossbow and loaded it with a dart. He had a feeling that this day was going to end in bloodshed. Probably his, he thought. One thing went through his mind. Don't get taken alive.

Bobbascow watched silently as Wringstone loaded the crossbow. He saw something in Wringstone that he'd never seen before: fear. In one sense, he was glad to see his grumpy boss flustered and nervous. But on the other hand, Wringstone did not get nervous easily. Bobbascow had seen him throw out the most violent of drunks and punched down the most notorious of crooks who wandered into Praschi. Maybe Bobbascow should be scared too.

"What are you doing, master?"

"None of your business, boy. And if you have any sense you'll go and hide in the back. And keep quiet for once."

Talkai walked in.

"I think I hurt the pig when I throwed it. This one didn't bounce very well," he said, genuinely remorseful.

"You stupid frog kissing git. Take the boy outback. Both of you go hide in the piggery. Wait there till I get you."

"Why," said Talkai. "It's not nap time already is it?"

"Just do as I say," he shouted at him.

Talkai shrugged his shoulders. "Come on, Bobba. Time to cuddle with piggy-Louise for a nice nap."

The two went off. Bobbascow looked behind him as he walked out only to see Wringstone concealing a knife in his boot. Suddenly, Bobbascow felt very sick in his stomach.

No sooner had the two servants left than three men in green tunics and silver helmets came in. They removed their helmets and walked towards Wringstone who pretended not to notice them as he cleaned a glass. Wringstone look down at the crossbow and sword he had hidden under the bench of the counter.

"Where is the publican of this establishment?" asked one of the men as he walked towards Wringstone. He was tall with long blond hair, dark eyes, and rigid cheek bones.

"That would be me. Now what will it be gents? A nice glass of rum for your journey?"

"We are not here for a drink."

The other two guards had began walking around the tavern and peeking into the adjacent hallway and rooms.

"We are looking for a young boy. The one you call Bobbascow. I believe he's your boy-servant. Is that true?"

"Yes, I have a servant by that name. What's he done? Did he assassinate the king or something?"

"Not quite," was the matter of fact reply. "But he is a person of interest to the crown. Where is he?"

Wringstone paused and looked around at the three men. "He's not here. I sent him out to do some errands and to fix a fence for a friend of mine."

The blond imperial guard stared at him blankly. "So the boy is not here then."

"That's what I said."

The rider came closer to Wringstone and placed his helmet on the desk. He smiled at Wringstone.

"Do you know who we are?"

"I'm assuming that you are three single men with an interest in young boys."

"We are imperial guards in case you hadn't noticed. We are not to be trifled with."

"Imperial guards you say." Wringstone pretended to be genuinely surprised. "Forgive me sirs, if I did not recognize you. The last time I saw imperial guards they had had their heads and hands chopped off and they were covered in blood. But come to think of it now as I look at you gents, you do bare an uncanny resemblance to the corpses left on the fields of Municia."

The rider smiled and looked away from Wringstone for a moment.

"You must have fought in the Munic wars then old man."

"That I did sir, and well may I add."

"Then you know all too well that we are not known for our merciful treatment of the enemy. And unless you want me to cut off your hands and feet and eyes and tongue, I suggest you tell me where the boy is."

"Look, I don't want any trouble. I came to this hick town to get away from you lot. Like I said, the boy is out doing errands. He should be back by end of the day. You can see him then."

"Good," said the man. "We look forward to being of his acquaintance. We will wait. Outside. When the boy returns, you be sure to bring him to us. Won't you, good fellow?"

"You can count on it," said Wringstone, dripping with sarcasm. "Whatever my king asks of me, I am his willing servant."

"For your sake I hope so, my beer-swilling friend."

He gestured to the other two imperial guards and walked towards the exit. Then he turned back to Wringstone. "Oh, by the way, what regiment of the Municians did you serve in? Out of curiosity."

"The royal hussars," replied Wringstone.

The man nodded to himself. "If I remember rightly, they were all killed at the bridge of Kefilcard."

"All but one," retorted Wringstone.

The rider locked eyes with Wringstone and then turned and left. The three guards went outside of the Motley Bulldog standing guard as if they were expecting royalty to enter.

Wringstone breathed a sigh of relief. He quickly opened a bottle of rum and took a long and deep swill. He sat down and rubbed his eyes. His dog Motley came to him and licked his hands.

"Motley, why do these things always happen to me?" Motley just barked and kept licking his master's hands, probably because they tasted of rum.

In the piggery, Talkai was snuggled up with a pig and snoring like a pig too. Bobbascow stood on a stool looking through a crack in the door to see if he could see anything in the tavern. He heard voices, but nothing he could make out.

"Don't worry, Bobbascow," muttered Talkai while half-asleep. "The worst thing that could happen is that the imperial guards take Wringstone off to jail and leave us to run the tavern. We could change the name of it to 'Talkai's House of Travelling Travellers.'"

"It's not Wringstone I'm worried about Talkai," said Bobbascow concerned. He looked down on the floor to see a pig licking Talkai's face. "It's us I'm worried about. What are imperial guards doing here?"

"Probably because Wringstone punched the king's butler in the face at some drunken party. Who cares, Bobbascow. It's nap time."

Suddenly, Wringstone came running out of the back door straight towards the piggery. Bobbascow jumped down on the floor to make it look like he hadn't been watching. Wringstone burst in and grabbed Bobbascow by the neck.

"What in the hell have you done boy?"

"Nothing, master. I've done nothing to no one."

Wringstone pushed him gently, but hard enough to make him fall onto the staw.

"Do you know who is out the front right now? Imperial guards! Do you know the kind of things they do? Do you, boy, do you know?"

"No," cried Bobbascow crawling backwards as Wringstone walked towards him. Bobbascow had seen Wringstone angry before, violently angry, but nothing like this. He could tell that Wringstone was scared.

"They do the kind of things that give you nightmares. At least they still do that to me." He looked down at Talkai who was lying down ignoring both of them. Wringstone lashed out and kicked him.

"Get up, you lazy toad."

"Ow, that really hurt." Talkai got up and rubbed his ribs.

"I don't know what the guards want with you boy. But I'll tell ya this much. You need to get far away from here as you can. So go now. Talkai you go with him, through the wood, as far as the Jedida falls. After that boy, you're on your own."

"But where will I go? Don't send me away, not alone out there."

"Look, Bobbascow. Whatever you fear the most in this life, that and a thousand other evils, are standing outside the front door of the tavern. So I suggest you stop your blubbering and get as far away from here as your little legs can carry you. Those guards will not give you a head start and you've only got a little time before they catch on to what is up. So get on with it boy, while you still can."

Bobbascow started shaking and crying a little. He rubbed his eyes as Talkai stroked his head.

"I know," said Talkai. "I have a brilliant plan. You tell them that I'm Bobbascow, and then what I'll do is . . ." He hadn't even finished the sentence before Wringstone had slapped him on the top of his head.

"You stupid mule of a man." Wringstone then gave Bobbascow a bag.

"What's this?" he asked.

"It's a loaf of bread, a flask of water, some fruit, and a knife."

"The knife is to fight off the imperial guards if they get too close," interjected Talkai.

"No," said Wringstone. "The knife is to slit your own throat in case you think you're about to get captured. Or to kill Talkai if he starts to drive you mad."

Wringstone lifted up Bobbascow and put him on the windowsill. He opened the shutters.

"Now go. You too, Talkai."

Bobbascow hesistated for a moment, but jumped outside the window and looked across the green fields and the woods only a few hundred yards away. Talkai jumped out behind him.

"Come on, then. Let's go," said Talkai as he started walking.

Bobbascow looked behind him and saw Wringstone watching them go. He turned to Wringstone and asked, "Master, why didn't you turn me over to them? It would have been easier."

"Hmpf," grunted Wringstone. "I could not have done that boy. I've always said that the pleasure of beating you to death would have to be mine and no one else's."

And for the first time Bobbascow saw Wringstone smile at him. Wringstone closed the shutters to the window of the piggery and Bobbascow and Talkai ran as fast as they could into the wood.

# Chapter 3

## Escape from Praschi

ONCE TALKAI AND BOBBASCOW reached the wood, they stopped running and slowed to a brisk walk.

"Did Wringstone seem a bit irritable today Bobbascow? More than normal you would say?"

"Very irritable, I think. Much more than normal. Something is bothering him."

"Do you think we should eat the bread now? I am awfully hungry."

"I think we should probably wait first. It could be a long journey."

Bobbascow looked behind him through the trees and back at the tavern and as much of the village that he could see. It had been his whole life, now he didn't know where his life was leading him, or even if he'd be alive at the end of the day.

"Don't worry, Bobba." Talkai knew that Bobbascow was scared. "We'll get you far from here and you'll probably end up working in a piggery for some nice old rich lady. That's the kind of life I dream of. Big fat pigs with a big fat masteress who likes to feed me bacon sandwiches, and stroke my chin. Ah yes, that'd be the life."

"Isn't that what Wringstone does for Motley his dog?"

"Well, yes, that dog has a good life you know."

Bobbascow smiled to himself and wondered how Talkai could be so oblivious to the dangers that they were escaping from.

Suddenly a blur of brown rushed from behind a tree. Talkai yelled "duck" as Bobbascow was pushed aside and fell to the ground. Bobbascow heard a thud. He looked over his shoulder to see Talkai lying on the ground unconscious with a huge lump on his head. Then standing over him was a man in a brown cape with a red hat, holding a huge stick and a whip.

"Going somewhere little man?"

Bobbascow rolled away as the man tried to hit him with his stick. Scurrying about, he got up and ran. He had only run a few steps before his legs became tangled in the whip that wrapped around his legs. He fell again this time knocking his chin on the ground. Bobbascow instantly felt the salty taste of blood in his mouth. The man was now on top of him and had begun tying him up with the whip. The last thing he saw was the man putting him into a huge sack. He tried to wriggle and squirm but it was no use. He was tied up and was being carried away somewhere.

The man carrying the bag spoke to him.

"Don't bother resisting little one. You're not going anywhere. And if I were you I'd save what strength you have for later. The gods know that you'll probably need it."

Bobbascow began to cry as he felt the constant bumps from the man jogging as he carried him along. He was scared like never before. For the first time he could ever remember, he caught himself saying, "Mamma, Papa, where are you? Come and get me."

After a while Bobbascow could recognize the sounds outside of the bag. A chorus of familiar voices, animal noises, and the clanking of tools. The recognizable smell of bread and smoke too. He was in the village. Then all of a sudden the walking stopped. The man in brown dropped the sack and Bobbascow landed with a thud. He could hear the man speaking to someone.

"I found something that might interest you commander."

Bobbascow had stopped crying now and was just waiting. Waiting to be let out of the bag, waiting for whatever was next. He briefly thought of Talkai, not knowing if his best friend was alive or dead.

The bag opened and the man in brown lifted him out of the sack by the hair and neck.

"This is the one you're looking for commander."

A blond-haired man in a green tunic came up to Bobbascow, who was shaking.

"What is your name?" the man asked him.

"B . . . B . . . Bob . . . Bobascow, sir. What have I done wrong sir? Please, I am sorry, I can repay . . ."

"How old are you?"

"I . . . I don't know."

The man grabbed Bobascow's chin. "What do you mean you don't know? Everyone knows how old they are."

"Honestly, sir, I don't know. I've been here 8 summers I think. Ever since I was a tot."

"He's got to be ten, eleven, or twelve at the most," said the man in brown.

"Then who are your parents?"

"I . . . I don't know."

"This is getting us nowhere. Get the publican."

Two men in green tunics dragged Wringstone in from the tavern. Bobascow could see that he was bleeding badly from the head and face. He looked weak, feeble, and broken. He'd never seen weakness in Wringstone before.

The imperial guard grabbed Wringstone by the throat and asked him, "How old is this boy? And who are his parents?"

Wringstone said nothing. The blond-haired man gripped his neck even harder and Wringstone's face turned red and then blue.

Finally he uttered, "He's eleven. I don't know who his parents are. He was brought in a slave train. He's an orphan."

It was the first time Bobbascow had heard the words "orphan." His whole life he had secretly hoped that one day his parents might find him and take him away from this awful place. Now he knew it was never going to happen.

"Why don't we just check him for the mark?" said the man in brown as he kept a firm grip on Bobbascow. The man in green nodded. One of the other imperial guards came up to Bobbascow, ripped open his shirt, and began searching his body.

"I don't see it," he said. "Wait, what's that?" They all bent down and peered at the tattoo on Bobbascow's right forearm. Two intertwined snakes. Small, but clearly visible.

"Where did you get that tattoo?" Bobbascow was asked.

"I don't know. I thought all slaves had it."

The blond imperial guard grinned. "No, boy, not all slaves have a mark like that. Most boys do not have a mark like that. Only one boy has it. One special boy in particular. And it seems that you are that special boy."

"I expect to get paid handsomely for this," spoke the man in brown with a sense of great joy.

"Oh, you will, but first, we have business to attend to. We have to bind him and take him to Morpeth. Once Morpeth confirms his identity you will be paid twice what you asked for."

Bobbascow felt his arms being pulled behind his back by the man in brown and his head was pushed to the ground as the man in brown prepared to tie him up again.

Wringstone shook his body and bucked away from one of the imperial guards holding him.

"You cowardly pigs. You imperial guards are the filth of rats and mice," said Wringstone from his swollen and bloodied face.

"I'll deal with you in a moment, you Munician traitor." The guard turned back towards Bobbascow. "It is time for you to go on a little trip my friend. I know someone who is positively dying to meet you." Bobbascow closed his eyes as his head was rubbed in the dirt some more. He could hear people in the town gasping and women yelling profanities at the guards. The next thing he heard was a scream of pain and then a thud on the ground next to his feet. He quickly opened his eyes to see the man in brown lying on the ground with an arrow sticking through his neck. Without thinking, Bobbascow rolled quickly to his right as an imperial guard tried to grab him. He looked up and the guards were standing in a small circle back to back with swords and shields at the ready.

"Where did that come from?" said one of them.

"Did you see anything?" said the other.

Their eyes darted around and then the leader turned his eye back to Bobbascow.

"Get the boy and let's leave. Now!" barked the blond headed leader.

One of the guards broke from their circle and grabbed Bobascow by the leg and began dragging him along the dirt road. But the man fell to the ground and released Bobbascow. As Bobboscow looked up to see what had happened, he saw Wringstone, on his knees, holding a knife behind the fallen guard.

"Run, Bobbascow, run," cried Wringstone.

Wringstone tried to get up to face the other two imperial guards, but before he was even off his knees, he was pierced by two swords. He stopped moving at once and died.

Bobbascow scurried backwards on all fours. He quickly unwound the cord from his ankles, and then ran down the main street. The imperial guards chased after him as townsfolk yelled and threw whatever they could at the guards in their pursuit. As he looked ahead he saw a man on a black horse riding straight towards him. He stopped and looked behind him, and then in front of him again. He was surrounded. He looked everywhere. There was nowhere to run. The black horse was only a few feet in front of him when he tried to dive to his left. It was no good. He felt the hand of the rider grab his arm and flip him in an arc. The next thing Bobbascow knew was that he was lying stomach down on a black horse with the rider holding him by the back of the neck.

"Hold on," came the unfamiliar voice.

No sooner had Bobbascow realized that he was on a horse than the horse leaped high in the air over the two imperial guards. There was a brief clanging of swords and the horse kept galloping away from the imperial guards. Bobbascow remained motionless, grateful to be alive, but confused as to why he still was. Then the horse came to a sudden halt and then fear returned to the pit of his bowels.

"Who are you?" Bobbascow asked still too afraid to look up.

"Just stay still and be quiet," came the reply from the rider. The horse turned around to face the two imperial guards who were now running towards them.

"Stay here and I promise that you will live," the mysterious rider said sternly as he dismounted. Bobbascow could see that he was wearing a black cloak and hood with a silver belt and green gloves. He carried two swords on his back and he drew both of them. Bobbascow thought to run, but something made him stay still.

The dark rider slowly walked towards the two imperial guards as they stopped in front of him. One of the guards lunged at the rider with a sword which the rider avoided and then counter-thrusted into the man's chest and fell him. The second guard, the blond one, was more cautious and slow in his approach. He feinted a few times and then finally came at the rider with a ferocious series of blows with his two handed sword. The rider blocked and swerved to avoid the huge sharp blade that sliced the air. The rider was being pushed backwards as he parried and blocked the aggressive attacks. Then he took two steps back and pointed his two swords at the imperial guard. Next, from the ground, several handfuls of tiny stones flew up into the imperial guard's face. It temporarily blinded the guard and he was then stabbed in the mid-section by the rider. The guard fell to his knees, grimacing in pain. The rider stood behind him with his two swords poised and plunged them into the back of the imperial guard. And then as if nothing had happened, he gently strolled back to the horse where Bobbascow was and remounted it.

"Are you alright?" the rider asked.

Bobbascow looked up and for the first time he saw the rider's face. It was young, handsome, and had a look of cold determination.

"Yes, I think so," Bobbascow uttered. "Who are you?"

"Questions later little one. We need to get far away from here as we can. When those imperial guards don't return to their camp, this place will be swarming with them before nightfall and you don't want to be here for that. You're lucky that I got here when I did."

They galloped off down the road away from the village. As the minutes passed the village looked further and further away. Bobbascow sat up and looked over the head of the horse as they galloped. It was odd. He had never ridden a horse before. Somehow he knew that his first ride would be one that he'd never forget. Then on the side of the road he heard a voice calling for him.

"Bobbascow, Bobbascow."

The rider brought the horse to a stop.

"Who is that?" he asked Bobbascow.

Bobbascow looked at the side of the road and saw Talkai sitting there looking very confused and rubbing his head.

"Bobba, take me with you, I can't go back. Wringstone will kill me for losing you."

"Do you know this man?" the rider asked

"Yes, he's my friend Talkai. He's a man-servant just like me."

Bobbascow turned to Talkai.

"Wringstone is dead Talkai. They killed him."

Talkai paused for a moment and looked down.

"But ... How ... What should I do? I can't go back. They'll come after me too."

"He's right," Bobbascow said. "The imperial guards will come for him too."

"That's not our problem," and the rider kicked the horse, but before it moved Bobbascow cried out, "Stop, we can't leave him. He's the only family I've got."

"We can't waste time picking up every servant and idiot from this rancid village that you know. Besides, he'll only slow us down."

Bobbascow slid off the horse. "Then I'll take my chances with him."

The rider was clearly annoyed.

"Come with me little man. I'm here to help you. Do as I say and do not try my patience."

"But I don't even know who you are. Why should I go with you? For all I know you could be one of them."

"In time you'll learn more my young friend. Now come, let's go, we don't have time for this nonsense."

"Not without Talkai."

"Yes, not without me," said Talkai in agreement.

The rider closed his eyes and grinded his teeth in annoyance.

"Fine, then. If we must. Both of you get on. Boy at the front and the serf on the back." He patted his horse. "Sorry, Infamy, but it's a heavier load for you today."

Talkai and Bobbascow mounted the big black horse and they set off at a blinding pace. The countryside seemed to fly by as the trio made their way easterward away from Praschi.

"My bottom hurts," said Talkai as he held on for dear life at the back.

"Not now," said the rider and Bobbascow in unison.

# Chapter 4

## The Wells of Mishina

AFTER MANY HOURS OF riding the trio came to a stop. The rider pulled the horse off to the side of the road and then walked into the forest for several minutes.

"Are we stopping?" asked Bobbascow.

"Yes," the rider said, avoiding eye-contact. "We'll camp here for the night and then continue our journey early on. We have to meet the others by noon tomorrow."

He tied the horse to a tree and then walked around for a few moments, looking and listening.

Talkai and Bobbascow hopped off the horse as well. Talkai got his foot stuck in one of the stirrups and tripped over. Bobbascow helped him up.

"You really are a clumsy clutz Talkai."

"I know," he said, "And thanks for bringing me with you. I can't imagine having to go into the village. I can't imagine Wringstone being dead."

Bobbascow stopped for a moment as the reality of the day's events dawned on him.

"He saved my life Talkai. He was a hard man. But he saved me. Twice in fact."

Talkai bent down and looked the little dark headed boy in the eye.

"I guess there was good in him after all."

"I guess." He hugged Talkai. "Why did they want me? What did I do? And why were they interested in my snake tattoo?"

Bobbascow lifted up the sleeve of his shirt and showed Talkai.

"I don't know Bobbascow. Perhaps you belong to someone important. Maybe your family offended Morpeth and they wanted revenge on you."

The rider walked up to the duo.

"Maybe it is because Morpeth is afraid of you!" he said beneath his hood.

"Scared of me? How could the king of Iona with his strange powers be afraid of me? I only a servant, a child."

"In time you'll learn why little boy. And I will show you how to make him afraid. You will strike fear into the heart of Morpeth and his army will quiver in fear before you."

"I think you have me confused with someone else."

The rider gently took Bobbascow by his right hand looked at his tattoo.

"No, child. It is you who is wrong. You have no idea how important you are and how powerful you will become. You will shatter a kingdom and warlords will lick the dust off your sandals."

The rider threw two blankets at Talkai and Bobbascow. "It will be dark soon. Get some sleep. We ride early tomorrow."

Talkai and Bobbascow cleared out a space on the ground and placed their blankets on the soft forest grass.

"Thank you," said Bobbascow to the stranger. "I mean, I don't know you, but I'm grateful for what you did."

"No, thank you," said the rider. "You are the answer to the prayers of many."

The rider turned away for a moment and began to make a fire.

"You're a good shot with an arrow too," said Bobbascow, getting under his blanket.

"What arrow?" asked the rider.

"You know, the arrow you used to kill the man wearing the brown cape with the red hat."

"I fired no arrow child. I think your memory fails you."

"But the man in brown was shot with an arrow. It went through his throat. I saw it."

"What man in brown? When I arrived in the village you were running from the guards, and then . . ."

Bobascow interrupted him, "But before that. When the man in brown first took me out of the bag. Then you shot him with your arrow."

Suddenly the rider looked confused. "I have no bow and no arrow. And I killed no man in brown. Are you sure?"

"Yes," said Bobbascow, "I saw the arrow. It had red feathers with a golden speckle."

The rider went from confused to concerned.

"That's impossible," he blurted back at Bobbascow.

"No. See? Some of the feathers got caught on my sandals when the man fell."

The rider peered over and looked at the sandals and saw little bits of feather that he ran between his fingers. He was staring at them most intently.

"These are golden eagle feathers. They are rare." He paused. "Golden eagle feathers used as fletching for an arrow, you say?"

"Yes."

"Now that is interesting."

"Why?"

"Because there is a tribe that once used golden eagle feathers in arrows."

"Who are they?"

"They were called the Minim."

"Were called? What are they called now?"

"Now they are called 'deceased,' since they died out ten years ago. They were great hunters in the far regions of the west. Now all gone, like many other tribes. Laid waste in one of many wars that they could not survive."

"What does it mean?" asked Bobbascow.

"It means, little one, that someone else is looking for you and probably wants to get you too."

"Who?"

"I don't know. But I promise you one thing. I'm sure we'll find out eventually."

The rider said that as he scruffed his hair with his hand. Then the rider stared at Bobbascow for a moment as if he was searching for something in his eyes.

"I know you are tired, confused, and afraid. But you have to trust me. You're safe with me. Even your friend Talkai."

They both looked at Talkai, who by now was snoring away.

"Tomorrow you will learn more about why Morpeth wants you. And you'll even learn more about who you are. But be patient. The questions you have will be answered."

"But I have one question for now, " the young boy asked.

"What is it?"

"Who are you? What is your name? "

"My name," he replied, "is Jakov. And I am here to help you and to protect you. That is all you need to know for now. For it is late, you look tired, and you need some urgent rest. I suggest you get some. There will be more time for questions tomorrow."

Bobbascow sighed and nodded in agreement. He layed down on the ground and faced towards Talkai as he felt the rider's hand on his shoulder. As the twilight turned to night, he fell asleep easily, feeling a strange sense of peace with the rider beside him.

The rider watched over Bobbascow till he was deep in sleep. After staying still for a few moments listening to the dark of the night, he arose and walked into the darkness. The rider walked for several minutes until he came to a small well.

The rider reached into his belt and took some silver dust from a small pouch and threw it into the well. Immediately the waters in the well began to bubble and glow. He spoke into the luminous ripples of water.

"I summon Morpeth, king of Iona."

The waters foamed and bubbled and then finally calmed. The image of Morpeth appeared on the surface of the water.

"Who are you and why have you summoned me?"

"You know who I am old man. Surely the resemblance of my face to your own should be clear enough."

There was a long pause and then Morpeth spoke.

"You . . . can it be . . . to think that after all of these years of searching and now it is you who seeks out me. For what purpose do I owe this meeting with my estranged son?"

"I bring you news, Morpeth."

"And what news is that Jakov?"

"I have found Iskandar. The boy is stronger than you can imagine. He will destroy you and your wicked kingdom and there is nothing you can do to stop it."

"Is that the news you bring your own father?"

"Yes, and what glorious news it is. Your sons are coming for you Morpeth, you and that conniving wife of yours, and justice is coming with us. We will crush you and rid the land of your tyranny once and for all."

"Don't be so confident of yourself boy. Your youth makes you arrogant. I will yet fulfil my vow to Marduk. Your blood and that of Iskandar will be spread upon Marduk's altar."

"My blood will remain in my veins and the breath in my body. I will yet avenge the blood of my brothers and sisters that you and that witch murdered and I will see you both die, Morpheth. Mark my words, I will turn you to dust."

"Jakov, do you really think you and your little brother are any match for me? You don't know what you're dealing with, boy."

"Oh, I know all too well, father, and now I have the tool I need to beat you."

"I look forward to seeing you again, my son; you and your little brother. We will have much catching up to do."

"I promise you this, Morpeth, the introductions will be brief."

"You won't even make it to the kingdom of Norella before I capture you both."

"Try your best, old man, but we are coming for you, and I will unleash all hell upon you."

"Why did you summon me through the wells of Mishina? Why would you give away the element of surprise?"

"I contacted you for one reason Morpeth"

"And what is that?"

"Fear."

"Do I sound afraid of you Jakov?"

"You voice betrays nothing my dear father. For you can change your voice, but your eyes, no, you cannot change them, and I see fear in them. I know what fear looks like in a man and I see it in you now. The very name 'Iskandar' strikes fear into your heart and so it should. The prophecy is coming true, your sons are coming to destroy you. Now for the first time in nearly ten years, I know that you are afraid."

"I am an immortal, Jakov, and you cannot kill a . . ."

And Jakov threw more silver dust into the well and the face of Morpeth disappeared into the blackness of the waters. Jakov took a moment to calm himself down as he noticed his hands slightly shaking with a mixture of joy and rage. He quickly walked back to the camp and saw the two figures curled up close together in their blankets. The moon beamed white shades of light onto the young boy's face. Jakov knelt down beside him.

"Little brother, it is good to see you again."

With that Jakov covered the boy with his cloak and lied down beside him. He looked up into the starry sky with his hands behind his head. He breathed deeply and then closed his eyes and began to dream as he dreamed nearly every night about his other brothers and sisters. He saw their faces, memories of childhood play, laughter, and the enduring emptiness of their absence.

# Chapter 5

## Discoveries in the Forest

TALKAI, BOBBASCOW, AND JAKOV got up before dawn. They buried the fire and tried to remove all trace of their presence. Jakov hurried them on as they got ready to ride on further. The morning's journey took them deeper and deeper into the woods. Finally they travelled where roads were no longer seen and the trees grew denser and thicker. As the trio sat on horseback, Talkai would continually fall asleep on Bobbascow's shoulder and drool down the back of his neck. Bobbascow would then nudge him and tell him to wake up. After a few hours a strange bird sound startled Jakov.

"Shh! Be quiet and very still," said Jakov in a faint whisper.

Jakov paused and he heard the sound again. He chuckled to himself and clapped his hands.

"We are here with our friends."

"What friends?" asked Bobbascow dismounting the horse.

Jakov laughed, "My friends and yours".

"I like friends," interjected Talkai.

"No doubt they will like you too Talkai," Jakov said as he scanned the wood with his eyes.

Then Bobbascow heard a whooshing of air and then behind him was standing a beautiful young lady with long black hair and a green tunic.

"Hello strangers," she said with a gentle voice.

Jakov turned around with a huge smile on his face, "Ayesha," and he ran to embrace her and they hugged.

"We weren't expecting you until dusk," the woman uttered.

"The imperial guards got there before me so I had to seize the boy before they took him."

Jakov pointed to Bobbascow. She bent over to look Bobbascow in the eyes. He felt shy before her, but her smile put him at ease.

"So you're the little man that everyone has been looking for. A pleasure to meet you Is . . ."

"Bobbascow" interrupted Jakov. "Call him Bobbascow for now."

Ayesha raised an eyebrow in curiosity.

"Bobbascow it is then."

"Oh," added Jakov, "And this is Talkai who was Bobbascow's fellow man-servant."

Ayesha courteously bowed to Talkai, who waved in return.

"Pleasure to meet you, your forestness. Are you the queen of the forest, princess of the pixies, grandma to the fairies?"

Jakov rolled his eyes. "Sadly, I don't think Talkai is quite all there, if you know what I mean." He turned to Talkai, "No, she's not the queen of the forest. Ayesha is from the Mijin tribe."

"Where is that?" asked Bobbascow.

"Far away from here. And sadly it's no longer a place that is warm and welcoming," she said.

Jakov placed his hand on Ayesha's shoulder. "One thing you should know about Ayesha is that she is very, very fast."

"You mean at running?" asked Bobbascow.

"At everything! Ayesha, give them an example."

"Okay." She took an apple from her pocket and gave it to Talkai.

"Throw it," she asked him.

"Why? It's a very nice apple."

"Just throw it, you dim witted fool," said Jakov in exasperation.

"But I like apples. Why would I throw away a perfectly good apple?"

"Just throw it you foolish man."

"Alright, but it's a waste of a perfectly fine apple."

With that Talkai threw the apple far as he could and just before it hit the ground Ayesha vanished in an instant and was suddenly back again before anyone could have blinked.

"Here's your apple," and she handed it back to Talkai.

"Wow, you are fast," said Bobbascow.

"And that was her taking it easy," added Jakov.

Then from behind a tree came another voice, deep, booming, and sounding quite serious.

"Do we have time for games, Jakov, or should we expect imperial guards any time soon?"

From behind the tree stepped a huge man, the largest man Bobbas-cow had ever seen. He was over seven feet tall. He was wide and sturdy, dressed also in green and brown, carrying a huge axe. And Bobbascow noticed, most of all, that he only had one eye. He was a Cyclops.

"We have a few minutes for introductions. But you are right. Imperial guards will be heading this way shortly, and we'll have to move on before nightfall." Jakov could see that Bobbascow was frozen, mesmerized at the sight of the Cyclops.

"Bobbascow, this is Sy. He is my most trusted friend and he will be our valiant guide for the rest of our journey."

"But he's a . . . a . . ."

"Cyclops," Sy finished his sentence, "Yes I am."

There was an awkward silence and Bobbascow spoke, "I'm sorry . . . it's just that . . . well . . . I've never met a Cyclops before. I never knew there really were people like that."

"Once there were many like me. But Morpeth put an end to that. I am the last of my kind."

Bobbascow looked at Jakov. "Did Morpeth kill all of your people? Your tribes, your families?"

"Yes he did. Most of us are survivors of his carnage."

"But why? Why would he do that?"

"He was looking for something," said Ayesha.

"He was looking for someone," corrected Sy.

"Who?" asked Bobbascow as everyone stared at him.

"It is you he is looking for, child." Ayesha told him.

"Me?" gasped Bobbascow in shock. "Why me? What have I done?"

"It's not what you've done. It's who you are. That is why he seeks you," stated Jakov.

"Then who am I?" There was a long pause and Sy and Ayesha looked away. "Please, tell me who I am!"

Jakov took him by both arms.

"Bobbascow, you were not always a man-slave. Your real name is Iskandar. You are the son of Morpeth and Prisca, the king and queen of Iona."

"What? No, that can't be true. You're wrong. I am not the son of Mor-peth. I can't be. I don't want to be. I'm not."

Iskandar's body began to shake with shock and confusion.

"There is no denying it. Iskandar is your name, your birth name, your holy name. To prove it, you have a special mark. The tattoo of the serpents on your right arm is no brand of slave ownership. That is a mark of prophecy. The holy and righteous god Vetrius has sealed you as the redemption child of the land. You will rise up and destroy Morpeth and Prisca, the immortal rulers of Iona. It is your destiny and your duty. I'm sorry to tell you this, but this is who you are and what you must do."

"I can't believe it."

"Believe it, child, for the weight of many hangs on your shoulders" spoke Sy this time, gently.

"But, how am I supposed to kill Morpeth? He's powerful, he's a like a god or something."

"He's not a god yet," said Jakov with much seriousness, "And there is a power inside you that you do not know about and we will teach you to unleash it with all the fury of hell and all the might of heaven. Mark my words Iskandar, let's use your real name from now on, you will free us all from the nightmare that has terrorized our land for ten years."

"My name is Bobbascow".

"Call yourself whatever you like," entreated Sy. "But you are Iskandar."

"How do you know for sure? How do you know I just don't have this tattoo because someone copied it from somewhere else?"

"There are other ways that we know, Iskandar."

Saying that, Jakov put his hands onto Iskandar's cheek.

"How do you know for sure?" was the boy's reply.

"I recognize your eyes."

"My eyes, what does that mean?" he protested with tears running down his cheek onto Jakov's glove.

"I knew your brothers and sisters, Iskandar. Before your father and mother murdered them. I knew them. I loved them. I know their eyes just as I know yours. You are their brother. You are the son of Morpeth and Prisca. And you are Iskandar. And you will fulfil the prophecy."

Iskandar wiped his face with his sleeve.

"I don't want to kill anyone. I just want to go home."

"Wringstone is dead, we have no home go to," said Talkai.

"But I don't want to . . . I don't understand."

"We don't understand everything ourselves," said Jakov as he rose up. "We don't know who hid you in the village with Wringstone. There are many questions that we simply do not have answers to."

"Where will you take me?"

"We are going to the eastern ice palace among the Nazvor Ranges. Morpeth's forces cannot reach us there. It is too cold and too hard to navigate through. We can rest there and carefully craft our plans. But for now, get some rest for you will need it Iskandar."

Ayesha walked over and took Iskandar to her side.

"Come, child. Let me cook you some mulla beans and hot tea. You must be hungry."

Iskandar walked away with Ayesha, followed by Talkai who walked behind licking his lips. Sy strolled over to Jakov and placed his axe handle on the ground and leaned on the axe head.

"You place such a great burden on one so young" said Sy.

"Some of us who are young often have great burdens placed upon us because we have no choice."

"You never game him a choice."

"No one gave me one either".

"Does he know that you're his brother?"

"No. For the moment it is better that he not know. It'll be too much for him to take in."

"Are you glad to see him?"

"Of course. He will destroy Morpeth and Prisca, and free us all. He will avenge the many deaths we have all suffered, Sy."

"Jakov, remember he's not just a secret magician you've discovered. He's a boy, he's your brother. You should be rejoicing that you found your lost brother."

"When Morpeth is dead, then I'll rejoice with my brother. Till then, we have a task to finish."

"Jakov, one more thing. Be careful."

"What do you mean?"

"I mean, don't let your lust for revenge destroy you as a person. Don't forget, you're little more than a boy yourself."

"This boy had to become a man very quickly. This boy woke up one day to find himself alone in a cave in the middle of nowhere. This boy learned that all of his brothers and sisters that he had played with and loved were murdered by his fanatical parents. And this boy will not rest until the blood of his brothers and sisters are atoned for."

"We used to have a saying back in my village, Jakov. Do you know what it was?"

"No, what?"

"If you have to kill a monster, be sure that it is not you who becomes a monster."

"Maybe if your tribe had become monsters you would still have a tribe."

"Careful Jakov. You go too far with your words. You are not the only one who has lost a family."

"I will be what I have to be to destroy Morpeth."

"We need a leader, not a madman, Jakov. Put your feelings of hate aside or else they will destroy you and us too."

Jakov paused for a moment. "I will take your words to heart old friend. I mean you no offence. You know I seek only the liberation of Iona from the evil that reigns upon it."

"I know that you are a very angry young man, but I warn you that your quest for vengeance may destroy your soul and make you no better than Morpeth."

"I promise you such things will never be."

"I hope so, Jakov."

Jakov began to walk away, but glanced back at Sy.

"Oh, one other thing Sy," added Jakov. "I spoke to Morpeth at the wells of Mishina. I told him we had Iskandar and that we are coming to destroy him."

"You did what? You foolish boy! He'll ambush us before we even leave the forest."

"Be of good cheer Sy. Morpeth was startled. He's afraid, though he wouldn't admit it. He knows where we are and where we going but he also knows he cannot stop us."

"The imperial guards will already be after us."

"They were after us as soon as I took Iskandar. With this knowledge it only means that he will be impulsive and erratic. He'll spend less time thinking about what to do and more time trying to get it done quickly. You know what he's like as a commander. Numbers and brute force are his way, not deftness and strategy. It only means that Morpeth will be forced to send his troops east to look for us and by the time they get into position we shall be at the ice palace."

"You take great risks with the lives of those entrusted to you."

"This war will only be won with risks."

"Some risks are unnecessary. Some risks are done out of pride."

"Then let us risk together, my friend, and see what glories follow us."

Ayesha served Iskandar and Talkai mulla beans and hot tea as they sat around a small fire. The two ate and drank to their hearts content.

"I'm more stuffed than a heifer who has been stuffed with pig fat and a thousand trees of broccoli," said Talkai.

"That was nice. Thank you Ayesha," Iskandar said to Ayesha.

"Glad you liked it," she replied, smiling back at the young boy, but wondering to herself if he really was the famed one who would destroy Morpeth.

Just then, two small men walked up to the trio around their camp fire.

"Quigon ji," said the first little man.

"Japhut lu," said the second.

They were about three foot high and holding canes that were slightly taller than them. The two little men both had stringy white hair, dark olive skin, tiny little goatie beards, and were dressed in overalls made of hessian.

"Hello Mo and Tar," Ayesha replied.

"Hala punici mar," said Mo scratching his hairy chin and staring at the pot of beans on the fire.

"Who are they?" asked Iskandar.

"Why, this is Mo and Tar. They are Triklite twins."

"Quigon ji," said Tar.

"They're saying hello to you both."

"Nice to meet you," said Iskandar as he shook their little hands.

"Aren't they vulnerable, two little men like these, out here in the forest?" asked Iskandar.

"Ha," Ayesha laughed. "Vulnerable, these two? I don't think so."

She turned and spoke something in Triktish to the two little men. They fell over laughing and pointed their fingers at Iskandar while squirming in amusement and kicking their legs wildly with tears streaming down their cheeks.

"They are not vulnerable at all. They are two of the most ferocious warriors you'll ever meet."

"Wait a second," interrupted Talkai. "Mountain lions are ferocious. Twenty imperial guards with sore bottoms are ferocious. These two midgets can't reach apples on trees, let alone fend for themselves against all the mean stingy thingies of the forest."

"Oh, want to bet?" Ayesha said, challenging Talkai.

"I most certainly think I do. Let them see if they can wrestle me to the ground."

"Okay, but don't say I didn't warn you."

Ayesha whispered something to Mo and Tar who started laughing even harder now. But eventually they got up and squared off in front of Talkai.

Talkai was muttering things to himself as he began to slowly walk around the two dwarves with a crouched posture. "Watch out little men cause I got moves. Mighty moves, deadly moves, I got moves, you want to see my moves, little men? Cause I got moves, alright."

Mo and Tar were poking faces at him and grunting like little piglets at the tall man. Then Mo jumped onto the shoulders of Tar and he grabbed Talkai around the neck and began choking him. Talkai squirmed and gasped and then grabbed Mo by the nose. Mo slapped him in the face while down below Tar kicked him in the shins and punched him in the groin. Talkai let out a squeal louder than any piglet could ever make. Then Mo dropped to the ground, Tar in turn jumped on his shoulders this time and climbed up and over Talkai until he was on his back facing doward. As Mo grabbed Talkai's legs, Tar sunk his teeth deep into Talkai's bottom. Talkai let out a loud scream.

"Ouch, the little sod bit my bum!"

Tar fell to the ground behind Talkai and Mo jumped up and kicked Talkai in the chest with both legs sending him falling backwards over Tar. Talkai fell smack bang on his bottom with a big thud.

Ayesha and Iskandar were laughing hysterically at the antics. Talkai just sat there looking very embarrassed and rubbing his bottom. Mo and Tar stood there looking at him with big smiles on their faces.

"They bit me. That is not fair, biting isn't allowed."

"Misquito elinois agava de swino registra," said Tar.

"What did he say?" asked Talkai.

"Tar says that you taste like a sweaty pig who has been sitting in the mud."

"It's not my fault. I haven't had a bath for a while."

"When was the last time you bathed?" asked Ayesha.

"August, I think."

"Oh that is so grotesque and filthy," she said with a look of disgust on her face.

Just then Jakov and Sy came over and Iskandar noticed that Jakov was dwarfed by the tall one eyed man.

"I see you've met the other two members of my tribe of survivors," spoke Jakov, looking at Iskandar.

"Survivors? Did Morpeth kill of all your people too?"

Ayesha put her hand on Iskandar's shoulder. "All of us had our tribes, our villages, and even our families killed by Morpeth and Prisca."

Iskandar paused for a moment and then looked up at her.

"Because of me?"

There was a silence all around, as no one dared answer the boy.

"No," said Jakov. "It is because of the madness of one man and one woman. It is they who would destroy anything and anyone who stands in their way. The fault is not yours."

"Far from it Iskandar," added Sy. "You are the only hope for those who survived. You can ensure that all this murder is finished once and for all."

"You want me to kill my own father."

Jakov knelt beside him. "Iskandar, that is the only way. Your father and your mother would kill you if they had the chance. Even now your father sends his forces after you, which is why we can't stay here for long. It is a hard burden to carry, I know. But I promise you – we all promise you, that you will never carry it alone."

Iskandar stared blankly at Jakov and then turned and looked each person in the eyes from Mo and Tar to Sy, Ayesha, and then Talkai.

"My name is Bobbascow and I don't want to kill anyone. I just want to go home."

Jakov grabbed his arm and pulled up his sleeve, revealing the tattoo of the snakes.

"You see this? This means you are Iskandar. You are the youngest son of Morpeth and Prisca and it is ordained by the highest heaven that you destroy him and free us all from the tyranny. There is no other way, do you hear me?"

"Find yourself another Iskandar. I am Bobbascow and I want to go home."

He pulled his hand violently from the grip of Jakov's gloves and walked off down the hill towards a stream.

"Wait, Iska . . . Bobbascow. Come here, lad."

Iskandar ignored him and kept walking.

"In time you'll learn your calling," Jakov yelled at him.

Jakov shook his head in annoyance and began walking after Iskandar. Ayesha caught up to him and poked him in the back of his ribs.

"He's only a child Jakov."

"He's our only saviour Ayesha. We don't have the luxury or time for children's tantrums. There is a kingdom to save and scores to settle."

"But first let the little boy discover who he is. Let him discover his power. And then, maybe, he'll be ready. But don't use him as your own hammer of revenge. Remember Jakov he is still your . . ."

"I know who he is to me."

"Then just enjoy finding your brother. Not all of us are blessed with family members still alive."

"Okay. I'll try."

Ayesha walked off and Jakov's eyes followed Iskandar as he walked down the hill. Jakov looked at Mo and Tar and nodded his head in the direction of Iskandar. The two little bearded men jumped up and slowly walked after Iskandar.

Iskandar sat beside a stream in the forest staring at the strange tattoo on his arm. So often before he had looked at it when lying in bed or when bathing, wondering what the symbols meant and who put them on him. He once thought it was the mark of a slave, but now it felt like it was the mark of a curse. He once hoped that his parents were still alive, that they'd come and take him home, or that they had died bravely trying to save him. But those hopes were gone now. In his imagination his mother had long blond hair and a gentle touch and his father was tall, strong, yet gentle and warm. Now he knew the truth that his parents hadn't lost him or tried to save him. His real parents were trying to kill him. Then Iskandar thought to himself, why him? Who had chosen him to do this? Couldn't it all be a mistake still? He picked up stones and began throwing them into the stream one at a time. He partly wished that he could throw one at Jakov for telling him all these things, all the truth or all the lies, whatever it was. Jakov had destroyed his world. It was a hard world, but a world that had happiness. Even in Wringstone's house there was happiness. But none of it mattered now. Nothing could ever be the same again.

"Good throw Iskandar."

Iskandar turned and saw Jakov not eight feet behind him.

"Go away, I want to be left alone."

"I know child. I haven't exactly made things easy for you."

"Why me? Why?"

"I don't know. It is who you are. It cannot be helped."

"I don't want to be Iskandar. I want to be Bobbascow. A boy working in a tavern."

"I'm sorry Iskandar, we can't go back now. The die is cast and fates are set in motion. We don't determine the path that we are given. All we can choose is how we intend to walk it."

"Then I want to walk away."

"Your path only goes in one direction. It goes to the royal palace at Dalazvar where Morpeth is."

"I cannot do this," Iskandar screamed.

Jakov came up behind him and put his arms around him.

"Can I ask you a question, Iskandar?"

"What?"

"Do you ever get a funny, tingly kind of sensation when you stand near water?"

"What kind of question is that?"

"I know it's odd, but think, do you have a strange, almost peculiar feeling when you sit by the stream?"

Iskandar paused for a moment and looked up.

Then Iskandar replied, "Sometimes. Sometimes when I'm near water, especially lots of it, I feel like . . . like . . ."

"Like there is someone in the room with you waiting for you to say something?"

"Yes, like you're supposed to talk to someone or someone is waiting for you to say something, but for some reason you never do. It's an odd feeling."

"That isn't odd Iskandar. I get the same feeling too."

"Really?"

"Yes, but for me it isn't water, it is stone and rock."

"You feel like the stones want you to talk to them?"

"It is far worse than that. Sometimes they even talk back."

"But that sounds quite silly, almost mad. Isn't it?"

"Not quite lad. Watch this."

Jakov raised his hand and several stones rose up into the air. Iskandar's mouth opened, gaping in wonder at the stones floating in the air. Jakov muttered something under his breath and then waved his hand. Suddenly the stones shot out like arrows across the stream and skimmed onto the water, going further and further.

"Are you a wizard Jakov?"

"No, not a wizard I'm afraid."

"But how? How did you do that? What magic is that?"

"I cannot explain it anymore than I can explain why the sky is blue and how the grass is green. All I know is that stones do what I tell them to do. Rocks obey me. Pebbles listen to my voice."

"Back in Praschi you made the stones fly into the imperial guard's face didn't you?"

"Yes, I did that. My power enables me to do such things. But more importantly, my little friend, you have a similar power."

"Me?" said Iskandar with his eyes almost falling out in disbelief. "But how could I possibly . . ."

Jakov leaned over closer to Iskandar.

"Just sit still for a moment and think about the water. Focus on the water, its ripples, waves, and currents going by you. Think of it as a playful dog or a curious cat that is playing right there in front of you. Call to it ever so quietly. Ask what its name is. And then tell it what you would have it do."

Iskandar sat for a moment and looked deeply into the stream before him for several moments. A tree could have fallen beside him and he wouldn't have noticed. Iskandar closed his eyes and whispered something to himself. Suddenly drops of water began lifting off the stream as if it were raining upwards. It was Jakov's eyes that now opened wide in amazement.

"Well done boy. That is astounding. Look at what you're doing."

Iskandar looked up as the droplets he sent up into the sky began raining down. He closed his eyes again and whispered some more and this time the water in the streamed shifted to the far side of the bank and then rushed towards them. Jakov tried to scramble back as fast as he could. But it was too late. A wave of water from the stream rose up from the bank towards them and half soaked him and Iskandar together.

"Did I do that?" asked Iskandar.

"You most certainly did," replied Jakov spitting the dirty water out of his mouth.

"I spoke to the water and it did what I asked it to do."

"See, I told you. You can speak and command the water."

"The water even spoke back to me."

"And what did it say?"

"It said 'Hello,' I think."

Jakov grinned as he tried to shake his black hair dry. Iskandar laughed for a moment as well at the wetness of the two of them, but he suddenly paused and looked again at Jakov

"This proves that I am Iskandar, doesn't it?"

"I have shown you that there is a unique power in you. And yes, it means that you are definitely Iskandar. But you knew that already before you came down here, didn't you?"

"I suppose."

"Iskandar, listen to me. I am your friend. I can be overbearing at times. But I am so glad to have found you. You are an answer to my prayers. I promise that I won't ever make you do anything that you don't want to do. But I do need you to trust me. You don't have to understand, you don't always have to agree. But I need you to trust me. Is that a deal?"

"It's a deal. But only on one condition."

"And what is that?"

"That you show me more on how to speak to the water."

"That we will most definitely do sooner rather than later."

At that very moment Mo and Tar came running down to Jakov and were yelling something frantically. Jakov heard and immediately the smile left Jakov's face. He grabbed Iskandar by the hand and they began running up the hill in great haste.

"What is it?" Iskandar asked.

"They are coming for us, sooner than I thought."

"Imperial guards?"

"No, something far worse, something the stuff of nightmares are made of."

"What is it?"

"Pray that you never find out!"

# Chapter 6

## A Gigantic Caterpillar
## and More Mysterious Arrows

JAKOV CONTINUED RUNNING UP the hill, pulling Iskandar by his sleeve. He was met by Sy who ran towards him, half out of breath. His one eye stared straight at Jakov with a cold determination in his countenance.

"They have a caterpillar and they are coming this way. Twenty or thirty troops with them," he said panting.

Suddenly a huge screech was heard a short distance away. Ayesha, Mo, and Tar also ran up to Jakov, waiting for his instructions. Talkai came as well, stumbling over a log and looking about somewhat confused by the ruckus.

Jakov took charge.

"Friends, listen in. We'll move in two groups north and east. Ayesha can take Iskandar on horseback with Mo and Tar following. Ayesha, head due east, straight for the ice desert. Don't stop for anything or anyone. In the meantime, Sy and I will hold them here for as long as we can. After that we'll head north to lead them away and then we'll go east and meet you at the border of the icelands. If we don't make it before sunset go ahead without us. Understood?"

"Yes," came the chorus of reply.

"What about me?" asked Talkai.

"You . . ." Jakov stuttered, deep in thought. "You . . . Talkai will have to stay with us."

"Do I fight too?"

"No," Sy answered. "But keep out of sight and try not to let the caterpillar eat you."

"Caterpillars don't eat people. They are only little bitsy things."

Jakov rolled his eyes in contempt. Suddenly the sound of the screeching got even louder and closer. Sy pointed to the distant clump of trees only a few hundred yards away.

"Oh, really? Then explain your theory to that beast over there."

Talkai squinted his eyes and through the foliage he could see a gigantic caterpillar munching through trees and rapidly coming towards the group. On top of it was a rider who controlled the enormous, green, hairy caterpillar with a harness. Several figures could be seen lurking to either side of the huge caterpillar as it marched towards them.

"Oh dear," said Talkai.

"Oh dear indeed," added Sy.

Jakov drew out his two swords from behind his back and walked towards the oncoming noise. He spat on the ground and watched the crashing of trees get closer and closer. The screeching of the caterpillar got louder with every passing moment. Jakov turned behind him and looked at the others.

"Now go Ayesha. May Vetrius give you speed and strength."

Iskandar had been silent, paralyzed by the sight of the huge caterpillar coming towards him. Before he knew it, Ayesha had grabbed his arm and he felt himself flying through the air. She ran with him in tow at a furious speed. The racing wind made his eyes water. Next thing he knew was that he was sitting behind her on a horse and they were galloping. Looking behind him a few moments later, he saw the two little men of Mo and Tar pursuing them on miniature horses.

"Hold on, Iskandar, this ride will be hard and long."

Iskandar closed his eyes and gripped the waist of Ayesha as tight as he could.

Sy came up beside Jakov and planted the head of his huge axe on the ground. Yawning, he turned, and looked down at Jakov on his left.

"You ever taken down a gigantic caterpillar before Jakov?"

"No. Have you?"

"No. Is there a trick to it?"

"Well, ordinarily, I tend to squish caterpillars with my foot. But I have a funny feeling that we might require a different strategy for a gigantic caterpillar."

Sy laughed at Jakov just as Talkai tip toed up behind them.

"What do I do now?" asked Talkai.

"If I were you, I would go and hide in that log over there," Jakov told him.

"Excellent idea. If you need me I'll be in the log. Come and get when the fighting is done."

Talkai sprinted over to a big log in a thicket of bushes and crawled into it and put his hands over his eyes.

Sy and Jakov watched as the crunching of trees got closer and closer. They could see the caterpillar clearly now and they leaned behind a huge oak tree to avoid being seen. Jakov looked on the ground and realized that there wasn't a single stone on the ground. Only dirt and mud around him. Those things were useless to him. He shook his head in disappointment.

"I guess we'll have to do this the old fashioned way," Jakov muttered to himself.

As they pressed their backs against the trees a number of imperial guards walked passed them but didn't notice them.

"Say when," whispered Sy.

"On my mark. One . . . two . . . three . . . now!"

In a burst of speed, Jakov jumped out from behind the tree and cut down two imperial guards with a whirlwind of steel. A thin spray of red mist followed behind him. Sy bellowed loudly an ancient battle cry of his people and began swinging his axe wildly. He struck the enemies in every direction. An imperial guard was knocked off his horse. Another had Sy's axe plunged into his chest, nearly cutting him in half.

Sy saw out of the left corner of his eye the caterpillar adjacent to them, not even forty feet away. Its huge hairy and lime green body was in view. Its screeching was almost as deafening as it was frightening, and the pungent odour was nearly as incapacitating. The rider of the caterpillar tightened the reins and directed the peculiar animal towards Sy and Jakov.

More imperial guards ran towards the duo only to be cut down either by a sword or an axe. Blows from Sy's axe knocked men onto each other and they fell three and four at a time. Jakov spun his two swords in a vicious circle that ripped up anything that came into contact with his steel spiral. As the caterpillar closed the gap, the imperial guards paused their assault and backed off to give room to the caterpillar.

Sy and Jakov took several steps backwards as the enormous beast came bearing down upon them with a momentum that surprised them. The caterpillar threw itself up onto its haunches and towered above the smaller trees in height. In then came crashing down where Sy and Jakov were standing. The beast crushed the tree they were hiding behind as the two men dived to the left and to the right. The animal screeched and bit the air around Jakov as it lunged towards him. Jakov scurried backwards and kept stabbing forward with his swords, occasionally clashing with the sharp teeth of the caterpillar. As Jakov dodged behind trees to avoid each lunge of the caterpillar towards him, he tripped on a vine and fell backwards onto the ground. The caterpillar rushed forward and was nearly on top of him. It rose up to pounce on him. Just then an arrow shot into its neck. Then another arrow struck. Four arrows in quick succession ripped into the caterpillar's neck. The beast screamed louder and shook itself in obvious pain and its movements became slower. Jakov quickly got to his feet and took several steps to the left side of the animal which again tried to bite him in its mouth. Jakov sliced directly into its eye and drew blood from the creature. The caterpillar thrashed about ferociously, nearly dislodging the rider from his mount.

Jakov ran behind another tree, only to have it knocked over and missing him by a few inches. Just then another flurry of arrows caught the caterpillar in the head but they did not stop the beast. From behind Jakov could hear Sy's voice calling to him.

"The rider, Jakov! Strike the rider!"

Hearing the call, Jakov ran towards the animal and jumped high in the air, narrowly missing its bite. He twisted himself in flight and drove one sword into the head of the caterpillar and with the other sword he threw at the rider. The huge blade pierced the air and landed in the chest of the rider who instantly fell sideways off the caterpillar. Jakov momentarily landed on the caterpillar but quickly bounced off and hit the ground, slightly dazed. The beast thrashed about and screeched loudly. With its new freedom the beast turned around and moved towards Jakov, Jakov's sword still protruding from its head.

The caterpillar advanced on the unarmed and slightly dazed Jakov who gingerly tried to get to his feet. Sy ran up to a huge oak tree and with three mighty blows from his axe the massive oak tree fell and landed right on top of the gigantic caterpillar, crushing the middle of its back. Jakov slowly came to his senses and then quickly ran up to the beast and pushed his protruding sword deeper into its head. He took his sword out after the caterpillar became motionless.

Sy and Jakov then rushed the few remaining imperial guards who watched the melee. Two ran to meet them but were cut down just as quickly as they moved. The remainder of imperial soldiers retreated with haste.

Jakov thought for a moment about running after them, but Sy placed his hand on Jakov's shoulder.

"No. There's no time. We must meet the others."

"You're right. Let's go."

Jakov ran over and collected his other sword from the body of the caterpillar driver. He then looked at the arrows in the head of the caterpillar and then looked at Sy in confusion.

"The arrows. Did you do this?"

"They are not mine."

Jakov grabbed one of the arrows from the caterpillar and noticed that its feathers were red with golden speckling. His eyes widened and then he turned and looked about in every direction around him. His eyes hunted the foliage and forest for movement, but he saw nothing.

"What is it Jakov?"

"We are not alone. I've seen these before."

Jakov handed Sy one of the arrows.

"Where have you seen these before?"

"I'll explain it to you later."

The two ran off heading north. Then Jakov stopped and skidded in his run.

"Stop. Wait. Talkai. The imbecile. We can't leave him behind."

Sy and Jakov walked over to the big log that Talkai was hiding in. Sy kicked it.

"Come out Talkai."

"Is it s-s-safe?" he muttered with trepidation.

"Yes. Come on, let's go. We have to try to catch the others."

Talkai crawled out and dusted himself off from the dirt and cobwebs that covered him. He looked down at his feet and noticed a caterpillar crawling up his leg. He shook it violently and flicked it off.

"Yuck, caterpillars. Horrible things aren't they?"

"You don't have to tell us," replied Jakov.

The three men jogged for a distance and then mounted the horses waiting for them. Talkai sat side saddle next to Jakov as their horses bolted off deep into the wood. They rode north for a time and stopped every so often to see if anyone was following. After that they headed east with the afternoon sun on their backs. Talkai began to notice that it was getting colder and colder the further that they went.

Ayesha gripped the reins tightly, looking over her shoulder every few seconds. Iskandar clung on for dear life, narrowly missing branches that flew passed his ears. Mo and Tar road on their own horses that were miniature but as fast as any other horse twice their size.

Then Ayesha lifted her right hand and clenched her first. Suddenly the trio of horses ran around a hedge of trees and came to a stop. The horses panted wildly for breath. Iskandar quickly reached for some water to drink, as he was thirsty from the race.

"Mo, Tar, can you see anyone following us?

The little men peered through the dense forest with their eyes, then they both dismounted, layed down, and listened to the ground. Then Mo sat up.

"Hipuchi marbat," Mo said to Ayesha.

"What does that mean?" asked Iskandar.

"They hear nothing." Even with that news, Ayesha still sounded concerned and looked fearful.

"Something is still following us, I can feel it."

Mo and Tar just shrugged their shoulders and muttered more of their language. And then a flurry of arrows from the sky hit the ground. The horses jumped up in fright and Iskandar was knocked off the horse.

With his back flat on the ground, Iskandar looked up to see a huge shadow pass over the top of him.

"Imperial gliders," cried Ayesha.

She lunged over and grabbed Iskandar by his shirt collar and dragged him back onto his horse. Then, more arrows hit the tree next to Iskandar's head. Ayesha moved the horse under the biggest tree that she could find and took her shield out which covered her and Iskandar.

"Can we outrun them Ayesha?" asked Iskandar.

"No," came the reply, "They move too fast on a day like this".

"The, what do we do?"

"Well, either they run out of arrows, or the wind dies, or ..."

"Or what?"

"Or we shoot them down like you would an eagle."

"How will we do that?" asked Iskandar, as two arrows struck Ayesha's shield.

She smiled at the young boy. Her face was beautiful even under threat. She raised an eyebrow and stared at Iskandar.

"Just you wait and see!"

Iskandar glimpsed up to see what looked like a huge bird hovering above the tree line they were taking shelter in. Despite the foliage, he could see two men holding onto some contraption that looked like a tent with wings like a bird. The men were holding onto some bar that allowed them to shoot arrows downwards. He pulled his head back in when another couple of arrows hit Ayesha's shield.

Ayesha was looking at Mo and Tar who had taken shelter under another tree. She looked at them and called out something in their language. Mo and Tar nodded and then kicked their horses and began riding around the tree that Ayesha and Iskandar were hiding under. Mo and Tar were riding in circles as the odd arrow missed them and were yelling unintelligible taunts at the glider above them. They even fired a few arrows upwards but missed by several yards whenever they did. Ayesha tied the reins of the horse to the tree and handed the shield to Iskandar.

"Hold onto this tightly. And for goodness' sake, don't poke your head out!"

Iskandar was motionless as he watched Ayesha climb up the tree they were under. Ayesha moved quickly, climbing with the speed and deftness of a cat. Eventually she got to the top of the tree where the branches were thin and weak. She could see that only thirty yards above her the glider was floating and shooting arrows at Mo and Tar below. Mo and Tar heckled out in laughter every time the glider pilots missed. Ayesha stayed completely still and watched the movement of the glider in the air, mapping its circuit with her mind. The two pilots took their eyes off the ground for a moment as they argued with each other over something. Sensing her chance, Ayesha lunged into the air and grabbed the apex of the tree and then swung her weight to one side. The top of the huge tree then began to bow over and bend to the left. Ayesha pulled back on the tree with all her strength until she was dangling over the edge. She then relaxed her grip. Then she felt like she had left her stomach behind as she was thrown through the air upwards towards the glider. Despite the force of her flight into the sky, she took out her knife and when she collided with the right side of the glider, she used the blade to rip completely through its right wing, tearing such a huge hole that she actually passed through it. She glanced behind her and saw the glider plummeting to the ground as she momentarily continued on her own upwards trajectory. She prepared for a lot of pain as she felt herself falling back down towards the tree from whence she had launched herself. She broke through two branches on impact but managed to grip onto the third branch without falling through it. The impact made her grimace in pain and momentarily left her winded. But slowly she made her way down the branches as she caught her breath and the excitement of the fight (and the flight) began to wane. She landed on the ground with two feet and began untying the reins of the horse. Iskandar looked at her with his eyes wide opened.

"Ayesha, I saw you fly."

"I told you not to poke your head out."

"I only did it for a second. But that was amazing. Can you fly like that all the time?"

"Only when I have a big enough sling shot."

Ayesha mounted the horse and called out to Mo and Tar who had already inspected the crashed glider to see if the pilots had survived. They hadn't. Then Ayesha handed Iskandar a cloak.

"What's this?" he asked.

"Something warm to put on."

"But I'm not cold."

"Soon you will be".

Ayesha set her eyes east and the three horses raced off as the sun began to set behind them.

# Chapter 7

## Journey into the Eastern Ice Desert

IT WAS DARK AND only the faintest glint of moonlight shone through the thick foliage of the wood. Iskandar could see the warmth of his breath steaming out of his mouth as he clinched his cloak closer to his chest. Ayesha sensed his discomfort and she used her hand to rub his back to warm him up. Mo and Tar were whining to each other about how cold it was and kept saying "brrr" as they shook off icicles growing on their little red hats. Ayesha gripped the reins of the horse tightly and raised her hand. Mo and Tar jumped off their small horses and unsheathed their swords and looked through the thick of the forest for movement.

"What is it?" asked Iskandar.

"Someone is out there," she answered.

"Who?"

Ayesha smiled at him.

"Let's find out."

Ayesha looked at Mo and Tar and pointed to the left and right and the little men fanned out in opposed direction as if they were stalking something. Ayesha turned around and drew her cloak over her head. Then in an instant she was gone. Her green tunic disappeared into the darkness in the blink of an eye as her supernatural speed propelled her through the shadowy trees before Iskandar. All Iskandar felt was the cold on the back on his neck and the darkness all around him. He knew Mo and Tar were nearby, but as he sat on the horse in the silence of the night, he felt very alone and very scared. His breath began to get faster and his heart was pounding.

Then Iskandar saw a shadow and gust of leaves rushing towards him and he gripped the reins of the horse and was about to kick the horse and gallop away for his life. But just before he did, Ayesha was standing in front of him. The first thing he noticed was that she wasn't even panting for breath. She smiled at him.

"We're here."

"Where's here?"

"With the others. Jakov, Sy, and . . ."

"Talkai," Iskandar added excitedly.

"Yes, Talkai too."

He had been worried about him all day, but he felt at ease knowing that Talkai was alright. He surprised himself when he felt glad that Jakov was there too. He wasn't even sure if he liked Jakov yet.

"Are they far?" he asked, as Ayesha mounted the horse.

"Just over the next rise."

Iskandar smiled as he saw Mo and Tar galloping ahead of them and kicking their tiny horses to make them run up the hill faster. After several minutes he could see a small fire ahead of them. He jumped off the horse that was trotting along. Iskandar ran the rest of the way on foot. He wanted to yell and scream for Talkai, but he knew that he shouldn't make too much noise. He got to the fire and saw Sy, Jakov, and Talkai sitting around it. He slumped on Talkai and gave him a big hug.

"Talkai, I was so worried about you."

"Bobba . . . Izzie, my lad. We were fine. We killed that enormous caterpillar".

"We?" asked Sy. "As I remember, Jakov and I did all the caterpillar killing".

"Well, I was cheering. And keeping out of the way. Which is just as good as helping if you were me," Talkai added, matter-of-fact like.

"We truly couldn't have done it with you," Jakov interjected dripping with sarcasm.

Mo and Tar ran up to the group and almost put their heads into the fire as they tried to warm them up. Ayesha sat down next to Jakov and let out a huge huff of breath in tiredness.

"That was a long and tense ride Jakov".

"Did you get away cleanly?" he asked.

"We were followed by an imperial glider. But we shot it down."

"Ayesha flew in the air like an arrow," Iskandar added in excitement.

"By the Sceptre of Mishkan, how did you do that?" asked Sy.

"Long story," she replied. "But what about you? How big was the caterpillar?"

"Big enough to eat me for an entrée, Sy for main, and Talkai for dessert," answered Jakov.

"I probably would have made him sick. I have an oily complexion," responded Talkai.

"But we got there in the end," uttered Sy.

"Then we are blessed," said Ayesha as she leaned forward and rubbed her feet.

"Except for one thing."

"And what is that?" she answered.

"This." Jakov leaned over and handed Ayesha the arrow with red and golden colored feathers at its end.

Ayesha held it up to her eyes, almost mesmerized by its feel.

"This is ... surely it can't be ... arrows with golden eagle feathers. These were only used by the Minim people, but I thought they were gone years ago".

"It seems as if they are making a come back of sorts," said Sy.

"Where did you get this?" she asked.

Jakov took the arrow back from her and placed it in his back pack.

We found it in the head of the caterpillar. As we were fighting it, someone shot at it. Quite effectively, I would add."

"Remarkable."

"Not only that," continued Jakov, "But someone with similar arrows shot one of the imperial guards in Praschi village moments before I arrived. Whoever did it probably saved Iskandar's life."

"Someone is following us Jakov," spoke Sy, with his one eye fixated on the fire.

"But who, and why?" asked Ayesha.

"I don't know," answered Jakov. "But as long as it appears that they are on our side all is well. Whoever it is obviously wants us to stay alive and succeed in our journey. We might not be the only ones who want Morpeth and Prisca destroyed. But then again . . ."

"But what?" Ayesha asked as she touched Jakov's arm.

"Imagine what someone like Iskandar could do for a local warlord or a small kingdom. He could grant them almost unlimited power. Or what if someone intends to capture Iskandar and take him to Morpeth for a ransom. Think of how much Morpeth would be willing to pay for Iskandar. Now that would be a king's ransom and a half."

"What should we do then?"

Sy took his single eye off the fire and gazed at Ayesha.

"The only thing we can do. Watch, wait, and stay ready. No doubt this Minim archer will not hesitate to make himself known again if he has to. And when he does . . ."

"Then we catch him and ask him several pressing questions about his interest in Iskandar," said Jakov.

Talkai and Iskandar were oblivious to the conversation around them as they traded stories about the day's events. Talkai described the battle with the gigantic caterpillar in exuberant terms that left Iskandar's mouth gaping open by the details. Similarly, Talkai was enamoured with Iskandar's description of how Ayesha turned herself into a human catapult to bring down an imperial glider. They laughed and joked by the fire, and soon, after some warm bread and tea, they slept soundly side by side in the cool of the night. One by one, the entire group fell asleep by the fire, relishing its warmth amidst the cold night air. Mo and Tar took the first watch of the night and they smoked their pipes, nearly as long as them, while they peered out into the darkness and whispered about what insects they'd like to put down Talkai's pants.

The travellers rose before dawn and ate a quick breakfast of barley bread and hot tea. Iskandar noticed that the water in his leather pouch had turned to ice overnight. The cold bit into his bones and made his fingers ache with pain. Talkai's teeth chattered as he spoke to Iskandar.

"Izzy, m-m-m-my b-b-b-bottom is c-c-c-c-cold. I-I-I-I c-c-c-can't f-f-f-feel m-m-m-my b-b-b-b-b-bo-t-t-t-tom".

Ayesha threw an extra poncho to Talkai and Iskandar.

"Don't worry, boys," she said, "You'll get warm soon enough".

"I th-th-thought it w-w-w-was s-s-s-s-s-s-s-supposedd to b-b-b-be sum-m-m-m-mer," complained Talkai, but no one besides Iskandar listened.

Soon everyone was up and wrapped up as warmly as they could be. Sy, Mo, and Tar unbridled their horses, caressed their noses, and fed them an apple. Then they slapped them on their rear ends and yelled at them loudly to leave. The horses bolted away.

"Aren't the horses going to carry us?" Iskandar asked Sy.

"No, they won't survive the cold. We have to go on by foot. The horses will meet us later when we return. No matter where we are, if we call them, they will come".

"Ice? Is that how we will get to the ice palace?"

"Yes, but we must go through the Nazvor Ranges, which are cold and treacherous. If we don't make it by nightfall, we will freeze to death."

"And what is there?"

Hearing the conversation, Jakov walked over.

"Beyond the Nazvor Ranges is a beautiful palace that its inhabitants call *Devora*, which in their language means 'Jewel of Ice.' It is the most eastern province of Iona. Few people ever see it because it is so remote and so cold. But to gaze upon it from afar is like looking upon heaven. The beauty of its citadel, its crystal towers, and golden gates are a spectacle that will remain with you your whole life. You will not soon forget the first time you lay your eyes on Devora."

"And who is the king that lives there?" Iskandar asked.

"There is no king in the eastern palace now. It is ruled by Princess Aurora who is as good as she is kind."

"You forgot to say 'beautiful,' as well, Jakov," added Sy with a wry smile.

"Indeed, she is beautiful too. She will give us shelter and allow us to plan our next move. You will meet her today."

"I've never met a princess before. But then again, up until yesterday I'd never seen a cyclops either. Before, I thought I was a slave, not a son of Morpeth, and now water talks to me."

Sy laid his hand on Iskandar's head.

"I sense that every day will be a new adventure for you from now on Iskandar. Every day you will learn more of a world that you never knew, and even learn more about yourself."

Jakov added, "And more of the power that grows inside of you."

Iskandar paused and thought about his few moments by the river the day before. He could actually talk to water and hear it talk back. Just then, he looked down at the snow at his feet and stared at it for a few seconds and then he began to speak to it under his breath. He grinned with excitement when he felt a little bit of snow move under his feet. He looked up to see Jakov watching him.

"You shall learn to do far greater things than that my friend."

"When?"

"When you need it the most. Necessity is often the best catalyst for combat".

"But it's a power to kill, isn't it?"

"Not always. It is a power to defend yourself and others. A power to bring light to those in darkness, liberty to those who are enslaved, life to those who are dying. It is a gift from the gods. It must be used wisely, justly, but if necessary, brutally."

"I've never killed anyone before. I don't know if I want to."

"When the time comes Iskandar, you may not have a choice. You will either kill or be killed yourself. And if you die, then ..."

"Then what?"

"Then hope is lost for the redemption of this land. So, you will not die. It is not ordained for you, I'm sure of that."

"Are you sure I am Iskandar? I keep thinking this is a big mistake."

Jakov kneeled down and looked Iskandar in the eyes. Seeing the reflection of his own eyes in that of Iskandar, he longed to embrace him, but resisted the desire.

"I am more sure of that than anything else in the world. I am more sure of who you are than who I am."

Jakov could see that under his poncho, Iskandar's hands were shaking with a mixture of cold and nervousness. He removed his gloves and gave them to the small boy.

"Take these and try to think warm thoughts. Once we get going you will warm up from the walk."

Soon the group was in a single line and walking down the hill into the snow that gradually got thicker and thicker. Mo and Tar were at the front trotting through the snow that at times came up to their waist. They used their shields as a sled and rode down the hills, much to their glee. Jakov then followed with Sy, Iskandar, and Talkai close by and Ayesha was last. Eventually the snow stopped and they were walking on ice. Talkai looked down and every so often he could see some fish swimming several inches under his feet.

"The salmon must be good here," he said to Sy.

Just then Mo and Tar stopped and began sniffing the air around them. They sensed something, but didn't know what it was. Jakov raised his hand to gesture to those behind him to stop. Sy looked around and listened carefully, but heard and saw nothing on the contours around them. There were ridges on either side of them and they were on a frozen river between the two crests. In the way ahead the ridges converged and came together through a narrow pass.

Sy turned to Jakov.

"This would be an awful place for an ambush".

"You're right. Let's keep moving."

Jakov called out to everyone.

"Everyone, shuffle along the ice. Glide as fast as you can. We need to make it to the pass very quickly."

Everyone started pushing themselves along the ice as quick as they could. Talkai was almost falling down every few steps and only holding Iskandar's hand kept him upright. In frustration, Sy and Jakov grabbed Talkai's hand and then launched him along the ice and he slid along for forty yards whereupon Sy and Jakov repeated the exercise to hasten their speed.

Ayesha kept peering over her shoulder to see what was behind them. After several minutes, she glanced behind and saw a blur of white in the distance. She stopped and focused her gaze upon the dots on the ice some ways behind her.

Ayesha called to Jakov, "Something is following us Jakov."

Jakov halted immediately. He looked behind him to where Ayesha was pointing. He took out a telescope from his pocket and looked through it onto the horizon. In the circular glass, he could see ten sleds being pulled by dogs, each sled carrying several men.

"No," he cried. "Why now?"

Jakov turned to Sy who was pointing up to the ridge on the left side. Jakov turned his eyes there and could see a single dark figure on top.

"It can't be."

"It is," said Sy.

Sensing the concern, Iskandar tugged on Jakov's sleeve, who was mesmerized by the man standing on the distant ridge. It took a moment for him to answer, but eventually, Jakov looked down at Iskandar.

"That man up there is your father. And he's come to kill us all."

Everyone stood still looking at the man high on the ridge. He was standing there with his hands on his hips looking down at them. Next to him, there gradually appeared rows of men in white tunics to his left and right until nearly the whole ridge was crowded with men in white that made the man in black stand out all the more. Then, overhead, two imperial gliders flew over in front of where the group was standing. Four barrels were dropped from above, and they burst when they hit the ice, spilling a liquid substance that began to cover the ice in front of them.

"What was that for?" asked Ayesha, as she watched the gliders fly away into the distance.

"I have a bad feeling about this," Jakov replied.

At that moment a huge beam of fire shot out from Morphet on top of the ridge and struck the ground exactly where the barrels had landed.

The ground then burst into flames, which caused Mo and Tar at the front to recoil back.

"They dropped oil," stated Sy as he hung his head down.

Jakov looked at the massive flames that now blocked their path towards the pass. He could see the sleighs behind them getting closer and closer, and up on the ridge to their left stood Morpeth with several hundred men to at his side.

"Are we finished?" asked Ayesha.

"We are never finished, not like this, not today," Jakov replied.

"There's no way out Jakov," said Sy.

Then a booming voice came from Morpeth upon the ridge.

"You are surrounded Jakov. Surrender yourself and Iskandar, and I will spare your friends."

Jakov half grunted and half laughed.

"Unless 'spare' means torture and behead, I wouldn't believe him," answered Ayesha.

Morpeth spoke again, "What is your answer Jakov? I shall not wait all day."

"What answer shall you give him," said Sy.

"How about this one?"

Jakov took several stones from his pocket. He threw them in the air and waved his hand as if to stop them. The stones froze in mid air, hanging by some strange power that suspended them before him. Jakov then whispered under his breath and violently waved his hands. The seven stones flew in the air up the ridge faster than arrows and struck a number of the men around Morpeth. Morpeth threw himself to the ground only moments before to avoid being struck by the rocketing stones. He stood up and yelled down into the valley.

"So you have chosen your fate. Die if you must, boy!"

With that, the men on the ridge next to Morpeth quickly began walking down towards the group.

"We can make a stand here if we have to," Sy said as he drew out his axe.

Jakov looked at each of his friends, who had unsheathed their weapons. They stood there bravely, ready to fight, and ready to die."

Jakov turned to Ayehsa.

"The other ridge over there. Do you think you could take Iskandar over it?"

"Yes, but what about you and Sy and the others."

"We'll hold them for as long as we can. Once you've got over it, head east, there should be another river on the other side. Follow it, and it will take you straight to the gates of Devora. You're our only hope now."

"But you'll all be killed."

"Do it," was Jakov's earnest reply.

Ayesha stopped for a moment and looked into Jakov's eyes, wondering if she'd ever see them again.

Jakov looked at the fire to his front, the men on the hill coming towards him from his left, the dog sleds he could now hear coming from behind him. He pushed Ayesha along and pointed up to the ridge to his right.

"Go Ayesha, before it's too late."

Iskandar had been motionless the whole time and frozen in fear. Ayesha grabbed him by his arm and quickly began running along the ice towards the other ridge, dragging Iskandar along.

Jakov turned and gestured to Mo, Tar, and Sy. They quickly formed a circle around Talkai, who had decided to sit down and pull his poncho over his head.

"Please tell me when it's over," Talkai uttered under his poncho as he watched Ayesha drag Iskandar off into the distance.

"To be honest Talkai, your option sounds like the most sensible one at the moment," Sy stated.

The men from both sides closed in on them as the flames from the huge fire ahead continued to roar.

Iskandar was dragged for a while along the ice, then he and Ayesha began their climb up the ridge. Iskandar looked over his shoulder and saw the men beginning to close all around his friends who were only a few hundred metres now from the incoming foes. He tried to hold back the tears but was unable. As he was dragged further up the steep incline, he grabbed some of the snow in his hand and squeezed it tight as he felt his fear turning to something he'd never felt before: rage. It welled up in his stomach until he could take it no more. He gritted his teeth and stuck his heels into the ground. Suddenly, he stopped and let go of Ayesha's hand.

"Wait. I have an idea."

"What?"

But Iskandar had completely let go of her hand and was now running down the hill back towards Jakov, Sy, Mo, Tar, and Talkai.

"Stop Iskandar. We must go. Stop," she cried and she tried to chase after him, but she slipped over and her leg was trapped in a crevice in the ice. Ayesha tried to pull her leg free. She watched helplessly as Iskandar ran further and further away from her, back towards the others.

Iskandar half slid and half ran along the frozen ground, stumbling every few paces, panting for breath in the cold air. He was running from the only direction that no one else was approaching his friends from. From the other three sides, men with weapons ebbed closer towards his friends.

Jakov took out another handful of stones that flew out from him like miniature catapults, knocking down several men. Mo and Tar fired arrows that hit a few other men in the melee as well. Jakov finally took out his two swords from his back and took one step forward in front of his friends.

"It's been a pleasure to know you brothers. Today we shall feast in paradise." Jakov looked at Sy and cast his gaze towards Talkai. Sy nodded, knowing full well what Jakov's concern was.

"I won't let them take him. It will be quick," the cyclops promised.

"I hope our fate is equally as good."

Just then Iskandar ran past Jakov and continued running towards the hundreds of men now sprinting down from the ridge, ready to engage the small band in combat.

"No!" Jakov yelled.

Immediately Iskandar stopped twenty feet in front of him. He looked over his shoulder and smiled at Jakov, his eyes still wet with tears.

"It will be alright Jakov. I know what I have to do now."

Jakov tried to run over to him, but Sy grabbed his shoulder.

"Wait Jakov. Let's see what the boy does. It is all or nothing now my friend."

As the men in white got closer Iskandar clenched his fists. The anger he felt running over was now ready to be released. He then raised his hands above his head, closed his eyes, and spoke to the snow and ice with an authority that it had never heard before. Instantly the snow behind, before, around, and under the men shifted and came rushing down the hill. All of the men fell over and dropped to the ground. The ground around them was wet, but now snowless, like the ground in early spring. The snow violently retreated towards Jakov and formed a twenty-foot mound of white in front of him, like a great wall of snow and ice twenty-feet high, ten feet deep, and two hundred feet wide. The men from Morpeth took back to their feet, stopped for a moment in surprise, but then they began running again down towards the wall of snow between them and their intended victims. Iskandar could hear them beginning to climb the great snow wall that he had created. He deliberately paused for a moment and pointed the palms of his hands towards the wall. With that, he waved his hands outwards and the snow wall suddenly collapsed and rolled up the ridge like a reverse avalanche crushing all in its path. The men were submerged beneath the wave of snow and crushed by the weight. Others were thrown about by the force of the tidal wave of snow engulfing them. The men's bodies lay strewn along the ridge as the immense wave of snow rushed further and further up the steep ridge.

When Morpeth had seen Iskandar running passed Jakov, he could scarcely believe his luck. He thought that with Jakov and Iskandar in front of him, this was the day that he'd finally become a god and be released from the torment of tasting divinity only in part. He thanked Marduk for his good fortune. Now as the tidal wave of snow came closer and closer up the ridge, thankfulness had vanished entirely and he began taking steps backwards. He raised he hands and launched fire ball after fire ball at the wave of snow that came rushing closer but they did nothing to impede the ferocity of its force. With only seconds to spare Morpeth ran backwards and dived to the ground as the wave of snow fell over him him.

Back in the middle of the valley, Jakov, Sy, Mo, and Tar could not believe what they were seeing. Sy dropped his axe, and his mouth fell wide open. No sooner had the wave of snow covered the hundreds of men than Iskandar turned to his left and focused his attention on the approaching sleds. He knelt down and placed his hands on the ice beneath him and could somehow sense the waters beneath. Standing up, he looked at the sleds one last time. He could see the men riding on the back preparing to disembark with their swords, and then he stamped his foot on the ground. A small crack in the ice opened up in front of him and then began splitting further, heading towards the sleds. The crack in the ice moved faster and faster. It got larger and it then divided into two parts, like a Y-shape on the ice. The huge crack then surrounded the sleds that had now stopped. As the four dozen men began disembarking and running towards him, Iskandar raised his hands and entire block of ice that the sleds and the men were on lifted into the air twenty feet. The men froze in fear as the ground beneath them literally lifted them up into the air like a huge white carpet. They dropped their weapons and began to look for places to run, jump, and even hide. But Iskandar flicked his wrist and the entire block of ice then capsized and cast the men and their sleds into the icy waters beneath them. The ice platform fell down top of them, leaving them trapped underneath its frozen seal.

Finally, Iskandar walked towards the flames that blocked their route towards the pass. He picked up some snow from the ground, rolled it into a ball in his hand, and threw it. As it hit the ground, the snowball continued rolling and rolling and rolling until it increased markedly in size and speed. When the snowball was the size of an eight foot boulder, it rolled over the fire from left to right and completely smothered it.

Iskandar looked behind him to see Jakov standing in disbelief and shock. Mo and Tar had their hands covering their mouth. Sy closed his mouth and began smiling. He hit Jakov on the back.

"You told me he was powerful, but I never imagined that he was . . . that he could . . . do feats like that!"

"Truth be told Sy, I'm still amazed that any of us are alive".

"Jehoora manui," said Tar.

"No, Tar, your eyes were not deceiving you. It happened alright," responded Sy.

"Quigon hijama wowi tis," added Mo.

"Yes, we might all have to change our underwear after that display Mo."

Iskandar turned around walked towards Jakov, who shook his head, smiled at him and held his arms open to receive him. Iskandar started running, but then felt something painfully hot behind him. Before he could realise it, a huge ball of flame had landed just behind him, melting the ice underneath him. The ice began to break up and Iskandar could feel himself slipping into a hole. A flash of green and yellow rushed before him and he felt someone grab his hand and pull him out of the freezing water. Iskandar felt cold, ice cold, worse than ever before. He felt his face turn blue and white as the numbness in his legs began to feel like the piercing of a thousand frozen daggers. He looked up and saw Ayesha's face looking into his own.

"You may have got away from me the first time, Iskie, but not a second time," she said to him.

Jakov looked up and saw Morpeth standing on top of the ridge, his black clothes now half covered with snow. He took a stone from his pouch and threw it up at Morpeth and it pierced through the air, narrowly avoiding his head. After that came the voice of Morpeth as he yelled in a strong voice from the top of the ridge.

"You may have won today, Jakov, but you cannot hide in this ice desert forever. When you return, I will be waiting for you and for Iskandar. This is not over."

Jakov turned to Sy.

"He's alone up there, Sy. We can take him now. All of us. We can finish this today and liberate Iona once and for all. Now I say."

"No, Jakov. We can't".

"But this might be the only chance we have to get him alone."

"We are not prepared for him. Not here, not like this."

"Then I'll go after him alone. I can take him by myself if I have to."

"No Jakov," Sy urged him.

"I've waited too long for this day."

"Then wait a few days more and do it properly."

Sy placed his hands on Jakov's chest and pointed to Iskandar who Ayesha had wrapped up in her cape on the frozen ground.

"He's hurt Jakov. He's freezing to death. We have to get him to the palace before nightfall or he might die of exposure to the cold."

Jakov looked up on the ridge as he saw Morpeth slowly walking away until he was finally out of sight. He closed his eyes and drew a deep breath. Waiting for a moment, he knelt beside Iskandar who was blue from the splash of water that struck his face.

"Iskandar, can you hear me?" asked Jakov.

"Yes, Jakov. D-d-d-d-did y-y-you s-s-s-see w-w-what I did?"

"Yes, lad, you did well. I'm proud of you. We all are."

"So am I," uttered Talkai, who then whispered to Jakov, "What did he do?"

"We'll get you to somewhere warm very quickly, my young friend."

"Good, because I'm r-r-really c-c-cold." Then he fell unconscious and Ayesha rubbed his face.

"We must hurry Jakov, he might not have long," she said to him.

Jakov looked at Mo and Tar.

"Make a stretcher for him and quick. Use some of the weapons from the dead imperial soldiers if you have to."

"What can I do?" asked Talkai.

"Talkai, I have a very important job for you."

"What is that?" asked Talkai excited.

"Take off all of your clothes except your underwear."

"What?"

"You heard me."

"Why?"

"No time to explain, just do it. It's for Iskandar's sake."

"I'll do it then."

Within a few minutes, they had stripped off the wet clothes from Iskandar and laid him with a semi-naked Talkai on a stretcher and covered them both with blankets. The body heat from Talkai returned the colour to Iskandar's cheeks, as he and Talkai were carried on the stretcher by Mo and Tar. Iskandar awoke.

"Talkai, why don't we have any clothes on besides our underwear?"

"It's a long story. Best if you try get some rest and best if we never talk about this again."

"Okay," he said as he drifted off to sleep, cuddling up to his good friend.

As the travellers moved on into the pass ahead of them, Jakov stopped for a moment. He looked all around him to see what was, from one perspective, an utter massacre. Hundreds of dead bodies strewn all over the side of the ridge. Jakov gazed up to the top of the ridge and wondered where Morpeth was now. He rubbed his hands into his short beard and wondered if that was the only chance he was ever going to get to kill Morpeth. He reflected for a moment in amazement and lament. He was still amazed at the extent of Iskandar's powers, yet he lamented his lost opportunity for revenge. The angst soon disappeared when he realized where it was that he was going. The ice palace of Devora. And he remembered who was there waiting for him. Great feelings of joy sang into his heart as he walked onwards towards the palace.

# Chapter 8

## Revelations at the City of Devora

WHEN ISKANDAR AWOKE, HE was lying in a bed with a mountain of blankets on him, wearing silk pyjamas. A fire was raging in a fireplace several feet away from the bed. The room was white, snow white, and the walls were adorned with mirrors and crystal ornaments. He looked about him for a moment and then called out.

"Is anybody here?"

There was no answer. So he waited for several seconds and then got out of bed. The floor, which was white like the ceiling and walls, was freezing cold. His feet stung just by standing on it, so he stepped onto the rug in the middle of the room to try to keep his feet warm. He saw some slippers under his bed and he put them on and they enabled him to walk over to the door and open it. The corridor was empty, but he could hear the sound of voices not far away. Iskandar slipped on a night gown from the back of the door and made his way towards the voices. As he walked down the corridor, he was again startled to see that everything was white: walls, floor, ceiling. The only non-white things were the row of red rugs that ran along the corridor and the odd mirror and crystal ornaments, shaped like stars, hanging on the walls. It was almost exactly how he imagined the heavenly kingdom of Vetrius to be.

As he walked on, somewhat apprehensively, he could feel the stiffness in his legs, partly from the cold and partly from the soreness of the battle in the valley the day before. It was only then that it just dawned on him what had happened and what he had done. As he turned a corner he saw Jakov and a young woman standing together. Jakov turned to him and smiled.

"Iskandar, you're awake."

Jakov seemed genuinely pleased to see him. His whole demeanor was different. Normally he seemed very intense, focused, and even angry. But now he looked, to Iskandar at least, Jakov was relaxed and even happy. He was wearing something other than black as well. A blue and yellow tunic with big white buttons. Iskandar smiled back.

"My legs hurt," he said.

"That's from walking in the snow and nearly having them blown off."

Iskandar looked at the young woman. Her hair was black like the pitch of night, her face white, with ruby red lips. Her beauty was hypnotic and Iskandar had to concentrate not to gaze at her with his mouth open.

"And you must be Iskandar. I am so happy to meet you," she said. "Jakov has told me so much about you." She beamed a warm smile at him and put her hand on his face and Iskandar blushed.

"Thank you."

Jakov put his arm around Iskandar.

"Iskandar, this fine lady is Princess Aurora. High Regent of Devora, city in the land of Nazvor, guardian of the eastern frontier, your friend, and my beloved wife."

"Wife," sputtered Iskandar with surprise.

"Yes Iskandar. We are married."

"So you're like a prince."

"Yes, but only by marriage."

Aurora smiled at him again. "But princes at Devora do not ordinarily galivant around the land kidnapping children, slaying a monster caterpillar, and fighting battles in narrow valleys like you do."

"I told you that I'd never make a good prince."

"I am starting to believe you Jakov."

"How did I get here?" Iskandar asked.

"You were carried here. You nearly died my friend. But we got you here in the end. Here where it is safe."

"And where is 'here' exactly?"

"Come with me and I'll show you." Aurora took Iskandar by the hand and led him outside with Jakov to a balcony. She pulled back the curtains and gave Iskandar a view of the surrounding area. Iskandar looked out into the wide open area and saw a small city below him with lights glistening against the twilight darkness and hundreds of houses built into the sides of hills and mountains with streets and street lights sparkling in the early dawn light. It was a city of white. Jakov kissed Aurora on the cheek, and spoke gently to her.

"I must go. I need to speak to Sy about our next move. I will see you at dinner my sweet."

Aurora winked at Jakov as he walked off and then at Iskandar. Iskandar felt a strange ease in her presence, as if he was resting in the glow of her beauty.

"Are you happy Iskandar?"

"With what?" he answered.

"Well, the past few days have been hard for you. Learning that you are the son of Morpeth, leaving your home town, people dying, being chased by an enormous caterpillar, and I heard about what you did against Morpeth's forces."

Iskandar blushed in embarassment.

"It's been very hard. Everything that I thought I knew has been changed. Everything I thought was true isn't true anymore. I thought my name was Bobascow. Now everyone calls me Iskandar. I thought I was an orphan, but now I know my parents are alive. I know who they are and what they did to all of my brothers and sisters."

"All of your brothers and sisters?" asked Aurora raised an eyebrow.

"Yes, Morpeth and Prisca killed them all. They are dead. I am the only one left. Jakov told me that it is my job to avenge them and bring peace to the land of Iona."

"Oh, I see," she replied, but Iskandar could sense something different in her voice. She paused for a moment and put her hand on his shoulder. Iskandar liked the warmth of her touch.

"Iskandar, I don't know how to tell you this, but I must. There is something you should know."

"What?"

"You are not completely alone. You have one brother who is alive," she stopped speaking as Iskandar's mouth opened wide.

"Jakov. Jakov is your brother, Iskandar. That is why he also has strange powers just like you."

Iskandar felt faint and then sick and then happy and then angry. Aurora felt his discomfort and strain and she rubbed her hands through his hair.

"I'm sorry to have to tell you about this. But I think you need to know. Jakov is your brother. You are not alone in this world child."

As Iskandar's face grimaced with frustrations he asked, "Then why didn't he tell me? Why?"

"He is a good man. Strong and noble. He is a complex man too. Jakov has a beautiful soul, but it is also a tortured soul. He is driven only by saving those whom he loves and by destroying those who would hurt them. He is a loving man, I know that in my heart, but he will stop at nothing to destroy those who would hurt his family. He lost his other brothers and sisters, his family, to the insanity of his parents. He doesn't want to lose you too. I suppose he was trying to protect you. Think of it that way."

"He could still have told me," Iskandar complained.

"I know he could have. He probably still means to do so when the time is right. But he, he just wants to . . ."

"To use me as a weapon? Is that all I am to him?"

"No, you're his brother. He loves you. He risked his life to protect you."

"Then why didn't he tell me that he's my brother? Anyone else would have!"

"Because he loves you. Maybe he didn't want to confuse you with feelings. I don't know. He'll have to explain it to you. However, I know this, there is nothing bad in him. He is not like his parents. He is noble, valiant, loving, and brave."

"Is he merciful?

Aurora paused. "He can be when he chooses to be."

"All these years I thought I was alone. Talkai was my only friend. But now I have a brother."

With that two small children ran up and hugged Aurora. A small boy and a smaller girl, no more than three years old. They had golden hair and bright smiles. They wore white bed clothes and buried their faces into Aurora's dress.

"Good morning mummy," they said in turn.

Aurora gripped them tightly and kissed their heads. She then turned to Iskandar and presented the children to him.

"Iskandar, this is Marius and Alexa. They are my children. Say hello children."

The two little blond children slowly and shyly turned to Iskandar and said, "Hello," with timid voices.

Iskandar struggled to smile at them. But then froze as he realized who these children were.

"Aurora, are these your children?

"Why, yes, of course."

"Does that mean that they are, I mean, I am, I mean we are ..."

Aurora guessed what he was trying to say.

"Yes, this is your niece and nephew."

Iskandar sat down for a moment on a small stool behind him in disbelief. He kept looking at the small children in astonishment. He noticed that little Marius looked almost identical to him.

"I'm an uncle," he said.

"Yes," laughed Aurora. "Children, give your uncle Iskandar a hug."

The children hesitated for a moment. They looked at Iskandar with their big brown eyes and sized him up to see if he was safe. Then suddenly they both launched themselves at him and hugged him, nearly knocking him off his chair. Iskandar enjoyed having their little arms wrapped around him.

"Come now, children. Off to breakfast. You need a big breakfast for a big day ahead of you."

"Yes mummy," they replied in unison, and scurried off.

Iskandar sat there stunned.

"They are very nice children," he said with a blank look on his face.

"They are nice, full of excitement and energy, and very curious. They are a bit like you I imagine."

"I always wanted to be part of a family. The only family I knew was Talkai and Wringstone."

"You are part of our family Iskandar. A brother, a sister, and nephews and nieces too. You are welcomed to stay as long as you like."

"But we'll have to go soon, won't we?"

Aurora turned her face away for a moment and then returned her gaze back to Iskandar.

"Yes, that is my understanding. Jakov needs to finish what he has started."

"A war with Morpeth."

"It's more like a quest. A quest to end the tyranny. A quest to bring justice to the land that has been plagued by evil. A quest to right a wrong of many years ago."

"And I have to go too."

"I don't want either of you to go. I wish you both could stay here, forever. But ..."

"But what?"

"But that cannot happen. Sooner or later, Morpeth will find us and he will come with his armies and do here what he did elsewhere."

"And what is that?"

"Kill everyone and destroy everything. Many lands have been laid waste, many cities burned to ashes, many have died, too many."

"Because of me?"

"No, because of the madness of one man who once was good."

"Morpeth was good?" Iskandar asked with surprised expression.

"He was not always evil. Morpeth and Prisca were corrupted by Marduk. He seduced them and his promise of divine power drove them to madness. Now they will stop at nothing to become fully divine, to be deified."

"No one has ever said anything good about him. Or about my mother. What became of them?"

"I'm told that after you and Jakov were rescued, they were so enraged that they fought each other. They were unable to share the blame for your escape and unable to share power. Morpeth was the more powerful and he subdued Prisca. Now Morpeth keeps Prisca locked up in a mountain fortress called Masavar. There she is unable to use her powers."

"Is she wicked as well?"

"They say she is worse than Morpeth. But people say lots of things."

"You said that Morpeth was good, once before."

"My father, the former king of Nazvor, considered Morpeth his closest friend and ally. Morpeth was wise, compassionate, and loving, but deeply committed to his god Marduk and that was his undoing. The undoing of many."

"What happened to your father?"

"Morpeth tricked him, betrayed him, and then killed him. Just as he did many of the kings, regents, and leaders of Iona. Royal assassins killed him on the way to a meeting with Morpeth. That was when I became Queen. I was twelve years old. It is only the ice desert that has kept his forces away and prevented him from penetrating deep into our land."

"I'm sorry," said Iskandar, genuinely sad.

"Don't be. It's not your fault. All we can do is the best we can."

"What will become of me?"

"Listen, fate is something that you discover, something you find unexpectedly, and even something that you create for yourself."

"Today I discovered that I have a brother."

"And tomorrow you may learn a whole lot more as well."

"I think I need to speak to Jakov."

"You will, but for now, why don't we go on a tour of the ice gardens. Did you know that some beautiful plants can grow in frozen conditions?"

"Yes, that would be nice."

Aurora led Iskandar around the gardens. But the whole time as she talked and showed him many things, all he could think about was having a brother, a family, and what tomorrow would have in store for him.

Jakov and Sy leaned over a map of Iona spread out on the table in front of them. They both stared at it, deep in thought.

"All roads to Dalazvar and Morpeth run through Norella," said Jakov. Dalazvar was the capital of Iona and housed the palace of the king of Iona and the headquarters of his military command.

"But even if we take the city we will have no escape route if Morpeth and the imperial army lays siege to us," Sy replied, rubbing his one eye.

"I am not planning an escape. This will be our single opportunity, our one and only chance to destroy his army. It is all or nothing. We defeat his forces in the open plains between the lake in the east and the great river running east west. Only two bridges in and out. They will be trapped once they traverse the northern bridge."

"But so will we, that's the problem. I see your point Jakov. Once Morpeth's army crosses the great river, they are trapped between the river and the lake, but we will be no different. What you're suggesting is to lock a mongoose in a cage with a cobra. You are the cobra and you are assuming that the cobra will win."

"This is the best terrain to fight on Sy. We will have the best strategic position from Norella. We will have the advantage of preparation, surprise, and ..."

"And what?" the cyclops asked.

"We will have Iskandar with us too."

Sy straightened up and took a deep breath. He wiped his sweaty hands on his tunic and looked back at Jakov.

"You have too much confidence in the boy."

"You saw what he did yesterday. If it wasn't for him, we'd already be dead."

"I saw a little boy nearly die in the frost. I know he has power Jakov, just like you, but I am not prepared to put my own fate, let alone the fate of the Freedom Legionnaires, into the hands of a boy."

"He will not fail us."

"How can you be so sure?"

"Call it fate, destiny, or the god Vetrius watching over us. I do not claim to know the what or the why. All I know is that everything that we've hoped for and worked for is coming to its end."

"But whose end? Morpeth's or ours?"

"Once we seize Norella and defeat the imperial army, we will have a clear run through the Yobi desert and straight to the gates of Dalazvar. Then it's only a matter of time."

"Will Norella open its gates to us so willingly? We both know the answer to that one."

"The people of Norella support us. Our army, the Freedom Legion, is filled with volunteers from the city. Men tired of the violence of Morpeth and his vassal who sits on the throne in Norella. Mazlo the Regent is despised for submitting the city to Morpeth's whim. The people want freedom and are willing to fight for it. Against Morpeth and even against Mazlo."

"What of Mazlo then?"

"He is wicked, but weak. He will surrender quickly. Once our forces are in the city he will either flee to Dalazvar or make peace with us. We can handle him."

"So you say."

Sy looked down at the map again and scanned over it, looking for an alternative option to Jakov's plan.

"Norella you say."

"It is the gateway to the north. There is no better place in all of Iona to fight the battle we want to fight. And we will fight it on the ground of our choosing, on our terms, and fight to our strengths."

"So be it then, Jakov. We place our trust in your hands. You haven't failed us yet. I just hope you know what you're doing. I will send word to our troops hiding on the outskirts of the icelands."

"But you are not fully convinced, are you?"

"You place too much confidence in a small boy."

"A boy who will lead us to freedom Sy."

"I hope so, for all our sakes."

Sy turned his eye towards the doorway and gestured with his hand.

"Speaking of small boys, the hero himself. I'll leave you two be, I obviously have work to do, cities to capture, kingdoms to liberate, and that's all before next week."

Jakov turned to Iskandar and gestured for him to come over to him, but Iskandar remained still, almost ignoring Jakov altogether. He stood there blankly, with his arms folded.

"Iskandar, what is the matter, you seem upset."

"I don't know ... brother. Maybe you could tell me."

Jakov leaned back on the table and ran his fingers through his dark beard.

"It is true. What you say is true. We are brothers. But I never . . ."

Iskandar leaped forward and burst out in anger, "Then why couldn't you tell me?"

Jakov paused for brief second.

"I wasn't sure how you would take it. I didn't know whether you could handle it. I thought it might affect your judgment. Cloud your thoughts with feelings. Threaten our mission."

"Mission? I never agreed to any mission."

"The mission is the purpose of our birth, the reason why we both survived. It is the destiny that awaits us both."

"I never agreed!" screamed Iskandar.

"You have no choice, and neither do I!" he screamed back. "People, villages, cities, and kingdoms all depend on you and me to save them. People are dying. Maybe you didn't see that in Praschi, but I see it every day."

"I am not anybody's saviour Jakov. I'm a boy. I just want to be a boy again, back in Praschi."

"That is not an option for either of us."

"You want me to kill my father."

"Our father! And if you remember rightly, he's already tried to kill us both, just yesterday."

"I don't want to fight, or kill, or die. I've always wanted a family to belong to. Just like other children."

Iskandar began to cry and Jakov bent over and looked him in the eye.

"And you have one. I'm your family. You are my family. Aurora and the children too. We are your family. All of us together, brother."

He touched Iskandar on the cheek, but Iskandar pushed his hand away.

"I still think you should have told me sooner."

"I wanted to, little brother. You have no idea how much I wanted to. Since the hour I plucked you out of Praschi. I've wanted to tell you and hug you. And I'm glad you know. But please understand I carry a heavy burden

Iskandar. And I have to carry it alone. Maybe when you realize that then you'll begin to understand. I have to put my own feelings aside and do what is required of me. Because if I fail, if we fail, there will be untold suffering for so many. I cannot afford to do that, for all our sakes."

"You carry the burden alone because you won't let anyone carry it with you."

"You don't understand my brother."

"I understand more than you think I do."

"Then what do you want of me Iskandar?"

"I want to have a brother."

"I am your brother."

"Back when I was in Praschi, men would visit the tavern. They always carried swords, they spoke only of war, death, and triumphs. Do you know what they were?

"What?"

"Mercenaries. Sometimes I think you are just like them. All you talk about is war, plans, and killing."

"Again, Iskandar, that's by necessity, not choice."

"Is it?"

With that Iskandar wiped his eyes and nose with his sleeve. He turned and left the room.

"Iskandar wait," called out Jakov, "Do you want to know how I found you?"

Iskandar turned around.

"How?" he asked.

Five days ago a snow falcon arrived on my window with a note attached to its talon. All the note said was "Iskandar is in Praschi." On the bird I also found a small drawing of you.

Jakov took a scrap of paper from his pocket and showed it to Iskandar. The boy looked at it and was amazed when he saw the picture. Its likeness to him was clear. It was as if he had posed for the drawing. His face in the drawing looked happy and full of joy, the opposite of what he felt now.

"Who sent it to you?"

"I do not have the foggiest idea. I wish I knew so I could thank them. The falcon flew away. At first I thought it was a trap. But you know what?"

"What?"

"As soon as I read that, trap or no trap, I came for you straight away. Nothing in Iona, in the heavens, or in hell was gonna keep me from you."

"Is it because of my power, a power you can use to kill Morpeth?"

"No, Iskandar, it's because you are my brother. I remember you from years ago. You can't remember me, but I remember you. When we were little, I mean very little, when you were no more than a baby and I was a little boy, we would play in the nursery together with toy soldiers, blocks, and games. I used to tickle you on your ribs and watch your laugh."

Jakov's countenance turned very dark and his face looked sad. The he added, "Along with our other brothers and sisters, who are no more."

"What were they like?"

"They were beautiful. Beautiful, naughty, mischievous, and fun. I miss them."

"I wish I could remember them."

"Me too."

"Jakov, what is going to happen to me?"

"I don't know for certain. But we are going to war."

"I'm afraid Jakov."

"I'm afraid too."

"What are you afraid of you? I thought you were brave."

"Being brave doesn't mean that you are not scared. I am scared. I am scared for myself, for Aurora, for the children. I am scared of losing you. I am scared of failing."

"Then why do we have to do this thing?"

"Bravery doesn't mean that you're not afraid. Bravery means that you believe that there is something more powerful than your fear. Bravery means that you won't let your fear stop you from protecting the people you love the most. Bravery means that your love is stronger than all the evil in the world. Bravery means that you will never give up, won't shut up, wont' lie down, fall down, or go down without the fight of your life. Bravery means that truth is more important than the lie. Bravery means I will walk through the darkness so that others can walk in the light. Bravery means that I will be alone so that others can be together. That is bravery Iskandar. It doesn't make your fears go away, but it makes you stand up and confront them, look them in the eye and say, 'Do your worst, for there is nothing that I cannot endure from you.' That is why we must fight. Can you be brave for me Iskandar?"

"I think so," he said softly

"I know you can be. That's why we are brothers. We can be brave together."

"I'll try."

"There is no 'try' for us. Decide now to be brave brother. Decide now that you will always do what you have to do, no matter how hard it is. I know that when the time comes you will do what is asked of you."

"I will then."

"Good."

"Brother?"

"Yes."

"Will we be okay?"

Jakov nodded and scruffed Iskandar's hair with his hand.

"Yes, it will work out in the end, I'm sure of it."

Iskandar hugged Jakov. Jakov was startled, but put his arms around the boy and embraced him. It was what he had always wanted to do but never had done. For a moment, he really wished that he believed it himself, that things were going to work out alright, but part of him knew otherwise.

That evening, Iskandar walked down into the garden. Rugged up in a coat and shoes, he walked through the garden where he felt the crackling of leaves under his feet and enjoyed seeing his breath in front of him in the cool night air. Everything was white, the roses, the flowers, and the ferns. It was snowing softly and he enjoyed the gentle coolness of the snowflakes on his face as he walked through the garden. He touched the white roses and noticed the drops of water that fell to the ground when his fingers pressed upon them. Just then Iskandar was startled as he heard footsteps behind him.

"What are you doing here all by yourself?" asked Talkai. His big lanky frame cast a big shadow over Iskandar in the moonlight.

"I'm just out for a walk. It's nice here. It never snowed in Praschi. It was only hot. Like a desert. And dry. It hardly even rained."

"I think it's freezing here. My toes hurt and my nose is numb," he said, rubbing his face for warmth.

"I like it here."

"It is more than the weather that makes it nice for you, Bobbascow – I mean, Iskandar – I keep calling you by your old name. I'm sorry."

"Bobbascow was my slave name. I don't know how I got that name. But my real name is Iskandar. I guess we both have got to get used to it."

"Well, it's hard for me. I'm always forgetting names. I can never re-member which one of the dwarves is 'Mo' and which one is 'Tar'. They are both as mischevious and naughty as the other. And all dwarfs look the same to me."

"I know. I remember that sometimes you used to call Wringstone 'Captain'. It made him so angry."

"Well, I think he was a captain, a captain stupid-head of course."

"But he's dead now, isn't he?" Iskandar looked at Talkai.

"I'm afraid so."

"He wasn't all bad was he?"

"He was a harsh man Iskandar. But, no, he wasn't all bad."

"So many people have died. We nearly died in the snow fields. I nearly died."

"I was afraid too. I thought I was going to die. Get chopped up into a thousand pieces or be thrown to ice bears to be eaten."

"I am afraid Talkai."

"Of what, Morpeth?"

"No, of Jakov."

"They tell me he's your brother. Is it true?"

"Yes, it is. Aurora told me and Jakov admitted it."

"I thought you'd be happy that you have a brother, a family. I wish I did."

"I am happy. But families don't go to war. They don't fight. They don't kill their parents."

"Yours is no ordinary family Iskandar. It's a rare family. A sad family. A family destined for important things."

"I want to be a normal family. I don't want to fight anyone. No sol diers of Iona and especially not a father that I don't even know. It's not fair."

"Then what will you do?"

"I will run away Talkai. Far away. Somewhere where there is no war or fighting."

"But if you did that, Jakov would find you again. Either him or Morpeth."

"Then I'll run to a place where no one will find me."

"Iskandar, you know you can't."

"Then I'll just stay here. I don't want to fight. I don't want to kill. I don't want to die."

"No one does. But if you run away, what will happen to your family? Aurora and the children, your niece and nephew?"

"Won't they be safe here?"

"Maybe, for a time, but you can't hide here forever. Morpeth knows we are here."

"Then I'll hide. I'm good at hiding, Talkai. You know I am."

"I know you are good. But some things you cannot hide from, not for too long."

"From battles?"

"From destiny. Ever since I've known you, I've known that you're destined for greatness. The fate of the whole land hinges on you. Your gift, your power, and your courage."

"I promised Jakov that I wouldn't be afraid. But I didn't promise him that I'd fight."

"I am not a wise man. I'm not a smart man. I'm not a clever man. I'm not even a brave man. But I trust in you. I believe in you. I believe that you'll always do the right thing."

"Will Jakov always do the right thing?"

"If he won't, then I know that you will."

Iskandar looked at the moon. It was pale, almost honey coloured, and then he cast his gaze on the mountains of ice that looked like blades cutting into the horizons.

"I don't trust him. There are things he's not telling me. I'm sure of it."

"He means you no harm. He's an angry young man, but he has no anger towards you."

"He'll stop at nothing to kill Morpeth."

"You don't know that. He has protected you, and risked his own life for both of us."

"But there is still something dark about him. Something not right."

"People say I'm not right in the head either, but you trust me, don't you?"

"Yes, of course. You're a funny man Talkai."

"Then trust me again. Stay with Jakov and see where he takes you. Then you'll see whether there is something good or bad in his heart."

"I think it would be easier to run away."

Talkai smiled at him, then he kneeled down and picked up a pile of show that he made into a ball.

"I'll make you wager. See that statue over there, the one by the tree with the man wearing the crown, do you see it?"

Iskandar looked about over his left shoulder where Talkai was pointing. He saw the outline of a statue in the distance, about a hundred yards away. He guessed that it was probably the same size as him.

"What about it?" Iskandar asked.

"Well, if I can hit it with this snow ball, you have to promise not to run away and that you'll stay close to Jakov if things ever get scary."

"You'll never hit it. It's too far away."

"Don't doubt me. I used to hit squirrels with rocks on the fence back in Praschi. I think I can hit an old statue."

"You'll never make it. I might as well leave now."

"Give me a chance. Do you accept my wager, do you?"

"Okay then, but you'll never hit it."

Talkai licked his finger to measure the wind, he licked his lips, leaned back and wound-up his arm and then threw the snow ball with a ferocity that surprised Iskandar. The ball of snow went high in the air and then landed right on top of the statue."

"Wow," said Iskandar, "That was amazing. I didn't know you could throw like that. How did you do that?"

"Did you ever remember seeing squirrels in Praschi?"

"No."

"Well now you know why. I am Talkai, the slayer of squirrels. But now you have to keep your side of the bet."

Iskandar sighed, and said, "I promise I won't runaway and I'll stay close to Jakov."

"Good, that makes me happy. You're the only friend I've got Iskandar. I don't want to lose you. Now let's go inside. I need some nice warm tea."

"Me too."

"But first, there is one important thing we need to do."

"What is that, Talkai?"

A wicked grin appeared on Talkai's face.

"Snowball fight!"

Talkai and Iskandar then started throwing snowballs at each other. Iskandar got Talkai on the face and he fell to the ground, pretending to be knocked out. When Iskandar ran over, Talkai put snow into his face and then ran off as Iskandar chased after him, throwing even more snowballs at him.

"Come on, that's enough, let's go inside. That tea sounds good after a snowball fight that I won."

"You so did not win. I got you at least eight times."

"As if. You couldn't hit a cow if it was tied to you."

"You're such a fibber Talkai."

Iskandar

The two ran back inside into the warmth of the indoors. Iskandar stopped for a moment and had one last look at the snow garden and the gentle fall of snow outside. Just then, he saw, sitting on the same statue that Talkai had a hit, a falcon, a snow falcon. It poked its neck out at him and screeched loudly as if to call for his attention. And then it flew away into the night. Iskandar watched it fly away. It was gone just as quickly as he had seen it, and for a moment he thought he was just imagining it. Then he heard Talkai's voice calling him. Iskandar shook the snow off his feet and then turned and ran after Talkai down the hall.

# Chapter 9

## The Journey to Glenn Wood

ISKANDAR WAS AWOKEN EARLY in the morning when it was still dark by Talkai, who gently stroked his head and then squeezed his nose. Iskandard pulled his face away in annoyance.

"Come on scallywag. It is time to get up and have another adventure," Talkai said.

Iskandar rolled over, still feeling very sleepy.

"Can't we have an adventure after a few more hours of sleep?"

Iskandar rubbed his eyes. He gave a big yawn, got out from underneath his blankets, and began to get dressed in his tunic, trousers, and boots. He was sure to grab his big cloak since he knew he'd be trekking through the snow soon. He then packed the few things that he had and put them into his knapsack. Out the window, in the first rays of the dawn, he could see Ayesha with Mo and Tar sharpening their swords and axes on a spinning wheel. Sparks flew in the morning light. Seeing Ayesha wielding her sword and practicing strikes and parries suddenly made him feel very afraid and very sick. For a moment, he thought about running to the water clauset, but he settled himself down. He had promised to be brave.

After he walked down the massive white corridor, he came into the hall where he normally ate and he was startled to see Aurora waiting for him. She was sitting down, looking sad, as if someone had given her terrible news. Aurora looked up and saw Iskandar and smiled at him. But Iskandar could tell that she was in no mood for smiling.

"Good morning Iskandar. Did you sleep well?"

"Yes, thank you. The bed was wonderfully warm."

"I'm glad."

Aurora was holding in her hand a long rectangular wooden box about the length of one of Iskandar's legs.

"I have something for you," she uttered, "It is something special for your journey. It's very precious, so you must take good care of it."

"What is it?" replied Iskandar excitedly. His mind started imagining what might be inside: a magic wand, indestructible armour, dragon's teeth, or exploding arrows. Aurora opened the box as Iskandar's eyes opened even wider. From it she pulled what was either a very long knife or a short sword. It had a silver handle encrusted with rubies and gold trimming. The sword glistened in the morning light as golden rays reflected off its steel blade. He took it in his hand. It was heavier than he thought it would be, and he grasped it tight and upright.

"Is this for me?"

"It certainly is. It belonged to my father. That is the royal dagger of Nazvor, the property of the regent and protector of the ice city of Devora. Used for the self-protection of the carrier in times of danger."

"Why are you giving it to me?"

"The dangers you face are real. I pray that you never have to use this, but that if you do," she paused with a deep breath, "that you will have the strength and power to use it properly."

"Thank you," said Iskandar, still hypnotized by the sword, which he began to swish through the air.

"Do come back to me safely Iskandar. And keep an eye on Jakov for me."

Iskandar smiled, "I will try to."

"I know you will."

Aurora kissed him on the forehead and walked out, leaving Iskandar in the dining hall. He stood there holding his new sword and then sheathed it in the belt that she had tied around his waist. Iskandar grabbed some bread from the table and a piece of cake that he saw as well. He ate the cake first and then munched on some bread as he walked down the hall with his cloak on, knapsack secure, and sword at his side. A servant opened the door for him as he went outside into the courtyard. There, he saw Ayesha, Mo, Tar, Sy, and Jakov kneeling in a circle and looking at the ground. Jakov was pointing at the ground with a big stick. Iskandar stood behind Mo and Tar who actually weren't kneeling but standing, but were the same height as everyone else now. Jakov spoke to them.

"And from there we move into the woods, gather our forces, follow the road north west until we come to Norella, and then launch our assault on the city."

"And the city will just fall into our hands without a fight?" Ayesha asked with a hint of sarcasm, "I have a feeling that Mazlo might a have a thing to say about that."

"There will be a fight," added Sy, "But Mazlo will be defeated quickly and easily."

"And how do you propose to do that? There must be nearly two thousand men garrisoned in the city: soldiers, mercenaries, and even imperial guards. We will have at best between eight hundred and a thousand men, hardly the numbers to take a city quickly, and we don't exactly have the time or resources to lay siege and starve them out."

Jakov smiled, "The walls of Norella will fall quickly my dear Ayesha. You just leave that to me."

"It's your funeral Jakov. I just hope that I don't have to light the pyre for you."

Iskandar grunted in laughter as it was the first time he'd seen anyone talk back to Jakov.

"Trust me Ayesha, have I let you down so far?"

"Well, no, but there is always a first time you know."

"Quicke eldebar quicke funkshie mar," added Mo.

"My thoughts exactly," uttered Ayesha.

"What did they say?" inquired Iskandar.

Ayesha replied, "Mo said that the cock that crows the loudest doesn't always win the fight."

"Wise words," Jakov responded, "But this cock is no chicken and even the wolves will flee when he ruffles his feathers."

Sy bellowed in laughter, "Jakov, you are a rock conjurer, a swordsman, and now a poet. You never cease to amaze me young man. I will follow you to Norella. Even if only out of a morbid curiosity to see what actually happens."

Sy turned towards Iskandar and patted him on the arm. Jakov then stared at his right hip most peculiarly. Iskandar wondered what he was staring at until he remembered that he was now carrying a sword.

"And what is that you carry my little friend?"

"It's a sword. Aurora gave it to me."

Iskandar took it out, very proud of its shine, though it still felt heavy. Sy took it in his hand and balanced the blade on his open palm."

"A fine sabre indeed. I have never seen one so finally balanced, and so lavishly decorated. Such a pity that something so small and so beautiful has to be put to such a vulgar use." He was looking at Iskandar with his one eye when he said it, but Iskandar knew that he said it so that Jakov could hear it.

Jakov pretended not to hear him. He kicked over his mud map on the ground, stood up and announced to everyone, "It is time to leave. We need to make way through the snow before dark, or else we'll freeze to death."

The group then tightened boots, filled water casks, and checked their knapsacks. Ayesha put on her black gloves that she wore everywhere. Mo and Tar snorted snot out of their noses and spat on the ground, with Ayesha shaking her head in disgust at the sight as she said, "Ooh, yuck".

Jakov stretched his legs. Iskandar put on his woollen hat and then turned around. As he looked about, he saw Aurora coming through the castle door with several attendants, as well as Talkai and the two children. Jakov turned and saw her. He paused for a moment, lost for words. Aurora walked up to him, with the children holding a hand each.

"Were you going to say goodbye before you left?"

"You were all asleep when I rose. I didn't want to disturb you. Besides that, we both hate goodbyes."

"Then promise me that you'll come back to us in one piece."

"I only make promises if I know I can keep them."

"Then tell me that it will be okay."

Jakov paused. "It will be okay, that much I can promise."

Jakov stroked her black hair with his hand and she touched the side of his bearded face with hers. Then he took her head in his hands and kissed her ruby red lips. As he did that, the two children grabbed onto his legs and hugged him.

"Bring us treasures back, daddy," said Marius.

"I want a golden wand and a new dress," pleaded Alexa.

"I will miss you two," said Jakov as he took them into his arms, "Both of you."

"Be good daddy."

"Me, be good! You be good my little munchins. Obey your tutors, do your exercises, and take good care of your mother. I will try return before the autumn festival and I will bring fireworks back with me."

"Will you bring us sweets?"

"As many as you can eat."

"Come children, father must go. Your nanny is waiting to give you breakfast," interjected Aurora as she guided them to their nanny.

"Bye father," said the two children in tandem as they ran off back into the castle.

"I lost my father when I was young Jakov. I don't want to lose another man in my life to Morpeth. Be careful."

"I will, my love. No power of Morpeth will ever keep me from you and the children."

"Keep him true to his word Sy."

"I will princess," replied the cyclops.

They hugged one last time before Jakov and the others began walking towards the front gate of the castle. Iskandar noticed that Talkai was still standing with the servants who were seeing them off and that Talkai had a very sullen look on his face. Iskandar tugged on Jakov's sleeve.

"Why isn't Talkai coming with us?"

"Because he's too stupid, too slow, and will get himself too killed. The idiot begged me to let him come but I told him no. That's my decision, and I'm sticking to it."

"What?" protested Iskandar. "Well, if he's not going, then I'm not going either."

"Iskanda, now is not the time for childish antics. Keep walking."

"No."

Iskandar pouted and stamped his foot. Jakov responded by forcefully grabbing him by the shoulders.

"Listen. I have seen so many of my friends die. More than I wish to remember. Are you in a hurry to have your last friend die too? Are you? Because if he comes with us I can almost guarantee you that he won't come back, not alive anyway. So think carefully about what you want my little brother. This is not a children's parlour game. People will die where we are going."

It was the word "brother" that stung Iskandar the most. As much as he hated to admit it, he knew that Jakov was right. He didn't want to be away from Talkai, but he certainly didn't want him to die either.

"Give me a moment then."

Iskandar ran back towards Talkai, who was still looking glum. He ran up and hugged him around the waist.

"I'm sorry you can't come with us Talkai."

"I did ask, but Jakov forbade it. He said I would be a liability. I don't know what a liability is, but I think it's a bad thing. Like a heavy weight that slows you down."

"You are not a liability or a heavy weight. You are my best friend. I will miss you. But it's probably best that you stay here."

"Probably true."

"It will be long and tiring, and we know how much you hate walking."

"That's true. And I'm sure it will be boring for you without me."

"Yes, it will."

"Stay safe, my little friend. I hope to see you sooner rather than later."

"Me too."

"Now go, before they leave without you."

Iskandar turned and saw that the others had kept walking on without him.

"Oh no," he cried. He ran off and looked back over his shoulder at Talkai as he waved and yelled, "Farewell."

Aurora waved at the group. Her gaze met Jakov's. When the group had passed through the gates and were out of sight, she placed her hand on Talkai's shoulder.

"Come Talkai. Let's get out of the cold. We must get on with the business of worrying about those whom we love."

"I suppose we must," replied Talkai as he began concocting a plan in his mind that made him smirk.

Mo and Tar slowly trotted through the snow, mumbling as they walked through the powdery ground, resenting the cold and how hard it was for them to walk in it. Ayesha was scouting the terrain ahead, her eyes constantly scanning the horizon. Sy and Jakov were talking about tactics and the resident army of the city of Norella. Iskandar felt lonely without Talkai, but contented himself with thoughts of adventures past and present. He occasionally looked down at the snow, skipped over it, and talked to the icy substance to see if it would listen to him. It always did. Iskandar raised his hand over some snow and made it roll along the ground until it rolled larger and larger. It formed a snow ball that kept rolling along the ground as Iskandar walked beside it. Soon it was big enough that he could touch it with his hand. As it rolled along the snow ball got bigger and bigger still. Then he had a naughty thought. He called to the snow ball and made it roll quickly towards Mo and Tar. The snow ball was now taller than the two dwarves and was hurdling after them. Mo saw it first and yelled, "Coochi mani." Mo and Tar both ran as fast as they could through the snow, which wasn't fast, as the snow ball chased them. Jakov and Sy laughed as they saw what was happening. Mo and Tar had desperation in their eyes as their little feet sprinted clumsily along. But it was no use. The snow ball caught them both and rolled over them, absorbing them into its spherical shape. The snow ball kept rolling along with Mo and Tar now trapped inside it, legs and arms protruding. Their muzzled voices could be heard screaming for help or cursing Iskandar (nobody really knew). Sy was bellowing in laughter, and Jakov just shook his head.

"That's enough Iskandar. Let them down," commanded Jakov.

With that, Iskandar called to the snow and it gently stopped. Then the now enormous snow ball fell apart and Mo and Tar's snowy faces emerged from the mess. Mo spat out some snow from his mouth and Tar shook his head to try and get the snow off his hair and beard. They both cast wicked glances at Iskandar and muttered unspeakable groans at him. They then looked at each other with their faces that had a mix of blue from the cold and red from anger, and then burst out in laughter themselves. The little dwarves were in hysterics as Iskandar ran over and helped them out of the snow. Mo and Tar dusted themselves off, but suddenly Mo grabbed Iskandar's trousers and pulled them down, while Tar thrust some snow down the back of Iskandar's undergarments.

Iskandar let out a great noise of "Aggh, that's so cold, so cold, so cold."

The two dwarves slapped Iskandar on the back and playfully poked him in the ribs. Iskandar smiled back at them as he wiped snow off Mo's tunic. There was much laughter as the group kept walking along.

Jakov looked at Sy.

"At least now we have something to laugh about."

"Perhaps in thirty years we will be able to do look back on this and laugh some more."

"Perhaps," Jakov replied, but he did not sound hopeful.

Just then Iskandar stopped.

"What is it?" asked Sy.

"Walking through this snow is hard, it's not fun, and it's tiring."

"Yes, it is. But unless you have a sleigh with dogs, a magical bird to carry us, or a rainbow bridge we can walk over, I think you'll find that it's the only way to the Glenn Wood."

"I have an idea," Iskandar said with a cheeky grin on his face.

He muttered something to the snow and it instantly turned into a sheet of ice about two feet long, a foot wide, and an inch thick.

"Watch this!" he exclaimed.

Iskandar mounted the piece of ice and pushed himself along on it with his right leg. He whispered to the snow a little more and then he began gliding along the snow. His movement got gradually faster, and faster, and then faster again. He was going so fast that the cold wind burned his face. He kept on going and struggled to keep balance with the wind and the bumps along the way. Within a few seconds, he had caught up to Ayesha who was out ahead. He leaned hard to his right and then circled around her three times before flying back towards the others.

"Ayesha, catch me if you can!"

"What on earth?" she exclaimed.

Iskandar then squatted lower to the ground as he went even faster. Mo and Tar were clapping in amazement as he whooshed passed them. Turning around tightly back towards them, he came to a slight mound of snow in front of him. He tried to slow down, but it was too late. The sheet of ice beneath him went over the mound and suddenly Iskandar was airborne twelve feet in the air.

"Whoa, oh no," he cried, with his hands and arms waving about as he spun upside down and around. Mo and Tar looked up as he flew right over them and landed in the big arms of Sy.

"That looked like good fun, you may have even invented a new sport. Ice gliding perhaps. But I don't see how it helps us walk faster," said Sy.

Iskandar got down to his feet.

"That was so much fun. But Sy, it can make us go faster."

"How?" added Jakov with a sense of bemusement and sarcasm.

"What if I make a sheet of ice big enough to carry us all over the snow? The snow will then just pass us along like many hands passing along a bucket."

"Go on then, show us," said Sy.

With that, Iskandar pointed his hands towards the snowy ground and spoke something soft and gentle that only he heard. Instantly some of the snow crystallized into a huge square piece of ice the size of a large bedsheet before them. He pushed it with his foot and it began moving at a brisk walking pace along the snow.

"Amazing," said Sy.

"Hop on," replied Iskandar.

Mo and Tar jumped on. They put their knapsacks on the ice and sat on them. They pointed ahead and banged their fists on the sheet of ice.

Mo uttered, "Googi mungi," which Iskandar guessed meant, "I want to go faster".

Jakov shrugged his shoulders and looked at Sy.

"I guess gliding on the snow is better than slowly trudging through it. It means we'll get to the woods sooner than dark, which will be nice."

"Seems a peculiar way to travel," Sy muttered.

The whole group mounted the ice sheet and they picked up speed after Ayesha jumped on with them.

The sheet of ice glided steadily along the snow trail, with Iskandar happily controlling the movements of the sheet along its path.

Sy leaned towards Jakov and whispered into his shoulder, "Why we are so eager to hasten what could be our deaths makes me want to get off and walk instead."

On the outskirts of the ice desert the snow dried up, grass grew, the sun was warmer, and finally Iskandar got to see something on the ground besides the never ending horizon of white. The group dismounted their ice raft and began walking along the green grass. Patches of snow and ice could still be seen scattered. Iskandar wished that Talkai was there so that he could throw one last snow ball at him. His absence made him feel sad inside. As usual, Ayesha scouted ahead and she would disappear in a flash of blinding speed every so often to go further ahead and see what she could find and hear. Eventually, the snow completely vanished from the ground, the sun beamed brightly, and the group came to a forest. Several minutes after entering the woods, Ayesha suddenly ran up in front of Jakov, and she stopped herself inches from him by digging her heels into the ground and skidding along several feet. It caught everyone off guard. It always did. Her freakish speed meant that she was forever sneaking up on people.

"They are up ahead. No further than a mile," she said, grinning, "I found their sentry. They are waiting for us in a clearing. The council has gathered ready for you."

Jakov nodded and looked around him.

"Be of good cheer my friends. Our brothers and sisters in arms are not far away."

They walked onwards. Mo and Tar skipped a bit in joy, knowing that they were soon to be reunited with old friends. Even Sy seemed strangely happy as opposed to his habitual melancholy.

"Who is ahead Jakov?" asked Iskandar.

"Our friends and our allies, the army of Freedom Legionnaires for the liberation of Iona."

"Who are they?"

"They are people like us. Refugees, survivors, victims of the evil of Morpeth. Those who have banded together and sworn by their own lives to destroy Morpeth or to die trying."

"Will they help us?

"They won't only help us. They will follow us wherever we go."

"How many are there?

"Several hundred, but not as many as there used to be."

"How many were there?"

"Once there was over two thousand men and women, but the war brought many casualties, many deaths, many losses to our side. Hopefully, that will be over soon."

"What are they gathered here for?"

"For a very important reason Iskandar."

"What is that?"

"They all want to meet you."

"Me?"

"Yes, they have come out from hiding and gathered together for one final battle. A battle to end them all. They are driven by the hope that the prophecy of Vetrius's prophet is coming true and the sons of Morpeth will soon free Iona from Morpeth."

Iskandar was genuinely impressed, but still very concerned that so many people thought he was some kind of hero. He didn't feel like one, but he hoped that one day he could be one.

Along the path, Iskandar saw a man in the distance, wearing a green tunic and leaning on a big stick with his right foot placed on his left knee. He had a well-trimmed black beard tinged with grey. His left cheek had a scar that stood out on his dark olive complexion.

"And what riff-raff blows in from the land of ice?" he said with a smile.

"No worse riff-raff that you find in a desert my friend," Jakov boasted back at him.

"I suppose not."

The man walked up to Jakov and hugged him.

"Welcome home, old friends."

He shook hands with Sy, patted Mo and Tar on the head, and kissed Ayesha on the cheek. Then his eyes became fixed on Iskandar.

"And is this the boy everyone has been talking about?" he said.

The man lifted up Iskandar's cheek with his gloved hands and stared deep into his eyes, as if he was searching for something.

"Iskandar," uttered Jakov, "this is our friend and brother, Mordecai, protector of the Forrest Glenn."

"If only there was a Glenn left to protect," was his rejoinder.

Just then he rolled up the sleeve on Iskandar's arm. He saw the tattoo of the snakes and his facial expression changed instantly. Mordecai's breathing became slightly faster with excitement and his eyes widened.

"Well, I guess the prophecy is true. You really are Iskandar the son of Morpeth. Everything is happening just as you said it would Jakov."

Sy, Mo, Tar, and Ayesha walked on ahead as the trio continued talking. Jakov stood behind Iskandar with his hands on Iskandar's shoulders.

"Did you ever doubt me Mordecai?"

"The only thing I doubted was your sanity."

Mordecai bent over and looked Iskandar in the eye.

"You are a quiet one lad. Anything to say for yourself?"

"No, sir. I'm just pleased to be here, with you, and with Jakov, my brother."

"If only all brothers were invested with such power from on high. I know growing up with my brothers would have been more exciting." Mordecai turned his attention back to Jakov. "The lad, he does have ... power? Does he wield the stones and rocks like you Jakov?"

"No, water is his gifting. He commands water like we give commands to a dog. It is really something to see. Water, ice, or snow. They all yield to him."

"Amazing. You can control water? Show me, please. I have to see this."

Iskandar looked up to Jakov and Jakov reluctantly nodded. Iskandar opened up his water pouch and waved his hand over the pouch.

"Is this some kind of conjuring trick? Are you going to pull a rabit out of that water pouch?" Moredecai asked.

And with a whisper of Iskandar's voice, the water squirted up into the air from the pouch and circled around the trio like a liquid ribbon being waved in the air. The stream of water moved about through the air going up and down and side to side. Iskandar waved his hands as if he were controlling the movement of the water the way a puppet master controls a puppet. The water jutted upward above the trees and then dispersed over the three of them like a misty rain in the autumn.

"Entertaining display, I have to admit," said Mordecai rubbing his scarred cheek, "If our enemies get bored or thirsty we have the perfect weapon to entertain them."

Then Jakov's faced was contorted with frustration "By the tar pits of Aponoch, why am I always surrounded by cynics and sceptics? You are just as bad as Sy. He can do far more than that."

"Too many years of battle, too many defeats, and too many fallen comrades makes men of war cautious and callous Jakov."

"We have never lost a battle, not while I've been in charge."

"I guess that's why the council voted to make you leader ahead of me, isn't it?"

"Trust me, trust him, trust us. There is enough power between the two of us to defeat Morpeth and his army. The Freedom Legionnaires shall prevail at last. Be assured."

"So be it then Jakov. May Vetrius bring you success and victory." Mordecai paused. "Oh, and I guess I should add revenge as well."

"Victory will be a fitting hope, thank you."

Iskandar could tell from the way that Jakov and Mordecai talked to each other that there was a mix of respect and rivalry between the two.

"But anyway, you must be tired. Let us go on. There is a warm fire up ahead, plenty of food, blankets to lay upon, and much to talk about."

# Chapter 10

## Savage Trolls and a Mysterious Dragon

FOR THE REMAINDER OF the evening the band of travellers greeted old friends and new ones. Several hundred men and women danced around fires, ate wild boar, and warmed themselves from the cold night air with rounds of mulled wine. Mo and Tar danced together as those around them clapped and the two little men did flips and cartwheels to the amusement of their audience. Sy and Jakov could be seen nearby, talking with Mordecai and they seemed uninterested in the festivities. Ayesha grabbed Iskandar by the hand and made him dance around the fire with her. Iskandar felt ever so embarrassed. Never before had he felt so self-conscious of his awkward and clumsy movements. His cheeks turned flush red as he had to put his hands around Ayesha's waist and hold her hands as they glided along beside the fire with onlookers singing and clanging mugs full of wine. Ayesha sensed that the poor boy had quite enough and she took him by the hand away from the fire and from the boisterous crowd around them, who booed their departure.

Ayesha sat down beside Iskandar on a blanket.

"You dance with the majesty of a swan."

"I've never actually danced before."

"Never before!"

Iskandar couldn't tell if her surprise was real or if she was just pretending.

"No."

"You worked in a tavern in Praschi and never danced even once? I thought many young wenches who haunt such a place would have found your soft little cheeks too irresistible."

This reminded Iskandar of the many nights working in Praschi where there often was dancing. Talkai would sometimes dance, but always stupidly, like he had something hot burning his underpants. His usual job was to fetch ale from the cellar and to clean up the horrid things that fell on the floor like ale, blood, and even people. As he thought about it, he never thought he'd ever like to dance. People always looked so stupid when they did. He promised himself once that he'd never look so silly in front of others. He smiled when he realized that he had broken his own promise.

"Do you miss Praschi?" she asked him in a tender voice.

"A bit. Things were simpler there. Not always nice, but easier. But I miss Talkai."

"He is a funny man."

"He is the closest thing I have to family. He's like a brother. No, more like a Father. But not that either. More like a, what do you call them?"

"An uncle," she finished for him.

"Yes, a bit like an uncle, a happy and harmless fool. Whenever I was sick he looked after me. He stopped Wringstone from being mean to me. He's looked after me ever since I can remember."

"What do you remember about your life before Praschi? Do you remember anything at all? Your parents, your brother, how you ended up in Praschi?"

Ayesha was no longer looking at him, but into him.

"No," he said and he looked down disappointed because he wished he had other memories. Then after a moment he looked up, "Wait, yes, there is one thing I remember."

"What?"

"I remember once playing in a room with other children. They were running around and laughing. Playing with a feather to tickle each other with. And the only other thing I can remember is crying in a forest with someone there. Someone is with me, a man, he is crying too, but I can't see his face. And then he goes away and leaves me. Then after that all I can remember is being in Praschi. Fetching water from a well every day. Wringstone yelling at me. Talkai being my friend. Nothing else."

"That is sad."

"It's okay, I'm grateful for Talkai. And now I have a brother, a sister of sorts, and even a nephew and niece." The thought of his niece and nephew filled his heart with warm feelings of joy.

"Well if any of them turn out to be good dancers at royal banquets, I'll know that they got their great skills from you and not from Jakov. Jakov dances like an ox with a sore foot."

"Have you seen him dance?"

"Oh yes, once before at Devora. After he had had too much wine. He danced with Aurora. Well, he danced until he stood on her feet, tripped over and landed in a water fountain. It was so funny. More so because it was his own wedding."

Iskandar snorted a laugh at the thought of Jakov dancing. Iskandar looked over to where Jakov was now. He was sitting beside a fire by himself and staring into it blankly. Every moment or so, he placed some food into his mouth. He was alone but didn't look lonely. It was the same look he always had. Thinking, remembering, planning, or whatever it was he did.

Iskandar yawned.

"I think it is time for bed," Ayesha said as she guided him down onto a pillow and covered him with a blanket.

"We shall have a big day tomorrow."

"What are we doing?"

"I believe we are going to capture a city."

"How long will that take?"

"I don't know. How long do you think it will take you?"

"Me? Am I going to do it?"

"Well, you and Jakov, I'm told."

"How are we supposed to capture a whole city by ourselves?"

"I'm sure Jakov has a plan. Well, he should have by the time you get there."

"What?"

"Be at peace Iskandar, I'm joking. Things will work out right. Don't worry, just rest my child. You have a big day ahead of you."

Ayesha gently took Iskandar's head to her chest and he liked the warmth of her body against his head. It made him feel safe, happy, and loved. He smiled.

He looked up to speak to her but he noticed that something had changed in her face. Ayesha was no longer looking at him. She was looking off into the darkness with a very concerned expression on her face.

"What is it Ayesha?"

"Shh. Be quiet child."

Ayesha was silent and she looked further into the darkness, listening intently.

Then her eyes widened. She took out her sword and she grabbed Iskandar before he could say anything. In a rush, she pulled him out of his blanket and ran quickly over to Jakov.

"Jakov," she screamed.

Jakov looked up from his aimless stare into the fire and stood up immediately as he heard the tone of her scream.

"Jakov, something is coming this way."

"What?"

"I don't know. But it's large and it's getting closer."

Iskandar couldn't believe that anyone could hear anything with all the noise going on. Jakov threw his cup of wine into the fire and unsheathed his sword. Then he screamed out, "Sound the call to arms. Trouble comes this way."

Someone nearby heard his order and took a horn and blew it. In a blink of an eye the festivities suddenly ceased as people heard the horn. There was a brief moment of silence and then people were running in all directions. Fires were put out. There was the scurrying of feet and the clanging of metal as people picked up swords, spears, and axes. Ayesha kept hold of Iskandar's hand and she followed Jakov as he walked to the edge of the camp. Jakov looked into the darkness that Ayesha pointed to. Iskandar could see nothing but blackness and hear nothing but the noise in the camp coming from behind him. Mordecai approached Jakov.

"This better not be one more of your rehearsals Jakov. The people need a chance to rest before the morrow. Surely even you need respite every so often."

"No rehearsal. Something comes. Something hunts us."

"What? The vilest beasts in this forest are rats and bats. Hardly anything to be afraid of."

Jakov put his ear to the ground.

"Something large comes this way. It is moving slowly. No, wait, there is more than one. They are moving slowly."

He stood up as Mo, Tar, and Sy joined them.

"Why the call to arms?" Sy asked as he approached.

"We shall find out soon enough," he replied. "Mordecai, order your men in ranks. I want two companies side by side facing north, spearmen on their left flank, archers behind them, with two more companies in the rear ready to encircle whatever comes this way."

"As you command, my captain." Mordecai ran off, but Iskandar noticed a certain degree of sarcasm in the way that Mordecai said "captain," like he didn't enjoy saying it.

"Ayesha, be a dear and have a quick look if you will at what it is that is coming this way."

"Sure thing."

She gently pushed Iskandar towards Sy, who sensed his fear and put his hand on the boy's shoulder to comfort him. She was about to move when Jakov grabbed her arm.

"Ayesha, do be careful."

She smiled at him, "I'll be back before you can say 'Morpeth soils his undergarments.'" In a blur of movement, she disappeared into the night.

Sy looked down at Iskandar and repeated Ayesha's words, "Morpeth soils his undergarments."

A few more moments elapsed, but it seemed like forever to Iskandar. Mo and Tar were slapping themselves in the face, shaking their heads, and pouring water on each other's head, presumably trying to sober up for the fight that was coming. In another blur of startling speed, Ayesha was back, panting this time. Iskandar had never seen her short of breath before.

"Mountain trolls," she said. "Three of them. Coming this way. They think they are sneaking up on us. They look hungry."

"Mountain trolls," said Sy in disbelief. "I thought they only lived in mountains."

"Well evidently they have decided to move to more serene and scenic pastures," said Jakov.

"They are hungry? What do they eat?" asked Iskandar.

"Anything that has flesh" was Jakov's reply.

"But I have flesh," retorted Iskandar, a bit concerned.

Sy looked down at him and nodded, "That's the problem we all have."

"Oh dear," Iskandar said.

Mo and Tar heard what was said, spat out of the corner of their mouths, and raised their axes high in the air and shook them aggressively.

Tar leaned over and muttered, "Gimme gibachi trollini amutsa".

"You might have to convince the trolls first before he lets you have him for supper rather than the other way round Tar," Ayesha spoke over to them.

Mordecai came up behind them.

"The men are in position Jakov. Now tell me, what is it that you fear?"

"Mountain trolls."

"Mountain trolls, here in the forest? How in hades could they get here?"

"I know, I know, but trust me, mountain trolls are coming."

"And what is your plan captain?"

"First, don't get eaten. Second, move one of the reserve companies to the front with the other two. Assign each company to one troll. Use the spearmen to engage them from the flanks to harass them and wear them down. Where possible, use the archers."

"The archers won't be much good, their skin is like armour," interjected Sy.

"True. Then use fire. Get the archers to shoot flaming arrows, dipped in oil and ignited with fire. It might not bring a troll down, but it will hurt them."

"Or make them even angrier," Sy added again.

Jakov rolled his eyes at Sy, but always with a half smile Iskandar noted.

"So be it," Mordecai stated matter-of-factly as he briskly walked off again and began yelling orders. Jakov looked at Ayesha.

"Take Iskandar and hide at the rear of the line. If it comes down to it, run away and meet us tomorrow morning at the crossroad to Norella."

Ayesha nodded and quickly walked off with Iskandar at her side.

"How come I don't get to fight?" he asked her.

"Believe me Iskandar this is one fight you don't want to be in. Have you ever seen a mountain troll die?"

"No" came the reply.

"Me either," she added, "And I've seen lots of them."

Ayesha took Iskandar behind the rows of men and some women who had formed ranks. Iskandar could see some men holding long spears pointing them upright. They were almost the height of small trees. Ayesha guided him to small dug-out hole that was covered by some shrubbery.

"Lay down here and try to be quiet."

Several ranks of soldiers had formed up in front of a clearing where they expected the mountain trolls to come. Over to the left of the clearing Jakov, Sy, Mo and Tar were laying down at the base of a clump of thick trees with weapons at the ready.

"What's the plan?" whispered Sy.

"We let the trolls go past us and then take them from behind as the spearmen hopefully spear them from the front."

"Sounds simple enough, as long as the spearmen don't spear us too.

Jakov looked at Mo and Tar, and pointed up towards the sky. The two little men nodded and climbed up the trees above them.

A noise could be heard ahead; bristling bushes and branches being broken.

"Thank goodness they are noisy, clumsy creatures even when they are trying to be quiet," Sy commented.

"I think you'll find that in battle they are anything but clumsy."

As Jakov looked between a fork in the trees, he could see one of the trolls crouched over and slowly walking into the clearing. It couldn't see the ranks of men ahead in the darkness because trolls did not have good eyesight, but Jakov guessed that it could smell them. It was eighteen feet tall, carried a huge club the size of a tree trunk, had a scarred body, deformed face, and a metal chain around its neck. This troll had once been in captivity. Then, beside it, another troll appeared from the darkness of the bushes. This one was even taller, with crooked and sharp teeth that protruded from its mouth like fangs on a wolf. The trolls were sniffing the air, sensing something but unsure as to what it was. The two trolls walked onwards and stopped for a moment, trying to make out what was to their front.

Sy and Jakov could hear Mordecai's voice as he yelled, "Fire." With that, a volley of flaming arrows pierced the air. Many landed on the bodies of the trolls. They let out a scream of anger that made the ears of men burn with pain for a moment, then the trolls charged wildly towards the ranks of soldiers in front of them.

As the trolls ran passed the clump of trees hiding Sy and Jakov, Mo and Tar leapt from above and landed on the left and right shoulder of one of the trolls. The troll reacted by trying to swat the little men with his hands. The troll violently twisted itself to and fro with no success, as Mo and Tar either evaded his grasps or else struck his hand with their axe while holding onto his ear to keep balanced on its shoulders. The troll then tried to hit Mo and Tar with its huge club but only managed to knock itself in the head and daze itself severely. The troll stumbled around off balance, still trying to swat Mo and Tar. It left him distracted long enough for twenty men with spears to charge at the creature. By the time the troll had noticed the spearmen, it only had time to swing his club at them once, striking several spearmen and sending them flying thirty feet sideways. The spearmen lunged at the troll in executed bursts and pierced it in the abdomen, chest, and throat, but it was not enough to completley stop it. The troll let out a blood-curdling scream and shook violently, which sent Mo and Tar falling off its shoulders. The two dwarves hit the ground and rolled away as the troll stomped near them, hoping to crush them with its immense feet. Then they both swung their axes high and wide and landed penetrating blows onto both of his ankles. The impact made the troll fall forward into the band of spearmen, who held their spears upright. The troll was impaled by the force of its fall. Seeing the dead troll lying there, still twitching in places, Mo and Tar raised their axes in triumph and started singing a peculiar dwarfish song.

The other troll had managed to scatter the spearmen who surrounded it and harassed it with stabs, but none powerful enough to seriously hurt the creature. With every swing of its club more spearmen and some soldiers were sent flying. Others had to dive to the ground to avoid its savage blows. Sy and Jakov ran towards the troll from behind, cautious of its club being swung in unpredictable directions. The troll was roaring in anger and hunger with every motion. At full sprint, Jakov took out his two swords tied diagonally across his back. He ran between the troll's legs and slashed at the flesh behind the knee caps and then slid ahead and turned to face the monster. The troll let out a cry of pain and fell to its knees, grunting ferociously as it looked at Jakov with its midnight black eyes. It raised its club and swung at Jakov, who narrowly missed being smashed by the blow. The three soldiers beside him were not so lucky. Jakov dodged another swift blow from the troll and fell back to the ground behind him. The troll seemed to snort in satisfaction and scurried forwards towards him on its knees. The troll raised its club high over its head and its shadow from the dim moonlight fell over Jakov. A huge thud was heard. The troll then crooked its head to the left in a strange gesture and then went still as a statue until it fell forward. Jakov quickly rolled to his left and jumped to his feet with his swords ready to strike. But the troll was motionless on the ground with Sy's axe firmly planted into the base of its skull. Sy stood there panting behind the troll and looked at Jakov.

"You know, I would have been there sooner if I could run as half as fast as you."

"Late is better than never."

"Glad to hear".

Jakov looked around and saw the second troll felled as well, with Mo and Tar doing a victory dance over it. Soldiers began tending to the wounded.

"Well done," yelled Sy across at them. The two dwarfs acknowledged him by dancing harder and singing even louder.

"I tell you Jakov, those dwarves are worth more than twenty men each. Such agility, such strength, and a strange absence of fear. Brilliant warriors even if they are, well, not all there in the head."

Jakov looked down at one of the trolls and he kicked the metal ring around its neck.

"These mountain trolls were captives. They had been put in chains and were probably trained as weapons of war. "

"Morpeth's work it seems."

"Most probably. Such ugly creatures."

Jakov wiped the sweat from his brow and put his swords away.

"Sy, this is the third time we've been ambushed. The giant caterpillar, Morpeth's snow battalion in the ice valley, and now mountain trolls fall upon us in Glenn Wood of all places. Morpeth is not that lucky. I'm beginning to think this is not a coincidence."

"Are you saying that there is a traitor in our midst?"

"I hate to say it, but it is starting to look like a real possibility."

"But who?"

"I don't know yet, but I'm sure we'll find out."

Sy shook his head in disgust as the two walked off towards the middle of the camp. And then Sy abruptly stopped walking and put his hand on Jakov's shoulder.

"Jakov."

"What is it?"

"Do you remember how many trolls Ayesha said were coming this way?"

Jakov stopped to try and remember.

"I thought she said three."

"That's what I thought. But where is the third?"

"I don't know. Maybe she counted wrong."

"It would not be like her to make such a mistake when . . ."

Sy was interrupted by the sound of a third troll stomping wildly through the middle of the camp as it knocked over soldiers and tents with its club.

"I guess she wasn't wrong after all," said Jakov on the run.

"Don't get too far ahead of me. I might not get there to save you at the last moment again."

Jakov kept on running ahead as the troll ran right towards the place where he had told Ayesha and Iskandar to hide. His heart was pounding faster and faster as he struggled to catch up to the monster. Jakov had to dodge people and horses who had managed to get out of the troll's way, and to jump over those who were not fortunate enough to do so. Behind him he could hear Sy panting and the distinctive noises of Mo and Tar as they followed as well.

Ayesha had thought that everything was clear when she heard the two trolls fall to the ground. She had assumed that the battle was over when people starting to look around for the wounded. She told Iskandar to stay put in the hole as she slowly crept out and walked over to inspect the battle area herself. She was in the middle of the camp when the third troll charged through the camp. The rampaging troll had caught her by surprise as well. She quickly turned to run back to Iskandar but she was knocked over by the stomping troll. She felt herself flying through the air and land on the grassy ground. She lifted up her head, feeling dazed and battered on her right side with blurry vision. But she noticed Jakov ran passed her and was racing after the troll as it moved towards Iskandar.

Iskandar popped his head out of the hole when he heard the second wave of commotion. The noise brought more panic among the soldiers than the first lot that he had heard only minutes before. He felt alone and very afraid without Ayesha next to him. His eyes flashed open wide as he saw the menacing troll coming towards him. He hoped that it hadn't seen him. But it was too late, their eyes locked together. The troll stopped, looked hard at him, and then ran towards him even faster. Iskandar ducked down immediately back into his little hole, not knowing what to do. He quickly got out his sword and then, without thinking, decided to run. He just managed to scramble out of the hole when the troll's hands narrowly missed him in its grasp. The troll let out a bellow of sickening noise as it saw him run away only inches from its grasp. Iskandar ran down the slope to his left as fast as his legs could carry him, with the troll pursuing from behind. The foliage and trees got thicker, which made it easier for his nimble body to move through, and harder for the troll who had to knock over branches and trees that got in its way. Beyond the trees was a clearing and then a river that Iskandar could just make out ahead through the moonlit night. If he could get to the river then he could use his power over the water on the troll. That is, if he made it that far.

The forest got thicker for a few more yards and Iskandar now had to make immense effort to pull himself through the vines, trees, and long grass in the dark of the night. He pulled himself out of the last vine and was at last in the clearing. With all his strength, he kept on running and he could see the river only four hundred yards ahead. He hoped that would be far enough for him to run without the troll catching him first. But the troll had also come out of the thicket into the clearing as well. The troll took four huge leaps and then dived and narrowly clipped Iskandar's feet with its club. Iskandar fell and before he could get up, he felt the troll's hand grab him around both legs and left him up so he was hanging upside down. He called to the river for help, but it was too far away. It could not hear him, but only because he was stuttering in fear.

The troll gave a triumphant cry as it had found its intended victim. It swung Iskandar over its shoulder and Iskandar's head was knocked against the troll's back. The impact rendered him dazed and he blacked out from being swung around and knocked about while upside down. As the troll turned around, Mo and Tar jumped up and landed on each leg of the troll. Hooking their own legs around the troll's legs, they struck their axes into its knee caps, causing the troll to grimace in pain and grunt loudly. But the troll responded by kicking each leg into the air, which sent Mo and Tar flying through the night sky like a child kicking a ball.

Sy then let out the war cry of his people and charged the troll with his axe in hand. He dodged several blows from the troll's club but was unable to land any blows himself. He raised his axe, poised to strike, but he only connected with the club as his axe sunk deep into the wood of the troll's weapon. He tightened his grip on his axe and tried to pull it out, but as he did that the troll simply threw his club over his shoulder and it took Sy with him part of the way until the Cyclops released his grasp and went tumbling along the ground for twenty feet and laid motionless where he stopped.

The troll kept one hand on Iskandar's back to stop him falling off and it looked down at Jakov, the last remaining person in its way.

"Just you and me now handsome," said Jakov, taunting the troll.

The troll lunged at him and tried to snatch at him with its one available hand. As it did so, Jakov slashed at the troll with one of his swords, cutting its hand several times, but the troll was unperturbed and kept on lunging at him.

Out of the corner of his eye, Jakov noticed two large stones, each the size of a chest, lying on the ground behind the troll. Jakov looked at them and whispered to the stones. The large pieces of stone uprooted themselves from the dirt, launched off the ground, rammed into the body of the troll and knocked it several feet to its left, but did not topple it. Jakov then ordered the stones to drop onto the troll's feet, leaving it screaming in pain. But the troll still had Iskandar tightly over his back as it now started retreating away from Jakov.

"Okay handsome. Looks like I have your measure now."

Jakov spoke to the stones again and they struck the troll its ribs, leaving him visibly winded and out of breath. Three or four times the stones struck the giant troll's body as it contorted with pain and cried out at Jakov. Jakov spoke once more, and this time the stones narrowly missed the head of the troll as they flew passed it. The troll swatted at them as if they were flies as it ducked its head to get out of their path. It then leaned down and picked up a fallen tree. When the two huge stones flew towards the troll again, it used the tree like a club and smashed both of them one after the other. The impact shattered both the stones and the tree. Splinters and shards of rock went flying everywhere, temporarily blinding Jakov.

The next thing he could see was the troll now rushing at him and again trying to swat him with its weighty arms.

"Not this again," Jakov said, as he took once more to parrying and slashing at the monster's immense reach.

The troll raised its fist high and thumped it down right in front of Jakov on the ground. In one smooth motion, Jakov leaned back to avoid the blow and then lunged forward driving his sword down through the arm of the troll and into the ground all the way to the handle, pinning the right arm of the troll to the earth. The creature screamed again as it released its grip on Iskandar's dangling body and tried to strike Jakov with its free hand.

With the troll off balance, weakened, and with its right hand pinned to the ground, Jakov took out his other sword and ran up the troll's pinned arm like a ledge. He ran up the arm and onto the troll's shoulder. He poised to strike and drove his other sword deep into the left shoulder of the troll, narrowly missing Iskandar in the process. The troll let out a blood-curdling scream that deafened Jakov for a moment, and then it shook so hard that Jakov fell off from the troll's shoulder and hit the ground hard, striking his head on a tree stump.

As Jakov tried to get up, slightly stunned from the blow, the troll ripped out the swords impaled into its hand and shoulder. It threw the two swords away and growled at Jakov, who was still getting to his feet. Then with both hands it grabbed Jakov around the waist and legs and began to squeeze him.

The troll started laughing as it could hear Jakov writhing in pain. Jakov felt the pressure around his ribs and hips like his body had been placed in a vice. He looked around for help to see if Mo, Tar, or Sy were anywhere to be seen. He tried to pry the troll's hand from around him but it was no use. All he could feel was the crushing pain on his body, the grizzly panting of the troll, and the air draining from his lungs. He looked up into the night sky, wondering if he'd see his wife and children again.

Jakov's head fell forward and he felt his entire body drained of breath and strength. He looked at the troll and his brother who was still on the troll's shoulder, lifeless and motionless. As the crushing pressure began to make him faint, he whispered a prayer, "Vetrius, save the boy."

In that strange place between consciousness and unconsciousness, Jakov felt a shadow pass over his head that hid the moonlight for a moment and then a small gust of wind blew past. With his eyes only half open, he could see the troll looking up into the sky as if staring at something. Then suddenenly two arrows landed right in the troll's eyes. The troll dropped Jakov, who suddenly took a deep breath and then another. The troll staggered back, screeching and yelling and drooling as blood poured from its eyes. The troll shook its head, covered its ears with its hands, and wandered around aimlessly.

Then Jakov could not believe what he saw next, and he wondered if he was already dead. There was another eclipse of moonlight over his face as a sheet of darkness seemed to pass over him for a moment, accompanied by a strong rush of wind. Then, in the midst of the clearing, there landed an enormous red dragon that screeched loudly at the troll. On top of the dragon was a rider. He wore dark purple armour with a helmet and visor that covered his face, a sword on his back, and a small bow in his hands. The rider in dark armour dismounted the dragon and patted it softly. He reloaded his crossbow and walked up to the troll, who was still staggering about blindly. The man in the purple armour then took aim with his crossbow and shot the troll in the head. The troll fell down, instantly dead. The mysterious knight then ran over to Iskandar and rolled him onto to his side and stroked his face. From his side, he took a water bottle and poured some water into Iskandar's mouth.

Jakov could feel the cool night air filling his lungs, his strength and sense of balance returning, and his dizziness subsiding. Although every muscle and bone in his ribs and chest ached beyond imagination, he forced himself to get up and he staggered over towards the knight, who was kneeling beside Iskandar.

As he approached, the dragon screeched and flew up and landed between his master and Jakov. The red dragon looked at Jakov and for the first time ever, even after facing the troll, Jakov's heart was filled with terror.

The mysterious knight called to the dragon, "Leave him Magnon. Let the boy approach."

With that, the dragon slowly walked backwards out of Jakov's path, but it did not take its gaze off him. Jakov walked passed slowly, also watching the dragon and he felt as if he were walking passed a guard dog from hades.

Jakov drew closer to the knight and Iskandar. The knight placed a vial of some kind under Iskandar's nose and it made Iskandar's face twitch. The little boy mumbled something.

"He will be alright Jakov. There is no need to worry. But he will need rest," said the purple knight.

"Who are you?" Jakov demanded, "And how do you know my name?"

The knight rose. He was tall. There were no distinguishing markings or emblems on his crystal-like purple armour. Jakov could barely make out the eyes through the slit in the man's helmet

"I am your friend Jakov. That is all you need to know for now."

"Have you been following us?"

The knight ignored his question. Jakov felt angry and frustrated and was not sure if it was wise to try to interrogate the knight who had just saved his life and the life of his brother.

The knight walked towards the red dragon and mounted up. The great beast knelt as its master climbed upon him. After taking the reins of the dragon like it were a horse, the rider turned to Jakov.

"Things are given for us to know in their proper time. It is not yet time for you to know everything. But know this. You and your brother are doing well. Keep pressing on with your plan. Wherever you go, I will always be watching. I have always been watching over you Jakov. You and Iskandar both. Four days will not pass before we meet again. I promise you that."

The red dragon then took off into the night sky with the purple knight and, in seconds, he was completely out of view. Jakov wondered if this was some kind of dream. But he looked down and heard Iskandar snoring loudly at his feet. Then he realised it was real. He rubbed his sore head and groaned a few times as every deep breath hurt his ribs. He then sat down on the ground next to Iskandar and rested.

# Chapter 11

## Explaining the Unexplainable

JAKOV HAD FALLEN ASLEEP next to Iskandar from exhaustion. He had slept for nearly an hour when he was suddenly awoken.

"Jakov, Jakov, wake up. Are you okay?"

Jakov quickly opened his eyes, feeling half asleep as if he had been awoken from a deep slumber. He sat up, looked around, and noticed Ayesha's hand on his shoulder. Her pretty face had a large cut on the left cheek and her pristine hair looked messy.

"Yes, I'm fine, I think. Where are the others? What happened to them?"

"They are fine. They are here too."

Ayesha pointed behind Jakov. Jakov turned around, groaning at the pain his ribs, and saw Sy standing behind him as well as Mo and Tar, with bandages on their little dwarfish heads. The two little men were tending to Iskandar, who was having his ankle strapped.

"Are you alright Iskandar?" Jakov asked him.

"Yes, I think so. My leg hurts a bit. But I think I'm okay. That was a crazy night."

"That was one lucky escape for all of us. Three mountain trolls in one night. That last one was a marauder from the gates of hell. And apparently you killed the last one all by yourself. Well done, I have to say," said Sy.

"No, I didn't," answered Jakov.

"You didn't?" Sy replied with a surprised expression. "The last thing I remember was being hurled through the air by that rogue monster. I saw you fighting it alone and then I blanked out."

Ayesha asked the question that was now on everyone's mind.

"But if you didn't slay the troll, then who did?"

"If I told you, you wouldn't believe me."

"Believe what?" Mordecai uttered as he approached.

"I didn't slay the troll. There was someone else. A man, a knight, in full armour. He killed the troll with his crossbow. Oh, yes, and one more thing. He rode on a red dragon."

"What?" responded Sy.

"You heard me."

"Let me get this right. A knight riding on a red dragon just swooped down and killed the troll just before it was about to kill you."

"That's what happened."

"No. Surely you're just being modest. You killed the troll Jakov."

"No Sy. It wasn't me. It was a knight on a red dragon. You all believe me don't you?"

Everyone looked at each other. There was a tense silence, then Ayesha answered.

"It's not that we don't believe you, it's just that . . ."

"The last of the dragons died four hundred years ago and none have been tamed since the time of the ancients. Whatever happened or whatever you think you saw Jakov, it can't have been a knight riding a dragon. Perhaps your mind is playing tricks on you. Battle can do that to a man, how much more for a boy," said Mordecai.

"I know what I saw Mordecai, and I am no boy."

"No offence meant my master. It's just that, well, I've seen what war can do to the minds of men. There is a certain madness that can set in. It goes eventually, but . . ."

"I saw it too," interjected Iskandar. "Only for a second. I thought I was dreaming. When I was laying down I looked up and saw Jakov talking to a man in armour and there was a dragon. I heard it screech. There was something there alright."

"By the undergarments of Ahura Mazada," added Sy.

Jakov rose to his feet, he walked away from the group, and looked intently at the ground ahead of him. After searching for a while, as if he was looking for a lost coin on the ground, he stopped and pointed at the ground.

"Look here! See the prints on the ground. This is where the dragon stood. Right here. I was over there. I saw it. As sure as I'm seeing all of you now."

"Unfortunately, none of us know what dragon footprints look like to compare them with Jakov. It could be the troll's markings or some oversized cow for all we know," Mordecai said, leaning on his walking stick.

Jakov bit his bottom lip in frustration and put his hands on his hips.

"I don't care if you don't believe me Mordecai. I know what happened. I know what I saw. If it wasn't for the knight, I'd be dead. Wait. There's something else."

"What?" asked Sy.

Jakov ran over to the troll and pulled one of the arrows from out of its head. He brought it over and held its feathers up for everyone else to see.

"Sy and Ayesha. Do you recognize the colour of the fletching? Ever seen these before?"

Sy stared at them intently.

"Those were the same one's that landed in the head of the giant caterpillar."

"And the same ones that felled the imperial guards back in Praschi when Iskandar was nearly captured," added Ayesha.

"Who was the knight?" asked Iskandar.

"I don't know. He wouldn't tell me who he was. Only that he was watching us. And that we'd meet him again in four days."

"Opooui magounoni ezcavan," added Tar.

"The dwarf asked if the knight was a wizard," Ayesha interpreted.

"I don't know," he answered. "But I do know that he is still out there and apparently he is on our side. At least for the time being."

"The tale is overly embellished for my liking. A story of mysterious knights, red dragons, and strange arrows sounds a bit concocted if you ask me," Mordecai added with a mocking smile.

"Doubt me or deny me if you like. But the dragon knight saved my life and that of Iskandar. And any man who can tame and ride a dragon deserves our attention."

"What now then?" asked Sy.

Mordecai spoke up.

"We need to rest and regroup. We took large casualties last night. We shall have to delay our assault on Norella for at least a week, perhaps a month."

"A month!" blurted Ayesha.

"You cannot take a city with half of your men dead, wounded, or afraid. It would be rash to attack now. We must err on the side of caution."

"This is most unfortunate. But perhaps you are right," added Sy. "We are in no state now to mount a serious assault. Not after a night like that."

Jakov could see the dawn light starting to break through over the horizon. Morning was coming. He paused and then turned to Mordecai.

"No. We fight now. Mordecai, prepare your men for the march to Norella. Take them via the king's highway. Tend the wounded, oil the weapons, and then leave in haste. I need your men there by sunset. Bring as many men as you can, or at least as many as can walk. The walls of Norella will fall to us by nightfall."

"The walls of Norella have not been breached in six hundred years. Even Morpeth couldn't seize the city by force. Morpeth and the entire imperial army laid siege to it for six months and then gave up. He purchased the allegiance of Mazlo the Regent when he couldn't force the city to surrender. How on earth do you intend to capture the city by sunset when it is a day's walk away?"

"I have a plan my friend. One that cannot fail. And don't forget, we have Iskandar with us. The one thing that Morpeth fears most. Iskandar and I will go ahead and arrange for the surrender of Norella. Negotiations will be quick. Mazlo will open his gates to let the Freedom Legionnaires in. If not, he will be destroyed."

"Now you are engaging in fantasy. Just how will you do that?" objected Mordecai. "Will you throw stones at the city? Taunt the garrison with childish insults? Will Iskandar amuse them to death with tricks of water conjuring?"

"Mordecai, I'm going to enjoy the look of surprise on your face when you sleep tonight in Mazlo's own private apartment."

"I'll enjoy it if I see it alright. But whether I see it tonight is another thing."

Sy walked between them, sensing the tension.

"I must warn you Mordecai. He's surprised me more than once. Don't make the mistake of underestimating him. I do that too often myself."

"True. I always have underestimated you Jakov. I guess that is why you are now the leader of the Freedom Legionnaires rather than me. Let me say that I am more than willing to be surprised on this matter and I'm willing to swallow my pride if you can prove me wrong. But life has taught me to be cynical of those who make great promises that defy reason."

"I shall do my best then to defy your sense of reason."

"I wouldn't expect anything less from a ... son of Morpeth," Mordecai commented, knowing that Jakov resented that title.

"I prefer to be called the man who is the thorn in the side of Morpeth, if you please."

"Of course, my mistake. No offence meant."

"None taken," though everyone knew otherwise.

Mordecai walked off and began yelling orders to several men around him.

"Come Iskandar. Let's go. We have a city to capture."

"Are we going now?" asked Iskandar.

"Right now. Grab your bag and let's go."

"Be careful," said Ayesha. "Friends here and far away need you to come home safe."

"We will do. I promise. Tonight we shall hold a banquet in the dining hall of the Regent of Norella. And we shall toast the glory of fallen comrades."

"I just hope it's not your death that I'm toasting there Jakov," said Sy.

"I'm surrounded by cynics Iskandar. Do you believe in me?"

"I do. I think. Most of the time that is."

"Most of the time! You cheeky rascal."

The two started walking away from the others who were stunned at their sudden departure.

Ayesha checked the bandages on Mo and Tar, and looked at Sy.

"I am fearful of the fact that Jakov has no fear. Morpeth, trolls, castles, and even death. There is nothing he is afraid of."

"Not true Ayesha. For there is one thing he fears."

"And what is that?"

"Failure."

# Chapter 12

## The Fall of Norella

"Where are we going Jakov?" asked Iskandar as the two walked through the forest together.

"We are going to capture the city of Norella," he replied matter-of-factly.

"Just the two us?"

"Well, I don't see anyone else, do you?"

Iskandar looked around.

"No."

"Then it is just us."

"My legs hurt. Can you carry me?"

"My legs hurt too. And so do my ribs, my arms, my feet, and my head. You're big enough to carry yourself."

"Not even for a little while?"

"No. You're meant to be a warrior. Warriors don't take naps or get piggy backs."

Iskandar sighed as he felt a wave of tiredness overcome him.

"Then could I not be a warrior for just a mile or so?"

Jakov shook his head.

"You can rest later tonight on a nice cosy bed."

Iskandar walked along, closing his eyes every few moments to see if he could sleep and walk at the same time. He couldn't, as it made him stumble and only reminded him of how tired he was. Lucky for him, Jakov was not walking all that fast for once. He tried to take his mind off things by thinking about his favourite things. Fields full of daffodils in Praschi, his niece and nephew, Talkai, and chocolate pudding.

All of a sudden, Jakov stopped and paused. He pushed Iskandar downwards and they both crouched to the ground. Jakov looked behind them and peered through the foliage. Iskandar was trying to see what it was he was looking for.

"What is it?" whispered Iskandar.

"Shhh," came the reply, as Jakov put his fingers on Iskandar's lips.

Jakov took Iskandar by the hand and, keeping low, they both moved slowly behind a large tree stump where they squatted. Jakov unsheathed his sword ever so gently so as not to make a sound. He peered over the tree stump. He then looked at Iskandar.

"Something or someone follows us."

"Not another troll," Iskandar muttered softly with a degree of concern.

"No, it's not a troll. Might be a patrol of scouts from Norella, hunters, or even bandits. But it's better if we are not seen. Or if they see us, they don't live to tell it."

Iskandar could hear a few bushes brustling behind them but he couldn't see over the tree stump. Then, he heard footsteps not far away. Jakov had changed his posture. He was holding his sword in one hand and had a large rock in the other hand. He was crouching, ready to strike like a cat about to leap onto a mouse. Then footsteps could be heard getting louder, stopping every so often, but still coming closer and closer.

"Stay out of sight," Jakov whispered ever so faintly right into Iskandar's ear.

Iskandar could feel his heart beating as the sound of footsteps got louder again. They were now just on the other side of the large tree stump. He slowly put his hand on the handle of his sword, hoping that he would not have to use it. Jakov then leapt into the air like a loaded spring. All Iskandar heard was a huge thud, someone making a funny "ooomf" noise like they'd been hit, and then the sound of a person hitting the ground.

Then Jakov could be heard yelling with his fighting voice, "Surrender or I will . . ." Jakov paused and spoke again, "What on earth?"

Iskandar noticed that Jakov's voice had changed.

"What by the highest heavens are you doing here?" Jakov yelled out.

Iskandar looked up and was so shocked at what he saw that he let out a gasp of amazement, the hair of the back of his neck stood up, and he could even feel small tears welling up in his eyes. Iskandar saw Jakov holding his sword and standing over Talkai.

"Ouch. Easy up Jakov. That really hurt. You hit my tummy. I need my tummy. That's where I like to put cakes and sweets."

"Talkai," Iskandar blurted out with an unrestrained joy.

Iskandar rushed over and jumped on Talkai and hugged him and Talkai again made that revolting "oomf" sound again.

"Talkai, I missed you."

Talkai embraced the boy with his arms, while still rubbing his stomach.

"And I missed you too. But I don't think Jakov did. He kicked my tummy and made me fall on my bummy."

Iskandar smiled and then looked up at Jakov, who was not smiling. He looked very serious, angry in fact.

"What are you doing out here, you half-witted, cow-sniffing baboon?" he said to Talkai, with a very piercing voice.

"Hey, I'm not a baboon, and cows smell very nice after being milked, thank you."

"Why were you following us?"

"I was looking for you." Talkai smiled. "I guess I found you, hey?"

"How did you find us? We must have had two days start on you."

Talkai sat up.

"Well, that is a rather funny story if I do say so myself. When I was a little lad, I once found my favourite acorn that was hiding out in the . . ."

"Give us the quick version Talkai. I don't have time for your frivolous stories."

"Okay. Umm. Well. To put it quickly, not long after you left, I felt lonely, bored, and a bit sad without my old chum, Iskandar – though I still think of him as Bobbascow, you know. So I took a dog sled into the forest, and then it was just a matter of following the dead bodies along the path. I saw three dead trolls. Nasty looking creatures too. I'd hate to have come across them in the dark of night I tell you."

"One of them nearly took me Talkai."

"Oh no," said Talkai putting his hands on his cheeks in shock. "I hope you got away. He didn't eat you for breakfast did he?"

"Of course he didn't eat me. Otherwise I wouldn't be here, would I?"

"Oh. That is true. But it must have been scary. Like that time that I got chased by that cat. Remember?"

"You just wondered into the forest and found us. Is that it?"

"Well, I knew you were heading west, towards Norella. So I just waited until after lunchtime and then followed the sun. Speaking of lunch, do you have any food? I could really go for a raspberry spongecake right now."

Jakov put away his sword, rolled his eyes, and rubbed his face with his gloved hands.

"I don't care how you got here, now it's time for you to go back."

"What? I just got here. Exactly where is 'here' anyway?"

"We're off to capture the city of Norella," uttered Iskandar.

"Great, can I come too? I'll be ever so good."

"No," interrupted Jakov, very unamused. "You cannot. You're going back to Devora or even Praschi if you wish. Wherever you feel the safest. Now go!"

"But Jakov," exclaimed Iskandar.

"But nothing," he interrupted, "He can't come with us. It's too dangerous, too important, and he's too stupid."

"He was smart enough to find us."

"That was his luck and my misfortune."

"Please let him come Jakov."

"Yes, please let me come Jakov. I'll be good."

Jakov looked at the boy and the man and saw the desperation in their faces. Talkai had even reduced himself to kneeling.

"Please," Talkai begged him.

"Alright then, if it will shut the both of you up. What did I do to be punished with this half witted imbecile I will never know. But since I can't get rid of you, I will still make use of you."

"And of what use can I be?" Talkai asked excitedly, "Do you want me to scout ahead looking for trolls, caterpillars, or imperial guards?"

Jakov smiled.

"Oh no, I've got a more suitable job in store for you."

Ten minutes later, Jakov was walking along a dirt trail up a steep hill with Talkai behind him carrying Iskandar on his shoulders.

"Man alive, you are a heavy boy. I think my shoulders are numb."

Iskandar just smiled and held onto Talkai's ears as they walked along.

"Don't complain," added Jakov, "I told you I'd find a use for you."

"But why this one? He's so heavy."

"Well, you're as dumb as a mule, so you might as well be treated as one."

"You are one unnice man Jakov."

As Jakov and Talkai got to the top of the hill they stopped in the middle of the road.

In front of them they could see the dirt road lead down the otherside of the hill where it turned into a cobblestone path that continued over a large bridge and stopped at the base of a huge city surrounded by massive walls.

"And there it is," Jakov muttered to himself.

"Wow," said Iskandar, mesmerised by the sight.

"That is one big city. Big walls. Big castle in the middle. Ah, let me get this right. We are going to capture the city before dark which is about one hour."

"That's correct."

Iskandar was still staring at the city behind the huge walls. He couldn't believe how enormous it was. He could see fires lit on its various corners, and little men walking along the top of the walls. They looked like ants with shiny helmets.

Jakov took Iskandar down off Talkai's shoulders. He looked the boy in the eye.

"Listen to me Iskandar. This is where the real fight begins. Everything up until now was merely a rehearsal, a practice. But this is real. This is where we fight and we win. We do it not only for ourselves, but for our family back in Devora, for our brothers and sisters who had their lives stolen from them. Today we will make a joyous noise that will strike fear in the heart of Morpeth. We will sound a trumpet of freedom to those enslaved under his tyranny. The freedom of the land depends on you and me, Iskandar. We cannot let them down."

Jakov rolled up his sleeve to reveal his dragon tattoo and he did the same to Iskandar.

"You see this? This means that we are brothers. We are servants of Vetrius. We were saved so that we could save others. We were marked to give hope to those who live in darkness. We were anointed with a special power to set the captives free. You and me together, my brother. Do you understand?"

Iskandar paused and then hesitantly answered, "Yes."

"Are you with me in your heart?"

Sensing his fear, Talkai put his hand on the boy's arm to comfort him.

"I am with you Jakov. All the way."

"Good, my brother."

"But I'm so afraid."

"I know Iskandar. It's okay to be afraid. Can I tell you something that I don't tell many people."

"What?"

"I'm afraid too."

"But you're not afraid of anyone. You're the bravest person I know."

"Iskandar, remember what I told you. Being brave doesn't mean that you're not afraid. It means that you believe in something greater than your fear. There is something that makes you face your fear and overcome it. Something that drives you on when every thought in your head and every muscle in your body is telling you turn around and hide. I am afraid too little brother. But I want to be afraid so that later on, one day, my two children will never have to be. I want to be afraid for a while so that my family can live in a world without fear. Do you understand now? It's okay to be afraid. Let's be afraid together and charge into our fears with all of our strength so that those who depend on us will never know the feeling of fear. Can you be afraid with me? Can you face your fears for others?"

"Then, I'm afraid with you," Iskandar replied with a smile.

"Good. Let us face our fears together and hope that one day our world will not know fear as it does now."

Jakov looked up at Talkai.

"Talkai, I want you to go back along this path until you come to a crossroad. It should only be half a mile away. Wait there. Within half an hour Mordecai, Sy and the rest of the Freedom Legionnaires will be coming through. Guide them up here towards the city. By the time they arrive the city's gates will be wide open and Mazlo will have surrendered. When they enter, they are to occupy the city immediately. I want them to take control of all towers and garrison the military quarters without delay. Just in case there is a counterattack. Do you understand?"

"Yes," he replied.

"Good, then go, give my instructions to Sy, and make haste. Tell our friends that we look forward to their company in the city."

Talkai nodded and then ran off back down the hill.

Jakov took Iskandar by the hand and slowly they began walking down the hill towards the city.

≈ ≈ ≈

Jakov and Iskandar walked hand in hand down the hill. Jakov was singing a children's song, trying to put Iskandar at ease. They came closer and closer to the city. Jakov could feel Iskandar's hand tightened around his own with each step they took towards the huge structure. After a few hundred metres they walked over a creaky old bridge that went over the moat surrounding the city.

"Are you friends with the water Iskandar?"

Iskandar waved at the water and it rippled a few waves as he passed over it on the bridge.

"Yes, the water hears me and it's glad to see us."

"Good. We shall need its help soon."

The brothers came to the foot of the castle and stood under the shadow of its mighty gates. It was now late afternoon and the sun was setting.

A man in a red tunic with a battle helmet and a spear yelled down at Jakov from the ledge over the gates.

"Who goes there? State your business."

Jakov smiled at Iskandar and rubbed his hand through his hair.

"My name is Jakov, son of Morpeth, prince of Devora in the Nazvor. I come here in the name of the people's rebellion, the Freedom Legionnaire. I am here to negotiate the unconditional surrender of the city and the arrest of Mazlo."

"What?" the man asked.

Jakov sighed in frustration and then repeated himself.

"My name is Jakov, son of Morpeth, prince of . . ."

"I heard you the first time. Are you mad or something?"

"No, I am of sound mind. Now go and summon Mazlo the Regent and inform him that he must surrender." Jakov paused and then said even louder, "Or Mazlo can face the consequences."

"I will do no such thing. Go away you daft fool, before you get yourself hurt."

The soldier shook his head and then walked away from the ledge.

"I don't think he believes us Jakov."

"Then I'll get his attention."

"Oi, you up there. I am not done talking to you."

After a few moments, the soldier popped his head back over the ledge.

"Are you still here?

"Yes, and I'd like you to surrender immediately, or face the consequences."

"Look. I don't know if you're a fool or deluded. But a man and a boy cannot capture a city. Where is your army?"

"They are on their way."

"Well, when they get here, let me know. We can arrange a battle then."

Two other guards heard the commotion and popped their heads over the ledge and looked down at Jakov and Iskandar.

They began talking to each other and pointing at Jakov and Iskandar.

Finally, the first guard spoke again to Jakov.

"Go away young man, or I shall have you arrested, and perhaps even killed."

"Then come and get me if you think you can."

Jakov took a large stone from his pocket, kissed it, and threw it with a ferocious speed that struck the man's helmet and knocked it clean off. The guard stumbled backwards from the fright and then slowly got back to his feet. He looked down at Jakov, this time with a look of anger on his face.

"I will have your head for that."

"You are welcomed to come and get it."

The guard then turned to the two other men beside him.

"Spear him! I want his head on a spike."

The two guards took their spears and threw them downward. The spears darted through the air towards them. Jakov grabbed Iskandar and the two rolled backwards and narrowly avoided being stabbed by the falling spears. Jakov grabbed two more stones from his pocket and threw them upward. The two guards who threw the spears did not even have time to blink as they were struck in the head by the stones. They fell to the ground instantly.

The single guard, who was obviously a chief guard, stood there without his helmet, looking at his fallen comrades either side of him. He turned his gaze to Jakov.

"Who are you boy? Really, who are you?"

"My name is Jakov, son of Morpeth, prince of Devora. I order the city of Norella to surrender itself and for the Regent Mazlo to hand himself over for arrest. Surrender the city, or my brother and I will take it by force."

"You have appealed to Mazlo, so I will let Mazlo himself deal with you. You stupid boy. I don't think you know who you are dealing with. Mazlo is not known for his mercy."

"Neither am I. Bring Mazlo out here and I will settle the matter quickly."

"So be it, boy."

Both Jakov and Iskandar breathed out a deep breath of relief as the chief guard walked away, rubbing his head where the stone had ricocheted off his helmet.

"Is this part of the plan Jakov?" asked Iskandar concerned

"It sure is. Let's wait and see what happens next."

Several minutes passed and then behind the wall there could be heard the sound of yelling, the rush of foot steps, the clanking of armour, and even more yelling. As if from nowhere, dozens and dozens of men were running along the ledge above them, carrying bows and arrows. They formed a line along the ledge. They drew the strings of their bows and took aim at Jakov and Iskandar. Iskandar gulped and he felt like a huge weight was hanging around his neck.

"Don't worry Iskandar. This is exactly what I thought would happen."

Next, there was heard a loud mechanical sound and ever so slowly the gate in front of them began to open. From behind the massive iron doors marched over a hundred men in formation with swords and shields held out in front of them. They marched in perfect timing, stomping their feet in sequence. The ground grew dusty with their footsteps, as the formation of guards marched around the two and encircled them. Jakov stayed perfectly still, with his eyes fixated on the ground in front of him. Iskandar was shaking with fear. He looked up and saw the archers with their arrows drawn and ready to fire. He looked to his left and right and saw the armed soldiers all around him. He looked up again and saw the chief guard leading a man in red robes towards the centre of the ledge. The chief then stopped and pointed down at Iskandar and Jakov.

The man wore red silk robes, had many rings on his fingers, gold chains around his neck, and a golden sash around his shoulder that fell to the left side of his hip. The man spoke.

"I am told that you are looking for Mazlo the Regent of Norella."

"That I am," retorted Jakov.

"I am told that you are calling for the city to surrender to you."

"That we do."

"I am told that you are the son of Morpeth."

"That I am too."

"You are either the bravest young men I've met, or the else the stupidest."

"My name is Jakov. I am here to liberate the city from the grip of Morpeth, who rules it through his puppet Mazlo."

"I am Mazlo and I do not suffer a boy to insult me and live. As you soon will learn."

"You will surrender the city to me now, or I will break the gates of the city on my own."

"On your own? Not even with a battering ram or a siege engine could you do that. I am beginning to think that you are a wandering madman, a vagabond or lunatic who stumbled across this city."

"I am no vagabond. You will taste my wrath if you do not obey me. Surrender Mazlo. This is my one and only warning."

"I have no intention of surrendering to a mere boy. If you are who you say you are, your capture will prove to be a great trophy for my dungeon and a timely gift for my friend Morpeth."

"Surrender Mazlo, or I will break the gates below you."

"Boy, these gates have not been breached in six hundred years. They are made of iron. What makes you think that you can do what no army has ever done?"

"Let's just say that I have my ways."

"Oh really? Well, I'd love to see them."

"If you don't surrender immediately, you will."

"Boy, your insolence was amusing at first, but now I have lost patience with your insults."

Mazlo turned to the chief guard.

"Kill them. Kill them right before me."

The chief guard nodded and then motioned for the archers to move closer to the edge. Mazlo stood there watching, leaning forward over the ledge, looking forward to the spectacle that was to come. Iskandar turned his face into Jakov and was shaking with fear. Jakov closed his eyes and raised one arm towards the sky with his hand open.

"Archers," the guard yelled, "Fire!"

The archers released their arrows and a volley of dozens of arrows zoomed in directly towards Jakov and Iskandar. Then, inches before the arrows should have struck the two, the arrows suddenly stopped, frozen and suspended in mid-air. Jakov opened his eyes. Iskandar looked up, surprised to be alive, and even more surprised to see the arrows hanging in the air.

Jakov reached out and grabbed one of the arrows and held it in his hand. He stroked the arrowhead with his fingers. There were gasps from the archers as they looked and saw their arrows hanging in the air. The soldiers surrounding the two took a step back in shock and disbelief at what they were seeing. Mazlo leaned forward even further with his mouth a gape and he cast his eyes over the two boys, wondering what manner of magic this was.

"Mazlo, one of the well-known things about the standing army of Norella is that their archers use sharpened stones carved from flint for arrowheads. They are superb arrows. They are lighter than iron, they travel much further, and are sharp enough to tear any flesh apart. The problem is that I have a very special way with stones."

Jakov threw the arrow in his hand down to the ground. He held up his hand and flicked his wrist upwards. Immediately the arrows turned around and were now facing back towards the castle. Jakov then waved his arm and the arrows suddenly flew back towards the archer and struck them all. Mazlo ducked and he saw the archers around him fall to the ground, screaming in pain and anguish.

"Surrender Mazlo. Or I will destroy you, your army, and these gates."

Mazlo peered over the ledge, his face twisted with a mix of fear and rage.

"I will not surrender. Not to a boy magician who does tricks with stones. You will die yet." He turned to the troops on the ground and screamed at them.

"Kill him! Kill the boy! The one who brings me their head will get a thousand talents of silver. Kill them now!"

The soldiers on the ground hesitated for a moment, but cautiously they began moving towards Iskandar and Jakov. Jakov drew his two swords and moved backwards towards the bridge with Iskandar clutching his belt behind him.

"Iskandar."

"Yes?"

"Could you ask the water under the bridge to do us a favour?"

The idea suddenly registered in Iskandar's mind and he felt a surge of strength and courage fall on him. The soldiers were getting perilously close. A few soldiers had even started swinging swords in their direction. They were still wary, but pressed on with more and more confidence. Iskandar looked at the murky water behind him under the bridge and he gently called to it. The waters bubbled and swelled until a huge tower of waters stood up from the moat. It rose into the air and spiralled into the shape of a cord. From its great height, even higher than the city, the water then crashed doward and lashed the men around Jakov and Iskandar like a gigantic whip, knocking the men down and backwards towards the gate. The immense wave of water lashed the soldiers again and again until they were all flattened and floored by the power of the attacking waters. The water then flew high into the air and dived back into the moat from whence it came.

"You are amazing Iskandar," Jakov said amazed at the spectacle.

A few more guards had now come onto the ledge and stood beside the Regent. Mazlo looked down at the muddy mayhem beneath him as two hundred of his men laid on the ground, half-conscious and half-drowned. He rubbed his hands on his face and bellowed out with rage.

"I don't know what magic you conjure boy. You may be powerful, but know this. Morpeth's army already marches this way. They shall arrive here by sunset tomorrow. You will not breach the walls of Norella before that time. Throw stones and water if you like. It will take more than that to sack this city. After first light, you will die out here. I will gut you like a fish and the last thing you shall see before you die is me ripping your lungs from your chest. You will die a hundred deaths before the walls of Norella fall to you."

Jakov half ignored Mazlo and reached into his pocket and took out another stone. He flicked it up with his thumb and caught the stone with the same hand. He looked up at Mazlo with a sardonic grin on his face.

"Mazlo. What are the walls of Norella made of?"

Mazlo yelled his answer "They are made of . . ."

Mazlo stopped mid-sentence and a look of terror came over his face. He looked all around him, at the towers, and even at the ledge that he was standing upon.

"Oh, no," he said.

"I believe that 'stone' is the word you're looking for," Jakov added.

Jakov drove his swords into the ground. He walked towards the gate and leancd forward with both hands outstretched. He closed his eyes tight, concentrated hard, whispered to the stone structure, and then threw his arms apart. With that, the huge wall of stone beside and above the iron gates crumbled and literally distintegrated in front of him. There was a defeaning noise as the large stones crashed down. Stone after stone fell, like dominoes, landing a pile. Dust flew up, a few screams were heard, and large bricks of stone rolled around in all directions.

Jakov took up his swords and walked over to the massive rubble, with dust obscuring his vision. He walked up a pile of rubble and he saw Mazlo lying down in front of him. His silk robe was now grey with dust. His face was covered in grit and dirt. Jakov pointed his sword to his throat. Mazlo looked up, dazed and blinking from the dust in his eyes.

"Surrender or die Mazlo."

Mazlo raised his hand.

"I surrender. I surrender."

Iskandar looked around behind him. He saw coming down the adjacent hill a large body of men in green uniforms with swords and spears. They were jogging along and cheering as they saw the wall of Norella flattened. Iskandar could also see Talkai at the head of the troops. He was dancing and doing cartwheels. He ran across the bridge and picked up Iskandar.

"Talkai, did you see what we did?" Iskandar said as he greeted him.

"I did. You and your brother just captured a whole city. All by yourselves."

"I know."

Troops faithful to Jakov began running over the rubble and into the city. The city guards had already begun laying down their arms and were being rounded up. Amidst the haze of the settling dust there was still chaos; yelling, and the odd sound of swords clashing. A group of men saluted Jakov and then seized Mazlo and took him away. Mordecai walked over to Jakov and beamed a smile at him.

"That was like nothing I've ever seen."

Mordecai gently punched him on the shoulder.

"You have done what no army has done in six hundred years."

"Then let us see what the morrow brings as well," came the reply from Jakov. "Perhaps greater things are still to come. Morpeth is on his way with the imperial army. We might have the entire war won by lunch time tomorrow."

Mordecai smiled, because he knew the truth was otherwise.

# Chapter 13

## A Traitor at Norella

IN WHAT WERE FORMERLY the royal chambers of the Regent of Norella, Iskdandar slept on a couch with a blanket over him and a soft cushion under his head. Nearby, Jakov sat on a chair with his boots planted on the table and a goblet of wine in his hand. Around the table sat Sy, Ayesha, Mo, and Tar. The two little dwarves had eaten well, drunk hard, and were passed out on the table with their faces in a bowl of food. They snored heavily into a plate of beef stew that soaked into their beards. Ayesha and Sy were in good spirits as they laughed and joked about the day's events with Jakov.

"You should have seen the look on Mazlo's face," said Jakov, who could hardly contain his laughter. "When he realized he was standing on a stone wall his face turned from anger to sheer panic. Then seconds later, it was all over."

"And the walls that even Morpeth could not capture were toppled by his son," responded Sy as he raised a goblet to Jakov.

Ayesha raised her glass as well. "Minstrels shall sing songs about you Jakov. Morpeth has killed his thousands and Jakov his tens of thousands. Jakov, the liberator of Norella!"

"No, Jakov the Great," added Sy.

Jakov put his goblet down and looked across at them. "Jakov the Executioner of Morpeth. That's the only title I aspire to."

Sy leaned back and stretched. "Perhaps that title will be yours soon too. All in good time."

"Perhaps," he replied in a more serious tone.

"There is one thing that I'm curious about," Ayesha said with inquisitive expression. "What about your mother, Prisca? What is to become of her?"

Jakov looked deep into his goblet of wine and after a few seconds he looked up at her.

"She is locked away in the mountain fortress at Masavar. She lost favour with Morpeth and he exiled her there. She is bound and chained. Even as an immortal, she is impotent. No threat to Morpeth and no threat to us either. She can rot there forever. She can spend the rest of her life wondering when someone will one day come to behead her."

"If that is your will, Jakov, then so be it," Ayesha replied.

"Did you ever love your parents Jakov?" the cyclops asked him.

"I don't know. I think so. Once. Long ago. All children love their parents I suppose. At least at first. Even the wicked can love their children. I'm sure Morpeth and Prisca did at one time. Before ... before they sold their souls to Marduk. Perhaps I loved them too. I don't remember any more. I do not want to remember their love. Whatever love I had for them died with my brothers and sisters. The most loving thing I can do now is to destroy them. Set them free from the monstrous evil that has consumed them. Avenge the blood of my siblings."

"It's a pity that any son must carry such a burden," noted Ayesha.

"Then I hope to hasten the day when we live in a land where no such burden need be carried."

"May it be so," added Sy as he lifted his goblet again. "May Vetrius give us victory for the sake of freedom, justice, and undying love."

"I agree. May there be victory for Jakov on the morrow," added Ayesha.

"I can't argue with my friends. A toast for victory," Jakov agreed with them.

The trio knocked goblets and Jakov drank the last of the wine in his goblet and wiped his mouth with his sleeve. There was a knock at the door.

"That will be Mordecai," declared Sy.

"Then bring him in," Jakov responded.

Sy led Mordecai into the room. He peered around the opulent surroundings and noted the place of Iskandar on the couch and the two dwarves asleep at the table.

"Jakov, I have my midnight briefing for you."

Jakov took his feet off the table and leaned forward in his chair towards Mordecai.

"Tell me how things go."

"The city is fully captured and occupied. Mazlo is in the dungeon. The last vestiges of resistance were defeated in the lower quarter near the eastern gate. The city's guards have either surrendered or offered to change sides. There was no shortage of volunteers to join our ranks. Mazlo was not particularly well-liked by his troops."

"Have the men eaten and rested?"

"Yes, rations have been provided from the local supplies. Most are billeted in houses in the city. Some are stationed in the garrison quarters."

"And what of security for the night?"

"Guards have been posted on all major walls. Thirty men guard the gate that you, well, destroyed. Before dawn, sentries will be sent out on horseback to monitor the horizon for signs of the imperial army."

"How is their morale?"

"The men are tired from the events of the last two days, but in good spirits. They are spurned on by our victory today. The sight of Norella falling before them has quickened their hearts. They are ready to follow you to the gates of hell if need be."

"That is good. But what of yourself? Does it go well with your soul Mordecai?"

Mordecai grinned and looked away.

"I'm a veteran soldier Jakov. I have spent a life time in the service of killing. There isn't much of my soul left."

"You know what I mean."

"I am doing well, master Jakov. I am most humbled to be under your command and to be part of such a great triumph."

Jakov stood up and slapped him on the elbow.

"Good. I am proud to have such an able commander with me. Now get some rest yourself, for I fear that tomorrow may be even more exhausting than today."

"Of course, master Jakov. As you wish."

Mordecai politely bowed, turned around, and walked away down the hall. Sy stretched again and yawned.

"I think it is time for me to retire to the sleeping quarters. I shall be down in the garrison chambers with the men."

"Sleep well, Sy," Jakov said.

Sy looked at two little dwarves sleeping soundly at the table. He shook his head.

"Mo and Tar might be able to handle an axe and trolls the size of trees. But they certainly can't handle their drink. Their heads shall hurt in the morning."

Sy picked up the two dwarves, one in each arm, and carried them out of the room. Neither Mo or Tar moved or grunted, but kept snoring as they were carried away.

"You should get some rest too," Ayesha spoke with her normal tender voice to Jakov.

"I will. In a moment."

Jakov walked over to Iskandar and stroked his head with his hand. He then leant down and kissed the small boy on his forehead.

"Good night my brother. I shall see you in the morning," Jakov whispered.

"I will sleep beside him."

"You don't have to Ayesha."

"No, it's alright. I am his bodyguard. I shall watch over him. You get some rest."

Jakov smiled at her and then went into the bedroom in the adjacent chamber. He slowly took off his boots, stripped off his tunic, and undid his belt. As soon as he lied down his eyes felt exceedingly heavy. He put his hands on his stomach and crossed one leg over the other. He thought over the events of the day and relived every instance of fear and violence in his mind. He forced himself to think of other things instead, pleasant things, his wife Aurora and his gorgeous children. Jakov longed to embrace them all. With that thought in his mind, he fell asleep.

In the adjacent chamber, Ayesha laid down on the ground next to Iskandar's couch. She used her cape for a blanket and her hands as a pillow. She looked at the candle flickering on the table nearby. The flicker became dimmer and dimmer as she also fell asleep.

In the bowels of the city, Mordecai walked down a dreary and dark staircase. It was poorly lit with only the faint glow of his torch providing any real light. Rats could be seen scurrying about and the place smelled of damp and filth the closer he got to the bottom of the staircase. After walking through a narrow and dark hallway, he came to a locked door with a small window, closed with iron bars. He tapped the door three times.

"Mazlo," he whispered.

A face peered out of the window.

"What do you want now? Can't you people let me sleep? I used to own this city."

Mordecai said nothing and merely offered him some bread.

Mazlo paused and then reached for it quickly with his hand and began scoffing it down.

"Thank you," Mazlor responded.

"Do you want to be free?" Mordecai asked him.

"What kind of question is that?" said Mazlo as he rammed more and more bread into his mouth. "Who wouldn't want to be free of this sewer?"

"Well, you sent enough down people here, so it is only fitting that you should learn what the quarters are like."

"Have you come here to mock me? If you have, I'd rather sleep."

"No, I am not here to mock you."

"Then what is your business with me?"

"Are you interested in escaping?"

Mazlo paused and looked Mordecai up and down.

"What kind of question is that?"

"I meant it in all seriousness. Are you interested in escaping?"

"Of course I am, what fool wouldn't be? That boy Jakov will probably execute me in the morning, anyway."

Mordecai dangled a key in front of him.

"I have the power to set you free, and I will, if you and I reach an understanding of sorts."

Mazlo tried grasping for the keys through the narrow bars but Mordecai pulled them away too quickly.

"Oh, not that easily, I'm afraid. Nothing is free."

"Who are you?"

"I am Mordecai. A commander of the Freedom Legionnaires, those who rebel against Morpeth."

"Then your loyalty is obviously faltering."

"That is no concern of yours. Do you want out of here or not?"

"Of course I do! How much?"

"How much do you have? Or should I say, how much is your life worth to you?"

"I can offer you gold, silver, even power if you wish."

"And am I to believe that once you're free you'll give it to me? I doubt that. You have a reputation Mazlo. Corruption, bribery, murder, and theft. Your wickedness knows no limits, I hear. So I shall not accept a promissory note from you."

"I don't exactly have a pound of gold in my pocket to offer you, do I?"

"Then I will accept the city as collateral, and you may pay me after Morpeth reinstates you as Regent, in the way of 5,000 talents of gold. And you will also deliver a message to Morpeth for me."

"What message is that?"

"For 10,000 talents of gold, I will deliver Iskandar to him by noon tomorrow."

"You and what army?" scoffed Mazlo.

"Leave that to me. I will bring the boy to Morpeth before noon. Tell Morpeth that he need only distract Jakov with the battle in the morning."

"So you want 5,000 to release me and 10,000 to kidnap the child?"

"That is correct."

"I agree to your terms. Now, release me."

"In a moment. How do I know Morpeth will agree to the terms?"

Mazlo laughed. "Morpeth would give you half the kingdom of Iona for Iskandar and the other half for Jakov. The price you ask is extravagant, but he won't hesitate. You have what he wants, the only thing he wants. The money is as good as yours. In this city, I am the eyes, ears, and voice of Morpeth. My master will reward you handsomely if you do what you plan to do."

"Good, just as I anticipated."

Mordecai inserted the key into the locked door and turned it. The bolts moved and the huge door swung open. Somewhat hesisitantly, Mazlo walked out, looking tired, and swollen on one side of his face. He kept his distance from Mordecai and studied his face intently.

"You seem very eager to enter the employ of Morpeth. How do I know that it is not a trap or a ruse? Why should Morpeth trust you?"

"I've sent messages to Morpeth before, given him information about Jakov's movements. That information proved to be true. Morpeth knows my name."

"So you are an ally of Morpeth, I assume?"

"You assume wrongly. I am a man tired of war, tired of not getting a share in the spoils of war, and rather weary of calling a teenage boy 'master.'"

"So it is not greed that motivates you but pride and envy. I might have known."

"My reasons are my own. I am not what I appear to be. War makes men cynical. It made me want to enjoy whatever life I have left and to enjoy it in the luxury that men like me do not normally find themselves in."

"Your motives are of no concern to me. But I will reward you as you wish, as will Morpeth, no doubt."

"Go up the stairs through the large doors and turn left."

"I know this city like the back of my hand. You have no need to direct me."

"But if you wish to avoid the guards I posted, then I suggest you avoid the high street, stick to the path along the canal, and remain in the shadows. The northern gate is unlocked and unmanned. Once you are outside of it, run across the paddock, and there under a fig tree you will find a horse, tied and ready to ride. Ride north and Morpeth's army will meet you on the way."

"So be it. Both I and Morpeth remain in your debt. Riches shall be poured upon you when the city is retaken."

"If you cross me Mazlo, I will kill you."

"I have no doubt of that. Traitors to their cause are the most wretched of men."

"I am no traitor. I am merely enlightened as to where my true loyalty lies."

"And where is that?"

"To myself."

"Ha, you remind me of myself when I was younger."

"You are wasting time, I suggest you make haste. In fifteen minutes, I shall raise the alarm that you have escaped, so you'd better be gone by then."

"You need not ask twice. Farewell Mordecai. I trust our paths will cross again."

With that Mazlo sprinted up the stairs and disappeared into the darkness.

As he walked up the flight of stairs towards the exit, Mordecai pondered for a moment at the treason he had just commited and the treachery that he had agreed to do. He had succumbed to the temptation that had enticed him for so long. It left a mixed taste in his mouth, but he had thought this over for a long time now. This was his one and only chance to escape the life of a soldier and to pay back Jakov for his humiliation. He resented Jakov for his power and success. Being replaced as the leader of the rebellion against Morpeth was shameful. A seasoned warrior displaced by a man who was not much more than a child. So he resolved to betray Jakov and to seek to profit from it along the way. Tonight was his one and only chance.

Once outside, Mordecai dropped his torch in a puddle of water and disappeared into the dark.

Iskandar was roused from his sleep by Ayesha who tapped him lightly on his foot. Gingerly he woke up, yawned several times, stretched and wandered about the room half asleep. He noted that it was still dark. Ayesha brought him a bowl of warm oats that he quickly devoured when he realized how hungry he was. While he was eating, Jakov entered the room dressed in his usual black garments and with his swords fixed on his back. Jakov looked surprised to see him awake.

"Good, you're up. Glad to see that you're eating too. You'll need your strength, we have a big day ahead."

"What are we doing today?" he said between spoonfuls of oats.

Jakov sat beside him at the table.

"Today could be the most decisive day of our lives, or even of the kingdom of Iona. Morpeth's forces are forming not far from here. We shall go out from here, fight them, and defeat them. Are you ready?

Iskandar nodded, but he wasn't really that sure.

"Good. Finish that and we'll go."

Jakov went outside the room and said some things to Sy and Ayesha that Iskandar couldn't hear. Talkai entered, holding a plate with some food on it.

"Look what I found in the kitchen. Pork sausages and bread! A breakfast fit for a king."

The smell was most attractive. Talkai placed the plate on the table and the two of them got stuck into it. Talkai made horrible chewing noises. Then Iskandar asked Talkai something that he had always wanted to.

"Do you have any family Talkai?"

"Yes, I have you."

"But besides me. Do you have any family? Real family. Like a mother or brothers?"

"Of course I have a mother, how else could I have been born?"

"But did you know them? I mean brothers and sisters. Did you grow up with any?"

Talkai paused and stopped chewing.

"I had a brother once."

"What happened to him?"

Talkai looked away and for the first time ever, Iskandar noticed that he looked sad.

"He died. Well, to be exact, he went mad and then he died."

"What drove him mad?"

"Whatever it is that drives people mad I suppose. This is an age of madness. Kings and paupers, everyone has gone crazy. Some even think I'm crazy."

"Were you good friends with him?"

"Very good friends. We were inseparable. We could have been twins. But we grew apart, went our different ways. That's what happens when you get older and grow up."

"Do you miss him?"

"Every day."

"I'm sorry."

"It is okay. You learn to live with things when you get bigger. Well, some things."

"Does it hurt to remember?"

"Not as much as forgetting."

Jakov came in and placed his hand on Iskandar's head.

"It is time for us to go, Iskandar."

Iskandar took a deep breath and stood up. Talkai adjusted his tunic and put his sword on his side for him. Just then, Mordecai entered.

"Jakov, Mazlo has escaped."

"What, when?"

"In the night sometime."

"How?"

"We don't know."

"Then what do we know?"

"He's not in his cell."

"Search the city."

"A search is already underway, but it is unlikely that he's still here. He would have fled the city and headed north at the first chance. That's what I would have done under the cover of night if I was him."

Jakov put his head into his gloved hands and yelled at them. He then sent a chair flying across the room with a ferocious kick. After a moment, he composed himself and looked back at Mordecai with a cantankerous expression on his face. Mordecai looked terribly apologetic. Then Jakov breathed out deeply and slapped his thigh with his hand.

"Well, no matter then. He was not essential to our plans anyway. He was at best a source of information about Morpeth's army and at worst an annoying hostage. It's too late for information on Morpeth's army anyway and we have no need for a hostage at the moment. Mazlo was not privy to our design for this morning."

"Do you still wish to proceed with the battle?"

"Yes."

"Even if Mazlo has alerted Morpeth to our campaign?"

"I doubt that Morpeth was unaware of it. Otherwise, he wouldn't be coming here in the first place. He knew we were coming and he is ready to meet us."

"But we have lost the element of surprise."

"I will have a surprise for Morpeth alright, when I ram his head onto a spike and parade it through the city and then use it to bludgeon Mazlo to death. That will be the surprise."

"Then what are your orders?" asked Moredecai.

"Assemble the troops exactly as planned. Keep them behind the hill on the southside of the fortress ruins. Use whatever cavalry we have as a screen, fanning out across the rear and flanks. Iskandar and I will take care of the army. After that, our men can pour across the plane and destroy whatever resistance they come across."

"As you command, master Jakov."

"Oh, Mordecai, one more thing."

"Yes."

"Don't fail on this. We have no room for error today."

"Of course."

"But I know you'll do well. You have my complete confidence."

"I am most grateful for your confidence and I remain your must humble servant."

Mordecai left the room with his head bowed and a peculiar smile on his face that Jakov didn't notice.

Jakov turned his attention to Iskandar.

"Come. It is time for us to leave."

"What about me?" Talkai asked. "Can I come too?"

"No. You shouldn't even be here. Stay in the city. If you want to make yourself useful, tend to the wounded when they are brought to the infirmary. That would be putting yourself to good use, which will make a pleasant change."

"Lovely. I always wanted to be a doctor."

"Then I already pity your patients. But if you do treat anyone for wounds or injuries try to make sure that they leave you in better shape than they came to you in."

"I'll do my best." And with that, Talkai saluted him.

Jakov just shook his head. As Jakov led Iskandar outside they were met by Sy, Mo, Tar, and Ayesha. They turned and walked down the great hall together.

"And so it begins again. Another day in the war" uttered Sy.

"Hopefully, this will be the last day of the war as well," Jakov responded.

# Chapter 14

## The Battle at the Abandoned Fort

ISKANDAR STOOD ON THE top of the hill. It was dawn, it was cold, and there was a heavy fog that was only just lifting. He stood among an abandoned and derelict old fort that was falling apart. It had no roof, its walls were mostly broken and large pieces of rock lay scattered all over the hillside. Down below at the foot of the hill was a large river at the mouth of a great lake and a wooden bridge that went over the river. Through the fog, he could see hundreds of torches forming a line like a giant worm of fire. The worm of fire slowly came over the bridge. Iskandar could make out the odd horseman and even catapaults being brought across the bridge. Iskandar looked behind him on the opposite side of the hill. There he could see the Freedom Legionnaires, several hundred men armed with spears and swords, ready to circle around the hill and to attack Morpeth's army. Jakov was tightening his boots and carefully watching the army of Morpeth cross the river through the fog. He winked at Iskandar.

"Do you enjoy this?" Iskandar asked his brother.

"What?"

"The fighting. Do you enjoy it?"

"No, I do not. I'd rather be back in Devora. But I do enjoy the notion of achieving a lifelong quest of bringing justice to Morpeth."

"After all of this is over, I never want to fight again."

"Then today we fight so we never shall have to fight again. So no child of Iona will ever have to again."

The two stood there watching the troops of Morpeth move into formation with ranks of soldiers, archers, horsemen, and catapaults. Eventually the fog lifted and Iskandar and Jakov could see all the troops in front of them. Iskandar felt afraid and turned to Jakov.

"There must be over 5,000 soldiers there."

"Closer to 10,000, I'd say," Jakov replied.

"And who is going to drive them back? Just us?"

"That's right."

"Are our troops going to attack at the same time?"

"No, they have strict orders not to pursue them until Morpeth's forces been completely routed."

"By us."

"Yes."

"So it's the two of us against ten thousand of them."

"That's what it looks like," Jakov said with a smile.

"This is going to be a massacre."

"That's the spirit Iskandar."

"I meant that we will be the ones massacred."

"Hey, we took the city of Norella with just the two of us, didn't we? We can handle a few thousand troops. In fact, they are surrounded."

"By what?"

"The river behind them, the lake to the right, us in front of them. And soon our troops will swing around our left flank like an axe and drive them into the lake."

"That's your plan?"

"Yes."

"But what if they surge up the hill towards us? What do we do then?"

"Well, I was rather counting on you and I kind of stopping them from doing that."

"And if we don't, then what?"

"Well, they'll run over us and then pounce on our troops who are hiding in a forming up position at the bottom of the hill behind us. Not very good if that happens, I'm afraid. We should probably try to avoid that."

"Try to avoid that? Are you serious? Can we run away instead?"

"No, it's too late for that. And why run, the battle is here. It's on the ground of our choosing. We have the high ground. We have them cornered."

"10,000 men cornered by two. That isn't cornered."

"Then wait and see what happens. Together, my brother, we will do magnificent deeds. Together we will drive a stake into the heart of Morpeth. Even if we don't capture him today, Morpeth will have nowhere to hide and no army left to protect him. This is the end for him. Today is the day of reckoning. This is where we stand and fight and this is where his army is finally destroyed. This is the end of Morpeth and his reign of evil."

"I might finally meet my father," Iskandar said pensively.

Jakov grabbed Iskandar by the collar.

"Don't ever call him that," Jakov scowled, "Whatever he is now, he is not our father. No father would do to his children the evil that he did. Never call him that, you hear me?"

Iskandar's face looked petrified with fear as he saw the rage in Jakov's face.

"I'm sorry, I won't say it again," the boy squirmed nervously.

Jakov saw the fear on his brother's face and he sensed the tightness of his own grip on Iskandar's collar. He released his grip and closed his eyes.

"No, it is me who should be sorry. Sometimes I lose my patience too easily. The problem is that I remember our brothers and sisters. You don't. If I seem callous and unfeeling toward him, then that is why. Do you understand?"

"I don't understand Jakov. But I trust you."

"And I believe in you brother. I am glad to be here with you. No matter what the day holds in store for us. I am grateful that we have been brought together. I could not do this without you little brother."

Jakov put his arm around his brother and kissed him on the top of his head. Then they both looked down the hill at the menacing army that was facing them.

Morpeth sat on his black horse high above the spearmen around him. The cold air filled his lungs with each breath. His horse was made restless by the clanging of armour and the noise of catapults being put into position. Morpeth himself was fixated on one thing alone. The grassy hill that gradually rose above him and the two figures he saw standing upon it between the ruins. A man in a black cloak approached Morpeth. He was bald. His eyes were sunk deep into his face and his thin lips had little colour. There was a tattoo of a skull in the middle of his forehead and an immense scar ran across his throat from battles long since fought. He kneeled before Morpeth.

"My lord."

"Rise, Balthasar. What news do you bring?"

"My lord, the Regent of Norella wishes to address you once more."

Morpeth was clearly annoyed, preferring to keep his gaze fixed on the grassy hill above. His eyes never left from them, not even to blink. Almost as if he was afraid to lose sight of the two boys on the hill. He replied to Balthasar, his imperial assassin.

"Then permit him to address me."

"As you wish my lord."

A few moments later Mazlo strolled up to Morpeth and the spearmen around Morpeth made a gap for Mazlo to walk through. Mazlo opened his arms and was about to speak but Morpeth interrupted him, without looking at him. Morpeth still looked up at the hill as he spoke.

"Mazlo, we have already made a bargain. If this man Mordecai brings me the boy, I will reward him with all the riches he wants. And after the city is retaken you will be reinstalled as Regent of Norella. I think we have nothing more to talk upon."

"I remain most grateful master for your benevolence and patronage as always. But I might simply request your assistance further as I try to make preparations for the security of our future."

"My future is secure Mazlo, it is your own you need only worry about."

"Of course master. But I have been thinking. Once the city is returned to my control, it will remain vulnerable, volatile, even unstable for a time. Revolution breeds contempt for all authorities. My small garrison has been destroyed or else has deserted me. I merely ask that you might grant me several thousand talents of silver in order to restore the walls and recruit a new army. A reasonable request, you see, in terms of future security for both of us. This is something we can never be complacent about. After all, Norella is the southern approach to your palace in Dalazvar, and your security is my highest priority."

"Mazlo, do you think that I am fooled by your pretentious ramblings about stability and security? Your request is nothing more than your brazen attempt to gain further monies from me. In recent years I have found you useful in the same way that a spider might find a web between branches useful. You have caught the fly in your web, but otherwise your services are no longer required."

"Master, my sincerity is genuine. I seek only what is best for your interests, the kingdom of Iona, the stability of Norella, and the . . ."

"The lining of your own pockets. Thus far you have found shelter in the harbour of my patience, but now the harbour is closed for the winter. I tire of your antics and I do not have the time or the need to entertain your drivel. You have affronted me."

"If I have, master Morpeth, then forgive me, please. I pledge my allegiance, my kingdom, my own life. Let me prove myself loyal."

"Mazlo, my deification draws near. By the genius of the highest god Marduk, I am an immortal and soon I shall be a god. So from this moment forth I wish to be addressed in a manner fitting of my station. From now on you shall address me as 'divinity'. And because you have offended a divine being I require sacrifice. As proof of your affections and devotion I wish you to kneel before me and then cut off your left hand as an offering to your new god."

Mazlo froze and then looked around at those about him to see if they could believe what he had just heard. The spearmen were all motionless and almost catatonic in their rigid stance. Only Balthasar acknowledged Mazlo's astonishment and he quickly looked away to avoid eye contact or having to speak to him. Mazlo took a moment to gather himself together and then kneeled down at the base of Morpeth's horse.

"Master, my lord, my king. Let us think this through. Let us reason together. No king of Iona has ever claimed the title of divinity for himself. No king has ever accepted or even demanded worship. And what possible token could my own mutilation be? How can I serve you in the devotion that you deserve if I am reduced to being a cripple? Master, I beg you to reconsider."

For the first time during their conversation Morpeth took his eyes from the hill ahead of him and looked down at Mazlo. He sneered in derision at the man who looked so pathetic too him.

"On second thought Mazlo, I think you might be right after all. Your mutilation would hardly be a trophy worthy of my divine greatness."

"Yes, master, you speak with great wisdom."

"Your death would be far more satisfying and worthy of me."

"No," Mazlo screamed as he rose, but two spearman grabbed him by his arms.

"Balthasar," said Morpeth.

"Yes, divinity," came the reply.

"This wretch offends me. I demand sacrifice. Kill him for me."

"Please, I beg you," cried Mazlo.

But before Mazlo could say another word, Balthasar had taken a sword with a curved blade from his side and at a lightning speed slashed it across Mazlo's throat. Blood gushed out everywhere and Mazlo fell to the ground, making a deathly gurgle as his life ebbed away. Morpeth looked down at him, completely unperturbed by the macabre scene.

"I think I shall make a burnt offering out of Mazlo."

Morpeth pointed his hand at Mazlo and a fireball rushed from his hand to the dying man and consumed his body in flames in an instant. His horse was temporily startled and jumped slightly, but soon clamed down. The spearmen moved away from the flames. Balthasar stared at the burning body and smiled in amusement at the spectacle.

"Balthasar," called Morpeth. "Are the troops ready for the attack?"

"Yes, divinity, everyone and everything is in place."

"Good, you may attack at will. Capture that hill, destroy any force that opposes you, and then sack the city. Beyond that, the men may take any booty that they find. Norella has always been a rather annoying city. Make it suffer and all who dwell in there. But ensure that the two boys are brought to me alive. I must take them alive. They must properly be prepared for sacrifice. Do you understand my instruction?"

"Perfectly, divinity. It shall be done exactly as you will."

"Good. Let it commence."

Morpeth returned his hypnotic gaze to the hill and he quickly searched out the two figures on top of it. He found them again and it made him smile in anticipation. He then whispered to himself.

"Now, my sons, it is time to be reunited with your father."

≈ ≈ ≈

From the top of the small knoll, Jakov looked down at the troops forming at the base of the steep incline. He moved behind part of the broken down wall of the ruined fort and turned to Iskandar.

"They are about to prepare their assault. Are you ready?"

"Yes," Iskandar said nervously.

"Good."

As Jakov turned around, he could see the catapults moving into forward positions and several men running about each one. A few seconds later, a ball of flame was launched from one of the catapult and sent flying through the air towards them.

"Hmph," laughed Jakov. "They haven't learned. Trying to crush us with flying rocks coated in oil and set alight. Well, we'll teach them a lesson on that one."

As the first burning ball of flame came closer, Jakov held out his hand and tried to command the incoming fireball to stop. It didn't stop. Instead it kept coming closer and closer. Jakov realized that he had no power over it and his eyes widened in fright as one fireball headed right towards him. He dived to his right, grabbed Iskandar, and rolled out of the path of the burning ball of flame. Crawling along the ground they took shelter in a crevice where two broken walls came together as more fire balls landed around them.

"What happened?" asked Iskandar.

"They aren't firing rocks at us."

Jakov got up and went over to the place where the fiery ball had fallen. He stuck his sword into the burning mix and pulled it out.

"Hmph. Tar, straw, oil, and fire. I was wrong. They are learning."

"What's wrong Jakov?"

"Morpeth isn't stupid enough to fire rocks or small boulders at us. He's launching volleys of tar mixed with straw that are coated with oil and set alight. Which means that I cannot stop the volleys from the catapults, since they have no stone or rock in them."

Several more balls of fire landed near and around them. Each time Jakov and Iskandar ducked their heads down as the incendiary volleys came near. Iskandar could feel the heat as the ground adjacent to them caught fire.

"What do we do? Do we run away?"

"No, it will take more than that," Jakov replied. "Give me a moment."

Jakov crawled around the broken wall to get a view of the area below. He looked down the hill and he saw hundreds of soldiers slowly walking up the steep hill towards him under the cover of the flurry of the fireballs. They had swords, spears, axes and were gradually getting closer to him and Iskandar.

As more fireballs fell in proximity to Jakov, he looked at Iskandar. Immediately, Iskandar could sense what Jakov was feeling. It was a facial expression that he had seen so many times before on the young man. Jakov's face looked contorted with sheer and utter rage. Jakov faced Iskandar as sparks from fireballs could be seen around him.

"Iskandar, this is it. This is where we kill them. This is where they die. This is the ground we have chosen. This is the ground we will hold. Do you hear me brother?"

Iskandar remained silent, paralyzed with fear, not just of the fireballs and the approaching army. He saw a madness in Jakov that left him terrified of his own brother.

Jakov stood erect, defying the threat of the balls of inferno, and with a single-minded expression on his face he took a deep breath he yelled at the top of his lungs.

"Morpeth, I send you my vengeance!"

The sound of his voice reverberated down the hill and along the river so that Morpeth heard it. The soldiers momentarily stopped when they heard it. Everyone heard it. Iskandar thought the voice sounded almost supernatural. It was a deafening yell of anger and defiance. But a few moments later the soldiers resumed walking up the steep hill towards them.

Jakov held his arms out to each side and gently raised them up to shoulder height. As he did that, two huge stones from the ruined fort, each the size of a large cart, lifted off the ground. The immense stones were suspended in the air for a moment, until Jakov flung his hands forward. At his gesture, the two stone slabs whisked high into the air and crashed into the two catapults. Many of Morpeth's men were crushed beneath the weight and impact of the cracking blow.

Jakov repeated the gesture again, and then again, and then again. Huge blocks of stone from the ruined fort kept raining down on Morpeth's army. Catapult after catapult was crushed by the onslaught of bricks from the sky. Jakov then turned his attention to the approaching army. He seemed to have no shortage of material as vestiges of the old fort fell upon the approaching soldiers. Many stopped in their tracks, some tried to run, and others were frozen by fear, but most were soon crushed. Jakov waved his left arm, then his right arm, then his left again and all over again. Each time that he did that, the heavy stones from the ruined fort lifted off the ground, shot into the air, and landed on the soldiers at a speed that made escape impossible. The battle field soon resembled absolute carnage and most of the frontline soldiers were running back towards Morpeth and were trying to make their way back over the bridge to the other side of the river. Soon, however, several projectiles of stone landed on the bridge and crushed it into multiple pieces. Men began trying to swim across the river to try and to escape the barrage from Jakov. Most of the army simply ran around in disarray, unable to cross the shattered bridge, unable to retreat, with their path blocked by the river behind them and the lake to their distant flank.

Morpeth had crossed the bridge only moments before it was shattered by a thundering rain of stone blocks. Several of his personal bodyguards were on it when it was struck and they fell into the river beneath the debris and did not emerge from it. Morpeth rode his horse to a safe range away from the savage blows of the raining boulders. Balthasar had also crossed the bridge with Morpeth. He was busy yelling instructions to the troops. Most of his words were ignored as men ran about in fear for their life and trying to avoid the seemingly never-ending onslaught of rocks and stone. Balthasar managed to rally several platoons of men that he sent up towards the hill, well spread out, on Jakov's left flank. At the same time, Balthasar jumped onto a horse that had lost its rider and he rode about, yelling commands and instructions to the scattered members of the cavalry. A cohort of horses and riders prepared for a charge up the right side of the hill.

Jakov paused for a moment and looked for another target. Most of the enemy was scattered in disarray. Bodies lay strewn all over the ground below him. The wreckage of the catapults could be seen, some burning from the fireballs that they failed to launch. He saw out of his peripheral vision to his left and his right that Morpeth's soldiers were at the base of the hill and preparing to advance. The hill was now depleted of stones and boulders available to him. Most of the stones were at the bottom of the hill and covered the battlefield between the hill and river below them. He called to the stones down there, but from so far away, they could not hear him.

Jakov jogged over to Iskandar, who had been watching the battle from the safey of a hidden crevice in the ground. Jakov took him by the arms and stared into his eyes.

"It is your turn now. There are too many of them. I cannot do this alone. You've got to unleash that power inside of you. And do it now."

"I can't. I don't know what to do," was all Iskandar could say.

"If you don't do something, Iskandar, we are both going to die."

"But ... I ... I can't."

"Iskandar," Jakov yelled inches from his face. "This is it. There is no place for us to retreat. There is no place for us to hide. Either we stop them or we die. What do you want?"

"I don't want to die," the boy whispered with his lips tremoring.

"Then do what you were born to do. Destroy them. Make them pay for what they did to our brothers and sisters. Kill them, Iskandar. Kill them all."

But Iskandar was motionless.

"Now, before it's too late, brother."

Iskandar could see the desperation in Jakov's eyes. There was something there. Not exactly fear, but a something far worse. Jakov was finally in a situation that he had no control over. Iskandar thought about his niece and nephew back in Devora. He closed his eyes and stood up. He took Jakov's hand as he stood up out of the crevice.

"I will do what I can. I will try my best."

"You can do no more than that. Try your hardest."

Hand in hand they walked along the top of the hill to its crest that towered over a steep incline, revealing the battle area in front of them. To their left and their right men were gathered, making their final preparations for their assault up the hill. It was the cavalry who broke the deadlock first. They began charging up the hill and edged closer by the moment. Although they were nearly half a mile away, they approached at a rate that made Iskandar's heart jump. Iskandar looked out over the battle field. He saw the river, the lake, the slumped bodies of men, the large blocks of the fortress spread all over the ground. Jakov squeezed his hand.

"Iskandar, I believe in you. End this, end this fight now so we can both go home."

Iskandar nodded.

He looked over at the river, closed his eyes, and he began whispering something, then speaking at a normal volume, and then finally screaming in a ferocious pitch towards the lake. He screamed so much that he fell forward from the effort. Jakov caught him and then held him upright. Together they waited, staring out at the river that stretched in front of them, but nothing happened. A few more moments passed by and nothing happened again. Jakov kneeled down beside Iskandar.

"Nothing is happening Iskandar. You must try again."

"No, it will work. Wait a moment."

"But nothing is happening. Maybe the river can't hear you."

"It heard me. Give it a moment."

Jakov could see the cavalry getting closer. On the other flank the other group of men was also speedingly running up towards them as well.

"Iskandar, I want you to run down the back side of the hill. Down below is ravine. Run into it and follow it. It will lead you to Sy with the forces waiting there. I will try to hold them as long as I can. Go now, run."

"No, it will be alright, Jakov."

"Iskandar, it hasn't worked. I'm ordering you to run."

"The water will save us."

"No it won't. We are too far away. I'm sorry. It's my fault. I underestimated the distance. The river can't hear you."

"It wasn't the river I spoke to."

"Then what was it?"

"The lake," Iskandar replied.

Jakov looked over to his right where the mouth of the river joined the great lake in the far distance. Then he saw the water on the shore of the lake quickly receding at a rapid rate. It was as if the water in the lake was being drained from the edges and was receding into the middle of the lake.

"What did you tell the lake to do?"

"You'll see," he replied in a serious tone.

Jakov kept watching as the water in the lake appeared to vanish as it was sucked away from the shoreline and disappeared over the horizon. The bottom of the lake, in some places over a hundred feet deep could be seen from the top of the hill where they stood. It was shocking. Wreckages of fishing boats and the various rocks and features of the underwater landscape could now be seen. The lake seemed to dry up in front of him.

Just then, Iskandar closed his eyes. He held his hands out wide and then pulled them back towards himself with a fist clenched as if he was pulling on a rope that was straining against him. The first thing that Jakov noticed was not the sight, it was the sound. Even from a distance, beyond his sight, he could hear a crushing sound on the horizon. The ground also began to tremble slightly and the tremor increased every several seconds. But then what he saw left him agasp. At the far side of the lake was a wall of water, at least 150 feet high, that was now rushing towards the coastline at the speed of racing horses.

The sensation of the ground trembling caused the advancing cavalry and the marauding chargers to stop for a moment. The horses became scared and the soldiers looked disoriented as they all struggled to keep balance. Balthasar pleaded with the cavaliers to calm their horses, who were restless and startled. They were only several hundred feet from the top of the hill and could see Jakov and Iskandar nearby. As Balthasar yelled instructions to his men to keep their ranks in order, his eyes met the sight of the lake. He froze at once, first in confusion, then in disbelief, and finally in fear. He yelled at his men to ride further up the hill lest they be killed, but it was no use. By now horses were throwing the men off and were bolting around the other side of the hill. Balthsasar only narrowly managed to stay on his horse as it bucked around and then galloped diagonally down the hill heading for the safety of the other side. He could do no more than hug its neck as the beast ran for its dear life. The men turned and now also saw the tsunami headed for them. But as they turned to run up the hill it was too late. The tsunami moved at a blinding speed. The gigantic wave of water struck the shoreline, followed the river along for a few hundred feet, then turned left and headed up the hill towards Jakov and Iskandar. The immense wave consumed and crushed all in its path. All of the low lying grounds before them were submerged in the blink of an eye. The colossal wave fell like a blanket on all the men and the wave appeared to suck them into its ferocious force.

Besides the amazement of the sight, Jakov noticed that the air smelt of salt. Iskandar was hypnotized by the sight and looked on as if he were watching a friend competing in a wrestling contest. Jakov noticed that after pounding the approaching soldiers with its ferocious power, the wall of water did not slow down or recede. Instead, it continued its ascent up the hill towards them. Acting out of reflex rather than thought, Jakov grabbed Iskandar, threw him to the ground, and tried to shield him from the ferocious wave. The action caught Iskandar by surprise, who found himself lying on the ground with Jakov strangely on top of him. Jakov had his eyes clenched, as if he were expected to be splashed at any moment.

The two of them heard a huge crashing of the wave and then a large spray of water covered them, but that was all. They looked up to the see the final motion of the wave smashing into into the steep edge of the hill before them, but it came no further than that. The wave slowly began receding back down the hill. As it did so, the current of the water now dragged into the lake as much as it had consumed when it had encroached upon the land.

Both of the boys stood up immediately to behold the sight before them. The waters from the lake were now retreating to the great pool of water from whence they came. The hill and all before it revealed a ground soaked in water and destruction. The river overflowed with its banks broken and the low-lying depressions of ground all filled with water. The ground was saturated and even the odd fish could be seen flipping about on the ground. The green grasslands had been turned into a swamp in a matter of seconds. Jakov put both of his hands on his mouth with a mixture of amazement and excitement at what had taken place. Iskandar just waved to the tsunami that had since returned to its original home. He whispered a thank you to it as the waters softly bubbled in reply.

Jakov turned to Iskandar very slowly, still in shock at the spectacle.

"Iskandar, what I saw you do in that valley in Nazvor ranges, with the snow, how you made it run up the hill, that was incredible. But this . . . words cannot express what this is. That was nothing short of a miracle. I still cannot believe what I saw." He paused. "Did that really happened the way I think it happened? Did the lake really … did it really come out as a gigantic wave?"

"Yes, it did."

"Did you do that? The lake, it was you?"

"It was. Are you proud of me?"

"Proud cannot begin to describe how I feel. I am in awe of you brother. Minstrels will write tales of your abilities for the next hundred years. Nothing like that has ever been seen in the land of Iona and I fear will never be seen again."

"Good, it wasn't as hard as I thought. I was going to ask the river to rise up, but then I asked the lake first. He said he would be more than happy to. He had been watching the battle and was wondering when I was gonna ask him for help."

"Well, he certainly didn't disappoint, did he?"

"No, he was ferocious."

"Indeed."

Iskandar began to stagger a bit and he fell to the ground. Jakov caught him. He noticed that Iskandar looked pale.

"Are you alright, Iskandar?"

"I feel very tired, very sleepy," he said groggily.

Iskandar closed his eyes and fell asleep in Jakov's arms. Jakov checked his face for warmth and his chest for a heart beat. He then picked him up and began heading towards the reverse side of the hill. Just before he began his descent a thought crossed his mind: Morpeth! Jakov quickly spun around and scanned the swampy grounds that lay below. He looked down near the river, on the shore of the lake, all around the base of the hill, and the horizon of the lands as far as he could see. Nothing. Not a soul could be seen moving. The only thing he could notice was the faint movement of the saturated grass being blown by a soft wind. He wondered if Morpeth had been killed by the tsunami from the lake. He imagined that he probably was dead along with all the others that lay strewn across the ground. But part of him secretly hoped that Morpeth was alive. He still wanted the pleasure of killing him face to face. He might have been robbed of that priviledge, but that was the price of their survival. He would send Sy with a search team to look for the body. And then Jakov smiled. He just realized that his quest for revenge might actually be over. It made him feel strange. A mixture of satisfaction, but also emptiness. The search for Morpeth's body would decide that. Jakov kept walking, carrying the boy to the rendezvous point he had with agreed Sy and Mordecai.

Morpeth slowly dragged his saturated body up the grassy ridge. His body ached with the pains of struggle as he had been knocked off his horse and had swam for his life. Only the debris of a broken siege engine had enabled him to swim to the nearby high ground. He rolled onto his back and tried to gain his breath. In the distance he could see the hill with the ruined fort, though now most of the ruins of the fort were spread across the field between the two hills near the river. He shook his head at the memory of being rained on by those infernal squares of stone and granite. The river was still overflowing into the adjacent areas. The first thing Morpeth noticed about the area was that everything looked wet.

Morpeth tried to remember what it was that exactly had happened. He remembered crossing the bridge just before one of Jakov's projectiles smashed it. He remembered seeing Balthasar's troops trying to outflank the two boys on the hill. He could remember the ground trembling. But after that, it was a blur. All he could recount was a wall of rushing water coming from nowhere. Then darkness and swimming for his life. The vision, the experience of it, was imprinted in his mind. It made him shudder a little. He began making his way again up the ridge. He started crawling, then climbing, and finally mustering the strength to walk the rest of the way up the ridge.

Morpeth stood up on the ridge and stretched his back and arms. He noticed that he was standing on a road. He remembered that it was the road to the Dalazvar. Just then, he heard the sound of galloping hooves at his right. He could see a soldier on a horse riding up the hill. The colours of the uniform were unmistakable. It was an imperial guard. He felt a sense of relief when he realized it was none other than Balthasar.

Morpeth folded his arms and stood in the middle of the road. Balthasar slowed up, stopped his horse, and dismounted.

"Divinity, praise be to Marduk who has protected you."

"Indeed he has, but I suspect at a great price. What happened out there? Do you remember?"

"The boy, the younger one. Iskandar. He controls the water. He somehow conjured the great lake. The lake attacked us, divinity. It attacked with a power that has never been seen before in Iona."

"Remarkable. The boy's powers are truly exceptional."

"But no match for your own power divinity."

"Of course," Morpeth didn't believe it and he even wondered if Balthasar did. But then he remembered that Balthasar was nothing more than a drone. "But their power now has to be reckoned with. We underestimated them. We should not have allowed them to pick the ground for battle. A mistake I shall not repeat."

"What are your orders, divinity?"

"Reassemble all the men. Get them rested and rearmed at once. We must prepare for a counter-attack tonight. We'll take them on as soon as it gets dark. While they are rejoicing from their victory we will strike them in Norella by surprise."

Morpeth noticed that Balthasar's face was blank and gaunt. He was unable to reply.

"What is it, Balthasar? Do you doubt my plan? Go, muster the men at once and prepare the army for battle."

"Divinity, I am sorry, but I there is no army to muster. They are destroyed, all of them."

"All of them?"

"Yes, divinity."

"What about the reserves, the cavalry, the rear eschelons, where . . ."

"They are no more majesty," Balthasar interrupted him.

Morpeth turned and looked around in the valley below. Now he paid attention to the bodies of men, men in the uniform of Iona, strewn across the soaked ground. Bodies could be seen floating down the river, while hundreds were piled up on the shore of the lake. The extent of his loss had now set in. It was not a minor loss. Rather, it had been a monumental defeat.

"Oh Marduk, my master, what did I do to deserve this? Why curse me with such misfortune? Why, master Marduk, why mock me with defeat like this?"

"Your orders, divinity, what are they?"

Morpeth could not answer as he was too consumed with anger. Those two boys had delayed his plans for deification long enough. Twice now he had had them in his grasp, only to lose them to the freakish power of Iskandar with his supernatural command of the elements. He formed a ball of fire in his hand and stared into it. He then threw the fire ball down the hill and it quickly extinguished as it rolled along the damp surface.

"I will retreat to the imperial palace at Dalazvar. I will wait there."

"Divinity, do you wish the garrison from Dalazvar to join you here to attack Norella and capture the boys?"

"No, I'm sure their next move will be to come to me. We need only wait for them. But this time I will be ready for them."

"As you wish divinity."

"Oh, Balthasar. See if you can get that package that Mordecai promised us. That will be the bait we need to lay a trap for young prince Jakov."

"It will be done as you wish divinity."

# Chapter 15

## Treachery by Friends

IN A SMALL CAMP hidden in a ravine behind the hill, Jakov and Iskandar came upon the rest of their army. Mordecai was screaming orders at soldiers as they began swinging around the hill in an orderly formation. He ordered their speed to change from a walk to a light jog. Their orders were to search the area between the fort and the river, looking for survivors and stragglers from the imperial army. Mordecai was on horseback and he gave his final instruction to a young officer who would oversee the men in the rest of their march through the grassy wetlands. At the same time, he despatched a cohort of cavalry to the site where the bridge had been, in order to secure the site in case imperial engineers tried to rebuild it. It was approaching mid-morning.

Sy approached Mordecai on foot and looked up to the man mounted on his tall stallion. Sy nodded his head towards the top of the hill and a silhouette could be seen running down the steep incline towards them.

"Jakov is coming Mordecai."

"Good. That battle was a resounding victory for us."

"Do you think the men will encounter much resistance?"

"No. There is nothing left to resist us. I saw part of the battle from a larger hill to our rear. Part of my vision was obscured, but I saw the main events take place."

"What happened?" the cyclops asked excitedly.

"To put it simply, it was an annihilation. Morpeth's men crossed the river over the only bridge, with infantry, catapults, and cavalry. They began their approach up the hill under the cover of balls of fire from the catapults. And then Jakov used the remnants of the old fort to rain down on them a barrage of boulders and stone."

"But what was that freakish noise we all heard?"

"That was the real amazing part. I still cannot believe it. As far as I can tell, Morpeth's army had been put into disarray. Still, somehow the army divided into two parts. What was left of the cavalry went to one flank, and the surviving infantry to the other flank. It was a good ploy. Jakov couldn't attack both simultaneously and he was running out of things to throw at them. They started advancing towards Jakov and Iskandar. And then," Mordecai paused, "And then there was the sound of a rushing wind. The ground shook like an earthquake. After that ..."

"What? What was it?"

"I'm not sure. But as far as I could see the waters from the lake swirled like water in a bathtub. There was a tidal wave of some kind. Morpeth's army was engulfed by it. It was formidable, almost terrifying."

"A tidal wave? That was the noise?"

"That's what I saw from up there."

"But how could Iskandar control the water so far away? I mean the river, I understand, but the lake is nearly a mile away."

"That will be something to ask Iskandar I believe."

Jakov was panting very hard as he ran down the hill into the ravine carrying Iskandar on his shoulder. Sy took the boy from his arms and held him like a babe.

"Is he wounded?" Sy asked.

"No," was the reply. "I think he is just exhausted."

"I fear that he's not the only one."

"I am alright. Slightly singed and a bit wet, but otherwise in good health."

"Mordecai told me that there was a tidal wave from the lake. Is that true?"

"Yes it is. Iskandar commanded the lake and it exploded over the land like a bucket of water being poured over an ants' nest."

"You need to rest Jakov."

"I will."

Jakov looked up at Mordecai on his horse.

"Mordecai, have you the sent the soldiers to sweep around the hill?"

"They are already on their way master Jakov. They shall complete their task before late afternoon."

"Make sure the bridge is secured."

"As if I needed to be told."

"Good. You've done well Mordecai."

"Not as well as you have done. That was a feat of power like none ever seen in Iona. Though I fear that generations will not believe the tale when it is told."

"And what tale would that be?"

"The tale of the two boys who defeated the imperial army of Morpeth with stones and water."

"Then build a memorial site here so that generations can remember what happened before it becomes legend or myth."

"So they shall remember the greatness of Jakov?" Mordecai provocatively asked.

"No, so they can remember the courage of the few who put aside their fear to fight against tyranny and injustice for the benefit of all."

"A worthy tribute to your memory."

"For those who have fallen and those who survived to tell the story."

Sy sensed the tension and decided to interject.

"Perhaps, friends, we can speak of memorials and tales later. For now there are more immediate things to deal with."

Then Iskandar coughed loudly and groaned.

Sy held him tighter and walked towards Jakov.

"Jakov, the boy must return to Norella. He needs rest immediately. Out here in the open is no place for him to recover."

"I agree."

Jakov looked at Mordecai.

"Take him back to the castle. Take him straight to Ayesha. She will nurse him to health."

"As you wish, so it will be done."

"Good. I look forward to dining tonight with you at my table. We shall feast again. You shall be toastmaster."

"Thank you. I look most forward to toasting you and your brother. Tonight, I know that I shall truly enjoy my celebrations. It shall be the sweetest feast of all."

"Good."

Sy handed the boy to Mordecai, who draped him over the front of his saddle.

"Take care of him Mordecai. He is the only reason why we are victorious today. He is also very precious to me."

"I shall ride with great safety until he gets to his destination. Trust me. Have I ever let you down before?"

"No you haven't. A fact for which I am most grateful. Ride with speed and I will see you at dinner."

Mordecai rode off up the hill, though Sy had a few suspicious thoughts in his mind, but he thought nothing of it.

Jakov sat down on the grass. He took off the swords tied to his back and loosened his belt. After removing his boots he layed back and rubbed his eyes.

"I tell you Sy, the power of the boy is astounding. What he did with that lake was beyond belief. Can you imagine a wall of water a hundred feet high crashing in front of you?"

"I can imagine it, I guess, but seeing it would be believing it."

"I've seen many strange things in my life, which hasn't been that long, but the boy is powerful. He wasn't meant for battle. He doesn't like it. But he is good at it, deadly in fact. The fighting you know."

"Who does like fighting?"

"I don't like the fighting. But coming closer to our goal, that is what drives me. That is what excites me."

"What will you do once this is all over Jakov? Take up farming, learn a trade, start a business?"

"I shall return to Devora. Be with my wife, my children. And live at peace with others."

"And find peace with yourself?"

"I hope for that too."

Jakov rolled up his sleeve and looked at the tattoo of the two snakes on his arm.

"I wonder if, when Morpeth is dead, the snakes will go away. Disappear off my arm."

"Tattoos do not normally go away of their own accord."

"This one was not applied in the normal way. It is no ordinary tattoo."

"Then what is it?"

"No one has ever been able to guess. But I think it's a seal."

"A seal of what?"

"For destiny."

"For what destiny do you think you were sealed?"

"To free men from the evil of Morpeth and to avenge my family for the slaughter of my brothers and sisters."

"We cyclops believe that a man may see many things, but he cannot see his own future. Not even in mystical tattoos."

"I think I have seen my destiny, my fate, my future."

"Where?"

"I can't say. It's not a vision, a hunch, or a hope. I think I know what will happen in the end."

"And what is that, Jakov?"

"We will defeat Morpeth. Iskandar will destroy him. But I will not live to see it. That is my destiny."

"You don't know that. No one can know that. You are depressed from too many years of fighting. Many warriors reach an age when they can only think of their eventual demise. Those who live by the sword will die by the sword. But it does not have to be so with you Jakov. Your destiny is not decided. It is still in your own hands."

"Nothing is in our own hands Sy. We are not pawns of fate, but there are powers at work in this world that go ahead of us and prepare for us paths that we must choose to walk. I fear failure, I fear losing my wife and children, but I do not fear death. If this is the path that has been chosen for me, if it is for the good of others, then I will walk it."

"Jakov, I don't care much for fates or destiny. I promise that you will never walk alone in any fate that follows you or fouls you."

"Thank you Sy. I am not ashamed to say that my best friend is a cyclops."

"I am only slightly ashamed to say that my best friend is a human boy. Though I'm learning to live with the shame of it."

The two men laughed. Jakov layed back with his hands behind his head and stared into the blue sky above. He wondered what the next day would have in store.

"You know Sy, this could all be over in three days."

"True. That's a more pleasant thought to consider."

"I told you what I would do when it's all over. What would you do?"

"I would continue my search to see if any other of my tribe and race are alive. I hear rumours of other cyclops imprisoned in Dalazvar. Perhaps some fled to the western mountains. Maybe some fled across the great sea. I want to be reunited with any of my people."

"If you cannot find them, then you are always welcomed to live among my people."

"There is only one problem with that."

"What is that?"

"Cyclops do not traditionally like snow."

"That could be a problem."

"We cyclops are more rural and rustic folk. Castles and cities are too cumbersome and closed. I much prefer the open air with four seasons rather than just slight variations of a never ending winter."

"What about a villa on the southern shores of Iona? Life by the sea. A big villa with a generous plot of farm lands. Could be attractive if you like the outdoors?"

"Then who would clean my villa and tend my farms?"

"I think Talkai would make a fine servant and Mo and Tar are apparently experts in animal husbandry."

"Jakov, I think I would much prefer whatever dark fate that you think awaits you than being confined to a country estate with Talkai inside the house and Mo and Tar outside it."

Sy took out two goblets and a flask. He poured wine into the two goblets and sat down beside Jakov.

"What is this?" Jakov asked.

"Wine from the regent's very own cellar."

The two clanked their goblets together and smiled.

"To victory for human and cyclops alike. May all of our dreams come true."

The two drank and relaxed with the thought of a bright future ahead of them.

Mordecai rode for a mile on his horse. But instead of going south towards Norella he turned west and headed for the only other bridge across the great river. It was a bridge at the town of Avorness. Balthasar would meet him there. After riding for a while he stopped his horse, dismounted, and checked that the boy was alive. He noticed that Iskandar was now stirring from his slimber. Mordecai knew that as long as he was near water the boy was a threat, a dangerous threat, to himself and to anyone else. So he blindfolded Iskandar, tied his his hands around his back, and tied a scarf tightly around his mouth. That way he couldn't do his magical conjuring with the water, or at least Mordecai hoped he couldn't. He then put the boy in a huge sack just to make extra sure that he couldn't see or do anything. He then remounted his horse with the sack tied firmly to the saddle. Mordecai then kept riding onwards, not a fast pace, but brisk enough to make good time. Every few moments, he nervously looked over his shoulder to see if anyone was following him. It was just after midday. Mordecai was ready to finish what he had begun. He had grown tired of taking orders from a boy who commanded the army that was once his. His humiliation would be reversed when the upstart boy from the icelands got his just desserts. Mordecai secretly feared Jakov but would never admit it. He knew the extent of his powers and most of all all he knew that Jakov had a temper and was not known for dealing mercifully with opponents. But on even terms, Mordecai knew he could easily beat him in a fight.

After riding for an hour, Mordecai came to the bridge across the river from Avorness. There was a man sitting on a horse in the middle of the bridge. Behind him at the other end of the bridge were seven men also on horseback, all dressed in imperial colours and holding spears. Their faces were hidden by scarves that hid all of their faces except for their eyes. Mordecai instantly knew who they were. Imperial assassins. The most trusted men in Morpeth's army. The ones he sent to kill people who were deemed to be dangerous or annoying to Morpeth. They had once tried to kill him before, back when he was commander of the Freedom Legionnaires. But he figured that if they wanted him dead then they could have easily have ambushed him already. He was alive and they wanted him that way. Mordecai slowly approached on his horse as it walked over the creaky bridge towards the rider in the middle of the bridge. The town of Avorness could be seen in the distance, but there was no one else in sight.

The rider spoke first.

"You must be Mordecai."

"And you must be Balthasar."

"Indeed I am."

"Where is Mazlo?" asked Mordecai curiously.

"He's dead."

"Should I ask how?"

"Probably better if you didn't."

Mordecai couldn't help but stare at the skull and cross bones tattooed on the front of Balthasar's forehead.

"I believe that you have something that belongs to my master, Morpeth the Divine."

"Morpeth the Divine. Since when did Morpeth assume divine honours?"

"Whenever his divinity wishes too."

"Fine, he can call himself the Prince of the Paupers for all I care."

"Do you have the package Mordecai?"

"Indeed I do. The package is a person."

"I know. Let me see him."

Mordecai positioned his horse right beside Balthasar's. He opened the sack and Balthsasar looked inside. He could see Iskandar. The boy was no longer asleep and was now awake. He started squirming, kicking, and trying to speak through the scarf that ruffled his voice."

"Well done Mordecai. The divine Morpeth promises great wealth and honours for you in doing this deed."

"I am so glad to hear that." Then Mordecai whispered, "But can I suggest that we get off the bridge before you know who realizes that we are standing above you know what."

Balthasar looked down on the bridge and the water beneath it.

"Ah, yes, good idea. We don't want a repeat of this morning's events, do we now? Let us go quickly. My master is very anxious to see this young man."

The two started walking along with the horses side by side. Soon the seven other men armed with spears joined them. One spearman was out ahead at some distance. Three were at the front of Balthasar and Mordecai and three spearmen behind them. Mordecai felt a little nervous among these men. They were killers, assassins, specializing in the art of death. However, if they were going to run into Jakov they were the best persons to have around he supposed. They were all silent. They did not speak. And they were alert, always looking about. Mordecai knew that these were perhaps the most dangerous men in all of Iona.

"What is to become of the boy?" Mordecai asked.

"Whatever his divinity Morpeth wishes."

"And what does his divine majesty wish?"

"The boy is to be dedicated as a sacrifice to Marduk. Then Morpeth shall experience deification and transform from an immortal into a god."

"Human sacrifice. Is that all?"

"No. He is also to be the bait to lure Jakov to Dalazvar. A trap is set and is ready to be sprung."

"Hmph. And I thought my father was bad."

A moment later, Iskandar tried squirming in the bag and kicking about. It made Mordecai's horse stop and jump a little.

Balthasar rushed over and slapped the sack very hard with the back of his hand. Iskandar stopped moving.

Balthasar leaned towards the sack and whispered into it.

"If I see one movement of you between now and Dalazvar, I will not hesistate in cutting out your eyes and cutting off your hands. You hear me little boy?"

There was only silence in the sack after that. Mordecai and Balthasar recommenced moving along the road. The horses walked at a steady pace. After a few moments Mordecai could hear the boy crying in the sack. It momentarily gave him feelings of guilt. He meant the boy no harm. But his lust for revenge against Jakov was too strong to resist.

He also whispered into the sack.

"Iskandar. Do as you are told and all the suffering will be over quickly. Be strong, little one. It will be over soon."

Balthasar cast a menacing glance at Mordecai that Mordecai pretended did not bother him.

"No more talking to it. Do you hear me Mordecai? I can take him to Morpeth by myself. Remember that."

"He's only a boy."

"He's a sacrificial victim. Like a lamb or a goat. And if he escapes, I promise you this, there is no suffering on earth comparable to what Morpeth would do to you."

"I shall be careful."

"Good, for all our sakes."

Without letting Balthasar see, Mordecai gently rubbed the bag and stroked Iskandar's head. The conflict in him was strong, but it was too late to turn back. He also knew that if he got out of line that Balthasar would not hesistate in killing him. It was then that he realized that revenge and wealth had its price. It had cost him an army, friends, and perhaps even his soul. He felt a little glum. But then he imagined what Jakov's face would look like when he found out what he had done. Just in case Jakov didn't quite figure out what had happened, he had wisely left behind something to explain it. He knew that the hunt would soon begin.

# Chapter 16

## The Pursuit

JAKOV WALKED INTO THE royal chambers of the regent and saw Ayesha sitting at a table polishing her boots. When he entered she put her boots down and stood up.

"Congratulations Jakov, I hear the battle was a great victory," she said.

"Yes, it was. Thanks to Iskandar. Speaking of Iskandar, how is he? Is he alright?"

"I haven't seen him," Ayesha replied, "I thought he was still with you."

"What? I sent Mordecai back to the city with Iskandar over an hour ago. It's not a far trip. I told him to come straight to you."

"Well, I haven't see him. Either of them. I don't think they came into the city."

"Then where are they?"

"I don't know. Iskandar has not returned to Norella."

"He should be with Mordecai."

"That is peculiar."

"Yes, it is."

"Have the legionnaires search the city for either of them. Maybe the horse was injured."

"Could they have been ambushed?"

"I doubt it. There was no one left to ambush them. Besides that, the area between the city and fort is teeming with our own men."

"Perhaps they are resting somewhere first."

"Perhaps."

"I'll arrange the city to be searched."

"Please, Ayesha, do that. But let us be quick about it."

Ayesha left the room and Jakov looked out the window. It was after midday, the sun was shining, and he could see a falcon high in the air. He could see the old ruined fort that was now even more ruined. But he had a strange, almost sick feeling in his stomach. He looked about the room and then something caught his eye. On the desk was a letter folded up with a red ribbon enclosing it. The front of the letter read "Jakov."

Jakov very quickly opened the letter and read it as Sy walked into the room.

"No," he yelled.

"What is it?" the cylcops asked, sensing the panic in Jakov's voice.

"It's Mordecai. The mongrel has kidnapped Iskandar."

Jakov threw the letter to the ground. He barged passed Sy and then ran for the door.

"Where are you going?"

"The road to Dalazvar, before it's too late."

"But Jakov, you can't possibly catch him."

"I will find him," Jakov yelled back.

"You could be captured."

"I'll take my chances."

Before Sy could say anything more, the young man was gone and running down the corridor. Sy noticed the letter on the ground. He picked it up and saw only a few words written on the page. They made his heart ache with pain and his stomach burn with anger. The letter read, "Dear Jakov, now you know what it feels like to be betrayed!" It was signed, "Mordecai".

Sy scrunched up the letter and threw it into the fire. Everything now was uncertain. Everthing now could be lost. The victory of today had just become a nightmarish loss. Sy knew what effect this would have on Jakov.

Talkai walked in with Mo and Tar at his side. Talkai was mid-conversation when the trio walked in.

" ... and that is why you should never put a jack rabbit in your bed to try to keep you warm at night."

The two dwarves nodded in agreement, impressed by the moral tale.

Talkai looked at Sy and knew instantly that something was wrong.

"What's wrong Sy? I thought Jakov and Iskandar won the battle for us. Hey, are they back yet?"

"I'm sorry Talkai. Iskandar has been kidnapped."

"Kidnapped? By who?"

"Mordecai."

Sy couldn't face Talkai as the foolish man's face froze with grief. Sy turned away and looked out the window. He saw below Jakov's horse suddenly burst out of the stall, galloping through the city and then through the northern gate at a blinding speed.

"I hope you find him Jakov. For all our sakes," he muttered.

Jakov rode his horse at a punishing speed. He knew that the river had only two crossing points. The bridge north of Norella and a western bridge at Avorness. Mordecai would have had to have taken the western bridge at Avorness which would have meant that he would have to detour around the great river both west and east before he could head north to Dalazvar, the capital of Iona, and home of Morpeth. If Jakov could cross the great river near the fort then he could gain on them easily. He could do that hopefully before they passed into the Yobi dessert. The Yobi desert was short from north to south, but it stretched wide across the northern half of Iona. It was a wastleland where nothing grew and nothing lived. No plants, no wildlife, and no wells. It was eight miles of desolation and death for travellers who got lost there. Its red sand was hot and relentless, especially in high winds. The road from Norella to Dalazvar went straight through it.

Jakov rode his horse along the main path heading north. He went past the abandoned fort where he had only been that morning. As he entered the valley he saw up close the carnage he and Iskandar had caused during the battle. Bodies of men were all over the place. Broken catapults and siege engines laid about in pieces. Some of the Freedom Legionnaires were still about, gathering the dead to be burned in a mass grave. Several saluted him as he rode past but he didn't take time to acknowledge them. The muddy and wet ground slowed up his horse, but he urged it on all the more. A few moments later he came to the broken bridge. A detachment of Freedom Legionnaire cavalry was there, guarding the broken bridge. One of the cavalry officers saluted him as his horse came to a halt.

"General Jakov. The bridge remains secure. There is no sign of an imperial counter-attack. No one is able to pass over the bridge sir."

"That is my problem. One I shall have to fix."

Jakov looked about around him and then stared at the river that was some 100 yards wide.

"Captain, how deep is the river?" He asked.

"By our measurements eight to ten feet deep. Shallower in some places, deeper in others."

"Okay then, this will have to be a non-traditional river crossing."

"A crossing sir? No one can cross it. The bridge is down. It is untraversable."

"Really? Then watch me."

Jakov turned around again, looking at the debris around him and he saw some of the huge stone bricks that he had hurled down this way only hours before.

"Everyone out of my way," Jakov cried out.

The Freedom Legionnaire cavalry all moved away from Jakov as they sensed that he was about to do something. Jakov waved both of his hands out to his side and then called to the stone blocks that lay around him. One after another raised off the ground, flew quickly through the air, and plunged into the river ahead of him. Each time a huge piece of stone hit the water there was an immense splash. This happened until an even path of stones littered the way through the river. All except the last several yards. Jakov grieved the lack of stones and bricks. He'd have to take his chance anyway.

Jakov kicked his horse and it began running over the newly made stone bridge. It was uneven and slightly slippery, but the horse held its way and its momentum. Coming to the end of the bridge that was still several feet short to the opposite river bank, Jakov kicked his horse even harder and yelled, "Hah." Taking a few final steps, the horse jumped through the air and landed safely on the river bank where it joined the road. Jakov turned around and all the cavaliers were applauding his efforts as if he had just performed a mighty trick for their amusement. He waved his hand to acknowledge them, but then urged his horse onwards at full speed as it ran up a slight incline leading to the top of a ridge.

Once at the top of the ridge, Jakov had a good view of everything around him. He knew he couldn't wait long, the Yobi desert was not far away. It was important that he caught Mordecai before he got there. But he let his horse rest for a minute. From here on the pace he needed to travel would have to be like lightning. He scanned the terrain all around him. He looked down at the road and the place where it met the junction leading to Avorness in the west. As he squinted a little he thought he could make out on the horizon several horses just going down the other side of a rise in front of him. They were at least half an hour ahead of him, but he knew he could catch them. He rubbed his horse on its neck and head.

"Let us make haste my dear Infamy. People are counting on us to win this race."

Jakov yelled, "Hah" as he kicked his horse Infamy and it raced down the other side of the ridge. Jakov sat up off the saddle trying to make the load as light for the horse as possible. The wind that ran through into his face made his eyes water. The flowing tears only reminded him of the sadness he felt at the loss of Iskandar.

The group of several riders with Mordecai and Iskandar continued their urgent pace along the road to Dalazvar. Mordecai could feel the air getting drier and hotter as they approached the Yobi desert.

"The boy will need a drink," Mordecai said to Balthasar.

"If you give him water, he might kill you with it. No drink for him."

"Then let him out of the sack, it must be sweltering in there."

"No, we cannot risk it. My master would not tolerate him escaping."

"Balthasar, tell me, will Morpeth tolerate his intended sacrificial victim, his very own son, dying of thirst in the Yobi desert?"

Balthasar glanced back at Mordecai and then at the sack that Mordecai was carrying.

"Take him out and give him a little water. But if escapes, you will pay for it."

Mordecai cut open the sack and grabbed Iskandar under his arms and put him on the saddle in front of him.

"Iskandar, if you move, speak, or try anything, the men nearby will kill you. Do you hear me?"

The blindfolded little boy nodded.

Mordecai took the scarf out of his mouth and gave him some water to drink. Iskandar drank down the water as quick as he could and licked his lips afterwards, wanting more.

"Where are we going?" he asked.

Balthasar unsheathed his sword and pointed it at him. Mordecai squeezed Iskandar's jaw with his hand and he knew it hurt him.

"My last warning Iskandar. Next time you speak these men will either cut out your tongue or run you through."

His lips trembled, but he nodded in agreement. Balthasar then put his sword away.

Suddenly one of the spearmen at the rear came running up to Balthasar.

"Captain Balthasar, we are being followed."

Balthasar looked behind and in the distance could see a small cloud of dust coming towards him. A single horse with a rider was at the front of it.

"No matter. He's only one man. And we'll be in the Yobi desert before he catches us. We will despatch him quickly. I will leave his body in the desert for the vultures to pick at."

"What if it's Jakov?"

"Then we will capture him and I will have two packages for my divine master. He will be most pleased."

"If it is Jakov, it will be harder than you think."

"We are imperial assassins. We are not afraid of a little boy."

"I don't know where you were this morning but that boy just destroyed the entire imperial army. So I suggest you think long and hard about your strategy for despatching him. Otherwise the only bodies strewn across the Yobi desert will be ours. Don't underestimate him Balthasar. I know what he can do. He is relentless and determined. Remember, this is a son of Morpeth. He's just as ruthless as his father. He does not give up. Never does, never will. And since we have his little brother I can guarantee you that he will be in a rather foul mood when he arrives."

"Fine. Everyone gather to me."

The spearmen all came towards Balthasar and awaited his instruction. Balthasar emerged from the huddle and addressed Mordecai.

"I will take the boy to Morpeth. I'll ride at full speed. The rest of you, you included Mordecai, can lay in ambush for him in the Yobi desert. Wound him if you have to, but he must be taken alive. Understood?"

The men nodded in agreement.

"Do you understand?" Balthasar asked Mordecai directly.

"Perfectly."

"Then let's go. Once we reach the Yobi, he will be easier to defeat."

"You'll be no match for Jakov," said Iskandar with a contemptuous voice. "He'll gut you all like a fish. Especially you, Mordecai."

Balthasar's fist slammed into Iskandar's jaw and knocked him off the horse. Iskandar lay there unconscious.

"Well, we did warn him, I suppose" said Mordecai.

"If Morpeth didn't need him alive, I would have killed him."

Balthasar picked the boy up and layed him across the saddle of his own horse.

"I ride for Dalazvar. The rest of you, hold Jakov off, and capture him if you can. Remember, he must be taken alive."

"It won't be easy," retorted Mordecai.

"Well if you fail, you can always explain it to Morpeth. That would be a short conversation at least."

# Chapter 17

## Jakov battles Mordecai

JAKOV SPED ALONG THE sandy road. His horse Infamy was panting heavily. He had slowed up in the last few miles, but he was definitely closing in on his target. He had seen them a few miles back and every now and then they came into his vision between the hills and turns of the road to Dalazvar. He had barely noticed the landscape become more and more barren as he rode along. The vegetation became sparser. Over the course of the ride the terrain shifted from rolling green hillsides to dry and rocky slopes, and finally to mounds of sandy red ground. As Jakov came over one small hill, he could see a lone figure sitting on a horse waiting for him. He pulled the reins of his horse to slow up and then came to a complete stop. He looked at the rider. Jakov recognized him at once.

"What have you done with him Mordecai?"

"With who, Jakov?"

"You know who. Where is Iskandar? What have you done with him?"

"He's on the way to Dalazvar with some fine company. Apparently his father is just dying to see him."

"Why, Mordecai? Why? Why did you do this? You were one of us. You were once the commander of the Freedom Legionnaires. Why did you commit this treachery? You were my friend."

"Jakov, I noticed that when you took control of the Freedom Legionnaires that there was no 'us,' only 'you'. You and your insane quest for vengeance. I was once the general of a fine army, feared throughout Iona. I could raid villages at will. The imperial army was powerless before me. I was the real rebel who threatened Morpeth. I was the most feared man in all of Iona. But then you came along. You and your trickery with stones. You and your rag tag band of vagabonds usurped my authority."

"I was made commander by the Legionaire council. I never asked for it."

"No, but you relished it. You enjoyed it, and I was humiliated. The finest rebel leader ever to roam the land replaced by a boy from who knows where."

"Your strategies were failing. The Legionnaires were taking heavy casualties. It was time for a change. Everyone knew that."

"That's your opinion Jakov. Being replaced by a child was bad enough. But I heard the songs that the men sung around the camp fires about me. 'Mordecai was great, but Jakov is greater. Mordecai was fearless, but Jakov is fearsome.'"

"I cannot believe that this whole thing was about your wounded pride. Are you so fickle that being replaced by someone younger than you was really so unbearable?"

"I lost my family Jakov. My wife and my children. When I fought Morpeth, they were captured and killed."

"And now you betray me to the man who butchered your family. What kind of justice is that?"

"My justice will be the rewards I reap. Morpeth will make me rich. He'll give me my own kingdom. I'll have a whole harem of wives and a plethora of heirs. I'm tired of fighting a foe I cannot beat. You can't kill an immortal Jakov. I've been trying for ten years and I give up. So if you can't beat them, then you might as well join them. I've learnt that lesson now. The whole time I was fighting on the wrong side. Might as well let him have what he wants and just enjoy the benefits if you can."

"Is that what you've learned through all of this? Then no wonder the Legionnaires replaced you. You are selfish and cowardly, with no love in your heart for anyone but yourself. You were never worthy."

"Think what you like. This is the end for you, my young friend. I will break you. I will beat you within an inch of your life and whatever is left I will serve up to Morpeth. I hear he knows the meaning of gratitude."

"You're a fool Mordecai, if you think he'll reward you. He'll destroy you whenever you become expendable. Don't you remember how this war started? Don't you remember what you were fighting for?"

"No, I don't remember. And that is the problem. I don't remember why I chose to fight any more. I don't know why I chose to live a life in god forsaken forests living off barley and cold rat meat. I don't remember why it all started. And the truth is that I don't care any more either. I only want to enjoy the rest of my life in whatever luxury and privilege that I can find."

"Whatever life you think you have left is going to be cut short, old friend. I will see you die Mordecai. I will kill you quickly."

"Always so confident, so full of talk, so brash, and so bold. I have had enough of that big mouth of yours Jakov. I am going to shut it once and for all. It is you who will be deafeated. Oh, in case you haven't noticed, there are no stones out here. No rocks. No boulders. Just me and a few friends."

Jakov's eyes darted around looking for others but he didn't see them. Then almost instantly he saw several flickers to his front and sides. Hiding under blankets covered with sand were several men armed with spears and swords. They jumped up from the hiding places, crouched into fighting positions, and surrounded Jakov on his horse.

"You are surrounded Jakov. You are no match for the imperial assassins. Better to surrender. I don't want you too bloodied up when I present you to Morpeth."

Jakov unsheathed the two swords on his back and held them in striking positions.

"We'll see about that."

With that, Jakov kicked his horse and charged towards Mordecai. In turn, Mordecai's eyes widened and he charged forward on his horse as well. The two came together. Their swords collided with such a ferocious force that they were both knocked from their horses. Jakov hit the ground and rolled to his feet. He looked up at his several adversaries, but off his horse he now felt very vulnerable. He took a few steps forward and then speedily turned around and saw behind him two imperial assassins running at him with spears. He quickly parried their thrusts with a circular movement of his own two swords. As one of the spearmen lunged again, Jakov sidestepped and spun around and struck a blow to his head with one sword and pierced his abdomen with the other sword. Jakov then heard movement behind him and he flipped through the air to his right, narrowly avoiding being impaled with a spear. Before the spearmen could retract his spear, Jakov had sliced him across his arm and chest.

The imperial assassins had lost two of their number, but the remaining five now formed a line towards him and began to encircle him. Before they could make a full circle around him, Jakov ran forward at them. As Jakov got closer three of the assassins lunged forward with spears ready to stab him. But Jakov launched himself into the air with a perfect front flip over the height of their spears. As he whirled through the air, he made a fast slicing motion with his swords that caught two of the assassins on their necks and they fell to the ground immediately. Now there were only three assasins left and Mordecai.

"You wretched fools," Mordecai yelled at them. "He's taking you apart two at a time. You must time your attack. Wear him down first if you must. No need to hurry. In this dry heat he won't endure long against you."

Mordecai himself joined the ranks of the imperial assassins. They now took turns of lunging at him with spears. They were pressing on him, but never too close to come near his swords that moved at lightning speed. They sallied upon him from his left, then his right. High and low. Sometimes from two directions at once. They timed their attacks with precision so that Jakov was constantly moving and parrying to avoid being struck. One of the spears got through his parry and narrowly struck him on the shoulder. It was not deep, but the force of the blow and its pain made Jakov drop his sword.

"That's it, men. We have him now," Mordecai encouraged them.

Jakov could feel his strength leaving him. He was sweating profusely, and his arms felt like they weighed more than a house. His shoulder throbbed with pain, and he panted for breath. He wasn't sure how much longer he could last. He counter-thrusted when he could, which was not often. Jakov found himself limited to defence and struggling to avoid the carefully timed attacks by the long spears.

As two spearmen attacked simultaneously from his right Mordecai charged from his left. Jakov was able to repel the two spears with his sword and then used a mighty kick to send Mordecai flying back across the dirt road. Then one of the imperial assassins charged directly into him with a sword. The break in formation gave Jakov a chance. He ducked down low and struck the man's knees as he ran by him. Using the momentum he leapt forward and swung his sword towards the remaining two imperial assassins. One tried to parry with his spear, but the sheer power of Jakov's blow broke the spear and his sword sunk into the top of the man's head. Pulling it out, Jakov turned his attention to the one remaining assassin. In desperation the man threw his spear at Jakov from close range. Jakov simply leaned to his right and the spear missed. Before the man could get his sword out, Jakov had run him through.

The seven imperial assassins were now dead. Jakov quickly spun around to turn his attention to Mordecai. But no sooner had he turned than he felt a burning sensation in his right knee that sent him crashing to the ground. Jakov's face twisted with anger and agony. He looked down and saw a spear lodged in the top of his right knee cap. The pain was excruciating and he nearly lost consciousness. Crouching onto one knee he reached down and, grimacing in pain, he pulled the spear from his knee. But it was too late. As he tried to get to his feet, Mordecai's boot landed in his face. Jakov felt the side of his face swell up immediately. He tried to swing his sword at Mordecai, but Mordecai stood on his arm, trapping it in its place. Mordecai lowered his sword so that it was just touching Jakov's throat.

"Impressive, I have to say, Jakov. To beat seven imperial assassins like that. But I guess it was just one adversary too many."

"If you kill me, Morpeth will kill you."

"I know. But I can hardly carry you to Dalazvar by myself. So I guess that I'll have to mortally wound you so that you are incapacited enough to be carried without being a threat to me on the way. That is probably my best chance. Cutting off your arm would probably do the trick. Leave you too weak to fight, but not quite dead yet. Morpeth is going to kill you in the end any way. What do you have to say about that?"

Jakov looked up into the sky. The sun was behind Mordecai and it left Jakov's own face shaded. He saw up in the sky what he thought at first was a vulture flying above. But it wasn't, it was something else. Jakov softly laughed at Mordecai.

"Come now, Jakov. Are you lost for words? What do you think of the prospect of having a limb removed and then being killed by your own father?"

"Mordecai, there is a dragon coming towards you. I suggest that you move and get out of the way before it strikes you."

"I'm not going to fall for that on. Really Jakov, a dragon, behind me? Is that your last ditch effort to survive. You know, I didn't really believe your dragon story the first time I heard it back in the Glenn forest and I'm certainly not going to fall for it now."

"Seriously, there is a dragon flying towards you. I see it behind you. It is going to strike you any moment now."

"I am not in the mood for charades. I'm going to cut you into little pieces. Don't you have something more noble or brave to say in the face of such imminent pain."

Jakov stayed silent and smiled all the more.

"Well, I guess that I'll just have to wipe that stupid smile off your face, won't I?"

Mordecai lifted his sword high and prepared to strike Jakov.

"You should have turned around Mordecai."

"Oh, really?" he replied.

The next thing Mordecai heard was a deafening shrill that startled him. He turned and looked behind him and saw a blur of red as the huge face of a dragon came into contact with his body. The dragon swooped low, knocked him over, and sent him flying across the road. He landed in the side of sand dune over forty feet away. The dragon's trajectory changed and it flew upwards into the sky again. Jakov could see its rider in a dark purple armour once more. The dragon and its rider circled the skies above them.

Jakov slowly stood up, picked up his swords, and limped over to where Mordecai lay. On the side of the sand dune Mordecai struggled to rise. He did manage to turn over from his stomach onto his back. His face was covered with a mixture of sand and blood. He looked at Jakov but had to squint due to the sun. Mordecai coughed up some blood and then struggled to speak.

"You were right. There really was a dragon."

"You ever known me to lie?"

"No."

"Where is Iskandar?"

Mordecai was coughing very hard but managed to spurt out a few words. "They've taken him to Dalazvar. They won't kill him until Morpeth has the both of you. They are settting a trap for you. That's all I know."

"Is this how you wanted it to end?"

"Does it matter any more?"

"I guess not."

"Do you know what Jakov?"

"What?"

"I know what happens now. And strangely enough, I really don't care. I don't care if Morpeth kills you or your brother. It doesn't matter to me any more."

"It matters to me."

"You care too much Jakov. You need to learn to be more selfish. You need to be more like your father."

"Do you remember when I told you that I was going to kill you quickly, Mordecai?"

"Yes."

"I lied."

With that, Jakov drove both of his swords into Mordecai's stomach.

"You can bleed into your own stomach for three days and die like the treacherous pig you are. You kidnapped my brother and sold him to the lunatic king of this land. You will suffer long and hard for that."

Mordecai doubled over in pain, coughed more, and convulsed in pain.

"Have mercy Jakov. Please. I'm sorry," he cried.

"The only mercy you'll get is from the vultures, hyenas, and the rats who will start eating your flesh before you're even dead. Ask them for a quick death."

Jakov turned and limped away as Mordecai lay there wailing in a pained and bloody mess. Ahead of him he saw the red dragon standing on the roadside. Its rider in his dark purple armour stood in front of him with his arms crossed. Jakov slowly approached.

"When you said that I would see you again, I didn't think it would be under these circumstances."

"Are you disappointed that I came when I did?" the rider responded.

"I can't complain about your timing. It's been immaculate on the two occasions that I've had the pleasure of your company."

The rider's eyes could only faintly be seen under the blackness of his visor. Jakov studied them closely.

"Morpeth has Iskandar," stated Jakov.

"I know," the knight replied. "That is most unfortunate."

"Then what do I do? I cannot take the city without Iskandar."

"If you are to rescue him, then you have no choice. You must capture the city."

"I cannot do it."

"Then all is lost and Morpeth has won. It's only a matter of time before he catches you. You can't hide in the eastern frontiers forever."

"I cannot capture a city by myself."

"You took Norella easy enough."

"Norella is not the same as Dalazvar. It was not garrisoned by the imperial army. Even if I doubled the Freedom Legionnaires, even if I ripped every stone from its walls, I still could not capture the city. It is hopeless."

"No it's not. As long as you and Iskandar are alive, there is hope."

"A fool's hope, perhaps."

"You could always try to enter the city by stealth. Sneak in and rescue Iskandar right under Morpeth's nose, without him ever knowing."

"Impossible," Jakov objected.

"There are many secret passages and hidden tunnels in the city and in the royal palace. They are only known to a few. But if you can get into them, you could enter the city undetected."

"And how am I supposed to do that?"

"Find someone who knows the secret entrances into the city."

"And who would that be?"

"Who do you think knows?"

"Besides Morpeth, hardly anyone else could know."

"There is at least one other who would know."

Jakov stopped and thought for a moment and then it dawned on him what the knight was getting at. His face showed a mixture of surprise and disgust.

"You could not possibly be thinking of asking . . ."

"There is no other way Jakov."

"I would sooner die than enlist assistance of that order."

"There is no other way," the knight was almost yelling at him. "And you know there is no other way."

"No, I can't."

"There is only one person who can lead you into the city."

"Then I'll find a way into the city myself."

"You don't have the time. Once Morpeth knows that you suspect a trap, he will sacrifice Iskandar to Marduk and be one step closer to deificiation."

"Never in a thousand years would I ever go to someone like that looking for help."

"Then your brother dies and Morpeth wins."

Jakov crouched down for a moment and it took the stress and pain away from his knee. He let out a mighty roar of anger and frustration. He slowly rose and faced the knight again.

"So be it. I will do this. I will go to ... to ... to that creature and get into the city."

"Good," the knight replied. "But one last thing we need to take care of."

"What?"

The knight took his crossbow from his back and aimed it at Jakov.

"Step to your left for a moment please."

Jakov was confused by the odd request, but he complied. Jakov stepped to his left. Then the knight fired his crossbow and Jakov saw the bolt land in Mordecai's chest. The old man died instantly.

"What did you do that for?" Jakov cried.

"It's called mercy."

"Mercy. He showed none to me, none to my brother. He was a traitor and an ally of Morpeth. For the love of Vetrius, he wounded me, can't you see?"

"Mercy is not deserved. It is given when you have every reason to withhold it. That's why it's called mercy."

"I will give mercy when and where I see fit. He was my adversary and I had the right to determine his manner of death."

"Life and death are not yours to give Jakov. They are for powers higher than ourselves. Don't try to play god, Jakov. It doesn't suit your father, and it doesn't suit you either."

"Don't compare me to my father."

"Then you need to make sure that you do not become what you are trying to destroy."

"I am not in the mood for your lectures on morality. I do what I have to do. I get the job done."

"Then watch out how you do the job. You show your family likeness when you surrender to your rage."

Jakov gritted his teeth, unimpressed by the knight's tone of voice and what he had to say. But he mostly took offence to the thought that he was in any way like his father.

The knight turned around, bent down, and picked up something large and metal and handed it to Jakov. It was a shield. As Jakov took it into his hands he noticed how light it was. The cover of the shield glistened in the sun, like it was covered in precious jewels. On the shield was a painting of two snakes intertwined, just like his tattoo.

"What is this?" Jakov asked.

"A gift from me. You'll need it when you face Morpeth."

"I already have a shield, thank you."

"But not like this one. It is made of diamonds taken from a volcano. It is indestructible. It cannot be broken by steel, stone, or even fire. It is the perfect shield."

"It looks nice, but I don't need it."

"Yes you do. You'll need it to repel the fire of Morpeth."

"I was hoping to dodge his fireballs rather than allow them to hit me."

"Trust me. Take the shield. It's your only chance to defeat Morpeth in close combat."

"Alright then, if it repels fire, then it will be useful. Thank you."

"You are welcome. Now excuse me, but we both have business to attend to."

"Wait," Jakov added, "Before you go there is one thing."

"What?"

"I want answers, from you. You know alot about me, my brother, and Morpeth. However, I know nothing about you. I must know, who are you and what is it that you want?"

"Who I am is no concern of yours. What I want is the same thing as you. I want the end to Morpeth's madness. I want peace. I want the tyranny to end. The rest you can learn later."

"Who are you, knight?" demanded Jakov more forcefully.

The knight turned around and began walking back towards the dragon.

"Hey, come back here. I am not done talking to you."

But the knight kept walking onwards.

"We are done Jakov. Go back to Norella. You know what you have to do."

"Come back here. I want answers from you," Jakov hobbled after him as quick as he could.

The knight kept walking and ignored Jakov.

"You have hidden behind that helmet for too long. You will give me answers. You will reveal yourself to me," he yelled as he limped.

Jakov grabbed the knight by his arm and then tried to grab his helmet.

"I am tired of this secrecy. Who are you?"

But the knight pushed aside Jakov's hands and then kicked him in his wounded knee. Jakov fell to the ground at once and let out a groan of pain.

"All things in good time Jakov. Everything will be revealed when the proper time comes. Have some faith lad."

The knight took a few more paces and mounted his dragon. The dragon screeched at Jakov, who sat there rubbing his leg in pain. In a matter of seconds the dragon and the mysterious knight flew off into the sky.

Jakov limped around clutching his knee and shoulder as he hobbled along the road. He called out to his horse Infamy. Then after several minutes it came to him. Jakov mounted up and began the long ride back to Norella. This time he didn't hurry. He was too weak and too confused to hurry. He needed rest in body and mind, since he knew that what he had to do next would be the hardest thing he'd ever attempted.

# Chapter 18

## A Daring Plan

IT WAS VERY LATE in the night when Jakov finally arrived back in Norella. Infamy was more exhausted than he was. Jakov greeted several of the soldiers from the Freedom Legionnaires when he entered the city. He saluted them, put Infamy into the stables, and then made his way up to the regent's residence. His wounded knee made each step up the stairs absolute agony, but he managed to make his way up into his sleeping quarters. He entered the room carrying only his swords on his back and his new diamond shield. Sy was there waiting for him. When the door opened, Sy immediately rose in anticipation.

"Jakov, thank goodness you're alive. How did you go? Where is Iskandar?"

Jakov barely acknowledged Sy, exhausted as he was. He limped across the room and put down his swords and shield on the table. He slowly sat into a chair and groaned as he put his feet up. He then took a deep breath and only then looked at Sy.

"Iskandar has been taken to Dalazvar. He is now a prisoner of Morpeth."

"What happened to Mordecai? Did you catch him?"

"Yeah, I caught him. In the Yobi desert."

"What became of him?"

"He is dead. Though he died far too quickly for my liking."

"I'm sorry, Jakov. I knew there was malice in him. But I didn't think he was capable of such treachery."

"Don't be sorry Sy. He fooled us all. He was proud and we were naive. It was nobody's fault. No one expects to be betrayed by someone within their own circle."

"What are we to do now, then? Without Iskandar, what chance do we have?"

"This war started without Iskandar and it can finish without him too if we have to."

"You assume Iskandar is as good as dead."

"He might already be, for all we know." There was a noticeable sadness in Jakov's voice as he said that.

"Morpeth means to sacrifice him to Marduk. But he will only become a god if he sacrifices the both of you. He will use your brother as bait to capture you and then to sacrifice you both. It is no good to him just to kill one of you."

"I know, I know." Jakov took water and then spoke again. "It would be unwise for Morpeth to kill him right away."

"You know what that means? There is still hope Jakov. There is hope for Iskandar, for you, for all of us. This is a tragedy, a disaster, but it is not the end."

"I believe you Sy. I believe you because it is only thing we have left to believe in."

"Do you have a plan?"

"Yes, I do."

"And what is that?"

"We sneak into Dalazvar, rescue Iskandar, and kill Morpeth."

Sy laughed.

"Surely you're joking. Sneak into Dalazvar? Sneak into the imperial palace? That is impossible."

"No, it's not. It can be done. There are secret passages, tunnels, entrances."

"But who would know such things? They are called 'secret' passages for a reason."

"There is someone who knows. Someone who can help us. Someone who knows all of the secrets of the imperial palace."

"And who is privy that that information?"

"My mother."

Sy was visibly shocked.

"Prisca. That witch. I cannot imagine that she would help us sneak into Dalazvar, rescue Iskandar, and kill Morpeth."

"She is our only chance."

"But she wants you dead just as much as Morpeth. She also will become divine once you are sacrificed to Marduk."

"She has also been imprisoned by Morpeth for almost ten years. Their madness drove them against each other. She might be far more willing to act against Morpeth than we think. Her lust for divinity may be surpassed by her hatred of Morpeth."

"Then what do you propose?"

Jakov smiled.

"I propose that we rescue her from the Masavar fortress. Then she can lead us into Dalazvar and to Morpeth."

"Listen to yourself. Rescue Prisca? This is lunacy."

"That is precisely why it will work."

"How do you know that?"

"Of all the things that Morpeth expects us to do, I doubt that he expects his own wife to lead us into Dalazvar. The madness is our method."

"Well, I guess that we'll certainly have the element of surprise. But how do you know she'll cooperate?"

"I'll make sure she will."

"And how is that?"

"If she doesn't assist, I will remove her head from her body. Then we can see how an immortal dies."

"Killing her might not be that easy, given her strange powers."

"If she's not a god, then she can bleed and die."

"Well, it is certainly a courageous plan. I hope it works."

Just then the door swung open and Talkai came in. He looked very tired and weary. For the first time, Jakov noticed just how old Talkai looked.

"Where is Iskandar?" he asked.

"Talkai," Jakov responded, "He was taken by Mordecai. He is now in Dalazvar. Morpeth has him."

"No," Talkai screamed and threw his hands into his face.

"I'm sorry Talkai. I did everything I could."

"Will he kill him?" he asked between the sobs.

"Not yet. We don't know for sure. There is a good chance that he will keep him alive, at least for a while."

"Why did you have to take him into battle Jakov? He's only a boy."

"I'm sorry Talkai. But this is a battle that we both had to fight."

"He's a boy. Can't you let him be one?"

"I will do everything I can to get him back."

"You better. He's like a son to me Jakov. You bring him back to me. I'm his best friend. I love him. Don't let anything bad happen to him."

"I love my brother too Talkai. There is nothing that I won't do to rescue him."

"Then take me with you."

"No, we've been through this before. I left you at Devora and you found your way here. I sharen't make the same mistake again. The best thing you can do is get out of my way and let me do what I need to do."

"I want to come and help. I'm not as stupid as everyone thinks I am. I can swing a sword when I have to. I'm not afaid."

"Talkai, listen to me. If you love Iskandar then you have to trust me. Wait in Norella and I will bring him to you. I promise on my own life, you will see your friend again."

Sy added a few words, "I promise you the same Talkai. We will find him for you, I swear."

"You better keep this promise Jakov. Bring him back to me. I want to see my little Bobbascow again. He'll always be Bobba to me."

Jakov stood and looked Talkai square in the eye.

"There are no forces in this world strong enough to keep me from my little brother. I will rescue him or die trying."

"I believe in you. I believe in him too. Bring him home to me."

"We will."

Talkai slowly left the room and closed the door. The room seemed empty, but more peaceful in his absence. Sy came over to where Jakov was standing near the table.

"He's a fool, but he's a loving fool. He is a good friend to Iskandar."

"I know. If he had half a brain more he might even make a good soldier."

Sy noticed the shield on the table.

"What on earth is this? Such ornate workmanship. Is this a weapon or a decoration?"

"Both, I think. It's a shield designed specifically to repel Morpeth's power over fire."

"Most interesting. Where did you get this from? I've never seen any-thing like it."

"Let's just say that it was a gift from an old friend."

"An old friend? And what old friend would that be?"

"If I told you, you wouldn't believe me."

"I'm learning to believe alot of strange things these days."

Jakov smiled, tired as he was, and added, "But this is another one of those unbelievable stories."

"Let me guess, does it involve a certain knight and a certain dragon?"

"That's only the start of it."

# Chapter 19

## Rescue at Masavar

ISKANDAR SAT IN A room blindfolded. He knew it was dark, dreary, and damp. Even without seeing it, he could feel it all around him. Iskandar occasionally heard footsteps and voices in the room outside him. He was tied up and too scared to move. Every now and then he cried, believing that he was to die soon. After some time, he heard the metal jiggling of a lock being turned. There were whispers about him and then more foot steps. He sensed a person now in the room with him and he began shaking uncontrollably. Then soft hands touched his face and startled him. Next the sleeves on Iskandar's shirt were rolled up and the person touched the tattoo on his forearm. The tattoo seemed to either alarm or annoy the person in the room as he let out a grunt at the sight of the tattoo. There was a slight pause then the same person undid the ropes around his arms and that brought instant relief from the tightness and constriction on his wrists. Next, the blindfold was removed. Iskandar looked up and saw a figure dressed in black who looked like a shadow in the room.

"Hello Iskandar," the man said.

"H-He-Hell-Hello" he sputtered, almost paralyzed in fear.

"Do you know who I am?"

Iskandar looked over the man. He had a dark olive complexion, and long hair that was dark as the night with hints of grey throughout. His beard was the same but more grey than black. His green eyes stood out as the only color on his face. The skin around his eyes looked wrinkled, but not aged. The man was dressed all in black from his boots to his cape. The only thing not black was a gold belt around his waist and a gold chain that clipped onto his cape.

"Are you Morpeth?" he asked timidly.

"I am your father. And forgive me child, for I am a poor one."

Morpeth bent down and looked into the boy's eyes. Iskandar looked away. He was confused since he felt so terrified by the strange man, but the man looked at him with great emotion, great feeling. It was almost like he was restraining his affection for Iskandar. Morpeth rubbed Iskandar's head with his hand and noticed part of his cheek was bruised and swollen.

"What a fine boy you've become. And powerful too. When sons fight their fathers in battle, usually trying to seize the throne, it is normally in their late teens or twenties, but you did it before reaching your teens. You have been victorious twice against me, with the help of your brother Jakov. Together you make a formidable force."

"Are you going to kill me?"

Morpeth stood up and looked away from him.

"Now is not the time to discuss morbid things. I haven't seen you for so long son. Ten years has been too long. I have missed you. I miss your brother. I miss all of your brothers and sisters."

"Then why did you kill them?" Iskandar boldly asked.

"There are realities in this world, the world above, and the next world that you cannot understand. But they have been revealed to me. You don't have to understand them Iskandar, but know that I act with the good cause and good concern for our family. Only in the end will you understand."

"You killed them and you're going to kill me and Jakov."

"I will explain it to you sometime soon, you don't have to understand, you only have to believe in me. Believe in my power. Let's not talk of death for now. I didn't come down here to kill you. I wanted to see my son, to hold your hand, and to look into your eyes. I have longed for this moment for so many years."

Morpeth took Iskandar by his hands and stared into him.

"You look like your mother."

"Is she dead?"

"No, she is very much alive. Though sadly she does not make for the best company these days. Immortality affected us differently and hurt our love for one another. Let's just say that since then we have gone our separate ways. I know she would love to see you. She'd be proud of you, just as I am."

"I want to leave here and go back to Jakov."

"I'm rather counting on Jakov coming to you."

"I know that you plan to catch him."

"Yes, it's true, I do plan that. I've been trying to catch him for eight years. He is quite elusive. Yet this time I hope to succeed."

"What makes you think that you can catch him this time?"

"This time I have something he wants: You. You will bring Jakov to me. And then the great rebirth can take place. I will be reborn as a god. And then I will put everything to right. Even the death of my children."

"Jakov said that your faith in Marduk has made you mad."

"Jakov does not know what he talks about."

"I miss my brother."

"So do I, son. So do I."

Morpeth sat next to Iskandar on another chair.

"They tell me that you were found in Praschi. A little hamlet in southern Iona. Full of farmers. I've never been there, though I hear it is nice, especially in spring. What was it like there?"

"Alright."

"Were your cared for there?"

"I was a servant."

"Outrageous. A prince of Iona living as a man servant. A travesty. Who raised you?"

"An inn-keeper named Wringstone. He and my friend Talkai both did."

"You don't know what happened to your uncle Fallkirk, do you?"

"Who?"

"Your uncle Fallkirk. He is the one who took you from me. He hid you and Jakov. He did it with the assistance of that do-gooding deity Vetrius and his priests. They blessed you and cursed me. But no matter. Marduk is stronger than Vetrius. We shall prevail. Did you know your uncle Fallkirk?"

"No. I don't know him."

"Pity. I have a score to settle with him. He was quite a nuisance to me. I understood his objection. My religion seems like madness to him. But I would like to teach him a lesson about meddling in affairs that don't concern him."

"I don't remember ever seeing or meeting a person named Fallkirk."

"Bah, no matter. What about friends? Did you have friends? Or school? Did you learn to read and write?"

Iskandar was silent.

"I don't feel like talking," he said.

Morpeth looked down at him.

"I understand entirely. Meeting your father is a big thing. You are no doubt scared and confused. I just wanted to see you. Make sure you got to meet your father properly before, well, before we attend to other things."

Morpeth walked towards the door and then turned.

"Iskandar, not everything that Jakov told you about me is true. I'm not some evil creature. I seek only to serve Marduk, my subjects, and my family. I am driven by devotion, not hatred."

Iskandar said nothing and looked away.

"I understand that this is hard for you, so I won't stay long. Get some rest. You will need it. Before long, I will be back to talk to you some more. We still have much to talk about. Much catching up to do. So rest easy my son."

Morpeth closed the door behind him, locked it, and walked down the corridor where Balthasar was waiting. Balthasar bowed, smiling as if he were pleased with himself.

"I trust that your son pleases you, divinity?" he said with his bald head bowed.

Morpeth responded by grabbing him by the throat and pinning him against the wall several inches off the ground.

"His face is bruised and swollen Balthsasar."

"It wasn't me, it was Mordecai," Balthasar said with a choking whisper.

"I ordered him not to be harmed and you were responsible."

"I'm sorry master, forgive me."

"I don't forgive. It is not in my divine nature."

Morpeth's hand glowed with warmth and it singed the skin of Balthasar who screamed out from the searing heat around his neck. Finally, Morpeth released him. Balthasar spat on his hands and applied the saliva to his neck that was red with a mild burn.

"You remain faithful to me Balthasar, which is why you are still alive. But I hold the power of life and death in this world and soon in the next. So be far more attentive to my orders or you will suffer in this life and in the next."

"Yes divinity," Balthasar responded with a mix of fear and contempt in his voice.

"Now let us go hence. We have another son to catch."

Jakov, Ayesha, and Sy slowly crawled up the rocky slope of the steep hillside. It was dawn, the sun was rising, and they were tired from the ride from Norella to the ridge overlooking the Masavar fortress. The fortress was locked deep within a rugged and barren range of mountains in the northeast of Iona. Trolls, bandits, and other creatures inhabited the mountain range, making it the most dangerous place in the country. The fortress itself consisted of four large towers in a diamond formation ringed by a wall over 70 feet high. In the centre of the fortress was another building, taller than all the others, almost 150 feet high. It was circular in shape and its thin neck became wider at its top. The central tower was called the carcerium which functioned either as an impregnable fortress or an imperial prison for members of the royal family who misbehaved. In the history of Iona many princes had been exiled there until the king or queen had died or until it was believed that the prince had learned his lesson. The carcerium was surrounded by a deep pit filled with terrifying animals ready to pounce on any prey that fell into it. The carcerium had no door, no stairs, or ladders. The only way into the carcerium was through a rope that was tied from the western tower of the fortress all the way up to the balcony of the carcerium. The rope stretched up diagonally over the pit of wild animals on an acute angle. The top of the carcerium contained an apartment furnished with all the trappings and luxuries that royalty liked, except for freedom. The rope reaching from the western tower to the carcerium had a pulley and a basket. This was how provisions and information was conveyed from the garrison to the hostage in the carcerium. The garrison consisted of twenty five soldiers commanded by a captain and a beastmaster who took care of the animals in the pit around the carcerium. The Masavar fortress was infamous for the motto inscribed on its front gate: "None shall enter, none shall depart." As a refuge against attack or a prison for wayward youths, either way, the edifice looked impregnable to Jakov, Ayesha, and Sy. They looked down on the fortress from the safety of their ridge, even though the carcerium rose up to nearly the height that they were at.

"Something tells me that this is not going to be easy," complained Sy to Ayesha.

"I never said it would be easy Sy," retorted Jakov, "I said it would harder than anything we've done."

"You have no objections from me on that assessment."

Ayesha looked over the fortress very closely and then spoke.

"There are at best only twenty to thirty men in the entire fortress. Only one or two guards are on watch in each tower at any one time. At this time of morning there are only four to eight guards on duty at the most.

They will be weary and tired from the night watch. Now is the best time to sneak in."

"Tell me again Jakov, why we cannot just reduce the fortress to rubble and drag that witch out from whatever rock she falls underneath?" uttered Sy.

"Because, my one-eyed friend, we don't want Morpeth to know we've been here and because we can't afford to kill Prisca in the process of trying to free her from this place."

"Understandable, I suppose."

Jakov looked at Ayesha.

"Are Mo and Tar in place?"

Ayesha looked down below at a goat trail that led into a narrow a pass between two escarpments that came to the western tower. It was that tower that had the pulley and the basket.

"Are we ready then?" Jakov asked.

Sy and Ayesha nodded.

"Ready as we shall ever be," replied Ayesha.

"Ready to see how you pull this one off," added Sy.

"Okay then," smiled Jakov, "Let's free Prisca from this prison."

≈ ≈ ≈

Mo and Tar sneaked along the canyon leading towards the fortress. The two dwarves moved from shadow to shadow to escape the exposing light of the crescent moon above them. Ayesha, Jakov, and Sy watched from the ridge above as the duo came closer and closer. Finally Mo and Tar came to the base of the western tower. Eighteen feet above them was a small window with a light inside. The occasional movement of a person could be seen therein.

"They are in place," muttered Jakov softly.

"Then, it is my turn to join them," responded Sy.

The Cyclops got up off the ground and slowly began to make his way down the ridge as quietly as he could. The ground was slippery. A mixture of sand and rocks made it hard to stay balanced at pace. Sy managed to move down the hill with stealth and silence so that he even surprised Mo and Tar as he emerged from the dark. The trio leaned up against the wall so as not to create a shadow with their silhouette.

Ayesha turned to Jakov.

"See you on the inside," she said as she rose from the ground as well.

Ayesha moved down the ridge more quickly than Sy. With her fantastic speed and poise she was able to glide down like someone riding a sled down a snowy mountain. Once at the bottom she slowly crept over towards where Mo, Tar, and Sy were standing as still as statues.

"Ready when you are," she whispered to Sy.

"Okay, let's get into position boys," Sy said to Mo and Tar.

At his word, Mo kneeled on the ground on all fours like he was pretending to be a puppy. A few paces away, Tar was bent over with his hands on his knees and his back facing towards Ayesha. Sy leaned against the wall on a sharp angle with his hands high above his head. Ayesha thought the sight looked funny, but it was the makeshift staircase she needed to climb up to be able to get into the tower.

"This going to hurt," Sy said to himself.

Ayesha took a few steps backwards and then she rushed forward at her superfast speed. She put her right foot on Mo's back, her left foot on Tar's back, and her right foot on Sy's head. The dwarves and Sy all let out a quiet "oomph" as she stomped on them. Yet her speed with the added height gave her enough momentum to scurry up the wall of the tower.

She treaded quickly up the jagged wall with the momentum helping her climb upwards. Reaching high, she was just able to grab hold of the roof of the tower with the window. Swinging herself back and forth, she then threw herself through the open and narrow window feet first. She landed inside with a light clap. A guard was sitting on the chair in a room with a single candle on the table between them. When Ayesha landed, the guard woke up, jolted by the noise and startled by the sight. He leaned over and grabbed his sword and stood up, though still looking half asleep. Yet before he could move or say anything, Ayesha jumped over the table and, spinning around, she drove her heel into his head. The force pushed him back against the wall and left him falling to the ground unconscious. There was a slight noise when his sword fell to the ground. Ayesha checked and the guard was out cold.

Ayesha looked about the room. It was circular with a high roof that narrowed in the middle. The room had two exits that followed the wall of the fortress and led to the southern and northern towers. She carefully glanced out of the doorways to see if anyone was coming. There was nothing. No noise, only silence coming from the other towers. Across the room she could see a basket and a pulley with a rope that led high up to the carcerium.

Turning around, Ayesha poked her head out of the window she had jumped through and whistled a bird noise.

"That's the signal," said Sy to Mo and Tar.

Tar took a deep breath and Mo swallowed as if they were very afraid of what was going to happen next. Sy just smiled as he grabbed Mo by the back of his shirt and the top of his trousers. After three big practice swings, Sy threw the little man high into the air towards the window.

Mo let out a quiet, nervous noise, "Ookiemamma" as he flew through the air.

Ayesha caught him and slowly pulled him into the window.

Next, Sy turned to Tar who was now shaking his head and mumbling something that Sy guessed meant, "I don't want to do it now."

Sy grinned as Tar tried to run away. The cyclops picked up the little man, who was squirming. In the same manner as before, he leaned back and then forward and with a big heave he tossed the little man high into the night sky where Ayesha caught him under his arm pits and helped him into the tower room.

"Chaniwowa fooki," Tar cried as he stood up in the room. In dwarfish that meant, "time for new underpants."

In the meantime, Jakov had come down the ridge and was now standing beside Sy.

"I do believe that the rest is up to you my friend," he muttered to Jakov.

"Be ready to catch me when I jump down," Jakov replied.

"Sure thing, I'll be waiting for you."

Jakov threw a rope up to Ayesha who caught it on the second try. Ayesha and the two dwarves held the rope tight as Jakov climbed up and finally entered the room as well. Jakov quickly surveyed the room and instantly noticed the rope, basket, and pulley. On the ground he then saw the unconscious guard. Looking at Ayesha, he cocked his eyebrow in surprise.

"Deadly and efficient as always, I see, Ayesha."

"I get the job done."

"Our next job is to get me into the carcerium."

Jakov inspected the basket.

"It is too small to hold me. Possibly one of the dwarves could fit into it."

Mo and Tar looked at themselves and then at Jakov and shook their heads violently.

"That is okay. I know that dwarves are afraid of heights. This climb is not for you, my friends. I'll do this one alone."

"Can you make it that high?" Ayesha asked.

Jakov looked over the rope that led high up into the carcerium. He looked at the tower and the pit beneath it. If he fell, he knew that the impact would kill him. If not the fall, then the beasts in the pit below would rip him apart in a matter of seconds.

"Let's just hope that I don't fall. But you'll have to use the pulley to get me up there faster."

Mo and Tar stood by the doors with their eyes fixed on the other towers, checking for movement and noise. Things looked clear so they gave Ayesha the thumbs up. Jakov climbed up onto the rope and positioned himself on top of the rope rather than underneath it. He did that by swinging himself on top of the rope and putting one leg on the rope behind him and another leg under the rope as a balance. He took only one sword with him so that his balance and speed would not be too badly inhibited. Once on the rope he began sliding upwards. It took a great deal of strength with his arms to drag himself along. But to make the journey quicker Ayesha was pushing him forward by using the rope as a pully and pulling on the parallel rope opposite Jakov. Jakov was smart enough to know not to look down and it didn't matter when he accidentally did because all he could see below him and above him was black. He felt enveloped by the dim twilight all around him. He could hear the sound of the odd animal in the pit below, growling and howling, but it was not overly loud. As Jakov looked up, he could see the carcerium coming closer and closer as he climbed towards it. The apartment had a little balcony which the rope connected to. Behind the balcony was a curtain and Jakov could see a faint light coming from behind it. As he thought about who layed behind it, he was filled with anger and also nervousness. His jaw tightened with hatred and his stomach soured with sickness. Now, for the first time in ten years, he would see his mother, and confront the murderer of his brothers and his sisters. As heavy and tight as his arms felt, the rage that set in made him climb even faster.

Iskandar layed on his bed unable to sleep. His mind was filled with fear. A fear for himself and a fear as to what would happen to Jakov. He knew Jakov would come for him. He knew that Morpeth was counting on it. He wondered what Jakov would do. For several moments, he began thinking about Morpeth. Before he found out that he was the son of Morpeth he had always pictured his father as a quiet, soft-spoken person, with light brown hair, a joyous expression, and bright clothes. Someone he felt that his very presence would make him feel warm and joyous. Meeting Morpeth was the opposite of that. Morpeth seemed dark, macabre, and morbid in comparison. Something not right, something wicked, like a poison that entered his brain. Yet he also saw in Morpeth something else. Not only evil, but also goodness. Morpeth was genuinely happy to see him, almost affectionate in his manner towards Iskandar. He was like a man who had once known the feeling of love, but had long since forgotten it. It was as if Iskandar was now reminding him of something that he'd forgotten or had been told to forget. Iskandar could sense the struggle in him. Morpeth's power and desire for a divine power consumed him, yet he somehow remained a father, even if only a broken one. Iskandar imagined for a moment what Morpeth would have been like if he had not been seduced by Marduk. Would he have been a good and noble man, a kind father, and a loving husband? But it didn't matter now. Now Morpeth was going to kill him, one way or the other, and that was the only thing he could dwell on now. Jakov was in danger as well. For the first time, his fear had begun to turn to hate as he remembered that he would probably never see Aurora again or his niece and nephew. He took a cup of water from the bedside table, the only other piece of furniture in the room, and he drank from it. He left some water at the bottom of the cup and using his power, he made it swirl around in the cup, dance about, make a little whirlpool, and splash about from side to side. It was then he decided that he had to do something rather than just wait for Jakov. He had to try to escape.

# Chapter 20

## Jakov Meets Prisca

JAKOV CAME TO THE balcony of the carcerium. He gently swung himself forward off the rope and landed with a light thud. His arms were sore and weary from the climb. He looked around to make sure no one could see him. The other towers showed no sign of movement and he could hear only the faintest growling of the wild beasts at the base of the carcerium. One thing that Jakov did notice was that he was incredibly high. The carcerium was a massive structure and it felt even larger when one stood on the balcony of the apartment.

Jakov stood on the balcony and in front of him was a curtain. On the other side of that curtain he knew was his mother. He took out his sword since he did not know what to expect. She would still be dangerous and he didn't trust her to help him. He was about to walk through the curtain when he froze. Jakov felt nervous and his hands were shaking slightly. Part of him wanted to charge into the apartment and behead the woman in there. He had imagined doing that so many times in the past. But then he experienced a flood of memories that he had long since tried to suppress. He remembered crying and his mother comforting him. He remembered kisses and cuddles in front of a warm fire. He remembered playing with toy horses and his mother clapping for him. He remembered the warmth of her smile and the tenderness of her touch.

Those glowing memories were eclipsed by another memory, that of his brothers and sisters being murdered. That was all that mattered now, to him at least. Windows of happiness in his youth were now replaced with anger, an anger that filled his mind again. Anger and purpose steadied his hands now. With his sword raised, Jakov delicately pushed apart the curtains and slowly began walking into the room.

It would soon be fully light. Talkai sat alone on a stool in the stalls of the horses. He patted several of the horses and fed sugar cubes to some of them. Jakov, Sy, Ayesha, Mo and Tar had left at dawn the previous day. Jakov had told Talkai to stay put as they set out for the Masavar fortress, but he had disobeyed that order before, and with good results when he left Devora to go to Norella to make sure that Iskandar was okay without him. Talkai knew more than he let on and he knew that he still had a crucial part to play in this story.

The faint glow of the sun was now on the horizon. A new day was breaking. He wondered what it might have in store for Iskandar, for Jakov, and especially for him. He knew all along that he wasn't going to stay put there. He wasn't meant to. It was not in his nature. Talkai picked up his knapsack, tucked a small knife into his belt, and walked towards the door. He left the warmth of the stables and entered into the cool dawn air. Talkai started walking towards the front gate of the city, knowing full well that it was time for him to do what he had to do.

Jakov slowly stepped into the room. The apartment was simple. A small desk in a corner. A table with flowers on it. Some paintings of the ocean and forests on the walls. In the middle, however, was a lavish bed with four posts surrounded by a veil. Beside it was a bedside table with a candle on it. He could see the outline of a body sleeping in the bed under the covers. Drawing back the veil he could hear the sound of deep breathing as the woman slept and he noticed the long locks of her red hair spread over her face. After coming to one side of the bed, with his sword still raised, he slowly placed his foot against her back. Then, pushing forcefully with his foot, he called, "Wake up woman. It is time to leave."

Prisca groaned as she felt the force in her back.

"Go away," she complained. "At least until after dawn. It is a godless hour."

Jakov could not believe her contempt. It was like she was trying to ignore him. He kicked her again, this time harder.

"Get up woman. I have no time for your games."

Finally Prisca rolled over and looked at Jakov with an expression of annoyance.

"You are not meant to be in my apartment. The last guard who disturbed me was thrown into the beast pit. You better have a good reason for being here."

"I am no guard."

Jakov noticed her face now as she threw her hair back by shaking her head. She had a young complexion, even beautiful, though her hair looked untidy and unkept.

"Then who are you may I ask? Has Morpeth finally sent an executioner for me? Or are you some young suitor who has come to rescue me from this prison and to seek my affections?"

"I am neither."

"Then who are you? It is too early for silliness boy. What do you want?"

Jakov lowered his sword to her throat.

"Who do you think I am?"

"I don't know. The imperial blanket folder? The cleaner of horse dung for Morpeth's horses? Oh, and get that thing out of my face before I lose my patience."

Prisca knocked his sword out of her way with her hands. It made a slightly clanging sound. Jakov noticed that her hands had been bound together with steel bonds. That was how Morpeth kept her here. If Prisca's hands were bound she could not summon the wind or call to it. He took a step back so she could see him in the faint candlelight.

"Strange you do not recognize me. No doubt the years have changed me woman. Perhaps you have even tried to forget. But surely the face of a boy, a child, laying on a sacrificial altar in the temple of Marduk is not too hard for you to remember. For that is where you saw me last."

Prisca gasped and her eyes widened. She began shaking uncontrollably. Her lips trembled and tears started to stream down her cheeks.

"Jakov, is that really you?" she said beneath her sobs. "Oh, Jakov."

She leaned forward to embrace him as her sob turned into uncontrollable crying.

As she moved forward, Jakov's foot struck her in the chest and sent her crashing back onto her own bed. He lifted his sword up and pointed it at her throat again.

"Keep your distance witch. I know what you are and what you can do. You will come with me, you will do precisely as I say, or I will not hesitate in removing your head from your body. Indeed, I will not even blink."

Prisca was still crying.

"Jakov, I'm sorry, I'm so sorry. Marduk drove me mad. I'm sorry. But I've changed son. I'm free from that wicked man Morpeth and his deranged god. You have to believe me son. I wish I could take it all back. I wish I could die instead. I'm so sorry."

"You can tell me your tragic story later. For now, we have to get out of here. I need your help. It'll be alot easier if you're not blubbering like a lost puppy."

"For what?" she said as her tears stopped flowing.

"I need you to get me into Dalazvar so I can rescue Iskandar."

"Iskandar is alive?"

"Yes, he is."

"Then the prophecy is true, it is coming true."

Jakov showed her the tattoo of the snakes on his arm.

"You better believe it woman. Morpeth's tyranny, and yours as well, are coming to an end."

"Why do you think Morpeth imprisoned me here?"

"I don't know, and I don't care. Lovers' tiff, greed, anger. It's all the same to me."

"I tried to stop him. I saw how far we went. I saw the suffering we were causing. I saw what immortality did to me. I tried to stop him searching for you both. I tried to save you from him. And that is why he imprisoned me up here, bound in chains like a slave. A queen living like a slave in this filth."

"I'm deeply touched by your plight and I really wish I could believe you, but I don't."

"Why not?"

"I know what evil dwells in your heart."

"You don't know the heart of a mother. Even a broken one, even an unworthy one. I did great evil, I know I did, but a mother's love can overcome the power of Marduk's seduction. It did for me."

"Then time will tell me, Prisca, won't it? Until then, you are my prisoner, and I will be watching you like a hawk. Come on, let's get out of here."

Jakov grabbed her by the shoulder and pushed her towards the curtains leading to the balcony.

"Where are we going?" she asked.

"Out of here."

"But what about the guards?"

"Hopefully they are still sleeping."

Jakov dragged Prisca to the balcony. The sun was now on the horizon. It was morning. He looked down below and what he saw sent a shiver up his spine. On the ground below he could see Ayesha, Mo, and Tar kneeling at the edge of the beast pit right underneath them. Around them were over thirty men, all armed with swords, axes, and crossbows. Three men held swords at the throats of his three friends. Jakov gritted his teeth in frustration and began thinking how he could possibly get himself, his friends, and Prisca out of here.

Iskandar knocked on the door of his locked room and called for assistance.

"Guards, guards," the boy called.

There was a long silence and then footsteps could be heard on the other side of the door. From behind the large wooden door came a voice.

"What do you want?" the voice said with a gruff accent.

"I am thirsty. I need a jug of water."

There was another pause and after the clinking of keys in a lock the door swung open. At the door stood a huge burley man with no hair, a huge stomach, and several keys hanging from his belt.

"I want water," Iskandar said again. "It is hot in here."

"I am under strict orders not to give you anymore than half a cup of water every few hours. Apparently you are some magician or something, and I have to keep water from you."

"But I'm thirsty," complained Iskandar.

"Orders are orders little boy. No water for you."

The jailer was about to shut the door when Iskandar spoke again.

"What about some wine then?"

"Wine? You're a child. You can't have wine. You'll get drunk."

"I am a son of Morpeth, a prince of Iona. I am used to the finest wine and the richest food. I demand wine for my thirst if I cannot have water. Bring me wine or shall I tell my father that you have mistreated me. And you know what he'll do, don't you?"

The jailer scratched his head and he looked confused. He knew what Morpeth did to guards and soldiers who displeased him and he did not fancy dying in a firery blaze like so many others did. He looked down at the boy.

"Wine you want?"

"Yes, a small clay jug would be nice."

The jailer thought some more then spoke to Iskandar.

"Okay then. Wait here for a moment."

The jailer shut the door, locked it, and went away.

After several minutes the door opened and the jailer returned holding a jug.

"This is wine," he said as he passed the jug to Iskandar. "But be warned. It ain't royal wine. It's the cheap wine that they give to the soldiers. It don't taste that nice, but it will help your thirst."

"This will do fine," Iskandar smiled.

Iskandar looked into the jug of wine. It didn't smell that nice, not bad, just not very alluring. Wringstone had much nicer wines in his tavern in Praschi. Iskandar took a deep breath and brought the jug to his lips. He took a sip. It tasted as bad as he expected but he tried not to show it to the jailer.

Iskandar licked his lips pretending that he liked it. He tasted in the wine exactly what he hoped it had.

"I love this wine," he said to the jailer.

"Really?" the jailer said in surprise. "It is cheap grog. It doesn't taste nice, but it does get you drunk quickly."

"Well, I don't like the taste. But what I do like is that the wine has been heavily watered down."

"Why does that make the wine good?" the jailed asked curiously.

"Because it means that I can do this."

Iskandar took his hands off the jug and it was levitating in the air and then floating to the left and right. The jailer was staring in awe. He looked entertained rather than afraid.

"By Marduk's trousers, that is incredible. You really can do magic. How do you do that?"

Iskandar winked at him as the jug floated upwards towards the ceiling and came to rest at the same height as the jailer's head.

"It's easy. I can do it the same way that I can do this."

"And what's 'this'?" the jailer inquired.

"Watch!"

Iskander pushed his hand towards the jailer and the jug of wine rushed through the room and hit the jailer right in the face. It struck him so hard in fact that the jug broke and the jailer fell to the ground unconscious and covered in wine. To anyone who came by it would probably look like the jailer had been drunk. Although he wasn't drunk, he would certainly have a huge headache when he woke up.

Iskandar

Iskandar grabbed the keys from the belt of the jailer. He stood up straight, walked out of the door, locked it and then began walking down the corridor, looking for a place to hide or a door out of the palace.

# Chapter 21

## The Battle of Masavar

JAKOV STOOD THERE WITH a sword in one hand and holding Prisca by the arm with the other. He looked down at his friends who were forcibly kneeling at the edge of the beast pit with armed men all around them.

"We are trapped," Prisca whispered to him.

"Not yet," he replied without looking at her.

Down below one of the soldiers stepped forward. He was dressed in grey armour but with a green helmet. He called out loudly so that his voice could be heard at the top of the carcerium.

"Jakov, my name is Grudim. I am the captain of the Masavar fortress, and the jailer of Prisca, wife of Morpeth. Your rescue attempt has failed. My men have caught your friends. Unless you do exactly as I say, they will be thrown into the beast pit. And that is a fate worse than death."

"What do you want of me?" Jakov yelled downward.

"Let's talk terms for a surrender."

"Very well, I accept. Lay down your weapons and I promise no harm shall come to you or your men, Grudim."

Grudim looked very confused.

"Not us, you fool. You. You surrender or I will throw your friends into the beast pit."

"If you do that, I will destroy you and all of your men."

"I find that most unlikely."

"Don't be so sure."

Grudim grabbed Ayesha by her arms and pushed her right to the edge of the beast pit.

"I do not have time for negotiations boy. Make your choice. Surrender, or I kill the girl now."

"Don't do it Jakov," cried Ayesha.

"Silence, you," said Grudim as he pulled her hair back.

"Wait," called Jakov. "Give me a moment."

"Fine, but I don't have all day."

Jakov desperately looked around. On one of the towers he could see that Sy had climbed up and was ready with his axe if needed. Prisca turned to him.

"Break my bonds Jakov, and I will destroy them."

"I don't need your help."

"Yes, you do son. Break my bonds and I can use my power to save your friends and save you."

"I don't need you to save me witch."

"If not for you, then do it for your friends. Must they die too?"

For the first time, Jakov looked his mother in the eye. He noticed that her eyes were just like his and Iskandar's. A deep blue, like the ocean. He realized that he was quite taller than her too. It made him feel less threatened by her.

"Very well then. I will release you. But if you betray us, I will behead you."

"I shall not betray you my son. Never again could I hurt you. I will atone for my evil with good deeds."

"What is your answer?" yelled Grudim.

"Watch and observe my answer."

Jakov pushed Prisca back. He nodded. She held out her bonded arms, and Jakov raised up his sword and slashed downward with all of his strength. The sword smashed the bonds, but also drove Prisca to the ground from the power of its impact.

She got up off the ground and rubbed her wrists and had a look of satisfaction and longing on her face.

"For eight years I have worn those bonds around my arms. For eight years I have suffered in this prison under that man."

Grudim saw what Jakov did in breaking Prisca's bonds.

"No," he yelled in panic. "You fool. What did you do that for? She will kill us all."

"Not all of you," Prisca replied. "Only most of you. But especially you, Grudim."

Prisca threw her hands forward and a huge storm of sands and dust swirled about, making vision impossible. The soldiers below shielded their faces from the wind and sand.

Mo and Tar turned their backs to avoid the wind. When the soldiers holding them weakened their grip, they turned around and head butted them in the groin. The two soldiers recoiled in pain and Mo and Tar grabbed two swords lying on the ground and ran towards one of the towers where Sy was stationed.

Grudim tried to block the sand from his eyes. Sensing his loss of sight, Ayesha elbowed him in the stomach. The blow made him grimace, yet before she could escape from his grasp, he pushed her forward and she fell into the beast pit. Grudim turned and ran.

Prisca waved her hands around as the sand and wind punished the men below. Several ran in all directions but miniature whirlwinds pursued each one and punished them by tossing them about. Several were struck against the side walls of the fortress, while two were cast into the beast pit. She was cackling in laughter as she watched the display of her own power.

Jakov saw Ayesha fall into the beast pit. He quickly leapt up and grabbed onto the rope that led down to the western tower. He quickly slid down the rope with his hand that was gloved. Although he felt his hand get very hot, his glove stopped it from burning. When he had slid far enough down the rope, he used his sword to cut it in front of him. Instantly, he began swinging back towards the carcerium, but he was swinging low enough that he was descending into the beast pit with the propulsion carrying him downwards.

He saw Ayesha running speedily around the carcerium, being chased by wolves the size of cows. With her speed she could dodge them easily. The beasts lunged at her only to miss again and again. Some of the other wolves were busy tearing apart the few soldiers who had fallen in, the rest chased after Ayesha. Ayesha was always a move ahead of the wolves. She jumped over some of the wolves, kicked some on the head as she dodged them, and tripped others. Ayesha was too fast for them, but Jakov knew that she couldn't do it forever.

As he swung downwards Jakov called out to to her.

"Ayesha, over here."

Jakov spoke to her as the momentum took him upwards and out of the pit. A few seconds later he was up in the sky, but then he began swinging downwards again into the beast pit.

Ayesha could see where he was and where Jakov was heading. Making even greater speed, she ran over to where she thought she could grab hold of Jakov as he swung through again. Two wolves dived at her simultaneously, but she jumped causing the two wolves to clash heads under her feet and fall down, sulking in pain. She jumped from the side of the base of the carcerium to the side of the pit, narrowly missing the claws that struck after her. Jakov swung past and held out his hand. Ayesha just got there in time to grab hold of his hand. A wolf scratched at her boot, but it was not enough to stop her. Holding onto Jakov, they swung upwards out of the beast pit and Ayesha let go when they were high enough. She landed on her feet and looked behind her to see where Jakov was. He was still holding the rope and before he could let go and land like Ayesha, the rope had changed direction again and was swinging back into the beast pit.

As he descended into the pit, he saw the pack of huge wolves with yellow eyes, growling, with ferocious fangs waiting for him to come closer. The wolves jumped at him and Jakov stabbed two with his sword and curled his legs up to narrowly avoid being bitten. The rope swung upwards again, but now the momentum was fading. It wasn't going high enough to rise above the edge of the beast bit. As the trajectory went upwards, Jakov tried to lift his legs high enough to reach the top of the pit. He got his feet on top and tried to use them to pull himself upwards, but it was no use. He began to swing downwards again into the beast pit back towards the wolf pack waiting to devour him.

Jakov started scurrying up the rope as fast as he could. By the time he got to the lowest part of the beast pit, he was now out of reach of the wolves. But the rope had lost its momentum completely. It swung from side to side a few times and then came to a stand still. Jakov kept climbing upwards towards the balcony on top of the carcerium. Below him two of the wolves had grabbed the rope and were violently pulling it and trying to make him lose his grip and fall. Jakov quit trying to climb and held on for dear life as the rope shook violently all about. He knocked into the side of the carcerium a few times and struggled to keep his senses. Finally, he felt his grip on the rope give away and he was falling downwards.

He fell on top of one wolf, but stabbed it with his sword on impact. Jakov got to his feet. The howling wolf made the others keep their distance for a moment. Yet not long long after they started barking, growling, and slowly moving towards Jakov. In the pit he was armed only with his sword and over a dozen wolves were pressing on him from his left and right.

Jakov saw several stones on the ground before him. They were small, but heavy. He kicked them and launched them into the air. Using his power, he made them strike the wolves right on their heads. The wolves slowed their movement towards him, growled in response to the annoying volley of rocks, but it was not enough to stop them. Jakov ran out of rocks and the wolves were getting closer.

All of a sudden there was a gust of wild wind in the pit, then it turned into a gale, and then it had the ferocity of a storm. Jakov stabbed his sword into the ground in order to stop himself from being blown over. The wolves barked at the wind and were gradually pushed backwards away from Jakov. Jakov looked up and saw Prisca pointing her hands downwards and controlling the wind. Despite the powerful wind, Jakov sheathed his sword and began climbing up the rope again as the wolves were tossed about the beast pit like ragdolls in a box.

Jakov reached the top carcerium, and lurched onto the balcony where Prisca was still. He was tired and out of breath. Prisca looked at him with genuine concern.

"Are you alright my son?"

"I am fine. You did well."

"Are you going to thank me?"

Point blank, Jakov said, "No."

Jakov looked over the balcony. Sy and Ayesha were fighting off the last of Grudim's men. The rest were lying strewn on the ground, partly buried in sand. For the past few minutes Prisca's mighty wind had tossed them about the fortress grounds and smashed them into walls. Grudim was lying on the ground with Mo and Tar standing on his arms, with their axes poised ready to strike in case he should try move. Once the last remaining guards were despatched, Sy and Ayesha come over to the edge of the beast pit and looked upwards towards Jakov and Prisca.

"How do you propose to get down now?" Sy called out.

"Good question," added Prisca.

"Watch," retorted Jakov.

Jakov raised his hands and clenched his fists. In that moment, the balcony came free from the carcerium. Prisca stumbled and looked about in a surprise.

"What manner of magic is this?" she asked.

"Mine," Jakov replied.

Slowly the stone balcony floated from on high until it rested down on the ground beneath.

"That was a rather direct route," commented Sy.

Jakov looked at Prisca and then at his two friends.

"By way of introduction, this is Prisca, wife of Morpeth. Prisca this is Sy, Ayesha, and over there is Mo and Tar."

"A pleasure to be freed by you, you have my utmost gratitude."

Sy and Ayesha were silent, stunned. They didn't know what to say. Ayesha managed a nervous smile and Sy grunted politely.

"What do we do with him?" asked Ayesha, pointing to Grudim.

"I have an idea," interjected Prisca.

The four walked over to Grudim who still had Mo and Tar standing over him. Along the way, Prisca picked up a sword that was lying on the ground. Jakov did not take his eyes off her as she held the sword and he noticed that she quickened her pace as she got closer to Grudim.

The group of friends and Prisca stood around Grudim. Mo and Tar backed away.

"You're a fool, letting that witch go. Morpeth sent her here for a reason you know. You have unleashed hell upon us all."

"Silence," demanded Prisca. "You kept me in that prison for eight long years. You kept me, a queen, prisoner here in this hole. I longed to have your head for what you put me through these years Grudim. I would have rewarded you if you set me free, but you would not listen. You treated me with contempt, like a slave, rather than with the honour that I deserve. For that, I will enjoy watching you die."

Prisca raised her sword and plunged it downwards towards Grudim. But its path was blocked by Jakov's sword.

"He doesn't die, Prisca."

"Why not? He's my imprisoner. He deserves to die. He dishonoured me. A queen. An immortal."

"I said he lives."

"Why should he live Jakov? After what he did?"

Jakov stopped and looked away from everyone and then looked Prisca in the eye.

"It is called mercy."

"I say he is to die."

"It is not yours to decide woman." Jakov raised his sword and pointed it at Prisca. "And you will submit to my commands from here on, or else."

Prisca stared at his sword and then dropped her own. Her annoyance was clear.

"If I wanted you dead Jakov, you would be dead by now. So don't threatenen me, son. There is a time for mercy and a time for compassion, but he does not deserve . . ."

Jakov interrupted her words with a scream of rage and he pushed her backwards with his hand, "What do you know about mercy and compassion? Did you show my brothers compassion? Did you show my sisters mercy? Your own children, Prisca! Did you?"

Prisca turned away from him, unable to look at him or to be looked at. Taking a moment to compose herself, she turned and spoke in a broken voice.

"Maybe one day you'll realize how sorry I am for what I've done. And soon, hopefully you'll learn how changed I am as well."

"I won't be holding my breath Prisca."

Sy loudly cleared his throat trying to remove the tension in the air.

"If we are not going to kill him, then what do we do with him?" the cyclops asked.

"Tie him up, place him in one of the towers. We'll have enough lead time on him before he can alert any one to what has happened here."

Sy and Ayesha grabbed Grudim by the collar and dragged him away.

"Thank you Jakov," Grudim said as he was led away.

Jakov ignored him and Prisca gave him a piercing look of utter hatred.

Jakov sent Mo and Tar out the front gate to get the horses as they would ride soon for Dalazvar. He walked towards the front gate and Prisca followed him, not knowing where else to go. As he walked along she questioned him.

"So where are we going?"

"I told you. Dalazvar," he said, still walking ahead of her.

"And what is there?"

"You will lead us into Dalazvar through the secret entrance. I will kill Morpeth and rescue Iskandar."

"What is to become of me after that?"

"That depends."

"On what?"

Jakov stopped and faced her.

"If you help us, I will let you live. If you betray us, I will not hesistate in severing your head from your body. Then the immortal Prisca will taste mortality."

"Why do you hate me so?"

"I'll give you four guesses."

Prisca froze, she had nothing to say.

"Brutoi, Karla, Crestin, and Izza. Do those names mean anything to you? The names of your own children that you slaughtered?"

"More than heaven and earth Jakov."

"More like hell. That is what you and that god of yours brought us. Hell on earth."

"Then do with me as you wish. I cannot change the past. I will help you. Not to save my life, but to save yours. I hope to prove to you that I have changed. I no longer serve Marduk. I will serve my children instead. Have some faith in me, I am your mother."

"When I refer to you, it will not be as my mother."

"Don't you remember life, our family, before ... before the unpleasantness? You had memories of happiness, laughter, frolicking, and fun"

"Those memories died with my brothers and sisters."

"Will killing Morpeth bring them back?"

"No, but his death will bring justice to pass. For me, and for the whole land of Iona. This country has been defiled by his wickedness and by yours. Tonight, we will cleanse the land of evil and a new era of purity and peace can begin."

"You are consumed by anger."

"I call it justice. But no more talk. Now we travel."

"I do love you, son."

"No more talk!" Jakov snapped at her. "You'll speak when spoken to."

Jakov and Prisca then passed through the gate of the Masavar Fortress. Behind them were Sy and Ayesha. They heard the conversation between Jakov and Prisca and exchanged whispers with one another. Mo and Tar brought over five horses including Jakov's Infamy. Prisca was quiet, clearly unsettled and hurt by Jakov's words. Sy helped her onto her horse. Mo and Tar took one horse together and Sy and Ayesha mounted up as well on their own horses.

"Where to now, Jakov?" asked Sy.

"Where do you think?" he answered back with a grin.

"Glory or death?" answered Ayesha.

"This will be one family reunion to remember," added Prisca, but Jakov ignored her.

"Krungi karzumi mi mufti," muttered Mo to Ayesha softly.

"I know. And I thought my family was messed up."

The group walked through the mountains for three hours and once they reached some plains they galloped at speed. Sy led the way with Ayesha close by, followed by Mo and Tar. Behind them was Prisca, who was carefully watched from behind by Jakov. He didn't take his eyes off her the whole ride. Along the way, though, he wondered if it was true. Had she really changed?

≈ ≈ ≈

It was now mid-morning as Iskandar walked through the hall. Lucky for him, the palace was so immense that one could walk for ages without seeing a single servant or soldier. Finally, he walked into a room that contained a big window. He looked out the window and saw that it was only several feet from the ground below. Iskandar gently opened the window and it made a click that was too loud for his liking. As he did that, he heard someone coming down the hall, some servants carrying trays. He froze and his heart was beating loudly, but they walked down an adajacent corridor without seeing him. Once they had gone away, he finished opening the window. Then he climbed up and gradually lowered himself out the window onto the ground. Iskandar landed on the cobblestone ground with a thud and he rolled along the ground and grazed his knee. It hurt, but it wasn't a bad injury.

He looked around. The palace was in the middle of the city near streets, people, and much movement. He quickly hid behind some bushes nearby. People were moving about the place. Markets were open, and he could even hear children playing in a nearby street. It would be easy to blend in and disappear. The problem was that everyone would be looking for him. It wouldn't be long before Morpeth had realized that he had escaped.

Iskandar ran over to another bunch of bushes near a road side. There were some clothes hung out on a clothes line nearby. Making sure that no one was watching, Iskandar leaned over and grabbed a yellow cloak with a hood that was just his size. He put it on and then walked out into the street. The hood covered his face. Although he felt virtually naked, like everyone was watching him, he walked down the street into the square. He moved quickly from the square to the streets that zig-zagged across the city, trying to blend in with the passers-by. He took shelter for a time behind some barrels of beer adjacent a tavern. He sat still for a while, listened to the conversations of people nearby, and looked out for guards in the area. After some time, he arose again and began walking about, wondering where the exit to the city was. The further he got away from the palace the better he felt, though he desperately hoped that no one thought him suspicious or recognized him. He also hoped that no one had seen him escape from the palace.

But he had been seen fleeing the palace. Two people had seen him jump out of the window in fact. He had been seen by one person in the tower above the palace and by another person outside the palace in the street who had already begun following him from a distance. Despite all his caution and care, Iskandar did not know that the whole time he was being followed.

# Chapter 22

## Iskandar's Escape and Jakov's Journey

BALTHASAR HAD SEEN ISKANDAR jump out the window when inspecting the guards on the watch tower on top of the palace. The tower gave a good view of the whole city. At first, Balthasar thought it was a thief who was sneaking out of the palace, but the movements and gestures of the boy were familiar enough. The last thing Balthasar saw was Iskandar putting on the yellow cloak and disappearing into the crowd.

He rubbed his bald head in frustration. Morpeth would not be happy about this. Someone was going to burn, hopefully not him. He dispatched a messenger to go and notify Morpeth of the escape. He sent the messenger knowing full well that he would probably not be seen alive again. Balthasar quickly dispatched another messenger to the local guard and to the imperial spies to be on the lookout for a boy in a yellow cloak.

Balthasar walked down the stairs of the palace, longing for the day where he would be rid of that horrid boy. The sooner Morpeth sacrificed him to his god the better. Morpeth could get whatever it was he wanted from the boy and hopefully then Balthasar would himself get some rest. The last three days had been a time of infinite insanity for the imperial forces in Morpeth's relentless quest to capture the two boys.

In the early afternoon, the travellers from the Masavar fortress stopped to rest in the forest on the eastern side of Dalazvar. Jakov sat down on the ground and rested from the tiresome journey. From the top of the hill, Jakov could make out the taller buildings of Dalazvar including the royal palace. The towers of the palace easily rose above the others. He had many fond memories of the city as a boy. But now he knew it to be the source of all the corruption and cruelty of Iona. It finally dawned on him that when Morpeth died, he would be the next rightful king of Iona. He was the heir to the throne, though it was a role that he did not aspire to or intend to fulfil. A quiet life in the winter wilderness of Devora was what he wanted with his young family. No more rebellion, no more violence. A life of peace and tranquility was all he desired when he thought of the future. The thought of ruling over Iona genuinely held no attraction for him.

Ayesha and Sy tied up the horses and stretched their legs and backs. Mo and Tar sat down to eat some dried beef and drink some water in the quietness of the forest. Prisca dismounted her horse and sat on a large rock beside Jakov. She also stared at the outline of the several buildings of Dalazvar that were visible through the trees. Prisca looked at the city differently than Jakov. Whereas Jakov looked at the city with a sense of disdain, she gazed at it with a feeling of homesickness and longing.

"Beautiful, isn't it?" she said to him.

"It's a city. They all look the same to me," Jakov replied.

"But surely not this one. It is the capital city, the royal city, the largest city of Iona."

"It is full of poverty and murder, populated by brigands, and the sewerage runs through the middle of the streets."

"On the contrary, it is full of markets, theatres, altars, a massive library, statues, and schools. There is so much history and life in the place. Our family line has reigned in Iona for over 200 hundred years. There is much in our family heritage to be proud of. It was your great-grandfather who unified the city states of Iona."

"It was my father who brought it to civil war in his relentless pursuit of his two sons."

"You are too judgmental. You see only the negatives, the darkness, the worst in people."

"The circumstances of my upbringing have made me cynical and untrusting. You can hardly blame me woman."

"I blame you for nothing. I blame myself for much. And I blame that scoundrel Morepth for the rest. It was he who enticed me to worship his god Marduk. It was he who seduced me to do . . . to do those things which are unspeakable."

Prisca become emotional for a second and Jakov looked away, feeling uncomfortable with her display of sorrow.

"You do believe me, don't you Jakov? You believe people can change, don't you, son?"

"Like I said, the circumstances of my life have made me cynical and untrusting. But, yes, I do believe people can change. Even you mother. However, the proof will be whether you lead us into Dalazvar and to rescue Iskandar, before his father kills him."

Prisca looked away for a moment and prepared to speak.

"There is something you should know Jakov. Something secret. Something that no one else knows about. Something shocking."

"And what is that?"

"Iskandar is not Morepth's son."

"What?"

"Morpeth is not his father."

"You lie. Of course he's Morpeth's son. Why else does Morpeth hunt him?"

"Morpeth doesn't know," she said, still unable to look Jakov in the eye.

"Who is his father, then?"

"He is your brother, your half-brother. You share the same mother, but a different father."

"Then who is his father?"

"I am ashamed to say. I have carried the guilt for so many years. I betrayed my husband."

"Who is the father?" demanded Jakov.

"Fallkirk. Your uncle Fallkirk. He is the father of Iskandar."

Jakov sat back and reflected for a moment. If this was true, it changed everything and nothing. Iskandar was still his brother and Morpeth still had to die. But Iskandar was now involved in a plot to kill a man who was not his father. He wondered how the boy would react to learning the news. Provided of course, that both of them lived long enough to see each other again.

"How?"

"Morpeth went away for two months touring the cities of Iona, celebrating twenty years since his coronation. I stayed in Iona to govern the city in his absence. Fallkirk and I were good friends, close friends. He was commander of the army and I was the queen. There was a royal banquet, much drinking and dancing. And later on ... later on, things happened. I am ashamed, but I cannot deny it. You and Iskandar deserve to know the truth."

"And Morpeth knows nothing of this?"

"No, I never told him. As far as I know, he thinks Iskandar is his true son."

"And what about Fallkirk? Did he know?"

"Yes, I told him. He was filled with sorrow and regret. He had betrayed his brother. We agreed never to see each other again and never to talk about it."

"That explains why he tried to save us in the temple. He wasn't only saving his nephews, he was trying to save his own son. Then where is he now?"

"Do you think I know? We searched for him for years and Morpeth continued his search long after I was imprisoned in that hell hole. We ransacked city after city and town after town. We found nothing. The only thing we achieved was to anger the people into revolt. It even led to the formation of the Freedom Legionnaires that you lead so ably against the imperial army, at least I hear as much."

"I have vague memories of Fallkirk as a child. Fleeting memories, pictures in my mind, but not much. I remember him being around, but never talking to him much."

"You owe him your life."

"I know."

"Where did he take you?"

"I don't know for sure. But I remember waking up with some people from the river tribe. I cried for days, calling for you and father. I was inconsolable. Then they told me what you had done. I didn't believe them at first. Then I saw first hand what the imperial army did to village after village. I saw the carnage. The army came to the village that was hiding me. They burnt the village and killed so many. But the people there hid me, they looked after me, they raised as one of their own. That was when I decided that I would stop Morpeth and end his madness. It was my duty to kill him. I knew of the prophecy and of my brother. And since I was fifteen years old I have thought about nothing else other than destroying Morpeth."

"Nothing else?" Prisca asked, now looking at Jakov. "Surely teenage boys have other interests."

"I did manage to find time for a wife and a family."

"A family? Do you mean I'm a grandmother?" Prisca laughed. It was the first time Jakov had seen her happy. It brought to him a rush of memories of long ago.

"Yes, I have a wife, a son and a daughter."

"And what are their names? Do they look like you? How old are they?"

Jakov smiled, but suddenly the smile left his face and he looked at Prisca coldly.

"From what I remember, you are not particularly good with children. And I don't want you anywhere near mine."

Jakov rose and began to walk away.

"A grandmother has the right to know her grandchildren's name."

Jakov turned to her.

"You may be their grandmother by birth. But you are still a child murderer, a witch of Marduk, and you have the sexual ethics of a stray dog."

"Why must you be so hurtful Jakov? Is there no pity in your heart? Don't you know the meaning of forgiveness? Do you think me incapable of remorse? I am still your mother you know, nothing will change that."

Jakov said nothing and walked further away.

"You are so like your father."

Jakov turned around once more.

"I am nothing like my father. And, may I add, nothing like my mother either. A fact for which my children should be especially thankful. Now rest in silence, you'll need your energy for the rest of the ride tonight."

Jakov walked over to Ayesha and Sy, who were away a distance near the horses. They were pretending not to hear the conversation between Jakov and Prisca but could not help hearing it.

"We should ride closer to the city soon as it gets dark," he said to Sy.

"I agree." Sy leaned close to Jakov so Prisca wouldn't hear his words. "Is meeting her everything you thought it would be?" he whispered.

"Far worse. I enjoyed hating her when I knew less about her."

"Her remorse may be genuine," added Ayesha. "Those years imprisoned in the carcerium may have given her time to reflect on the depth of her sins."

"Or maybe she is playing the part of the penitent woman so she can betray us at first opportunity," replied Jakov.

"You don't trust her?" asked Sy.

"Only as far as I could throw her."

Iskandar walked along one of the cobblestone streets of the city. He went into the market place where it was crowded and where he hopefully wouldn't be noticed. People were walking in all directions, yelling out about produce and prices. A seller of fine cloth pushed some material into Iskandar's face and pleaded with him to buy it. Iskandar avoided eye contact and walked on ahead. The sounds, smells, and sights of the market were overwhelming to his senses, especially after being locked in a cell for nearly two days.

At the far end of the market, Iskandar saw a detachment of soldiers busily making their way through they crowd. They were heading right towards him. The soldier leading them was calling out to people, ordering them to get out of his way. The soldiers were carefully searching everything and everyone they came across. They looked in baskets, under tables, and every young boy passing nearby was interrogated and searched on his arm. Iskandar knew that they were looking for him. It didn't take long then for Morpeth to realize that he had escaped. The boy froze on the spot and wondered what he should do. If he ran, it would be too obvious. If he tried to hide, there was a chance that they might find him. Slowly he turned around, pretending to be very natural, and started walking in the opposite direction. He walked quickly, but not too quickly to make it look like he was in a hurry. He noticed that he was actually walking back towards the palace and he felt trapped. Iskandar stopped for a moment and had to decide what to do next. He could hear the soldiers behind him still making their way through the market and annoying people with their intrusive inspection of shoppers and shopkeepers.

To his right he saw a small alley between some stalls. He made sure that the hood of his cloak covered his face and he quickly darted off into the alley way. He leaned up against a doorway that sunk into a dwelling. From there, no one in the market could see him. It was dark and damp in the alley and smelled of onions and raw meat. Every few seconds he popped his head out to see if the soldiers had passed by yet.

Suddenly, the door behind him opened and he felt a hand around his mouth.Another hand grabbed him around his waist and held him tightly as he was pulled backwards into the dwelling. The door closed in front of him and he was sandwhiched between the door and the man behind him. He froze in terror, not knowing what to do. Iskandar tried to resist and squirm, but he was being held too tight around his mouth and waist. He didn't know whether to yell or to try to fight. As he struggled there was a voice.

"Be very quiet right now. For your own good," the voice whispered.

In the corner of his eye he could see through a window and outside the window he noticed soldiers coming through alley way. The person holding him inside the dwelling had hidden him from their view. It was then that he realized that whoever had him now was trying to keep him safe from the soliders. Iskandar held his breath as the soldiers passed into the alley peering into windows and knocking on doors. The door in front of him was knocked, but after what seemed like an eternity the soldiers moved on. Iskandar and his captor remained motionless and silent for several seconds more.

"Do not make any sudden moves," the voice whispered. "They might come back."

The hands around him were forceful, but were not painful. The voice was assertive, but not threatening.

After a minute or so, the man holding him slowly relaxed his grip around his face and stomach. As he did, Iskandar wondered whether he should elbow the man in the ribs and try to make a dash for it. Still, the stranger had saved him from certain capture. As his grip relaxed, Iskandar turned around to see the man. His eyes nearly jumped out of his head as he found himself staring Talkai in the face.

"Talkai, what are you doing here?" the boy asked excitedly.

"I'm here to rescue you, what do you think I'm doing?"

"Is Jakov with you?"

"No, he told me to stay in Norella. But that sounded boring. Just like when he told me to stay in Devora. That was boring too. So here I am. Again! Are you glad to see me?"

"Of course I am. But how did you get here? Did you walk through the Yobi desert?"

"That is a long story, but I got here in the end, even with sore feet."

"What do we do now?"

"Well, I never really thought that far ahead. I came here to find you, but had no idea where to look. It was pure luck that I saw you. I broke into this house looking for some food, then out of the window, I saw you sneak passed, and I grabbed you when I saw the soldiers coming down the same way. I guess we should probably try to leave the city. Then head towards Masavar and see if we can find Jakov along the way."

"That sounds like a good plan."

"Then let's go."

The two stepped outside the abandoned dwelling and went into the alley. Iskandar looked about carefully and then nodded to Talkai. Talkai took Iskandar by the hand and they walked out of the alley into the market. Iskandar enjoyed the feel of sunshine on his face as opposed to the damp and darkness of the alley. They turned to their right and began walking down beside the various stalls and shops of the market when a bald man stood in their way. It was Balthasar.

"Young master Iskandar. Where do you think you're going?" Balthasar said slyly.

Iskandar stopped and looked at Talkai. Fear was in both of their eyes.

"Your father misses you dearly. He has a big celebration planned for you. You don't want to miss that, do you?"

Iskandar turned around and saw ten soldiers behind him. Trying to run would have been pointless.

"Iskandar," asked Talkai, "Do you know this man?"

"Yes, I do. He works for Morpeth."

"The divine Morpeth, actually," added Balthasar. "Or at least he will be divine once a certain person is properly sacrificed."

"I wish Jakov was here," commented Talkai. "We could use his swords about now."

"Tie them up," Balthasar ordered. "Morpeth is accelerating his plan. Their presence is needed back in the palace."

Talkai and Iskandar were seized, tied up, and then carried like sacks of potatoes along the main street as the cohort of soldiers took them back towards the imperial palace.

As they were carried along, Talkai said, "I'm starting to think that staying in Norella would have been a good idea after all."

"Don't worry, Talkai. Jakov will come for us, I'm sure of it."

"I hope so too," added Balthasar. "Morpeth is counting on him as well."

Iskandar's heart sank. He had been so close to escaping the city. Now his life was in danger again. But not only his, also Jakov's, and even Talkai's. He hated himself for it. But he consoled himself that he had tried his best and it was not over yet. Jakov was coming. He knew it in his heart.

# Chapter 23

## The Tunnel

IT WAS TWILIGHT IN the forest. Evening was coming. Prisca led the four-some through a goat trail just outside the city.

"There is a secret entrance nearby," she said. "It goes under the aqueduct, under the armoury, and comes out in the bottom of the royal kitchen. That will get us into the palace."

"How do I know you're telling the truth?" asked Jakov.

Prisca looked at him rather coldly. For once she felt in control.

"You don't Jakov. You shall simply have to trust me for now."

Jakov grumbled to himself.

As they continued on, they came to a slight clearing. Ahead, the walls of the city could be seen several hundred yards away. But the clearing was still out of view of any of the watch towers.

Prisca paused and looked around several times trying to orient herself to her environs. She walked around the area, looking for something. At last she came across a large rock, the size of a cow, behind some bushes.

"Here we are," she said contentedly. "A doorway into Dalazvar, the imperial capital of Iona."

Somewhat confused, Sy asked, "Where is the entrance?"

"It is underneath the rock," she answered. "All you need to do is lift it. It is heavy so you'll have to . . ."

Before she had finished speaking, Jakov pointed his hand at the large rock and rolled his wrist. At his gesture the large rock rolled sideways to its left, exposing a large hole with a ladder underneath it.

"Aha," noted Sy.

"What now?" asked Ayesha.

"Now, you go in and I lead you to Morpeth," Prisca stated.

Jakov stopped for a moment to think. Everyone was looking at him. Sy walked up closely to him.

"What do you say we do now Jakov? Everyone down the hole? Last one to the throne is a rotten tomato?"

Jakov looked at Prisca, who seemed a little tense and even nervous. Finally Jakov spoke.

"No. Not yet. We need to know if it is safe. We have no idea who or what is down there."

"Nothing, I assure you," Prisca snarled. "Hardly anyone knows of this secret passage, and even those who do know have probably forgotten about it."

"For all we know this could be a trap Prisca, and I won't risk my own life or my friends going down there with you."

"Then what are we to do Jakov? You've come this far and now you stop because you've lost your nerve. You want to kill Morpeth. Well, Morpeth is on the other side of this tunnel. Make up your mind child. You brought me here to lead you to a secret passage into the city. Well, here is your secret passage."

"Something is not right Prisca. I think you're up to something."

"Again with the mistrust. If I wanted to hurt you Jakov, I could have done that a hundred times since we left Masavar. I have my powers and I could have used them. And you forget that I even saved your life in the beast pit."

"She's right," noted Sy.

Jakov was deep in thought and he drove his fist into the palm of his hand and cracked at his knuckles. He looked over Prisca, trying to read the expression on her face. He gazed at the city walls and then back at his friends. Finally he spoke to them.

"Mo and Tar," I want you to stay here and keep an eye out for any sign of imperial forces. They probably aren't looking for us, but once they get news of Prisca's escape, every blade of grass from here to Masavar will be swarming with soldiers. Keep out of sight, but keep your eyes peeled."

The two dwarves nodded and ran into the shrubbery behind them.

"Sy and Ayesha, stay right here at the entrance to the tunnel. I will go with Prisca. If I'm not back in half an hour, you'll know that I have succumbed to foul play. If so, retreat to Norella and Devora. Defend them at all costs."

"Wait," interjected Ayesha. "I have an idea."

"What?" asked Jakov.

"Let me go down the tunnel with Prisca. I will make sure that it is clear and safe for us. If anything happens, I can at least run. My speed will protect me."

"Ayesha, you don't have to. I'm not afraid of what is down there."

"But I am. If we lose you and Iskandar we are ruined. If it comes to that, then, well, everything is over. Everything is for nothing. Everyone who has died and all who gave given up their lives. We can't let that happen. Let me check it first with Prisca."

"Is this really necessary?" complained Prisca. "It would be so much easier and simpler if all of us just walked through the tunnel at once. The royal kitchen is no more than a fifteen minute walk underground. Surely we can go together?"

"No," interrupted Jakov. "No. I won't endanger all of us. We are too vulnerable down there. I don't know what is down there or where this comes out. I won't endanger all of us. Especially when our only witness is known to be unreliable."

"Then I will go," said Ayesha in a commanding tone.

"Very well, then, Ayesha. Go with Prisca. Check out the tunnel. But if you are not back in half an hour, I will be coming down there looking for you."

Prisca rolled her eyes in frustration.

"This would be so much easier if we did things my way."

"Sy and I will wait for the two of you to return. Go. Go now."

Ayesha smiled, pleased with Jakov's confidence in her. Prisca climbed down the ladder first into the darkness of the tunnel. Sy ripped up some fabric, and tied it to the top of a stick. He poured some oil on it from a flask and then lit it up using some flint. He handed it to Ayesha who took the torch in her hand, and also descended into the darkenss of the tunnel.

As the two descended, Jakov felt very apprehensive. He wasn't sure if letting Prisca out of his sight was a good idea. He didn't trust her, but deep down inside he really wanted to. He wanted to believe that she was different. He wanted to believe that she had changed. It was now that he would learn if his mother had really changed.

At the bottom of the tunnel, Prisca used a stick to knock over some cobwebs. Ayesha looked up from the bottom of the tunnel at Iskandar and Sy.

"See you soon," she said with her usual pleasantness and grace.

With that, the two women walked off into the darkness of the tunnel and were no longer visible from above.

Jakov sat down and looked at Sy, but the two of them said nothing. It was just then that Sy noticed that the sky above was getting dark and a light pitter patter of rain could be heard on the ground.

"Rain," said Sy annoyingly.

"We are in for a wet night old friend. I hope you have an exta cloak."

For the next few moments Jakov did nothing but stare into the darkness of the tunnel beneath, hoping that Ayesha and Prisca would emerge at any moment.

Talkai and Iskandar were carried into the imperial palace by Balthasar and his men. As they went through the front entrance, several soldiers saluted Balthasar. The group continued down several corridors and up several flights of stairs. Then they came to a large foyer with several doors. Balthasar turned to the men holding Talkai.

"Take him to the dungeon. He can stay there until we have further instructions."

"No," yelled Iskandar. "Don't take him. He's my friend."

"Silence," Balthasar yelled back at him. "He's my prisoner. He goes to the dungeon."

"Don't worry Iskandar," called Talkai as they carried him away. "I'll be alright. I'll see you later on. Be brave." His voice got fainter and fainter as he was carried away.

Iskandar felt overwhelmed with sorrow. He was afraid now too. For Talkai most of all. He wasn't very good at looking after himself and he wondered what was going to happen to his friend.

Balthasar came over to him and looked him in the eye.

"Where are you going to take me?" Iskandar asked him.

"Morpeth has a special room prepared for you. His own private altar dedicated to Marduk. The last room you will ever see."

The soldiers continued carrying Iskandar further into the palace. Iskandar noticed that they were constantly walking up stairs and going into the upper floors of the palace. Eventually they came to a room with golden doors and all sorts of graven images and pictures carved into the door. Balthasar pushed it open.

Iskandar looked inside the room. The first thing he noticed was that it had no windows. The room was illuminated by several torches in the corners of the room. In the middle of the room was large stone table with a large ornamented knife lying in the middle of it. To one side of the stone table was a wooden table and on it was a metal basin. At the far end of the room was a statue of a man with six arms and a wolf's head. In front of the statue, Morpeth was kneeling with his arms raised and he was chanting something very softly.

The soldiers sat Iskandar on the stone table, but they removed the knife and placed it on the nearby wooden table next to the basin. They did not untie him. Iskandar looked about for one thing: water, and lots of it, but none was to be found.

"Did you enjoy your tour of the markets my son?" asked Morpeth, still kneeling before the statue. But there was no answer from Iskandar.

"I hear the turnips and custard fruit are delicious this time of year."

Morpeth rose and came over to Iskandar. He looked visibly agitated, enraged in fact.

"That was very close. You almost escaped from me. I underestimated your resilience and your intelligence."

"I will escape again. Jakov will rescue me."

"The next time you see Jakov, he will be lying where you are now. And I will sacrifice you both to my master Marduk. I shall fulfil my promise to him and he shall reward me."

Iskandar just realized that the room was an altar to Marduk.

"Do you like this place? It is an altar to my god, Marduk. Simple and yet elegant, I feel. The temple of Marduk was destroyed and in its place I changed this room into a private altar to my god. Ironically, it used to be your nursery. Your life began here, it will end here, and it will begin again here. It is a room of birth, death, and new birth. It is the room where I shall be reborn as a god."

"You are no god," retorted Iskandar. "It is you who will die in here. Jakov will kill you."

"We will see, little one."

Balthasar stepped forward and bowed before Morpeth.

"Divine master, we captured him in the market. But he was not alone."

"Not alone?" responded Morpeth in a surprised tone. "Who was with him?"

"Some simpleton, some nitwit from the country. A friend of his, I believe"

"And where is this simpleton now?"

"In the dungeon. We wait for your instruction as to what to do with him."

Moreph stroked his chin and stared coldly into Iskandar's eyes.

"Kill him. I have no need for a dim-witted fool."

"No, please, no," pleaded Iskandar. "Don't kill him. I beg you. Father, please, no."

Iskandar started to cry.

"It is a punishment for your insolence. I do not tolerate rebellion or contempt. Not even from my own son."

"Take my life if you must, but spare his. He's innocent. He is no threat to you. I beg you, father. If I am your son then show mercy to him. Show mercy to me."

"I am sorry son, but a lesson must be learned. Not only by you, but by all who live under my reign. One thing I have learned as a king is that it is better to be feared than to be loved."

"Please, father."

"Enough," shrieked Morpeth at him. "I command death and death it will be. You have no right to protest. You defied me and for that your friend dies. The time for mercy has ended. The time for my coming of age as a god has begun."

Iskandar wept as quietly as he could. He felt great sorrow and grief for Talkai. Now he felt utter hate and rage for Morpeth. He looked out the corner of his eye and saw the knife near the basin. He wished he had it now. He wished he was unbound. And for a moment he imagined what he would like to do to Morpeth and to Balthasar with that knife.

"It shall be done as you wish divinity," said Balthasar as he bowed and departed. He promptly left the room, but the soldiers remained in the room with Morpeth and Iskandar.

"I hate you," cried Iskandar at Morpeth.

"Good, then at last you will know how to rule as a king one day."

"I hope Jakov cuts you into a thousand pieces."

"But then you'll never see your brothers and sisters again."

Iskandar was confused at these words.

"But they are dead. I'll never see them again because of you."

"Not true. You will see them again. Indeed, after I sacrifice you, you will live again. Jakov too."

"What are you talking about?"

"The reason why I am so consumed with sacrificing you and Jakov is because Marduk will reward me with divinity. I am immortal now. I cannot die, unless my head is taken from my body. But once I am divine, I will have unlimited power. Power over the elements. Power over nature. And even power over death. I will be able to stop people from dying. I will have the ability to end disease and make death itself work backwards. I will be able to bring you, Jakov, and your brothers and sisters back to life. That is why I am so relentless. I want to bring my children back to life. All of them."

"That is impossible."

"Not for a god like me. When I am a god, I will do the impossible. I will grant immortal life to all of my subjects, including my children."

"It cannot be."

"It will be. I will make it be. That is why you must die. Without your death, I cannot bring your brothers and sisters back to life. They remain in the dark clutches of death until you die. You must enter into the darkness of death so that you can lead them out of it. Your death and Jakov's will set them free. Do you realize that?"

"This is crazy. No god, not even Marduk, can grant you that power."

"He will grant it and I will use it. I will be a god to this world."

"But why sacrifice your children to Marduk in the first place? Why, father?"

"A kingdom can last a lifetime, several generations, even an age. However, once I become a god, my kingdom shall last for eternity. It shall be the kingdom to reign over all others. I shall be the king of all other kings. I shall be the god king of Iona and you and Jakov will rule as immortal princes in a realm that is filled with the life of the heavens. I offer you that. Yet first, you must die."

"This is not how things are meant to be. It is not natural."

"The natural world is full of death and decay. I offer an alternative to that. I offer unlimited life and never-ending purity. I offer you immortality, but it comes only through death."

"I do not want an immortal life paid for by the life of my brothers and sisters. I would rather die than reign with you. What you say is a lie. No god can give this. You have been tricked and deceived by Marduk. You are a fool Morpeth. A fool."

"You don't have to believe me, or even understand. I only ask you to trust in me that I will bring you and your brothers and sisters back to life."

"It is madness."

"If I am wrong, then there is no hope for your siblings, for Jakov, and not even for your friend Talkai. Yes, your love for him runs deep. I could bring him back to life too. Perhaps he is already dead. Balthasar is very efficient at killing."

Iskandar foamed at the mouth in anger.

"I hate you. You are a cruel, monstrous wretch."

"You will learn to love me son. Once you are given an immortal inheritance you will change your mind I'm sure."

"No, I will never love you."

"So be it, but that does not change the present. Your death will bring me divine glory. And I sense that my time for deification is very near. Perhaps this evening shall not pass by before I drink of the nectar of the gods and sit among the pantheon of the divine. 'The Most High God Morpeth' shall be my title."

"The title 'lunatic' is all you will be remembered for."

"I grow weary of your lack of faith and understanding. Tonight I shall be deified, I know it. I feel that Jakov approaches, I sense it. My destiny is soon to be fulfilled. And you will be there to see it. Then, after a while, you will understand. In time you will thank me for what I've done. You will rejoice when I make you a son of a god."

"I'll only rejoice in your death."

"No, it is I who will rejoice in your death, and then in your new birth. For now, I tire of your insolence. The hour comes. I must prepare myself for the ceremony."

Morpeth nodded to the men who proceeded to lay Iskandar down and to tie him to the stone table with ropes.

"Are you going to kill me now?" asked Iskandar, curious, but strangely not afraid.

"No, I shall wait until Jakov gets here. You will die together. I think it will be more fitting that way. More worthy of Marduk my master to kill you together."

Iskandar felt the tightness of the ropes around his wrists and ankles and it made him grimace. He had nothing more to say. He turned away and gazed at a torch in the corner of the room and the flicker of its flame and the shadows that it created behind it. Morpeth came near and whispered to Iskandar.

"Rest if you can my son. The end for both of our mortal lives is not far away."

From his position tied to the stone table, Iskandar spat on him and Morpeth wiped the spittle off his cheek with his glove.

"You will learn, little boy. You will learn."

Morpeth left the room and the guards followed him out of the golden doors. By himself in the dim lit room, Iskandar prayed. Not to Marduk, but to Vetrius. He prayed that he, Talkai, and Jakov would be spared. But he felt only the silence in return and wondered if there was even anybody there to hear such prayers. He closed his eyes, a few tears ran down his cheek, and he passed out from mental, physical, and emotional exhaustion.

Prisca and Ayesha slowly moved along the dark tunnel with only Ayesha's torch for light. The narrow passage was low, forcing the two girls to crouch slightly as they walked through. The corridor was filled with cobwebs and the odd rat could be heard scurrying away from them over the ground that smelled of damp.

"Have you been through this tunnel before?" asked Ayesha, who led the duo.

"Once or twice. Mainly when I wanted to sneak out from the castle for some privacy. The sad thing about being a queen is that there is little chance for rest and respite. There is always someone who wants to see you, beg you, bribe you, or even kill you. A walk in the forest alone is a luxury that I had to steal when I could."

"How many passages are there?"

"Three or four, from memory. The main reason we had them was in case of an attack on Dalazvar. Never used them for that purpose. It was the case that sneaking about the city or out of the city was called for every so often."

"I can imagine."

"Can I ask you one question?" said Prisca has they continued to walk along the dark path.

"What?"

"Why did you volunteer to accompany me down here?"

"Someone had to go with you, and Jakov doesn't trust you."

"But you do?"

Ayesha turned around and looked at Prisca with what little glow her torch gave.

"I believe you are a mother. Mothers can make mistakes, but their maternal instincts overpower them soon enough. No matter what you've done, you still have a mother's heart, I'm sure of it."

"Are you a mother yourself?"

"No. My people were killed. The one I was promised to marry died with them."

"I'm sorry, so sorry. I know part of the fault lies with me. I tried to restrain Morpeth, but to no good. And all I got for my efforts was eight years locked up in that god-forsaken fortress. But I will make amends for it today, I swear."

"If you show your loyalty and faithfulness to Jakov and to us, I'm sure you'll get what you need."

"Jakov's trust?"

"Something you need far more."

"And what is that?"

"Redemption," she said with warmth in her face. "A chance to forget the wrongs and start again. It is something we all need from time to time. To be brought back from darkness and taken into the light. Even when the only thing that dwells in us is darkness. A dark power that veils anger, pain, and hate."

"You speak as if you know the experience."

"Take it from me. Letting go of our pain and our failures and seeking reconciliation or forgiveness, even when you don't deserve it, is one of the most liberating things any person can do."

"I believe you. I hope I am reconciled with Jakov. I hope that I earn this chance at redemption."

"Me too. Heaven knows that Jakov could use some motherly advice from time to time."

Ayesha turned back around and the two kept on moving along the dark passage. Eventually the path slanted upwards and they ascended up on a slight incline. After turning a corner, they could see a faint light at the far end of the passage.

"Ah," said Prisca. "The inside entrance to this tunnel is close by. Up ahead is the secret door into the kitchen cellar. From there we can enter the kitchen cellar and sneak up into the royal apartments and seek out Iskandar and Morpeth.

"Sounds simple, I suppose."

"It should be," Prisca laughed lightly.

The two finally came upon the entrance and they could see the origin of the faint shard of light that pierced the darkness of the tunnel. It was a small hole that allowed an ember of light into the maze of darkness and cobwebs.

"How do we open it?" Ayesha inquired.

"There is a latch here somewhere. Once we find it, we can push the door open."

Prisca felt around the wall feeling for the latch, with Ayesha holding the torch for her.

"Aha, here it is, our key into the castle."

"Can you hear anyone outside the door?"

The two leaned against the door for several moments but heard nothing on the other side.

"All is quiet," commented Prisca. "Which is normal for this time of night. The kitchen servants will be upstairs serving dinner. Only the scullery maid might be lurking about, and she'd be easily despatched."

"We need only peek in to see if the way is clear, then we can go back and tell Jakov that the passage into the castle is safe and clear. The end of our little underground adventure is near."

"In more ways that one, my dear. More that is over."

With those words, Prisca took a dagger from under her leg and plunged it into the back of Ayesha. Ayesha did not scream, but she reacted in a convulsion of agony and clutched her back and slumped forward. She turned slightly to face Prisca as she collapsed to the grounded and held one of her arms out, partly in defence and partly pleading for mercy.

"No, Prisca. Please!" was all she could manage, with little more than a whisper as the burning steel and racking pain took her breath from her.

The torch fell to the ground and was partly extinguished, but its slight glow illuminated Prisca's motionless and cold face.

"This is the end of you, young lady. It is also the end of my exile. It is the end of my waiting for divine life and divine power. It is the end of Jakov's stupid rebellion."

Ayesha panted for breath as her face convulsed with waves of agony.

Prisca dropped her knife and lunged forward at Ayesha with her hands pointing up and downward. From the still tunnel came a powerful wind that picked up Ayesha from the ground. It sent her flying down the dark tunnel where she landed with a thud. Her small body was rammed into the wall like a ragdoll. Prisca looked and listened for her movements, cries, or shrieks. There was only silence. Though it was dark, Prisca could tell that Ayesha did not move and made no noise.

Next, Prisca turned around in the dark and pulled the latch with her hand. There was a soft clicking sound. She then slowly pushed the door open and it creaked a little, revealing a large bedroom with lavish furnishings. It was no kitchen cellar, it was the royal bedroom. She smiled widely as she looked on the bed and saw there Morpeth sleeping deeply and completely unaware of her presence. Prisca closed the secret passage door and then sat on the bed next to Morpeth.

She looked at him with mixed feelings. A mixture of love, anger, and need. She needed him more than ever, just as he now needed her more than ever. Only by working together could they finally become gods and be released from the tormenting lust for divine power. She cleared her throat, hoping that it would wake him. But all it did was make him grunt and roll over on his side. Prisca rolled her eyes and finally tapped him on his shoulder.

"Did you sleep well, my love?" she asked him.

Morpeth yawned, scratched his head, and slowly opened his eyes. He closed his eyes and then suddenly opened his eyes again when he saw her beside him. He sat up and rubbed his eyes. Morpeth stared at her in shock and disbelief and looked about the room to see if anyone else was nearby.

"How did you get in here?" he demanded.

"I escaped from Masavar with the help of a mutual friend. I believe you know him. His name is Jakov, our son."

"Jakov brought you to me? Then where is he?"

"He is on the other side of the secret passage, just outside the city wall. He is ready to walk down that passage and then, he thinks, he's going to rescue Iskandar and kill you."

"Why would you lead him to me? We have nothing in common any more."

"Oh, but we do, my beloved. We both have the same hunger, the same yearning, the same unsatisfied longings we have had for these ten years."

Prisca moved very close to him and was deliberately sensual in how she spoke to him.

"We both lust for more than immortality, we want the divine power that yet eludes us. That is why we must work together."

"The last time we worked together, you tried to kill me. The last time we worked together, you tried to convince me to sacrifice every child under the age of ten in the kingdom to Marduk to make sure that we killed Jakov and Iskandar. The last time we worked together, your bloodlust and rage nearly cost me my army. The last time we worked together, I had to stop you from massacring half of the kingdom of Iona. I have the same desires as you Prisca. Yet your insatiable bloodlust and complete disrespect for the office of the king is too much even for me to handle. Some call me a tyrant, but you are a positively evil woman. I wish that I restrained your relentless violence long before I finally had you sent to Masavar. There is no point becoming a god if none of your subjects are alive to worship you."

"I may have been evil Morpeth, but at least I got the job done."

"If by job you mean trying to betray your husband and start a rebellion, then you were a riotous success."

"I promise to be more self-controlled and disciplined this time. I shall not resort to the normal bloodletting that I do so efficiently. The stakes are too high. You have Iskandar and I have Jakov. We are mutually dependent on each other now. We need only sacrifice them and then our dreams and longings will be complete. We shall not be shackled in this semi-mortal state any longer. Our souls will be fully and finally divine at last."

"What do you propose?"

"Where is Iskandar?"

"Since your exile, I built an altar to Marduk in the upper quarter of the palace. He is up there, ready to be offered up to our sovereign master Marduk."

"Good. I shall lead Jakov up the corridor and into your waiting arms. Make sure you have men outside the city who can secure and seal the tunnel once he enters into it. Then he'll have no escape. You can wait here with as many men as you can fit into this room. We capture him and take him to your altar and then ..."

"And then we finish what we started all those years ago."

"Yes, we finish it once and for all."

Prisca reclined on the bed next to Morepth and stretched out, trying to relax. She gently leaned over towards him with her head leaning on his hand.

"Do you miss me, Morpeth?"

"At times."

"Well now my sweet you can have me back forever. And soon you can tell me what it is like to be married to a goddess."

Morpeth looked away briefly and looked back at her and searched for something in her eyes.

"Is that all you ever think about? How or when we will become divine?"

"It has preoccupied my mind most days. That and how to escape from Masavar."

"Do you ever regret what we did, sacrificing our own children?"

"No, of course not. It was an act worthy of Marduk, our magnificent god. Anyway, as we always intended, once we become gods we will have the power to resurrect them and bring them back to life. A happy reunion of parents and children where our children can share in the life and joy of an everlasting kingdom. Surely immortality is the greatest gift we can give to our children. Even if they must walk through the darkness first."

"I suppose," Morpeth said, though half-hearted.

"Do you doubt what we did?" asked Prisca.

"Some days I wonder. But it is too late for turning back. Too late for apologies. We must finish what we started. I believe in Marduk. Marduk will honour our service and sacrifice."

"Be of good cheer husband. Our day, our day of reckoning, our day of transformation into a whole new mode of existence draws near."

"Then bring Jakov to me. I will be waiting here. Together we can finish this. Once and for all."

"Half an hour Morpeth. In half an hour I will return with Jakov. Be ready. I look forward to the ceremony."

Prisca sat up from the bed, she got up to her feet and walked over to the secret passage. After opening the entrance she turned to face Morpeth one more time.

"Oh, for what it matters, I did miss you, Morpeth."

She blew him a kiss, walked into the passage, and the door slammed behind her.

Morpeth shook his head and said to himself, "That woman is as beautiful as she is wicked."

He stood up and called out for his attendants. Once they entered he spoke to them.

"Get every guard and soldier in the palace into this room immediately. I want every man at arms in my employ in this room within ten minutes. And find Balthasar too. I need him as well. Go."

The two guards ran off as if their lives depended upon it.

Morpeth rubbed his hands and stared at the secret doorway. He was relishing his chance to finally meet Jakov face to face.

# Chapter 24

## Balthasar is sent to kill Talkai

TALKAI SAT IN THE cell, very still and quiet, listening for the noises outside. Suddenly, the door swung open and Balthasar walked in with a sword at his side.

"Good evening. My name is Balthasar. I am your executioner."

"Well, that's disappointing. I was rather hoping that you were the chef. I could really go for some salted pork, roast potatoes, and some beer. The food here is terrible you know."

"These lodgings are not made for comfort and generally they are not permanent either. Most who lodge do not stay long and they never see the light of day again."

"That does sound rather ominous. Do they go and live underground and live with moles or foxes or something?"

"They do go underground. But that's because we bury them once we kill them."

"How rude!" Talkai objected. "I mean, really. You cannot go around just killing people. It is not right you know. What kind of kingdom are you running here?"

"The divine Morpeth commands the kingdom as he sees fit. And he has commanded that you be killed. You are guilty of conspiring against Morpeth and assisting in the escape of a fugitive."

"To be honest, I cannot deny it. So what happens now?"

Balthasar took out his sword.

"Now would be that part where I kill you with my sword, you die, then I tell Morpeth that you're dead, and then I go and have a nice dinner."

"Really, what are you having for dinner? Pork, by any chance?"

"I believe beef stew is on the menu actually. But that is of no concern to you any more."

Balthasar grabbed Talkai by the shoulder and threw him on the ground and then stood over him. He held his blade upright and wondered which side of the blade was sharper. He hoped that he could behead him in one motion. It was always a feat of strength and some necks were thicker than others.

Talkai remained upright on his knees and just smiled cheekily back at Balthasar as Balthsar inspected his sword. Balthasar looked closely at him for a moment with a confused look on his face.

"There is something about you that is very familiar. I feel like I've seen you somewhere before. Who are you?"

"My name is Talkai. I was a servant in Praschi. Have you ever been to Praschi? It is absolutely gorgeous this time of year. Birds singing, bees buzzing, and children playing in the fields. It is remote, but it has a rustic charm about it."

"I've never been to Praschi."

"We could have met in alot of places. Perhaps on the battlefield near Norella. I do have a memorable face, I'm told"

"No, that is not it either. Bah, it is no matter. I've killed many men. They all look the same after a while."

Balthasar waved his blade around, ready to use it, and he looked at Talkai who was there, kneeling with a very odd grin on his face.

"Usually when a man is about to die he cries, begs for mercy, or struggles. Why on earth are you smiling at me? Do you understand what is going to happen now? Why do you smile at me as if I were some court jester?"

"Because," replied Talkai, grinning even wider.

"Because what?" demanded Balthasar.

"I'm smiling because I know something that you don't know."

"And what is that?"

"It's a secret. I'm not supposed to tell you."

"You should tell me. It'd be a shame to take such a secret to the grave. Tell me your secret, you fool, and I promise to kill you quickly with a nice clean blow."

"I can tell you if you promise not to tell anyone else."

"You have my word."

Talkai looked around to make sure no one was around. Still on his knees he leaned forward and began whispering upwards to Balthasar.

"Well, rumour has it, that in a few moments from now ... no, you wouldn't be interested in hearing it."

"I am interested."

"No, you wouldn't be. It's not your thing."

Balthasar lost his patients and now screamed at Talkai.

"Tell me, you damned fool. Why are you smiling at me? What is this stupid secret? Tell me now, or I'll bleed you slowly."

"Alright, then. No need to get your undergarments in a twist. The secret is, and let me stress that this is just between us, the secret is that in a few moments from now, you will be dead."

Balthasar laughed with a snort.

"That is it? That is your secret? I'll be dead in a few moments? I don't want to dampen your hopes, a fool's hope it may be, but in a few moments you will be dead and I'll be enjoying a beef stew."

"Are you sure?" Talkai asked, still smiling.

"Very sure," replied Balthasar as he lifted his blade above his head.

"Then, get used to disappointment," Talkai spoke, but now his expression and voice had changed. He smile was gone, his face was cold, his stare was penetrating, and his voice had an air of authority and command.

With his sword still raised above his head, Balthasar's hands froze, and his eyes widened. As Talkai looked up at him, Balthasar experienced two things, recognition and fear.

"It can't be," he complained. "It's impossible. They said you were dead."

The shock sent Balthasar stumbling backwards in momentary panic. Talkai rose to his feet and smiled again, but with a different kind of smile.

"I told you to get used to disappointment."

# Chapter 25

## Prisca's Treachery

PRISCA WALKED QUICKLY THROUGH the tunnel in the dark. The torch had long since gone out, but she knew this corridor well enough to be able to move through it unassisted. She walked past Ayesha and noticed that she was still there. Her body was cold and no sound of breath could be heard. Prisca assumed that she was dead. If not, she would be soon enough. As she went on further down the dark tunnel, she rehearsed her lines in her head and made sure her story was straight. Jakov would not be convinced easily and she would need a great performance to fool him. He was pessimistic and suspicious by nature. But she had the charm and eloquence of any player or actress. She could ordinarily twist any man around her finger, her son included. As she neared the exit where Jakov and Sy waited, she stopped. She picked up a stone and struck herself on the head with it. She did as hard as she could, hard enough to draw some blood. Then she ran towards the entrance and towards the light.

Prisca climbed the ladder and emerged from the tunnel panting as if out of breath. She felt the rain hit her face as soon as she stood up. Jakov ran over as soon as she came out. He noticed that she was alone.

"Where is Ayesha?" he asked.

"When we came to the entrance we opened the door to go into the kitchen cellar. It was all clear and we were about to come back. But then, out of nowhere, two guards appeared. We fought them off, but, Ayesha. Ayesha was ..." Prisca's eyes filled with tears and she pressed her lips to her hands, "I'm sorry, Ayesha was killed. But thanks to her, I escaped. The way is clear. I hid the bodies of the guards and even Ayesha. I'm sorry, I had to. I had no choice."

Jakov stared at her blankly and then walked away. Sy fell to the ground also with a gaunt and lifeless look on his face. Mo and Tar were within ear shot and they began weeping at the news. They hugged each other and wept as quiet as they could, which wasn't very quiet at all.

"She's really gone," uttered Sy.

Jakov said nothing, he couldn't look anyone in the eye. He felt a mixture of emotions. Grief, loss, and shame.

"It is my fault," Jakov added. "I should have gone. We all should have gone together."

"My son, you didn't know. The guards were only in the kitchen cellar by a freakish chance. They caught us by surprise. There was nothing anyone could have done. I'm sorry, I wish I could have saved her. I tried, but it was all over too quickly."

There was an eerie silence among them all.

"What now?" asked Sy. "Do we go on, or go back?"

"There is no going back. We have come this far. We must end this tonight," added Jakov.

Suddenly the gloom of the rainy night seemed fitting for the sullen atmosphere.

"But without Ayesha, we are without one of our best swords, one of our best friends."

"Then, let us make sure that her death was not for nothing. Let us remember what Ayesha fought for. She fought for us, for freedom, for liberty. We will honour her the best way we can. By bringing Morpeth to justice this night."

"Whatever you do, son, I will support you," interjected Prisca. "You have all the power and strength that I posses at your disposal. I owe Ayesha my life and I will not rest until that debt is repaid in full. Let me help you Jakov. Let me prove my love to you as your mother."

Jakov nodded at her.

"Friends, the time for grieving will be soon. But for now the time for battle is upon us. I do not know what lays in store for us when we go into the tunnel. I do not know if we will come out. But one thing I do know. Our friend and sister has died this night, this hour. I will not let her sacrifice be for nothing. I will not let her death be in vain. Whatever our destiny is, whatever Vetrius has appointed for us, let us rise now and embrace it. Let us go and meet Morpeth the destroyer. Let's end this madness, this war, once and for all. Are you with me?"

"Oikoi mou," cried Mo and Tar, which meant, "We are" in their dwarfish language.

"To the very end," responded Sy.

Prisca put her hand on Jakov's soldier, "You can count on me too. In life or in death."

For the first time Jakov almost smiled at her.

"Thanks," he said.

But Jakov's faint smile turned to alarm when he looked over Prisca's shoulder and behind her saw Ayesha slowly climbing out of the tunnel, clutching her lower back.

"No, Jakov. She means to betray us. She turned on me in the tunnel. Prisca is a traitor," Ayesha called out with a frail voice. After saying that, she collapsed before them all.

Everyone stared at Ayesha in disbelief and joy. Mo and Tar rushed over to help her. At the same time Prisca, took several steps to her left to move away from Jakov. Jakov felt a flurry of feelings, joy and then anger. He turned towards Prisca and Sy quickly came up beside him.

"I should have made sure she was dead. It was my own oversight. I was in a hurry to return here. Rest assured, I will not make the mistake again with her or the others."

Jakov drew both of his swords from his back.

"You lying wench. You nearly fooled me. For a moment there you nearly fooled me. I almost thought you had changed, but I should have known better. I should have expected that you would try to kill us all. I knew your heart was full of evil. You'll rot in hell for this treachery Prisca. I will do what I should have done when I first found you in that apartment.

"You can try, my son, but your meagre powers are no match for mine. I will gift wrap you for Morpeth and then we'll finish you off the way I finished off your brothers and sisters."

"Oh no you won't," yelled Sy, and the cyclops charged at the woman with his axe at the ready.

Prisca waved her hands and conjured a wind that blew harder and harder at the cyclops as he tried to run at her. At first Sy was slowed down, then stopped, and finally the brute strength of the wind pushed him backwards. The wind was so strong that he was sent flying backwards over several feet. He stayed on the ground, trying to get back up.

As the wind gushed, Mo and Tar laid on top of Ayesha to protect her injured and frail body from the powerful blast of wind. Jakov kneeled down and got closer to the ground and tried not to let the force of the wind push him back. He kept as low to the ground as he could and using all of his physical strength, he gradually started crawling towards Prisca.

"It is useless to resist Jakov. You are no match for me. I control the elemental powers of wind and air. You cannot stop me boy."

Sy kept trying to get up, but every time he tried the wind forced him either down or backwards. He was losing ground on her. Only Jakov was able to advance.

As Jakov moved he could see the trees around him nearly blown sideways. The rain stung as the wet wind struck his face with slaps of cold water. He grit his teeth and kept moving along the ground. He looked up to see Prisca standing over twenty feet away. He grabbed onto grass, pushed his feet into the dirt, and did everything he could to move towards her. Jakov looked behind him and saw Mo, Tar, and Ayesha blown back several feet away. Desperately, the dwarves tried to shield her, but her groans of pain filled the air. By now Sy was holding onto a tree trying to prevent himself from being blown any further. The foliage and loose twigs on the ground swirled about in the air like a miniature tornado. In desperation, Jakov tried once again to rise up off the ground and to run at her, but he was quickly driven back to his knees and then onto his stomach. All he could hear after that was the cackling laughter of Prisca, mocking his efforts.

"It is useless Jakov. You might as well give up now."

By now Jakov's eyes were hurting from the constant impact of rainwater. His arms strained from trying to hold himself to the ground. But the pit of his stomach swelled with anger as he looked up at Prisca.

"Jakov," cried Sy. "Do something. Do something now or we are doomed."

Jakov looked up and saw Prisca commanding the wind. She used it like it was a rolling pin that grinded over Jakov and Sy again and again. Behind Prisca he saw the large rock that formerly covered the entrance into the secret tunnel. With the little strength he had left he reached forward with his arm and called to the rock, unsure if it could hear him over the roaring wind and rain.

Instantly, the immense rock was uprooted from the ground and struck Prisca from behind. The blow knocked her down to the ground and towards Jakov. The wind suddenly stopped and, sensing his chance, Jakov rose up and sprinted towards Prisca. Prisca also began to rise, winded and groggy. She tried to raise her hands up, but as she did, Jakov's sword sliced across, cutting her two hands clean off. Prisca fell to the ground and cried out in agony. Jakov looked down at her.

"That will be the last wind you conjure," and with that he drove his sword into her abdomen and withdrew it again. The sword went all the way through and protruded from her back.

Prisca rolled over and began coughing up blood straight away. She clutched her stomach with her handless arms. Jakov kicked her in rage. Her face went white as snow and blood the same colour as her hair covered the lower part of her dress. Jakov could see the wound he had made, the tear in the skin, and the profuse bleeding. What was equally astounding was that he saw that the wounds were already beginning to heal.

"It will take more than that," Prisca struggled to say. "I am an immortal, remember?"

The pain was still visible on her face. Her movements and gestures were slow and she hunched onto the ground, facing dowards. Sy had come over to Jakov's side.

Prisca looked up at him, "I am a quick healer these days," she said. "But not quick enough to fight you any further tonight."

"What is down that tunnel?"

"It does not lead to a kitchen cellar. It leads to Morpeth's royal quarters. He's waiting for you there. It will be an ambush."

"Where is Iskandar?"

"Morpeth has built an altar in the upper quarter of the palace. Once inside, any of the staircases will take you to it," Prisca said, coughing up more blood.

"You know I can't leave you alive."

"Yes, yes I know. End this madness for me Jakov. End my torment."

Jakov nodded.

Prisca coughed some more and rolled over once or twice. Grinding her blood-stained teeth, she managed to get up on her knees. She looked up again and this time Jakov noticed that she was crying. She spoke again, but this time her voice was different. It was the voice of his mother that he truly remembered as child.

"Jakov, please don't remember me for what I became. Remember me as I was long ago. Before the terror, before Marduk enslaved me. Don't remember me like this. End it son. End this evil now, before it is too late for me."

Jakov said nothing. He simply nodded again.

Prisca doubled over and leaned forward, knowing full well what Jakov would do, what he had to do.

Jakov raised his sword up, but Sy stopped him by putting his hand on his shoulder.

"Wait, do you want me to do it?"

"No," he replied. "Let me. It is better if I do it."

Sy took his hand away.

Jakov took a deep breath and swung his sword downward as hard as he could. The blow struck Prisca on the neck and severed her head from her body. Jakov dropped his sword and closed his eyes, unable to look at her any longer. He turned around and Sy put his arm around him.

"She had to die Jakov. You did the right thing."

"I know I did. I did not flinch from it."

"What now?" the cyclops asked.

"Go and attend to Ayesha. She is perilously injured. I need a moment to myself."

"Yes, of course."

Sy ran over towards Ayesha, Mo, and Tar.

Jakov picked up his sword and walked away into the forest to clear his mind. He drove his sword into the ground and fell onto his knees from exhaustion. This was a day he had longed for, imagined, pictured, rehearsed in his mind, and hoped for. Jakov had half realized his short life's vision for the revenge of his murdered brothers and sisters. This should have been a victorious moment for him, but instead it felt bitter and ugly. There was no surge of triumph, only a feeling of emptiness and loss. He gripped the handle of his sword and leaned his head upon it. The rain still fell, but it became gentler in its volume and weight. For the first time that Jakov could remember, he wept.

In the royal apartment, Morpeth stood hypnotically fixated on the doorway to the secret passage. He waited for it to open and for Jakov to walk through it at any second. Virtually every available guard in the palace was in the hallway outside, ready to pounce in at his word. Ten soldiers were in the room beside him and six more hiding under the bed and behind curtains. It was the perfect trap. Jakov would have no place to go. Soon, another detachment of men would be at the entrance to the tunnel just outside the city. There was nowhere for anyone to escape. Morpeth firmly believed that his day for deification had come.

But as Morpeth stood there he felt a strange sensation come over him. It was a feeling of joy, pain, and power all at once, like pins and needles moving through his body. It was a sensation that he had not experienced since that fateful day in the temple of Marduk when his body began to be filled with immortality and other mysterious powers upon the death of his children. Feeling almost giddy, Morpeth sat down for a moment. He felt himself growing in power. He looked at his hands and then clenched his fist and the strength he felt was peculiar, but recognizable. It was then that he realized what had happened.

"My wife is dead," he said aloud. "Her power has passed to me. All praise be to Marduk who has blessed me for this battle."

For a moment he was genuinely grieved, but the mystic experience of more power invading his body made him feel joyous and invincible. He was even more confident in facing Jakov. It was unfortunate that Prisca had died, but it was not without its advantages.

"Guards," called Morpeth. "Rip the door down. I have a feeling that Jakov is onto our plan. Go in there and bring whoever you find to me. But make sure you bring them alive."

With no pause or hesitation the guards opened the secret door and began running through it one after another. Morpeth sensed that now might be a good time to check on Iskandar. The boy had escaped once, it would be important to make sure that he had not done so again.

≈ ≈ ≈

Jakov looked down at Ayesha and held her hand.

"How are you Ayesha?" he asked her.

"Bruised, battered, and bleeding, in other words, just like any other day following you around Iona."

Jakov laughed at her, though it was more pretending than anything else.

"I believe she will live," added Sy. "But she needs to get out of this weather as soon as we can."

"Yes, I agree. Mo and Tar, take her to the nearest village. Find a doctor if you can. Do whatever must be done. Once she is well enough, ride hard and fast for Devora. Let nothing stop you."

The little dwarves nodded in agreement and they helped Ayesha up and she leaned on their heads like crutches as she made her way along the forest.

"Just one thing, Jakov, before I go," Ayesha said.

"What?" answered Jakov.

"Find your brother and bring him home to us. Revenge can wait another day. Your mission is to rescue Iskandar."

"I will retrieve him Ayesha. No more talking. Go. Go and get some rest dear woman. The next time I see you I want to see you in a bed with a blanket and a crazy doctor sticking all kinds of potions and medicines down your throat."

The dwarves helped her onto a horse and they mounted up with her. Slowly, they rode off into the night.

Sy and Jakov walked towards the wall of the city. They walked passed Prisca's body and Jakov did his best not to look down at it.

"What do we do now?" Sy questioned.

"We do what we should have done the first time"

"And what is that?"

"Break into the city, the palace, and Morpeth's altar, and get Iskandar back."

"Getting into the city will be easy. Even sneaking into the palace might not be that hard. But once in the royal palace, what then?"

"You go down to the dungeon. Find any allies, any of the Freedom Legionnaires, and set them free. We might need their help to get out. Even if it is only to create a diversion."

"What about you, then?"

"I'll be looking for Morpeth's new altar on the upper quarter of the palace."

"Is all that there is to the plan?"

"Yep."

"Jakov, a cyclops and a teenager who can juggle rocks storming a heavily armed palace really ain't much of a plan."

"True. But we can make up the rest as we go along. And you are forgetting one crucial thing."

"What is that?"

"Morpeth may possess supernatural powers, he may have a palace with hundred of armed soldiers, but we have a secret weapon."

"You? Iskandar? What?"

"We have the element of surprise. He's not expecting us to charge in the front door is he?"

"Probably not. But besides that, how do we get into the city?"

Jakov and Sy looked about the massive city wall in front of them.

"Do you have a rope or a grappling hook so we can climb up?" asked Sy. "We need to sneak into the city very stealthily, like a cat on a roof, or like a fox in a chicken yard."

"Or how about like a sledge hammer on an iron roof?"

Jakov slapped the wall of the city with the front of his hand. Slowly the wall began to shake and a massive hole appeared at the bottom where part of the wall just crumbled away. Debris covered the ground and dust floated all among them.

"Or I guess we could just do that," commented Sy.

Jakov went back to his horse and grabbed his diamond studded shield. He came back to Sy.

"You know Jakov, there are places in Dalazvar where it is not safe to go wearing a diamond necklace, let alone carrying a diamond shield around."

"The thieves of Dalazvar are the last people I'm worried about. This shield is my new toy. I hope to give it a proper testing from Morpeth's bolts of fire. Carrying this is better than being burned alive."

"Whatever you think best Jakov".

Both men headed towards the hole in the city wall.

"After you," said Jakov.

With that Sy and then Jakov walked through the freshly made hole in the city wall and then began running down the city streets of Dalazvar.

# Chapter 26

## Jakov and Sy enter the palace

Iskandar fell asleep on the stone table for a while, he wasn't sure how long. Although it was cold and hard, his body simply needed to sleep. He woke to the sound of thunder and lightning in the night sky outside. The sound of rain on the roof of the palace combined with the dim light made him feel almost relaxed in its serene atmosphere, though the altar to Marduk still looked as gloomy as ever. He could see four soldiers standing about the room. They milled about, mumbling to each other every so often, and casting the odd look at him.

He stared up at the wooden ceiling. He noticed that there were cob webs up above and a spider was crawling away from a drip of water that ran along one of the beams. The water then fell off the beam and landed near him. He heard a soft and slow dripping of water falling from the roof onto the water basin near him. The sound gave him hope. If it could fill with water, he might have a chance against the guards.

Iskandar sighed deeply and wondered what was going to happen next. He worried that Morpeth would come through that door at any moment and pick up the knife and kill him. There would be nothing that he could do to stop him. Then his mind turned to Talkai and he became even sadder.

"Where are you Jakov? I need you," he whispered to himself.

Sy and Jakov ran through the streets of Dalazvar. Jakov sprinted like a leopard and Sy did his best to try and keep up.

The streets were mostly empty. The odd lone person could be seen about. The lights of several houses were on. The taverns were filled with people and several sat outside, cheering as they ran past. The rain made it hard to see, the streets were filling with running water and mud, and the odd flash of lightning was all there was to illuminate their way. Rather than tire, Jakov ran even faster, as he could see the palace in the distance.

Jakov reached the road that led into the front entrance of the palace. The palace itself was surrounded by a small three foot wall that was more symbolic of the limits of the palace grounds rather than an actual barrier. A small cobblestone path lead up to the palace doors from the road that ran adjacent to it. Two guards could be seen standing at the front of the entrance. They were soaked with rain, but stood still as statues nonetheless. As Jakov came closer to the front gate he slowed up his run to a brisk walk and then hid behind a wagon that was parked off to the edge of the road. Several moments later, Sy arrived and came up to him.

"I am far too old for this Jakov," said Sy panting.

"Then save your breath, because we will need it once we are inside."

"How do we get past the guards without them sounding the alarm?"

"Easy."

Jakov reached down and used his sword to jimmy out two pieces of stone from the jagged cobblestone path. He took them into his hand and began walking down the cobblestone path towards the palace. The soldiers saw him coming towards them but they paid him no attention. When he got close they raised their spears simultaneously.

"Halt," one of them cried.

"This is the imperial palace, what business have you here?" asked the other.

But that was all he could say as Jakov threw the two pieces of stone from his hands. They darted out like arrows and hit the guards in the head and knocked them out cold.

"My business is with Morpeth," answered Jakov belatedly.

He walked over to the front of the massive door and looked it over. Sy peered behind them to see if anyone had seen them. It would be hard for anyone to hear anything under the cover of the noisy rain and thunder.

"Ready?" asked Jakov.

"I'm not getting any readier, if that is what you mean," the cyclops replied.

"Once we are in we must be relentless, ruthless, and destructive. We need to take down as many men in there as we find. Strike the fear of hell into them through a mixture of surprise and power. No one that comes across us can be left alive. Understood?"

"No objections from me. You watch my back and I'll watch yours."

"Then, let us do this thing we came to do."

Jakov took a few paces back and grabbed his shield with both hands. Then him and Sy both charged at the enormous door and yelled "Yah" as they impacted it. Much to their surprise the door smashed open and they burst into the room, falling onto their stomachs. They were expecting a mass of soldiers and guards to be around them. Yet as they looked about all they could see was a few furnishings, paintings, mirrors, and chairs. There was nothing else and no one else. Except for the sound of the storm behind them outside, they could hear nothing. It was an eerie silence.

"Hello?" called out Jakov.

"Anybody home?" asked Sy.

"We are are here to storm the palace. If anyone would like to come out and fight us, now would be a good time."

"Where is everyone?"

"On holiday, out to dinner, on the lavatory," Jakov conjectured.

"Oh well, guess it must be our lucky night."

"I hope the rest of the night is as lucky."

"If only."

Jakov looked at the staircase and how it led upwards to the upper floors of the palace.

"This is where we part ways Sy. I'm going up there," and he pointed to the staircase.

"Then, I'm going down to the dungeon. I'll find any freedom Legionnaires if they are there. Then I'll join you upstairs."

"See you on the top floor."

"The grace of Vetrius be with you Jakov."

"And with you Sy."

The two men hugged and then ran off in separate directions. Jakov headed up the staircase and Sy ran down the corridor to his left.

Iskandar bit his lip in frustration as he waited for the water basin nearby to fill with water. The dripping from the roof was so slow and he wished it could hurry up.

The door then slowly crept open. There was a pause as the soldiers in the room instantly stood to attention and saluted. They expected Morpeth, but their stance changed from upright to a readiness for action when Jakov stood at the doorway.

"Surrender or be killed," called one guard as he pointed his spear at Jakov.

Jakov ignored the threat and charged at him with his diamond encrusted shield and his sword.

"Jakov," cried Iskandar with his heart filled with exhilaration. "I knew you'd come for me."

As much as Jakov wanted to respond with equal joy he found himself rather busy. He was slicing and blocking the attacks of the four guards. The soldiers' blows bounced off his shield and one soldier even broke his sword as he tried to strike through it. Jakov focused on quick movements, sharp changes in direction, and varied his line of attack against them.

Jakov raised his shield to block one sword strike from above and simultaneously drove his sword into the guard's stomach. Then he kicked out his right leg and drove another guard into the wall and then spun around and sliced him across throat. The two remaining guards charged forward, but Jakov jumped up and flipped behind them and slashed them both across their legs and back from behind. They fell to the ground and soon became motionless.

Jakov ran over to Iskandar and noticed the restraints placed on Iskandar. With a ferocious strike, he cut through the ropes and broke the chains binding his brother. Iskandar sat up and embraced Jakov, who in turn hugged him and kissed him.

"Are you alright Iskandar?"

"Yes, I think so."

"I'm sorry. I'm sorry you were captured. It was my fault. I shouldn't have trusted Mordecai. I should have rescued you back in the Yobi desert, but I failed. I'm sorry, brother."

"It's okay. You're here. I knew you'd come."

"Nothing on earth could stop me."

"Where are the others? Where is Sy and Ayesha and the dwarves?"

"Sy is in the dungeon looking for prisoners. Ayesha was hurt. She will be okay, but she was badly injured. Mo and Tar and looking after her."

"How did you get into the palace?"

"It is kind of strange. But the place is basically deserted. I don't know where all the guards are. But they are not here. I only saw three or four servants as I ran up the stairs. Those servants just dived out of the way as I ran passed."

"I'm glad you came. I didn't stop believing in you."

"We should get out of here then. We can fight Morpeth another day."

"No we can't," said Iskandar with a serious voice.

"Why not?" he asked, seeing a fear in Iskandar's eyes.

Then there was a voice from behind him.

"That's because he's standing behind you Jakov"

Jakov turned around and saw Morpeth standing there with his arms folded.

Jakov clenched his shield to his chest and raised his sword upright. Iskandar stood on the stone table and tried to hide behind Jakov. The eyes of Jakov and Morpeth locked onto each other.

"It seems that our game of combat will end tonight Jakov. One way or the other," said Morpeth.

"It will end alright old man. You can take my word for that."

Sy ran through the corridor and finally came to a flight of stairs that descended downwards in what looked like a dull and gloomy lower chamber. He went down the poorly lit corridor and could finally see rows of doors. These were obviously prison rooms. As he went along he came across only one man, a jailer, who tried to hit Sy with a chair. But Sy smashed the chair with his axe and the jailer ran into one of the rooms and locked himself in. Sy just shook his head at the man and kept moving along the corridor.

Sy checked each room for persons. Most were empty. But in three of them he did find Freedom Legionnaires who had been captured. He knew two of them by name and the third was the son of a friend. He smashed the doors open with his axe and ordered the three men to make their way out of the palace and to wait for him at the junction on the King's Highway. They thanked him for his efforts and they ran out of the dungeon as Sy continued his search for Freedom Legionnaires.

Finally, Sy came to the last room. He peered in through a small slot and saw a man lying on the ground.

"Oi, you in there. Wake up! Wake up, I say. I'm here to free you. Can you hear me? Are you alright?"

But the man didn't move.

Sy leaned back and again smashed the door with the ferocious power of his axe. He went up to the man and gently shook him on his shoulder. Yet he did not move. Sy rolled him over onto his back and looked at the man. It was Balthasar. He had been the chief commander of the imperial army. Sy supposed that he had recently lost favour with Morpeth and had died in the cell. His death looked gruesome. Someone had impaled him on his own sword. Sy had no grief for the man since he had been the main adversary to the Freedom Legionnaires for so many years.

Sy's mind now turned to Jakov and Iskandar. He stood up and began running back along the corridor, thinking only of what could be happening to his dear friends.

# Chapter 27

## Morpeth versus His Sons

MORPETH STOOD HIS GROUND and blocked the only way out of the room.

"The reason why you found it so easy to enter the palace is because every man I could find is currently looking for you in an underground tunnel or else combing the grounds outside the city for you. There was meant to be a trap, but it seems that my trap did not go to plan."

"That is the least of your worries now Morpeth," Jakov blurted back, while Iskandar was gripping the hem of his cloak.

"I have reason to believe that Prisca is dead. Am I right?"

"Yes, I killed her the same way that I will kill you."

Iskandar heard the news that Prisca was dead, but he didn't know what to think, what he should feel, or how he should respond. All he could think about was how he and Jakov could escape from Morpeth. He looked to his left to the table near him. The knife was still there and the basin of water was still filling up.

"Jakov, my son, we don't have to do this. Submit to me, my boy. The only hope that there is for you and for your brother is death. If you die, then you will live again. If you die, your brothers and sisters will live again too. Lay your life down Jakov, and I will raise it up again for you."

"I have no time for riddles or for your ridiculous devotion to that false god Marduk."

"You have already tasted Marduk's power. But that power has doubled since we last met Jakov. I have not only my own power, but that of Prisca also flows through my body now. Unless you surrender, you will taste the full extent of my powers."

"I will die first before I give in to you."

"Then you have made your choice son. I will take you by force."

"You can try old man, but it won't be as easy as you think."

"You two are the only things that stand in the way of my deification. Now, it is time for me to be reborn as a god. I will not hold back."

"Me either."

With that, Jakov waved his hand and some bricks came out of the wall behind him and flew towards Morpeth. Morpeth in turn wielded his hands and an immense wind blew the bricks off course and sent them smashing into the wall. The impact caused the entire wall to shake, and part of the roof gave way, revealing the stormy night outside. More water poured into the room and Iskandar saw that more landed into the copper water basin on the table. The wind and rain that ebbed in caused the torches in the room to go out, leaving it darkened and only the light from the corridor and from the gap in the roof above provided any light.

In the near darkness, Morpeth placed his fist into his palm and formed a fire ball that grew in size. In one quick motion, he threw his hands forward and the blazing ball of flame carved through the air right towards Jakov. Jakov ducked his head behind his shield and Iskandar ducked behind Jakov. Then Jakov lunged forward with his shield in front of him and the ball of fire bounced off his shield like a stone and rebounded back towards Morpeth. Morpeth dived out of the way just in time and narrowly avoided being fried by his own ball of fire. The fireball hit the wall behind Morpeth and set alight the curtains and furnishings there. Suddenly, the room was far from dark, but aglow from the fire. The room contained a strange mix of cold night air from the storm outside and searing heat from the fire.

Jakov sent another brick from the wall flying through the air at Morpeth. Morpeth again responded by using his power over the wind to shift the flight path of the brick and force it to hit the wall behind him. The walls again shook and more of the wooden roof fell down. This time the fallen debris caught fire. In return, Morpeth created another fireball with his hands, even larger than the first. But no sooner had he thrown it at Jakov than it again ricocheted off his sparkling shield and nearly slammed into Morpeth.

"This contest is becoming tedious and predictable Jakov. Our powers over the elements are at an impasse. We can play this game of stone and fire all night if you wish. But I think we might be better off trying to settle things the old fashioned way."

"Steel over magic is my choice any day. So I'll give you the chance to taste my steel now," Jakov retorted.

Morpeth took out his sword and clutched it with both hands tightly and looked at Jakov with a penetrating stare. Jakov in turn stepped forward with his shield and sword at the ready. Iskandar jumped to the ground behind the stone table since it looked like the safest spot in the room, but he kept his eyes fixed on Jakov and Morpeth, who moved closer towards each other.

Morpeth attacked first. He was much taller than Jakov. His blows were fast and powerful. Despite his age, he moved with the prowess and speed of a young man. Jakov was at first caught off guard by the swiftness and power of his blows. Jakov dodged and parried.

Morpeth raised his sword over his shoulder and swung it downwards. Jakov sidestepped and struck Morpeth across the face with his shield. The blow sent Morpeth staggering backwards.

"That was for my brother, Brutoi," said Jakov.

While Morpeth was off balance, Jakov kicked him in the stomach. Morpeth staggered back further. Iskandar could hear the wind knocked out of Morpeth from the strike.

"That was for my sister, Karla," Jakov yelled at him.

Morpeth took a moment to regain himself and then pressed forward with two stabbing blows. Both were deflected off Jakov's shield. Jakov allowed Morpeth to overrun him and as he went passed Jakov sliced Morpeth across his arms. Morpeth hissed in pain.

"That was for my sister, Izza."

Morpeth swung his sword horizontally and Jakov ducked the blow and then sliced his sword along Morpeth's shoulder. Morpeth let out a cry of pain and frustration.

"That was for my brother, Crestin."

"Shut up, Jakov."

"No, Morpeth. I will remind you of your sins before I kill you."

The two men traded further blows of swords. The room became more ablaze with fire and the roof continued to give way. More water spilled into the room from the roof and some of it extinguished the burning items. Smoke and ash mixed about in the air, creating a musty odour in the room.

Morpeth then sent a ball of flame at Jakov. It caught Jakov by surprise, but he had enough time to duck behind his shield. Yet the momentum of the fire ball knocked him to the ground. As he was on the ground and vulnerable, Morpeth rushed at him and slashed downwards at him. Jakov rolled to his left and to his right to avoid the blows. Then, just as Morpeth was about to strike downwards again, Jakov drove his sword into

Morpeth's chest and drew it back just as quickly. The old man let out a cry of pain and stumbled backwards. Jakov rose to his feet.

"That was for my brother, Iskandar, whom you nearly killed."

Morpeth stumbled about, gripping his chest in clear agony. He was barely conscious as he swayed back and fro. He dropped his sword and fell sideways onto the wall, but managed to upright himself again. Finally, he fell to his knees and lifted his hands up.

"Please, son, have mercy on me. I can survive these blows. But I cannot survive a beheading. Take pity on me."

"I will show you the same mercy you showed my brothers and sisters. None!"

Jakov slowly walked up behind Morpeth and took up his sword and prepared to strike.

"And this, this one is for me."

Jakov then drove his sword into the back of Morpeth so that it came through the other side. Iskandar turned his eyes away at the hideous sight. Morpeth screamed out loudly once more. He collapsed forward onto all fours with the sword still protruding out of his chest.

Jakov had no emotion on his face. He dropped his shield and then took up his other sword that was still on his back. As Morpeth was still leaning forward, Jakov moved around to Morpeth's side.

"I'm ending this now Morpeth. Once and for all."

Morpeth looked up at Iskandar with a countenance of hatred on his face as he panted for breath. Jakov looked at Morpeth's neck, gripped his sword in both hands, and then swung his sword up high over his head to gain enough force to land the killing blow. But as the sword came down, Morpeth raised his hands and latched onto Jakov's arms. Morpeth then pushed Jakov's arms apart awkwardly so that he dropped his sword. Springing up with his last vestiges of strength, Morpeth wrapped his arms around Jakov and pressed his body against his in a type of bear hug. As he did that, the sword that protruded through Morpeth penetrated into Jakov's own chest.

Jakov's eyes went wide opened and his mouth shut in the agony of pain.

"And that is for my god, Marduk," said Morpeth.

"No," cried Iskandar, who felt a wave of grief and a strange surge of power in his own body. His heart sank, his eyes welled with tears, but his fingers and feet tingled with a peculiar sensation.

Morpeth squeezed Jakov as tight as he could until he felt the life leave the young man. He let go and Jakov dropped to the floor motionless and lifeless. Morpeth then reached behind him with one hand and with great anguish on his face he pulled the sword out from behind him. He shrieked from the pain, but enjoyed the instant relief it gave him. He turned his attention to Iskandar.

"I am an immortal boy. Soon I am to be a god. You cannot kill an immortal. Not one like me."

"You're a murderer," Iskandar responded, cowering from the far side of the stone table.

"I had no choice. And neither do you. You must die Iskandar. Then we all will be free of this mess."

Morpeth slowly advanced towards Iskandar. Iskandar momentarily froze in terror and tried moving to the opposite side of the table. Morpeth, still slow and wounded, struggled to keep up with the boy as Iskandar squirmed and dodged around the other side of the table.

"There is no point in resisting. You are delaying the inevitable," said Morpeth, with the rain and wind from the broken roof falling upon him. Despite the stormy conditions that now entered the room, the fires kept burning, fueled by the gusty wind that entered the room.

Iskandar lost his footing on the wet ground and Morpeth grabbed him by the neck, picked him up, and laid him on the stone table. Morpeth put his hands around the small boy's neck and began to squeeze. Iskandar could not breathe and he tried grasping Morpeth's hands but it was too late.

"Forgive me child. But there is no other way. My deification is nigh."

Iskandar looked up at the water basin adjacent to him. The basin was now full of water and was even overflowing. As the pressure around his neck tightened, Iskandar reached upward and called to the water. In a second, the water turned cold and crystallized into ice. Iskandar bent his fingers and the ice burst from the copper basin and was propelled into the air. A large block of ice struck Morpth across the head and sent him sprawling backwards.

Iskandar gasped for breath and wasted no time as he got up and ran towards the door. But just before he got through the door, a ball of fire struck the door and flames blocked his path. He looked about for another exit. He thought about trying to jump through the door even though it was ablaze. He thought about trying to use his power over the water to extinguish the flames on the door, but his indecision cost him. As he turned around, he saw that Morpeth was back up and was on top of him. Morpeth grabbed him by the back of his neck, picked him up, and threw him down very hard on the stone table. Morpeth leaned on top of him with his knee in Iskandar's back. Morpeth leaned over and took the dagger from the wooden table near the stone table.

Morpeth held the dagger upright and prepared to stab down at Iskandar.

"I do this in the name of my god, Marduk. I do this for the divine power I have been promised. I do this for my family."

Before Morpeth could plunge the dagger into Iskandar, Iskandar saw a blur of movement from the roof descending downwards at a rapid speed. He saw what looked like a physical form and a mass of purple fall through the air.

The purple knight dived through the hole in the wooden roof and his foot collided with Morpeth's chin. Morpeth fell to the ground dazed and rolled across the ground for several feet. The knight grabbed Iskandar under his arms and lifted him off the table.

"Get behind me," the knight said.

Not knowing what to do, Iskandar moved behind the knight in the dark purple armour and waited. The two of them moved backwards still facing towards Morpeth who was gingerly getting up off the ground. The two walked passed Jakov's lifeless body. Iskandar had to turn his face away. Reaching down, the knight picked up the diamond studded shield and held it up. The knight also drew out his sword.

Morpeth got up to his feet.

"And who are you?" Morpeth asked the knight.

"An old family friend," the knight replied.

"I have no time for games. Who are you, really?"

"You know who I am Morpeth. You know why I am here."

Morpeth stopped for a moment. He looked the knight up and down, shook his head, and spat on the ground clearing the blood from his mouth.

"I should have known that you'd be back. You were behind this all along. Still jealous of my power and my greatness."

"I am a servant of Vetrius, Morpeth. He will suffer your murderous lusts no more. The day of your judgment has arrived."

"The only day that has arrived is my day of divine glory. Vetrius will serve me in the heavens. I will make him my slave."

"I think otherwise."

"Do you just? That is easily changed."

Morpeth unleashed a fireball at the knight and Iskandar. The two crouched down behind the shield. Morpeth launched more fireballs and the knight in armour struggled to keep hold of the shield. He turned to Iskandar and looked at him through the visor in his helmet.

"Iskandar, I cannot hold him forever. It is up to you now. Only you can stop him."

"But how?"

"Remember what you did at the battlefield at Norella?"

"Yes," answered Iskandar, as another fireball crashed around them and Morpeth bellowed out in laughter.

"What you do now must be a shadow of what you did that day."

"I can't. It's impossible."

Fireballs kept landing and the fire around them grew more and more intense.

"I can do this all day," called Morpeth. "You can surrender to me or surrender your flesh to the flames."

"Iskandar," the knight yelled at him. "Do it for Jakov. Do it for all of us who have suffered."

Iskandar kneeled down and put his hands in his face and thought for a moment about what to do. He then peered around the shield that the knight held and saw the body of Jakov lying there as the rain from the broken roof pelted his body. As hot as the room was with the flames and fire around him, it was now nothing compared to the sheer rage that burned inside him.

After another fireball, the knight was knocked over backwards and Iskandar rolled to his left. Seeing Iskandar move, Morpeth turned his attention towards him and began briskly walking to him.

"Don't resist, Iskandar. There is no escape. It must be this way."

"No, Morpeth. It will not be this way."

Iskandar clenched his fists tight as he could and then he called in his mind to every drop of water and every inch of rain that might hear him.

Morpeth prepared a fireball and threw it at Iskandar. Iskandar opened his fist and raised his hand at Morpeth with his palm facing him. At that gesture all the water in the room somehow rushed together and formed a shield of water that blocked the ball of flame. The flame itself was extinguished on impact with the wall of water.

In frustration, Morpeth sent more raging blows of fire at Iskandar. One fireball after another came flying, but the wall of water stopped them all. Morpeth then sent the fireballs combined with wind, but again he was unable to break the wall of water.

"An impressive weapon of defence, my boy. But it will take more than water to hurt me, I'm afraid."

"Don't be so sure," Iskandar called back.

Iskandar clenched his fists again and the wall of water separated into two parts. Morpeth stared in amazement as the two parts of water then changed into the shape of fists and also crystallized into ice. The iced fists were roughly the size of a small wagon and looked dense.

"What is this?" he asked.

Iskandar raised his fists upwards and the fist-shaped ice also turned upwards. Iskandar moved his fists and the ice mirrored his actions.

Iskandar then threw a punch into the air and the ice mimicked the motion and struck Morpeth across the body. Iskandar then punched into the air again, and again, and again. Each time the ice fists collided with Morpeth on his head, body, or legs. Morpeth was sent reeling across the room from the blows. He tried to steady himself, yet each time he regained balance he was knocked down again. Iskandar's rage continued as the fists of ice pummelled Morpeth all across the room. Soon his face was bloodied from the blows. Iskandar wound himself up for one particular blow and at that, Morpeth was belted across the room and landed on the stone table.

Morpeth lay on the stone table, unable to get up. He groaned and leaned to his left, hoping to fall off the table. As he did that, Iskandar raised both of his fists high into the air and slammed them downwards. The fists of ice imitated the motion and Morpeth was pounded with such force that the stone table underneath him broke.

Crawling along the floor, Morpeth tried to scurry towards the door with what strength he had left.

"Oh no, you don't," said Iskandar. "You will not escape this time."

Iskandar reached his right arm across the body and let fly with his hand in front of him. One of the ice fists replicated the movement and Morpeth was once more thrown across the room.

Next Iskandar opened his fists and reached out and made a grabbing motion. The fingers in the fists of ice likewise extended and encased Morpeth in their grasp. Iskandar squeezed his hand and the ice squeezed around Morpeth so much so that Morpeth struggled for breath. Iskandar squeezed tighter again and then stopped.

Morpeth remained there trapped in the grip of ice and his face contorted with pain. Iskandar walked across the room and picked up the dagger that only moments ago Morpeth had almost used to stab him with. Morpeth panted for breath. His face was bruised, and bleeding all over. Iskandar advanced on him with the knife.

Just then Iskandar felt the knight's hand on his shoulder.

"Wait," he said.

"For what? He must die."

"I know, but let me do it."

Iskandar did not understand but nodded.

Iskandar clapped his hands and the ice around Morpeth disintegrated. Morpeth fell downwards with his head bowed low to the ground.

The knight took out his sword from his side.

"Step back, please, Iskandar."

Iskandar obeyed, but kept his eyes on Morpeth in case he tried anything. As he did, Iskandar saw that Morpeth now looked old, weak, and powerless. He looked more like he expected an old man to be. He was not the menacing figure he recognized from only minutes earlier. He looked vulnerable, almost pitiable.

The knight gently kicked Morpeth in the stomach.

"I am sorry for this Morpeth, but this is for the best, for everyone" said the knight.

"I know," Morpeth struggled to say.

"Your release will be quick. Your suffering will be over."

"Good, that is good news. End it for me. End it now. Stop me from committing any more evil. Set me free brother. Free me from this insanity."

Iskandar was surprised, even slightly annoyed, when he saw the knight kneel down beside Morpeth and softly stroked Morpeth's head with his hand. Morpeth did not seem to mind.

"Do it now, before I recover," Morpeth demanded.

The knight raised up his sword and swung it downwards. The blow was swift, hard, and brutal. The knight beheaded Morpeth and then stared down at the dead body of the former king of Iona. The knight looked genuinely sad, even regretful at what he had done. It was then Iskandar also began to feel some grief. For Jakov, for Talkai, and now even for Morpeth. It was a sad sight. He had seen some good in the man. But the good had been consumed with a lust for divine power.

Iskandar then felt very peculiar. It was like a buzzing feeling in his mind, butterflies in his stomach, and pins and needles in his hands and feet.

"Is it over?" Iskandar asked.

"Yes," the knight replied. "Almost over, that is."

"What is left? Morpeth is dead. Prisca is dead. Even Jakov is dead. It must be over."

"It is not the end yet, Iskandar. There is still one last thing you must do. There is still one last miracle you must perform."

"What? There is no one left to fight."

"The last foe you must beat is death. Death is the ally of Marduk and you have the power to defeat him here."

"Defeat death? What are you talking about?"

"Do you feel different Iskandar? Do you feel strange? Almost peculiar?"

"Yes," he answered wondering how the knight knew.

"You are now an immortal. You cannot be killed, unless your head is removed from your body. You have a choice. You can live forever in this state or you can give up your immortality and impart life to another. You can impart life to someone else like Jakov."

"I am immortal? How?"

"The life and power that was in Jakov, Prisca, and Morpeth has passed onto you. You are the last survivor of them all. The life of the others now flows into you. It is up to you how you will use that power."

"How can I be immortal? I feel peculiar, but not immortal."

"Then, how do you think immortality would feel?" he asked.

"I don't want to be immortal. I saw what it did to Morpeth and Prisca. I don't want this curse. I want to give life to Jakov."

"A good choice."

The knight took Iskandar by the hand and led him over to Jakov.

Iskandar touched Jakov's face and it was cold, clammy, and his clothes were soaked with water.

"What do I do?" Iskandar asked the knight.

"Lay your hands upon his face and then breathe upon him. Then it will be done."

"Okay."

"Wait," interjected the knight. "Are you sure you want to do this? This is immortality that you have. Are you so quick to give it up?"

"Jakov gave up his life to save mine. The least I can do is give life back to him. For the sake of his children, I have to."

"Very well, then let it be so."

Iskandar layed his hands on Jakov and then breathed on him as the knight instructed. Nothing happened at first, but then Iskandar felt the strange sensation all through his body drain away. At the same time, he saw colour return to Jakov's cheeks. His skin became warmer, and Jakov coughed.

"He's alive," Iskandar said with jubilation. "He's alive," he called again, almost crying.

Jakov slowly started moving and looked like he was coming out of a deep sleep.

Then Iskandar froze for a moment.

"What about Talkai? Can I use this power again to bring him to life as well?"

"No, I'm afraid not. It can only be used once."

"But what about Talkai?"

"He is not dead. He is very much alive."

"How do you know that?" Iskandar pleaded.

"Because, I just do. You must trust me."

"I know who you are," asserted Iskandar, as he noted Jakov making more movements. "You are Fallkirk, our uncle. Morpeth's brother. You're the one who saved us from Morpeth in the temple and from the mountain trolls. I thought it was you. I knew it in my heart."

"Yes, I am Fallkirk," the knight then put his hands on his helmet and lifted it off to show Iskandar his face. "But for most of your life, you have known me as Talkai."

Iskandar's face turned ashen with shock at what he was seeing. In the purple armour was the body of a great warrior, but on top of it was the head of Talkai.

"But how . . . how could you be the one who saved us? Talkai is . . . I mean, you are . . . you are not very smart or very brave. I mean, you were always so silly, so clumsy, so scared all the time. How can you be Fallkirk, the man who fights trolls and rides a dragon?"

Talkai smiled at him.

"It is a long story. But I had to protect you until the day came when you and Jakov were to fight Morpeth and Prisca. That day was today."

"But everyone thinks that you are some kind of fool or imbecile. Even I did."

"Iskandar, in order to remain by your side and to avoid detection I played the part of a fool. And I believe that I played it well. I did it to protect you and to protect Jakov."

"But how? How did this all happen?"

"After I rescued you and Jakov from the temple of Marduk, I intended for all of us to go into the western ranges looking for shelter among the hermits and nomads of the plain. But before I got there something happened to me. I went to rest under a tree, but while I was there a snake bit me on my arm. I don't know how to explain it, or if I even understand it, but I died. The next thing I remembered was a shining citadel and a great white throne and upon the throne was one like a man. He had a look of mercy and compassion in his eyes. His clothes shone like no fabric I've ever seen and a feeling of peace overcame me as I came close to him. He told me to go back to the world of men. He said that he had heard the prayers of those who suffered and I was chosen to protect the two of you until the day of redemption for Iona. I was ordained to be the guardian of the two children who would bring peace to the kingdom and healing to the land."

"Who was the man on the throne?" asked Iskandar.

"I believe that he was Vetrius. When I woke up I was alive, but different. I knew what I had to do. I hid Jakov with the Zeniti tribe among the forests. I hid you in Praschi with an old friend of mine called Wringstone."

"Wringstone was your friend?"

"A retired soldier whom I knew well. A good man and a dear friend."

"But he always used to beat you," Iskandar complained.

"He only pretended to. After you went to bed every night we would share a cup of wine or ale together and laugh about the whole thing. He acted mean and harsh in public, but he was in fact a good man. He gave his life to protect yours."

"So the whole time, it was you?"

"I've done my best to orchestrate things so that we would come to this point. It was me who sent the snow falcon to Jakov with a note saying that you were in Praschi. It was me who also told Morpeth's spies that you were in Praschi so that Morpeth's hand would be forced to act. It was me shot the imperial guards in Praschi with special arrows made by the Minim tribe with my crossbow. It was me who shot the giant capterpillar with the same arrows. It was me who killed the trolls. It was me who rescued Jakov in the Yobi desert. It was me who came to Dalazvar to find you."

"But what about the red dragon?"

"The dragon is a gift from Vetrius. He sent it to me several years ago to help me in my service to him. His name is Magnon, and he is the most wonderful pet anyone could have."

"I cannot believe this. The whole time you were with me, watching over me, looking after me. Vetrius sent you to guard us."

"Vetrius means to liberate this world from the evil power of Marduk and his servants. Morpeth and Prisca were seduced and then betrayed by Marduk. They would not have become gods by killing their children. They would have become his servants in whatever nether region that Marduk inhabits. They were granted immortality, but Marduk cannot grant divinity to anyone since he is not divine himself. Marduk was once a mortal like us. He was a man, a priest of an ancient cult. It was through treachery and murder that he ascended to the pantheon of the demigods. He is no more divine than you or me. He is only a god to those foolish enough to worship him. Marduk's day is still yet to come, that I'm sure of."

"I still find it hard to believe."

"There is one more thing you must know Iskandar. I must warn you that it is shocking."

"What could be more shocking than to find out that my best friend is also my uncle."

"I am not your uncle, Iskandar. I am your father. Your mother was Prisca, but I am your father by flesh and blood. I am sorry. It needs to be explained someday. In the fullness of time I will do so, but there is no time right now. One day there will be."

Jakov coughed and sputtered some more. "Where am I?" he asked groggerly.

Iskandar looked up at Fallirk. "You're my father?"

"Yes, I am, my son. And I want you to know that I am so proud of you and I love you. And no matter where I am, I will always be thinking about you."

Fallkirk stood up.

"Where are you going?" Iskandar asked.

"I am a servant of Vetrius. Your work here is done, but mine continues. The battle against Marduk rages on. What we have done here is but a small battle in a larger war. One that I must fight in."

"Will I ever see you again?"

Fallkirk smiled and hugged the boy.

"Yes, I promise you that. Sooner than you think. And even when you can't see me, know this, I will always be watching over you."

The rain had stopped and the first rays of the dawn light could be seen through the roof.

"Magnon," yelled Fallkirk.

After a few seconds there was a shrieking sound and more of the roof collapsed as the large dragon landed on it. Fallkirk mounted up, but looked back at Iskandar.

"We will be reunited soon, son. Oh, and when you get back to Devora, Vetrius has some old friends waiting for you and Jakov. Take care my son!"

All Iskandar could do was wave as Fallkirk took off into the sky on the back of the dragon.

# Chapter 28

## The New King and Regent of Iona

JAKOV SLOWLY BEGAN TO rouse. He rubbed his face, sat upright, and looked at Iskandar in confusion.

"What happened? Why aren't I dead?"

Iskandar put his hand on Jakov's shoulder.

"I'm not sure if I know how to explain it. I don't know if you'll even believe it."

"Where is Morpeth?" Jakov interrupted.

"He is dead. The battle is over."

"Did we win?"

"Yes, but only just."

Jakov searched the room and then saw the headless body of Morpeth. It grieved him and shocked him. Jakov felt relief, but not joy.

"Then you defeated him, Iskandar. I knew you could do it. I believed in you."

"I did have some help."

"From who?"

"From my father."

"Do you mean Fallkirk?" Jakov asked with some hesitation.

"No, from Talkai."

"What?"

"I'll explain that to you later too. It has been one confusing day."

At that moment, Sy ran into the room and he stopped when he saw the two boys sitting there.

"Is the battle over?" he asked.

"You're late again Sy," responded Jakov. "You missed the whole thing, as usual."

"You're the one who told me to go and check the dungeons."

"No matter, let's just get out of here while we still can."

Jakov and Sy walked out of the door, while Iskandar stood still, looking through the broken roof up into the sky.

Noticing that he wasn't with them, Jakov came back into the room.

"What are you looking for?"

"Nothing, I'll tell you later."

The trio hastily walked through the corridor and down the stairs. They encountered the odd servant who only stared at them as they walked passed. Jakov rubbed his shoulder and stretched his neck. Iskandar himself limped a bit from the frantic exhaustion of the fight with Morpeth. The three came to the front entrance of the parlour and saw there the door that Sy and Jakov had knocked down. The palace was mostly empty and there was an eerie silence.

Jakov looked about.

"This isn't right. There should be shoulders and guards here by now."

They slowly walked towards the door and as they stood in the entrance way they could see hundres of men in uniforms standing in the grounds of the palace.

"Oh dear," said Sy.

Jakov's shoulders slumped.

"Getting out of here might prove harder then getting in."

"Do you think we can talk our way out of this one?" the cyclops asked.

Jakov shook his head.

"Probably not. We just killed their king and queen. Custom tells me that such feats often annoy people."

"Okay then," said Sy as he lifted up his axe. "I'll take the two hundred on the left, you take the two hundred on the right, and I'll meet you in Devora before tea time."

"Maybe not," added Iskandar as one of the soldiers approached.

A soldier came forward with his sword sheathed and his imperial helmet on. Sy and Jakov could tell by his insignia and decorations that he was a high-ranking soldier in the imperial army. All the soldiers stood behind him at attention. Everyone was staring at Sy, Jakov, and Iskandar.

"Are you sons of the divine Morpeth and Prisca?" the soldier asked in an alarmed tone.

"We are," anwered Jakov confidently.

"Do the king and queen live? Have they ascended into the heavens as gods yet?"

"No, they are both dead. And you are looking at their killers."

The soldier paused, swallowed slowly, and look back over the troops behind him.

"How are we to believe you?"

"If you go up to the altar that Morpeth made, you'll find a corpse that has been beheaded. That is all that is left of Morpeth."

"What of Queen Prisca, where is she?"

"Just outside the eastern wall of the city. Same thing."

On hearing those words, the soldier took out his swords and pointed it at Jakov. He then turned around and punched the sword high into the air as he faced the many troops.

With a mighty voice the soldier called out to them, "Morpeth is slain. The king is dead. Morpeth is slain."

The crowd of soldier then let out a might cry of triumph, applause, and joy. Many threw their helmets high into the air, others clapped, and some even danced. It was a scene of unbridled celebration and great jubilation.

The soldiers turned back around to face Jakov. He bent down on one knee before Jakov and laid his sword across his hands.

"My name is Aquinas. I am the warden of the palace. I offer you my sword. For you are the heir of Morpeth and you are our new king."

Jakov's face lit up with surprise and he looked astounded at Aquinas' words.

"Listen up my good man, I am no king. You have mistaken me for someone else."

"You are the heir and you are the king." Aquinas insisted.

"I think we might have to talk this over some other time."

But it was no good. The soldier turned around and yelled at the rejoicing soldiers.

"The king is dead," then, lifting up Jakov's hand, he shouted even louder, "Long live the king! Long live king Jakov!"

The men responded in an anthem of agreement.

"The king is dead. Long live the king. Long live king Jakov."

"Oh no, they just made me king," Jakov opined.

"I can think of worse things, Jakov," Sy said to him.

Iskandar giggled at the soldiers calling out Jakov's name. He tugged on Jakov's sleeve.

"I guess you were right. Getting out of here might be harder than we thought."

"I really can't wait to see how you talk yourself out of this one Jakov," Sy whispered in his ear.

"Wait," announced Jakov to the men with a booming voice. "Listen to me. Listen to me, men of Dalazvar. As your king, I wish to make my first royal decree."

At his word the men fell immediately silent.

"This day we celebrate our liberty from the tyranny of Morpeth. I, Jakov, hereby appoint Sy of the Glenn as Regent of the city and Protector of Iona."

Sy's single eye nearly popped out of his head and he stared at Jakov in disbelief.

"What? Are you mad? You can't be serious. You can't appoint me Regent of the city."

"Can and just did. And why not? I think you'll make a fine Regent. You have nothing else to do. There are no more wars to fight. You are a great leader of men. You need a home and they need a leader. And besides, it means that I have an excuse to leave now."

Several men picked up Sy, somewhat against his will, and they put him up on their shoulders and carried him about. As they did so, they cheered and praised him. Many called out, "Hail Sy, the Regent of Dalazvar. Hail Sy, the Protector of Iona."

Over the rejoicing and merriment, Sy could only just be heard as he called out to Jakov, himself half laughing at what was happening, "I'll get you for this Jakov."

After that the men carried Sy away in their enthusiasm and took him on a tour of the streets of Dalazvar. They danced underneath him and sang songs of his greatness.

Jakov and Iskandar just stood there laughing. Jakov then turned to Aquinas.

"May I trouble you for two of your finest horses. My brother and I have a long ride ahead of us."

"At once, your majesty."

Aquinas clicked his fingers and two attendants came to him. They were instructed and several minutes later two fresh horses were presented to Jakov and Iskandar.

The two boys mounted the horses and began walking down the street of Dalazvar. People rushed out of their houses to see what the excitement wall all about. As the news spread of Morpeth's death there was cheering and dancing in the streets. People let out cries of joy and people followed

Sy and his cavalcade around the city. The streets became so crowded with merriment that the two found it hard to walk through the streets on their horses. Everyone who saw them came up and shook their hand and offered them cake and wine.

Eventually, they left the crowd behind and they go to the front entrance of the city. They looked behind them to take one last look at the palace which still towered in the air. Although smoke could still be seen to be coming from one of the far corners where Morpeth's altar had been.

"Do you think Sy will be happy here?" asked Iskandar.

"I know Sy very well. I know he'll be happy here. The people of Dalazvar could not have a finer ruler."

"Why did you make Sy the Regent? Why not reign as king yourself?"

"Because I already have something far more precious than any kingdom. I have a wife and a family. Looking after them is the only kingdom I need."

Jakov leaned over and hugged Iskandar and scruffed his hair with his hand.

"And looking after my little brother as well will keep me far more occupied than the affairs of state. Shall we go, brother?"

"Where to?"

"Where do you think?"

"To Devora, I guess."

"Home to Devora, for sure."

Jakov and Iskandar kicked their horses and trotted along down the road. The early morning light warmed their faces as they travelled into towards morning sun that was still coming over the horizon.

# Chapter 29

## Reunion at Devora

THE RIDE LASTED A day, a night, and most of the next morning. Along the way they talked and relived the whole adventure of the last several days. Jakov was still unable to believe that Fallkirk, the mysterious knight, and Talkai were the same person. The unseasonable warmth meant that it was possible to ride their horses the whole way into Nazvor, through the ice desert, and towards the famous eastern ice palace Devora. Despite the cold air around them, there was warmth in Jakov's soul as he saw the great ice palace ahead of them. With only a few miles to go, they galloped the final distance with their horses at full pace. As they neared the gates, trumpets were sounded by men on watchtowers who saw them coming. Jakov punched into the air as he passed the front gates. There was a frantic movement of people about the ice gardens as servants helped them down from their horses.

Jakov shook hands with several attendants that he knew and he exchanged greetings with them. More trumplets blew, murmering could be heard about the grounds, and several persons went inside and outside of the palace doors. Iskandar felt a slight shiver from the cold as he had forgotten how chilly Nazvor was.

"We are home at last Iskandar. Home, where we belong."

"How does it feel?"

"It feels good, brother."

Some attendants brought them larger coats as they walked towards one of the palace doors. Before they reached the door it was opened and Marius and Alexa came running out with arms open.

"Marius, Alexa," Jakov called.

"Daddy," they called in reply.

The children hugged each leg of Jakov as he showered their heads with kisses and squeezed them hard. He rubbed his face on theirs and kissed their cheeks.

"Daddy, you smell," said Alexa. Jakov laughed.

"Then, go hug your uncle Iskandar, he smells far smellier than me."

The children left Jakov and jumped up on Iskandar and knocked him over onto the snowy ground.

"Uncle Iskandar," they kept calling out. "Did you bring us presents?"

Jakov looked up next and saw Aurora walking towards him softly. Her head was covered with a white scarf and her ruby red lips stood out from her pale skin, ebony hair, and white dress.

She smiled at him and the couple ran towards each other and embraced. They kissed long and hard, hugged, and kissed some more. Finally they just held each other for a moment and Aurora ran her fingers through Jakov's hair.

"I thought you might never come back," she confided in him.

"I nearly didn't come back."

"Is it over?" she asked.

"Yes, it is over. It is finished."

"At last, we can have you home for good."

Iskandar only just managed to get off the ground from Marius and Alexa jumping on him when Mo and Tar leaped on him too and began tickling him on his ribs.

"Stop it," he cried as he giggled, but the two dwarves tickled him all the more.

Ayesha hobbled out from the doorway as well on crutches. Her face looked full of colour even if her movements were slow and deliberate.

"You are looking much better Ayesha," Jakov commented, with his arm still wrapped around Aurora.

"I am feeling much improved. Amazing what some medicine, a bandage, and a hot bath can do for a girl. But where is Sy? Is he okay?"

"Sy is fine. He is probably enjoying his new job."

"What job could that possibly be?"

"He's the new Regent of Dalazvar."

"Sy is the Regent of Dalazvar?" she chuckled. "How did he come upon that job?"

"Let's just say that he didn't quite volunteer for the post, but he didn't exactly object to it either. He will be fine."

The group of friends stayed in the garden and chatted for a moment. Then Aurora took Jakov by the hand and led him to the side, away from everyone else.

"Half an hour before we came, some refugees arrived here. They said that they were looking for a man named Jakov and his brother Iskandar. They were cold from the weather and hungry so I took them in. Do you want to see them?"

"Yes, of course."

Aurora motioned to her attendant to bring the visitors. After a few moments, four young teenagers walked towards Jakov. Two girls and two boys. They were all wearing white and looked disoriented and confused.

"Greetings," said Jakov warmly. "My name is Jakov. I am the husband of Aurora the queen of Nazvor. I'm told that you are looking for me."

"We are looking for you," the eldest boy answered.

"Where are you from, then? You must have come a great distance to get here."

The boy paused and answered.

"We don't know where we are from. Nor do we know how we got here."

"What on earth do you mean?" asked Jakov.

"I mean, all we remember is that a man told us to come here and to look for Jakov and Iskandar. He told us to find you and then all would be well."

"Who was this man who sent you here?"

The boy looked at the others to see if any of them had an answer, but no one did so he spoke for them all.

"I'm sorry, but we do not know that either."

Jakov did not know whether the young teens were mad or had lost their senses in their travels.

"Then what are your names?"

The young man pointed to himself and spoke.

"I am Brutoi, these are my brothers and sisters. This is Karla, this is Izza, and this is ..."

"Crestin," Jakov finished for him, in shock as he gripped Aurora's hand very hard.

Brutoi was confused.

"Sir, do you know us?"

"Yes, yes I do."

Tears slowly fell down his cheek as he looked the boys and girls over. He could see now that it was them. They looked older, but there was no mistake about it.

"Can you tell us where we have been and why we are here? We can remember nothing sir."

"I am your older brother Jakov. And this is your younger brother Iskandar."

The four teenagers looked at Jakov and Iskandar. Something happened and their minds were opened to remember and to understand. They recognized the two boys and their hearts became filled with joy.

Jakov lunged forward and embraced them one after another and he called their names out. "Brutoi, Karla, Izza, Crestin. Welcome thome."

Iskandar came over as well and stood besides Aurora.

"Who are they?" he asked her.

"These are your brothers and sisters."

"They are alive!" he exclaimed.

"So it seems."

Iskandar rushed over and waved hello to them, unable to speak as he was too consumed with emotion. Karla touched his hand with hers as did Crestin. They did not speak to each other. There was no need to, but they smiled.

"These children are deathly cold Aurora. Let us take them in and get them something warm to eat and drink. Let us dine together. We have much catching up to do."

Aurora smiled and guided the children into the palace doors. Jakov put his arms around Izza and Brutoi and accompanied them down the corridor. Ayesha, Mo, and Tar went with them chatting as they walked along.

Iskandar was about to follow when he felt a snow ball strike the back of his head. For a second he thought it was Mo or Tar. But he realized that they were already inside. Turning around, Iskandar saw someone ducking behind some bushes in the garden and walking away. He paused for a moment and then ran into the garden and behind the bushes. Ahead of him someone was running, running away from him, through the hedges and around the statues. He ran faster and tried to catch up.

Eventually he got to a clearing and there he saw the person he had been chasing. It was his father, Fallkirk. Next to Fallkirk was a red dragon.

"Hello my son," Fallkirk replied.

Iskandar stopped and looked Fallkirk in the eyes.

"I knew you'd be back."

"Did you see your brothers and sisters?"

"Yes. That is amazing. How did they come here?"

"I know the secrets to many mysteries of earth and the heavens. However, the return of your brothers and sisters is a mystery that even I cannot explain. There are powers in this world that none of us can understand. All I can say is that there are things more powerful than death, murder, and hatred."

"What is that?"

"Love. Love conquers all. Love always triumphs. Love always wins. It was a type of magical love that brought your brothers and sisters here."

Even though the two talked Iskandar could not take his eyes off the dragon.

"Can I touch him?"

"Of course," Fallkirk said, patting the nose of the large dragon, who grunted in approval.

Very slowly and very cautiously, Iskandar walked over towards the dragon. Magnon moved his head about and smelt Iskandar and then finally licked him with his long tongue. Iskandar thought it was like a lizard's tongue, except a hundred times bigger."

He giggled and patted the dragon on the side of his face.

"Would you like to go for a ride on Magnon?"

"Would I?" exclaimed Iskandar in excitement.

"Then, let's go."

Magnon lowered his back as Fallkirk and Iskandar mounted up. Fallkirk sat Iskandar between his legs and held the reins with Iskandar's head cushioned between his arms.

"Let us soar, Magnon."

The dragon jumped up and started flapping its massive wings. Iskandar looked down and noticed the ground was getting further and further away. Looking around he could see things far away that were not visible even from the watch towers of the palace. Iskandar laughed loudly at the sensation that was exhilarating as it was scary. Fallkirk shook the reins and Magnon began flying forward at a quick speed and they flew in circles high above the castle.

As Iskandar looked down he saw Jakov walk out of the castle door. Jakov was looking about for something or someone. He could hear Jakov calling.

"Iskandar, Iskandar, where are you?"

"Shall we scare him?" asked Fallkirk.

"Yes," agreed Iskandar.

Jakov stood there in the snow, scanning the garden and grounds for Iskandar.

"Where could that boy be?" he said to himself. "It is so much like him to wonder off at the wrong time."

Just then a huge surge of wind and a flash of red flew past Jakov from behind and nearly knocked him down. He ducked down quickly unawares as to what had just flown over his head. In front of him just off the ground Magnon was circling back. Jakov was startled but his heart stopped fluttering when he recognized the dragon and its two riders. Magnon slowly descended to the ground and landed in front of Jakov. Jakov stared not at the dragon, but at Fallkirk in disbelief.

"It really was you," uttered Jakov in disbelief. "You are Talkai, I mean Fallkirk. It was you who saved me."

"It was, nephew. But it was you and your brother who saved the kingdom. I was your guardian and guide. It was the two of you working together that brought us victory."

"And to think that I regarded you as nothing more than a clumsy fool."

"It takes a fool to know a fool Jakov."

"I think the proverb is true."

Iskandar popped his head up and looked down at Jakov.

"Look at me, Jakov, I'm riding a dragon."

"So you are. How is it?"

"So much fun. It's like riding a thousand horses in the air."

Jakov slowly and hesitantly moved forward, but Magnon growled at him.

"Easy boy," called Fallkirk to the dragon. "Sorry Jakov, but old Magnon here simply doesn't like you."

"Well, tell him that the feeling is mutual."

"I sure will."

"Where are the two of you going?"

"I'm taking my son for a ride."

"When will you be back?"

Iskandar looked up at Fallkirk.

"I shall have him home for supper."

"I will be here waiting."

Aurora came out of the doorway as well.

"What is taking you so long?" she asked. Then, seeing the dragon, she took a step backwards, "Oh my goodness. That's a dragon. What is a dragon doing in the garden of my palace?"

"Whatever it likes," commented Iskandar cheekily.

"Ha ha," yelled Fallkirk as he shook the reins of Magnon.

The red dragon jumped up once more, flapped its wings, and took them off into the clear sky.

"Oh dear, I can't believe this," Aurora spoke softly to Jakov.

"Seeing is believing, my love."

Jakov and Aurora waved as the two riders waved back and then went further way into the deep blue sky.

"Where are we going father?"

"Wherever you want to my son," he said, kissing the top of Iskandar's head.

"I'd like to see Praschi, see it from high above."

"Very well, then, to Praschi it is."

As they passed through a small white cloud Fallkirk pulled the reigns to the left and Magnon veered to his left and kept on flying.

"Come on Magnon. Let's show my boy the heights of the heavens."

The dragon groaned and then flew even faster into the sky.

Iskandar relished the cool breeze flowing through his hair and the arms of his father around his waist. He noticed that the ground looked like a mass of green and white underneath them. He snuggled up into the warmth of his father's chest and Fallkirk placed his chin on Iskandar's head. Fallkirk looked down with a grin and saw Iskandar smiling up at him.

"This is fun," the boy said.

"Oh, Iskandar, the fun is only just beginning for us."

www.ingramcontent.com/pod-product-compliance
Lightning Source LLC
Chambersburg PA
CBHW051145030726
47504CB00004B/1041